BAGGED

BAGGED

Jo Bailey

A THOMAS DUNNE BOOK

ST. MARTIN'S PRESS   NEW YORK

All opinions and inaccuracies are the author's. Everything in this book is fictional but the diseases.

Design by Glen M. Edelstein

Library of Congress Cataloging-in-Publication Data
Bailey, Jo.
    Bagged / Jo Bailey.
       p.   cm.
    "A Thomas Dunne book."
    ISBN 0-312-06296-6
    I. Title.
  PS3552.A3722B3   1991
  813'.54—dc20   91-21842
                                                                 CIP

First Edition: November 1991

10 9 8 7 6 5 4 3 2 1

For Papa Cacoethes, Mrs. Schwartz, and Scooter Bee

Acknowledgments

I want to thank Dr. L. Stefan for his patience in helping me to understand some of the technical matters included in this book.

Part One

1

THE body bag was hand sewn with fine leather and cured with red quebracho that turned it a rich lobster color. Its full-grained texture was so supple to the touch that the man in the driver's seat of the hearse couldn't resist reaching in back to stroke the head of the bag while murmuring, "Don't be so impatient." When the body inside the bag jerked upright into a sitting position, the man forced it back down. "No need to hurry." After that, the body lay motionless as a roll of carpet.

The hearse, an executive model, complete with silk curtains, sat in the emergency parking lot at Jackson General, affectionately—or not so affectionately—called General Jack by the citizenry of the city. The driver, who was in his mid-twenties, wore his thin, dark hair in a shaggy, shoulder-length cut that was uncommonly fashionable for one of the boys in mortuary science. He held a star chart in his gloved hands and kept leaning forward to peer upward through the top of the windshield, hoping to identify the Hercules constellation. His face wasn't handsome or homely, maybe somewhat goofy, the way his nose crooked a degree or two to the side, and his dark eyebrows were so narrow, as if plucked. He kept fluttering his lips as if giving himself frequent advice, although no sounds escaped. No luck with Hercules. On a sweltering Friday evening in mid-August, with half a harvest moon slicing above the city's glass skyline, there was too much haze and airborne grit to make it possible to locate more than the brightest stars; but since the task helped him forget his companion in back, he kept trying. The driver would never have admitted to fear, nervousness, or the need for distractions. He was too much man for that. He carried a club, needed reinforced Jockeys, and would have freely given up his rib back in Genesis. He was that generous.

A quarter hour passed. He moved his scan of the heavens eastward for Pegasus. Not much luck there either, maybe a hoof. By General Jack's Emergency entrance several smokebirds gathered for cigarettes, their fogged-in flocks a fixture since the hospital had banned smoking across the board. A drunk or two stagger-limped in. A husband squealed up to the entrance with his ten-month-pregnant wife and almost sideswiped a wino. The man in the hearse waited, not so calmly, glancing more frequently toward the entrance as the minutes passed. Finally, two ambulances arrived within moments of each other, the smokebirds flew their roost, and the man went into action.

Stepping out of the hearse, he shot his cuffs beyond the dark sleeves of his coat and with a surgeon's manner tugged at his perforated driving gloves as if they weren't tight enough. While stepping to the back of the hearse, he ran a hand lovingly over the vehicle's contours. Pulling a cart out, he cranked up its accordion legs and slid the body bag easily on top of it. As he wheeled across the lot, a third ambulance whooped in under the Emergency Room's portico and backed up to the pneumatic doors. A security guard popped open the rear of the latest ambulance; nurses in faded-blue scrubs helped rush a bare-chested, elderly man inside. A sweat-drenched fireman thumped up and down on the patient's chest as they went. Covering the dying man's gaping mouth was a clear plastic oxygen mask that made his face look lifeless.

Nobody had time to pay attention to a stylish mortuary attendant wheeling a cart across the parking lot. Amidst all the activity no one thought anything about a funeral home delivering a body to a hospital rather than picking one up.

The man patted the shoulder of the body bag and whispered, "Not much longer." He followed the cardiac arrest inside, through the automatic doors, and into the air-conditioned triage area.

Forget that from the outside General Jack looked like a geriatric case soon to be visited by the city's dynamiters. On the inside, at least in the vicinity of the Emergency Room, ferocious arthroplasty surgery had been done. Image-conscious administrators had had their way with aging walls and corroded pipes. Toothpaste and soap detergents weren't the only items that had to be new and improved to attract customers. The triage area just inside the sliding doors looked like a space station receiving wounded from the Alpha Centauri wars. The word *triage* itself was French and came from Europe's battlefields, where it designated a space set aside for deciding which soldiers needed immediate treatment and which could wait. Bright lithium-crystal lights zapped everything a faint amber hue. The nurse behind the glassed-in desk forcefully explained to a disorderly fighter-pilot type that the gash on his forearm would have to wait until more serious casualties had been attended to. Pent-up antiseptic odors replaced the frothy smells of the overheated city streets. A volunteer chaplain with a clerical collar and long white beard ushered a sobbing wife into a dimly lit waiting room.

The man in the black linen suit guided his delivery against a wall, carefully aligning it with an empty gurney. With a final pat on the foot of the body bag, he whispered, "Nothing personal," and slipped back outside without anyone noticing his entrance, delivery, or exit.

Twice, he drove through the city's adult entertainment district because he liked the sensation the hearse caused at intersections. People looked away, then back, then quickly away again. Finally, being a thoughtful, sensitive hearse thief, he parked his transportation less than six blocks from where he'd boosted it, the Bundleweiss Funeral Chapel, and transferred to his gutsy little midnight blue Mazda RX-7. He removed his gloves to grip its steering wheel bare-handed, its contours giving him much satisfaction. Once he'd rolled over its engine, he took a good thirty seconds to lovingly tick off gauges and to fine-tune his stereo before finally preparing to depart. If he'd given his on-again, off-again girlfriend half as much foreplay, she'd have been satisfied. But then he noticed that he'd forgotten his star chart in the hearse. He retrieved it, realizing too late that he'd taken his gloves off and left fingerprints. Well, that could be fixed. He wiped everything with a silk handkerchief that had been a Christmas present from his sister and hopped gears off into the city night, pleased with a job well done.

The body bag was abandoned at 9:28 P.M., by which time the man inside the bag had slipped completely into a coma and was beyond rolling off the cart or calling for help. Any of the physicians parading past would have diagnosed bradycardia, possibly resulting from an overdose—the body's heartbeat had dropped below fifty per minute.

At 9:29 two security guards physically escorted a drunk to a holding room where he was locked safely—although hardly quietly—away. Muffled and quavering, his rendition of the

"Star-Spangled Banner" rang in the halls. No one had time to applaud. Fifteen seconds after the drunk, a mother rushed in with her infant who had ingested lye. For the next three minutes the triage desk was staffed only by the nursing assistant, who accepted a twenty-dollar bribe from a nattily dressed man who wanted a speedy gonorrhea test. The playboy was placed in a cubicle just before a family of three with possible exposure to chicken pox arrived. The man with the gash on his forearm kept bellyaching while a fellow beside him held an ice pack to an ear and moaned, "Thelma, Thelma, Thelma."

At 9:37 reinforcements arrived at triage, giving the nurse and nursing assistant a breather. Shortly thereafter a roving camera plus reporter from a local television station appeared, wanting to quiz employees on their reactions to the late-breaking story of a thirty-six-year-old mother of four who had sued the county hospital for sexual discrimination in its promotion practices. For five years she'd worked as a security guard at General Jack and twice had been passed over for promotion. Early that evening she'd been awarded the whole ball of wax: reinstatement, promotion, back pay, and a lump sum payment of fifty thousand dollars for compensatory damages. The irony was that she worked in one of the few male-dominated positions at the hospital. Of the thirty-six security guards employed at General Jack, three were female. Of the 3,221 workers at General Jack, 81 percent were women. Did one of those women care to comment? The new nurse at triage did: "It's no money in my pocket."

A balding security guard gave the news team one beleaguered, crusty word: "Nuts."

At 9:40 the interview ended when a gunshot wound was hustled in through the doors and into the same stabilization room where the earlier cardiac arrest had gone. It looked as though a .38 had shattered the attempted suicide's jaw. The breakneck pace rattled on for another twenty-five minutes, during which time the original nurse and nursing assistant returned. Then, shortly after ten P.M., the tumult suddenly slackened.

At 10:20 the nursing assistant, returning from a smoke outside, finally noticed the high-quality body bag lining the wall. "Who's bagged?"

The nurse, who was studying the Emergency Room work schedule, said without glancing up, "Some democracy—three Fridays in a row."

"Dissatisfied customer?"

"I don't know." She pushed aside the schedule and glared at where the nursing assistant was pointing. "A mortician is probably getting his hearse."

Another relatively quiet half hour passed before the nurse said, "Tony, why don't you see if there's a name on that bag."

"Isn't that a job for a more highly trained type of person?"

"Tony . . ."

"I'm shuffling. I'm shuffling."

Pretending decrepitude, the nursing assistant worked his way across the entry and to the body bag, zipping it open from the toes as far as the shins. What he found were tailored pant legs and patent leather shoes in which he could see his reflection. Even if he'd reached under the pants and felt the clammy warmth of the leg, it was a long shot that there would have been a chance to save the man. But the nursing assistant didn't do that. It didn't make sense that a live body would be zipped up tight in a body bag. Without thinking about it, he assumed the man had been dressed for his funeral and closed the bag. Feigning a bad lower back, the assistant hobbled toward the nurse, who eyed him suspiciously all the way. He pulled his chair next to hers and whispered, "What we have here is a problem."

"Why's that?"

"Because in ten minutes we're out of here."

"You mean that in ten minutes you're getting together

with that slinky X-ray technician? Isn't that what you mean, Tony?"

Looking wrongly accused, the nursing assistant said, "I just thought maybe this once you'd like to get out of here on time. That's all I was thinking." Lifting the work schedule off the telephone extension and carefully setting it in front of the nurse, so that she couldn't avoid seeing the three Fridays she'd been scheduled in a row, the assistant began punching the number for the nurse's desk in the ER, but before he'd finished, the nurse grabbed his wrist.

The discovery of the body would initiate a lengthy round of questions. The Emergency Room's charge nurse would want to know how it had alighted in front of them without their noticing who left it. Whichever doc was pit boss—the pit being the central area where all the ER doctors gathered to trade second, third, and fourth opinions—would repeat all the questions the charge nurse asked, and then add a few more to show who was in command. Security would get involved. The nursing supervisor would be called in for a consult. Someone would suggest calling the county morgue. Someone else would suggest checking with Admissions to see who had passed away that evening. If there were likely candidates, the nurse and her sidekick would have to call the nursing station involved to see if they would claim the body. At each point they'd have to repeat their story, feeling a little more foolish and impatient with each retelling. And what would happen in the end? Someone from a funeral home would sheepishly arrive and claim the body.

"Hold on that, Tony."

When the shock troops from the next shift arrived, the nurse passed on the baton, saying, "Nothing much to report. Some guy from a funeral home should be picking up that body bag over there."

So the body inside the bag lay in quiet repose for another hour, all the while slowly fading away, at times surfacing from unconsciousness and able to hear people walking past but too weak to beckon. This continued until the new triage nurse, cranky because her teething infant daughter had kept her awake all day, ordered the new nursing assistant to quit asking her simpleminded questions and return the body bag to the morgue. "We're not holding visitation hours, after all."

Because the nursing assistant had never been to the morgue before, she drew him a little map, complete with a skull and crossbones marking his destination, and told him to ask the charge nurse for the key. The nursing assistant's only question was, "What if I get lost?"

"Call collect." The nurse scribbled down the triage extension number on the bottom of the map. "Or sprinkle bread crumbs."

The nursing assistant was relatively new to his job and completely new to the graveyard shift. To stay awake through the long vigil ahead of him, he'd toked some A-number-one Colombian to stimulate his corpuscles and keep himself alert. It was for the good of the patients that he experimented with these controlled substances. On the way to the morgue he had a series of body rushes, after which his imagination cut loose and bony arms and legs started reaching out of the decaying walls for him. Beyond the Emergency Room and Admissions area, the hospital reverted to its true Dorian Gray self. Guiding the cart down the absolute center of the corridor, he started humming a ditty entitled "Green Berets" to keep his spirits up. At 12:15 A.M. the basement hallways that he traveled were poorly lit and empty, except for linen bins that were deep enough to conceal any number of ghastly shapes. The wheels of the cart he pushed echoed eerily. He got lost repeatedly and once, rounding a corner, almost collided with a maintenance man riding a three-wheel scooter. To prevent the cart from toppling, he had to push hard against the body bag and for the first time felt the dead weight inside it. That set his heart thumping.

By the time he reached the morgue, he was singing snatches of his song out loud and checking over his shoulder every ten to fifteen seconds. It wasn't until then that he realized he'd forgotten to ask the charge nurse for the key. A minute passed before he mustered the courage to try the handle on the door that simply had 060 numbered on it. He knew from the map that this was his destination. Locked. He cleared his throat, knocked, and called out hello. No one answered. But then who would be answering from such a place? He checked twice up and down the long, dim hall before blocking the entrance to room 060 with the cart and walking stiff-leggedly away without looking back.

There the body bag dropped anchor until seven the next morning. By that time the heartbeat of the man inside had stilled and rigor mortis slowly began to settle throughout his body. Two housekeeping workers wandered by the doorway, on their way to an equipment room, but otherwise no one else passed by.

In Jackson County, the medical examiner was housed in a separate facility some miles away, so there was no permanent staff in the hospital's morgue. Primarily, it was a holding area for bodies. Either a technician from the medical examiner or a mortician from a private funeral home picked up the last remains.

At seven that morning, an associate director from the Eternal Rest Funeral Chapel arrived to claim the remains of Mrs. Selma Thiessen, who had passed away the previous evening from an aneurysm. Having gone through the routine before, he picked a key up from Admissions and proceeded alone to the morgue. When he found the red-colored body bag blocking the doorway, he briefly admired the craftsmanship, then nudged it aside, unlocked the door, and let himself in. The room beyond was empty except for a small table with a log book, which the funeral director unflinchingly called the Death Book. A side room that held dual autopsy tables used for teaching fledgling physicians was empty as well.

The stainless steel door to the cooler had no lock. Inside the walk-in cooler were three bodies, covered by thin plastic sheets and identified by toe tags. Finding Mrs. Thiessen, he pulled back the sheet to see how much work her face would require. He lifted her eyelids to see if she'd donated her eyes—she hadn't. Transferring her to his cart, he tucked her in his own flat-black leather bag, signed the body out in the Death Book, turned off the lights, and locked the outer door of the morgue.

As he turned to leave, he again saw the misplaced body bag and made a little whistling noise through his nostrils, as he did whenever he had to finish someone else's work. In rapid succession, he unlocked the door, turned on the lights, stowed the red bag inside the cooler, and left without making any notation in the log book. The body rested there in the dark over the weekend and then for another week, and then longer.

Bodies came, bodies went.

Thirteen days elapsed before a nursing assistant who worked on the Oncology ward happened to bring down two bodies within three days of each other and remembered the rich-red bag, which by then had been shuffled into the corner of the cooler. This particular NA had an offbeat sense of humor, and beyond that, she relished pointing out how ineffectually Jackson General was run. When she checked the log book and could find no mention of the body within the red leather bag, she smiled like a Cheshire cat who has discovered the state's fishery.

2

THERE were three of them filling up the chairs in Security's subbasement office when Jan Gallagher reported back for duty that first night, the Friday before the start of the Labor Day weekend. They didn't say a word in greeting, simply filled their chairs, and they were none too expert at even that elementary task. Their posture wasn't exemplary, for one thing. For another, despite all their effort at indifference, they didn't look comfortable. Three more of them slouched against file cabinets or were bucked up by a wall. Her newly awarded crew. The town without pity. Six sets of eyes and pin-drop silence. Five men, one woman. No, make that six men; the single woman's efforts at masculinity had earned her honorary status. What was it about men that made a group of them seem so dense?—as in stupid, although they certainly were impenetrable too.

"She's here," Jan said, delivering the obvious joke, but even in her uniform she wouldn't be mistaken for a stand-up comic who played police retirement parties. If not for her mane of zip-black hair, she might have been completely lost inside the stiff white shirt, black trousers, and mirror-buffed shoes, for she was small, slight of build, and despite being in her midthirties a bit girlish in the eyes. She had a clear complexion with a few wandering freckles. Her general inclination was toward laughter, but her crew uneasily shifted their position without succumbing to humor. So that was how it was going to be.

She zeroed in on Gavin Larsen, who lounged behind the desk that belonged to the shift supervisor, meaning the desk Jan had been awarded in court two weeks before as a result of sexual discrimination in the hospital's promotion practices. Larsen was the man whom the court had dictated she would replace, the man who was supposed to help train her in. Nobody laughed about that either.

"We've been waiting," Gavin Larsen said. "Right here." Pause. "All breathless."

The last laconic crack caused a stir on the edges of her vision, but she concentrated on Larsen, who returned the favor. Roughly the same age as Jan, Larsen leaned in the other direction—toward old age—balding, sour-stomach thin, and so standoffish that he enforced the use of his proper first name; no nicknames like Gav or Gravy crept in. Shifting her eyes to the soles of Larsen's shoes, which were propped up on the desk—her desk—Texan style, Jan decided there was no reason to wait. *Take the plunge now,* she told herself.

"Resting up?" she asked. "Or is there some other reason you're sitting behind my desk?" Before Larsen could wipe the smirk off his lean face and regroup, Jan continued. "Or was the chair just empty?" Holding up her lunch bag for everyone to see, she stepped toward the break room, saying, "Nobody move."

Once out of sight, she could hear them muttering their

grievances, and she silently mimicked their bitching but then stopped, realizing that her attitude wasn't going to win friends or influence people. Holding her breath, she bent over and pushed her lunch bag into a half-size refrigerator. It smelled as though the medical examiner was working after hours in there. No one ever cleaned it, unless it was herself or one of the two other women on Security's staff, and that thought caused a gleam to slowly backfill her dusky-green eyes. Crazy shine, her mother had long ago called it. From a box next to a coffee machine, she lifted seven toothpicks, broke one in half, and arranged them between her thumb and index finger so that no one could tell which was short.

Back to the office she went, moving lightly on the balls of her feet, a habit learned as a teenager trying to stretch her five-two height to match her brothers'. As she reappeared, the whispering drained away and her crew solidified into a mass that had the sparkle of a police lineup. Stan Charais reacted late, hustling his baby face back to a corner, apparently arguing with Larsen about something. The rest of Mount Rushmore included Leo "Shoptalk" Kennedy, department father figure; Cindi Paige, who didn't count as a woman because she was trying so hard not to be; Jackson Martin, big on naming muscle groups; and Willie "Smokey" Smokeham, big on talking, talking, talking. Smokey should have had his own late-night show for interviewing criminals. Jan held the toothpicks up, swinging them about for all to see.

"My first act as your supervisor," she announced, completely serious. "Short stick cleans the refrigerator. Democracy here, so I'll draw with you."

It looked bleak. No one budged. She offered first chance to Larsen, who kept his arms folded on his chest and snorted. The rest of them stared at her clenched hand as if being asked to play Russian roulette. The glances the boys shot to each other said, Did you want to know what it would be like, working under a woman? Did you have any doubts? Clean the goddamn appliances? Why, we're supposed to be protecting staff and patients. Laying hands on criminals.

The moment's weight multiplied geometrically until Jan felt as though she was back in that sterile courtroom with all those eyes focused on her. At one point her lawyer had leaned close and whispered sage advice: *Fuck 'em.* An attitude that Jan saw the intrinsic value of. She stared at each of her crew in turn until Smokey, who had no love for Larsen, could bear the lack of talk no longer and broke rank, saying, "That's mean work," while plucking a toothpick out of her hand.

The established pecking order cracked ever so slightly. Down the line they went, Leo Kennedy shaking his gray head as he drew, acting as if an era had passed. Action Jackson said nothing—perfectly. Stan the Man blushed. Cindi waited until next to last, saying that housekeeping ought to do it for them. That left Jan and Gavin untested.

"What the hell does this have to do with our job?" he asked.

"Fair question." She forced herself to smile, semisweetly, she hoped. "If we can't police ourselves, how can we expect to keep order out there?" She gestured beyond the door. "And another thing." She pointed to his feet, which remained propped on the desk. "Put a better polish on those shoes. You're hired to represent this hospital, and appearances are important."

Larsen slowly pulled himself up to his majestic six-three height, from where he looked fairly ludicrous trying to stare the much shorter Jan down, which he was unable to do anyway.

"You don't like the rules the way they are?" he said. "You want to change them? To what? Lady, I don't think you know what in the hell you're doing." He brushed her hand aside and started toward the door.

"This mean I can have my chair?" she asked.

He hesitated, then jerked open the door and was gone.

She let the chair remain unclaimed and said to the rest of her troops, "Anyone else have an opinion they'd like to share?"

"Plenty," Leo Kennedy said, "but the excitement's tuckered me out."

"Sorry to hear that, Leo. You're on clock tour tonight." A groan. Jan raised her hand for quiet. "Just following the pattern already laid out. Cindi, you're with Larsen in A building."

"Shit," Cindi said, never skipping an opportunity to swear like one of the boys.

"Absolutely," Jan said. "Stan and Jackson, B building. Smokey and I will start in the ER and Pharmacy. Any questions?" She'd rattled this off so quickly and competently that they all simply stared at her. "Good. I want to go through this new procedure on gunshot wounds in the Stabilization Room, then we're off."

She ran through a checklist for securing the Emergency Department's Stab Room whenever the patient being treated was the victim of a violent crime. No one appeared to be listening too carefully. They all kept glancing toward the hallway door, expecting Larsen's return. She read on, ignoring their inattentiveness. Their new procedure was the result of a youth-gang member bursting into the Stabilization Room with a seven-inch knife and trying to finish off the job he'd earlier started on a street corner. Now the Stab Room's doors had to be secured. Security guards visible. Potential troublemakers were to be identified and the city cops notified.

"OK," she said, satisfied that they'd absorbed maybe a quarter of it, "one last thing and we're off. Jackson, pick a stick for Larsen." She held up the two toothpicks left in her hand.

Everybody immediately became interested and admired the sense in this choice. Nobody argued with Jackson's integrity, and nobody, particularly a nobody named Gavin

Larsen, intimidated him. A short scan of Jackson's six-foot height and 230 weight—none of it cellulite—made the explanation for that obvious. Squinting at Jan, Jackson apparently liked what he saw because his usual contrariness flagged and his large mouth broke into a generous smile. His black hand, double the size of Jan's, covered the white of her knuckles, and when he pulled away, he held a broken toothpick in it.

"Larsen cleans," she said. "I'll tell him."

Once they'd all left, she sat alone in the office, suddenly melancholy, and found herself wondering all over again what in the world she was trying to prove. So her promotion galled her second ex, a city cop. So what? She liked to imagine she'd outgrown him. The hours on this job weren't soothing, and the ideal of bringing law and order to the corridors of General Jack struck her as laughable, something fit for Wonder Woman. Through its entrances the hospital received in concentrate all that was violent and unjust in a city whose crime rate and homicide count was aimed toward the moon. She'd long ago realized the only way to make General Jack's halls safe would be to lock its doors.

But the publicity of her lawsuit had—temporarily at least—removed her inclination to quit. The issues had ballooned larger than any one person. She'd blinked and become some kind of symbol. What kind she didn't know. Nor did she know if she liked it. She doubted it was real. Originally, she'd applied for the promotion out of stubbornness and because of four daughters and two ex-husbands whose flow of child support was dependable as a dry wash. It wasn't as if she could sit at home all day and worry about what the maid should clean next. More of the same kind of motivation had moved her into court where she was quickly shunted onto the news escalator. Women had actually stopped her on the street to give her support. Try turning your foolish back on that.

None of these thoughts helped her step out of the protective confines of the office to start her first night as a landmark case for women's rights. It took a code three from the ER to pull her away from all that wonderful privacy. When she did emerge, there weren't any television cameras to mark the occasion. Her fifteen minutes' worth of being a celebrity had been all used up. The real world wasn't quite as bright.

Her shift started at eleven and zigzagged, uphill all the way, to seven-thirty the following morning. Until two, when the bars closed, her entire time was spent in the ER helping control a bar rush amplified by its being Friday night, the moon being full, and the first of the month having recently arrived. The start of a new month meant that welfare checks had been received, cashed, and in hard cases thoroughly squandered, which wasn't to say that the poor were the only drunkards causing mayhem on the streets; they were simply the most uninhibited. By the time the staff had strapped down the last drunk, she'd begun to think that maybe she could pull this off. A security supervisor had to be good with people, not a nightstick, and people-smart she was, willing to talk and listen, and then apply leverage when neither of those worked. And the little stunt with the toothpicks hadn't hurt. At least her staff was cooperating.

When the delirium tremens hours had passed, the building remained standing and settled into the fitful sleep of the sick. Patients rested uneasily, lying still to avoid pain, sleeping with the aid of little helpers, staring at shadowy ceiling tile, and sweating about going under the knife in the morning. Nurses trod lightly on shadowy floors. Residents crept off to try nabbing sleep and ended up dreaming about suburban practices and summer cottages on lakes far removed from the call of emesis basins and small-bowel obstructions.

Through all that roved Jan Gallagher, new security supervisor. Nobody gave her a round of applause or pat on the back. One ER clerk did ask how it felt to win. It felt all right, she thought. A little pick-me-up of power went with the authority, the responsibility, and she quietly told herself to watch that good feeling. Overconfidence could get her in trouble.

Her crew took turns breaking for supper, or whatever you choose to call a meal taken in the middle of the night. Bolstered by coffee, they made rounds to secure General Jack's hidden nooks and crannies. When she searched out Gavin Larsen and Cindi Paige in Old General and passed on the broken toothpick, Larsen didn't say a word, although his eyes almost set that little stick ablaze. She accepted that and without asking if he intended to do anything to help train her in, left him standing beside Paige, who suggested in her practiced streetwise voice that Jan should lighten up. All in all, not bad advice, but pretty hard to follow considering the radio call she got a half hour later from the morgue.

As she wound through the corridors to the morgue, her sixth sense acted up. She hated it when that happened. Wasn't it enough that her other five senses were constantly unloading information on what was about to go haywire? Nevertheless, an unexplainable something made her cautious as her destination grew closer, but on rounding the last corner, she found Stan Charais, alone and straining for nonchalance by leaning against a wall.

A measure of relief entered her tone. "What do you have, Stan?"

He pushed away from the wall with his shoulder. "This one may puzzle you, Chief."

"Oh?"

Forget Stan's angelic face. He sounded as sincere as Jan's first ex had when phoning from the Holiday Inn.

"The trail started with this." He rapped a knuckle against the metal fire door of the morgue.

Taped to the door was a piece of white paper—the back of

a physician's assessment sheet, actually—that said in red felt-tip ink:

HELP ME

She peeled the homemade notice off the door and checked its front side, finding it blank.

"This wouldn't be something you and Leo cooked up?"

"Why, Chief," Stan modestly said, straining as always for a mature voice, "I'm surprised you'd think such a thing."

Unblinking, she swung her gaze toward him. He frequently made a point of reminding people that in five months he'd be thirty, but his creamy complexion and china-doll blue eyes threw him clear back to twenty. Some weeks he coaxed forth an anemic blond mustache that either made him appear younger than voting age, or else inscrutable, but of late he'd discarded that attempt at storming adulthood. Tall and solid at the shoulders, he possessed a self-conscious yet fluid way of nervously turning and rotating his upper torso and neck, like a swimmer coming up for air.

One other thing about Stan: his romances belonged in a country-western jukebox. He had a way of spooking a woman's maternal instincts. Twice he'd turned to Jan for lonely-hearts advice—she belonged to the opposite sex, didn't she?—and the first time she'd made the mistake of listening so well that she soon found herself grappling for breath in a vacant surgery waiting room. She'd had to slap him. And then he'd slapped her—not hard but with a full hand—and that was that until the second time he'd needed a shoulder and she'd coolly informed him that her own four kids soaked up all the momsy she had to spare. He hadn't appreciated the frankness, bearing a grudge that surfaced during her discrimination trial.

"Stan," Jan flatly said, "drop the Chief business, or I might start to think you have a problem with what happened in court." Her lawyer had so shredded Stan's innuendos about Jan's seductive behavior that he'd stumbled when leaving the witness box.

He momentarily stiffened, the rosiness of his cheeks blanched, and he said as if he had no idea what she was referring to, "Didn't realize you'd be so touchy."

"Now you know."

"You'll have my unending cooperation."

"Let's back off a step, OK? Whatever's going on here, we'll find out faster if we work together, right? So, anything more you wanted to tell me?" She watched closely but glimpsed no telltale smugness as he stubbornly shook his head. She prodded gently. "We were talking about how this might be a joke."

"That's what I thought at first, but then I investigated. I mean, that's what I'm paid for, right?"

"OK, I'll ask. And what did you find?" She had to subtract the sarcasm and ask again—real nice—before he would proceed.

"It appears that we've collected a nonpaying customer down here."

"For shame."

He ignored that, apparently wanting to share with someone what he'd discovered. "As near as I can tell, nobody knows how it arrived here. I've already called Admissions"— he made an unnecessary digression to explain—"they do discharges too, and checked the morgue's book. I hope this all meets with your approval."

"So far. What'd you find?"

"There's nothing listed in the book and Admissions said they've got trouble enough keeping track of the live ones and didn't know a thing about any extra dead ones." Sounding hopeful, he concluded, "I haven't exceeded my bounds, have I?"

The last dig clinched it. As she opened the door and stepped into the morgue, she asked, "You still dating Melody?"

"What gives you the right to ask a thing like that?"

"We're about to find out, aren't we?"

Ignoring his indignation, she surveyed the room. Nothing appeared out of place, but then there was very little that could appear out of the ordinary in such a setting. The entry room contained only a small wooden table for the log book, two empty gurneys, and a stainless steel door for the cooler. Taped to the cooler was a second hand-lettered note saying:

HELP ME

That described all the entry room's furnishings but one, and that last item was a palpable silence that seemed to stir the very molecules of air. The dead weren't completely inert. She definitely felt a draft.

Off to the left of the cooler was the closed door of the autopsy room, which she crossed to and checked inside of, finding nothing more than two porcelain autopsy tables and empty counter space. There certainly wasn't any place for a Leo Kennedy or Gavin Larsen to conceal himself. This slowed her, made her more thoughtful. Sense number six started throbbing again.

"The outer door was locked when you got here?"

"Yes, ma'am."

She stared at him. "What brought you down here in the first place? Leo's supposed to be on clock tour."

To ensure diligence and lower insurance premiums, the hospital had installed time clocks throughout the complex. Guards making security rounds had to punch in at each location, thus proving they'd been there.

"We traded," Stan said uneasily. "His foot's acting up."

"OK. Go on. Tell the rest."

"That's it," he said, acting relieved that she didn't comment on the switch in duties. "I read the note. I went inside. I read the second note. I opened the cooler. The inn's full up. Five stiffs waiting for disposition, one with another note. But when I check in the book, I only find four unclaimed names listed."

Turning toward the log book, she tried to envision a sequence of possible events. "You went back a few days in the log?"

"A week. Say, believe me, I wouldn't have bothered you if I didn't think this was something that needed checking into."

"Sure, Stan. You take a look at the extra body yet?"

He admitted he hadn't.

"Let's," she said.

"You're the boss, but don't you think you might be tampering with evidence?"

"You tell me, Stan—how are we going to know this body doesn't belong here unless we take a look-see?"

"I was only thinking that if there's a homicide investigation . . ."

"That's an interesting conclusion to jump to."

She thought she had him there, but instead of explaining himself, he went to work trying to loosen his shoulders.

"Until we're absolutely certain this body doesn't belong here," she said, "there's no need to involve the police. Am I right?"

"Sounds reasonable."

She shook her head in resignation and stepped inside the cooler. A single light glinted off the crosshatched metal sheeting of the walls. With the forty-degree temperature suspending all odor, the room might have been the walk-in freezer of a restaurant kitchen. The light, positioned above the door, cast shadows from the five carts. Four forms were covered with thin plastic sheets, their features a bluish outline beneath the covering; one of them stretched too long for his sheet; his toes pointed up. The fifth body was concealed within a stiff, M&M-red leather bag with another note taped to its chest:

HELP ME
PLEASE!!!!!

Aside from two wire baskets, the cooler contained nothing more. One of the baskets held tubes of blood kept in plastic bags; the other, covered with a linen, held a spare upper leg which resembled a petrified log more than flesh and blood. It had been fished out of the lake years before, never identified, and today was used to educate young residents doing a tour through pathology.

"The red bag?" she said, not yet stepping close.

"That's the one with the note."

"You checked the name tags against the log?"

That crossed him up. "I didn't think it necessary."

She stepped around Stan to retrieve the log book, which contained column headings for the patient name, autopsy number, date of death, medical records number, age, sex, medical examiner, mortician license number, mortuary, station, and initials of the person delivering the remains to the morgue. With nothing in General Jack safe from theft, the log was chained to its desk, which she had to drag to the cooler door. The last four names didn't have any entries for being picked up. The fifth entry from the top did.

"I'll read off these last four, you compare them to the IDs."

Each corpse had a plastic hospital ID strapped around the wrist and a tag on the big toe, which Stan, who didn't wear glasses because they made him appear even younger, had to lean over and squint at. Proximity to the bodies didn't appear to bother him, which surprised Jan because she could feel icy little feet skating up and down the back of her arms. The log book and toe tags matched, and when he'd finished he looked at her with a smart-alecky satisfaction that said he hoped she'd have the decency never to doubt his word again.

Still not satisfied, she pushed the desk back and returned to the cooler to stand over the leather body bag, holding her breath to listen for any sounds of life, sounds such as a practical joker waiting to lurch out might make. She detected nothing. Checking over her shoulder, she asked Stan to step aside so that he wasn't blocking the light, then in one swift motion zipped the bag open from foot to head.

No one popped out. She stood above the body of a man who was dressed in a frilly white shirt, black bow tie and tuxedo, red cummerbund, and a blue carnation—brown on the edges—pinned in his lapel. The end of an unlit cigar stuck out of his small mouth, which was clamped shut with a cloth chinstrap tied to the top of his head. Because so little of the cigar was showing, it appeared that he must have swallowed most of it. His cheeks had five o'clock shadow, and the side of his jaw had a long ugly bruise running from the round lobe of his ear to beneath the oval of his chin. His hands were tied together at the wrists and rested over his groin. An odor of overly ripe baby diapers began to rise up from the bag. She thought his face familiar, but where she might have seen him, she couldn't pinpoint. It was an intelligent face, a finely knit, aristocratic one in which the cigar looked crudely out of place. Now it was a dead face. For the first time the thought occurred to her that this might be something more malicious than a simple prank.

"Give me a hand with rolling him over."

"He's going to look just as dead from the back." The notion that he might have overlooked something made Stan more attentive, but the corpse's rear pockets were empty unless you counted the mess made from the emptying of his bowels. Whoever had tucked him away had foreseen this eventuality and laid an absorbent pad beneath him.

"He look familiar to you?" Jan asked, once they'd righted him again.

"Can't tell."

"And you don't know anything about where this guy came from?"

"I already told you so."

She looked across the corpse at Stan, who quickly averted his eyes.

"Something's bothering you, Stan. Spill it."

He denied it but looked uneasy.

"Come on," she coaxed.

"All right," he said in an agitated burst. "You were right about Melody. We quit seeing each other. She's developed this thing about not doing my laundry anymore."

She lowered her vision to the dead man between them, counting to ten before zipping up the bag, then assaulting ten again before gesturing toward the door and saying very carefully, "Sorry to hear it, but I'm sure you'll work it out."

That's all she said, and for once, all Stan asked. This all happened two weeks after the body had been delivered to General Jack, a fact that Jan would have been very grateful to know.

3

CALL it paranoia—Jan did—but she continued to sense a man's clammy hand behind this. Except that no matter how long she looked at the note she'd brought back from the morgue, the printing appeared feminine. At intervals the muffled voices of staff or the coasting of equipment wheels rumbled by in the hallway outside Security's subbasement office, but neither was enough to disturb her concentration. The office was windowless, an afterthought of the architects who back in 1922 had failed to foresee the need for an entire squad of officers— thirty-six of them—to protect patients from patients, staff from visitors, staff from patients, and any other combinations of patients, staff, visitors, and nonvisitors you care to think of. She, herself, found it difficult to imagine such a time as 1922. At least the lack of windows meant that no one could look in at her bewilderment over whether the John Doe in the morgue was legitimate or whether her staff was pulling some sophomoric stunt to humiliate her.

When exactly five minutes had elapsed, she rose from her desk and returned to the morgue to poke about privately. She half expected the note on the inner door and the fifth body to be gone. No such luck. Sucking in a deep breath and rubbing her hands on her pant legs, she crossed herself and zipped the body bag open to conduct a lengthier, more conscientious search. This was the kind of intimacy she could do without, although the body was no less responsive than her second husband had been in the months before their split. All that she discovered was that the tux's labels had been snipped away. Throughout it all she kept expecting the man's eyes to flutter open and to hear him haughtily say, *Take your hands off me.* She imagined his voice would have an upper-class English accent, why she couldn't say. Twice, she addressed him rather than talk to herself, which seemed impolite given the circumstances. Raising four daughters, most of the time minus a spouse, had fostered a habit of talking to herself. "Really? Really." This time she didn't limit her investigation to the corpse but examined the body bag and cart as well, without results, except to note that whoever had done the job of removing all identification had done it thoroughly.

Satisfied that she'd learned all she could from the deceased, she moved to the log book to transfer the last eight names and the stations where they had expired to her pad. She flipped to the previous page and copied two more names for an even ten. Once again she surveyed the outer room and the walk-in freezer but discovered nothing. "Back to the drawing board." Hard to remember that her New Year's resolution had been to quit talking to herself. The habit itself she didn't mind; it was the clichés she uttered that made her clench her teeth.

* * *

The clerks in Emergency Admissions, two of them with sleep-hungry eyes that looked turned inside out, weren't exactly fountains of information. Nor graciousness.

"You're the third one to ask us," the older of the two testily said. The bridge of her eyeglasses had a rubber band spun around it, holding the halves together. The woman savagely sorted through a stack of patient billing sheets without finding what she wanted. Her wrinkled face was missing a wart on her nose, that was about all.

"Third?" Jan asked. She stood apart from the two women, trying to act friendly, probably too friendly. The two clerks looked at her without trust. Pulling a chair closer, Jan sat so that she wasn't standing above them and looking down. It helped minutely.

"That tall moon-eyed one called us," eyeglasses said.

"Stanley," the second clerk filled in, sounding as though she was about to swoon. College age, she was overdressed in a glittery top and at the moment was leaning far sideways in her chair to watch an orderly pass down the hall. When he was out of sight, she sighed passionately, then tugged on her bra straps to bring herself back to reality.

"And that tall bald one," eyeglasses sourly said. "He was number two. The one who wraps a strand of hair across his forehead. You know, the one who always looks as though he wants to give you a ticket."

"Gavin? How did he get involved?"

"I don't know."

Jan looked to the young-love clerk who had so breathlessly provided Stan's name, but this time she shrugged.

"What did Gavin want?" Jan asked.

"Same as you. Asked about some unidentified white male down in the morgue. Then wanted to know how we handle the stiffs."

"Arlene . . ." young-love said, embarrassed by her co-worker's choice of words.

"What?" said Arlene, who was beginning to enjoy herself.

"How long ago was the other guard here?" Jan asked.

"Ten minutes."

"Well, what did you tell him?"

"Same as we'll tell you. We don't keep track of that. Ralph does." Arlene pushed her eyeglasses up her nose and rapped a knuckle against the computer screen before her. "Or doesn't."

"Ralph's the computer," young-love explained.

"You can't trust them," said Arlene, raising her hand to the computer terminal as if expecting back talk.

"Her husband's named Ralph too," young-love said.

"Not my husband anymore."

The younger one shook her head to show that Arlene was hopeless.

"Well," Jan said, "if we could believe what Ralph had to say"—she patted the terminal—"this Ralph, that is, what would he have to tell me about patients who've recently died in-house?"

Wrong question to ask. You couldn't under any circumstances believe Ralph, any Ralph. Five tangled minutes later she'd heard a great deal about the new computer system General Jack had installed over a year ago and which, when it bothered to work, still didn't work as well as the old system, which hadn't been any prize catch either. People put information in, who knew where it came out?

"Two mules would be better."

What two mules were going to accomplish with the hordes of paperwork generated at General Jack, no one bothered to explain. It was now 3:20 A.M. Women were saying all sorts of ridiculous things all over the hospital. Men were too, of course, but on the graveyard shift the number of employees at General Jack who were women rose even higher than the 81 percent of the overall total. The percentage rose to somewhere in the low nineties. Staff in positions dominated by men—doctors, administrators, supervisors—weren't about to show up at midnight and work until dawn with any regularity. That wasn't part of the scheme of things. Security and on-call doctors were the only male-dominated positions with that luck.

"But you do have to discharge a patient when they die. Right?"

They both looked at Jan as if they could see blue sky through her ears. Arlene suspiciously said, "Aren't you the one who won the big bucks in court?"

"Depends what you mean by big."

"Sure don't act smart."

"What are you going to do with all that money?" younglove dreamily asked.

"Mostly pay lawyers."

"That's right," Arlene said, but you could tell she was curious too. "So was it worth it?"

"Ask me a year from now. What can you tell me about the first four people on this list? They all died recently."

"Not much," Arlene said, pointing to a blank computer screen before her. "Ralph's limp. For how long, we don't know. We never know." She snatched the sheet from Jan and moved it in and out until finding a proper reading distance from her face. "Even if Ralph was hard . . ."

"Arlene . . ."

"What?"

"Go on," Jan said.

"Even if Ralph was hard," Arlene said, "he wouldn't have anything more than what you have here. And what you have here's going to be more accurate. Someone with a brain wrote it down."

"Can you at least tell me what it is you're supposed to do when someone dies?"

"Oh yeah. We scratch them off Ralph."

"That's it?"

"We divide up the dead guy's stuff."

"Arlene . . ." the younger one said, then explained to Jan.

"Valuables go over to Carrie's desk, that's In-Patient. No one there until morning, though."

"What about dealing with funeral homes?"

"We give out the fridge key," Arlene said, then snapped her fingers. "Hey, we could check the cards at the Reception Control Center."

"The what?" Jan said, feeling uneducated.

"Information desk, they used to call it. In the old days. Back when people needed information and didn't need control. They keep a card that tracks every patient."

Arlene adjusted her eyeglasses again before retrieving a four-by-six file-card drawer from another room and helping Jan sort through the cards. The search provided the ten names she'd copied from the morgue's log, plus the names of three other patients who had died in the last week but hadn't appeared in the log. The nursing station, plus date was also included on the card. Jan jotted these facts down.

"Where did these three go?" she asked. "There's no record of them in the morgue."

"How the hell would we know?" Arlene said. "Ask the nursing supervisor. She should know how the floors deal with the stiffs."

"Arlene . . ."

"Say," Arlene suddenly said, "do you want to hear about our phone calls?"

"Should I?" Jan asked, suspicious but getting no clue from young-love about how to react.

"He's called four times now," Arlene said, grinning.

"Arlene," said a disgusted young-love, "you're so gross."

"What do you mean? The officer here said she wanted to know what we told the other guard. Well, we told him this."

"You don't have to act like you enjoy it."

"I'm not the one racing to the phone at two o'clock. That's when he calls," Arlene explained to Jan. "On the dot."

Young-love huffed but then giggled by way of confession and said, "He's got a sexy voice."

"Cripes," said Arlene. "It's a wonder you're not pregnant twice a month."

"Surgical procedures," young-love fired back. The meaning of that barb wasn't entirely clear, but it served to immediately silence Arlene. The two clerks glared at each other.

"You were going to tell me about a phone caller?" Jan said. Neither answered. "You two related? Or something?"

"Yuk."

"Gross."

But now they were talking again, Arlene saying, "This guy calls up four times and asks if we found an extra stiff down here."

"That's not how he says it."

"How then?"

Young-love deepened her voice. "I left a guy down there . . ."

"He doesn't say *guy*."

"He did to me."

"He says *corpse*."

"Whatever he says, he says he left it in a red body bag." Young-love's voice deepened to imitate the caller. "Have you found him yet?"

"I asked if he wanted to take the stiff back," Arlene said, terribly pleased with herself.

"Arlene . . ."

"He hung up."

"That's all he said to you?" Jan asked.

"Yup."

"We thought it was some creep," young-love said.

"It was."

"Calls at two o'clock?" Jan said.

"But not tonight. Not for two or three nights."

"Arlene scared him off," said young-love. "Told him we were tracing his call."

"Well, we had work to do," Arlene said.

Jan thanked them and asked them to let her know if they

remembered anything else. In addition to the phone caller, she'd learned one important fact: Gavin was taking this seriously enough to conduct his own investigation. He wanted to make her look incompetent, no doubt. But his interest also meant this wasn't a prank. That knowledge was a relief, of sorts. Unless of course it was all part of an extremely elaborate put-down that included Gavin Larsen, whose sense of humor could have fit under a walnut shell. In other words, it was unlikely this was a joke.

"Hey," Arlene said, "you really think you can do that job as good as a man?"

"Maybe better."

"You're no taller than I am," she said, looking Jan over. "All bones too. What if you've got to wrestle some big baboon down?"

"Karate," Jan said as if explaining a secret.

Arlene glanced about to check their privacy. "I don't believe in that crap. Kick him in the balls. That's what works."

"Arlene . . ."

"Well, it does."

Jan left them quibbling. Back at the office, she used the phone-paging system to beep the nursing supervisor, then arranged to meet her near Surgical Intensive Care Unit number four, where the supervisor was handling staffing problems. To get there was a three-block walk and up two flights. Most of the doors she passed were closed with no sounds from within, and those that did have sounds, they weren't anything that Jan cared to listen to.

Despite the lateness of the hour, no hallowed tones for Faye Maygren, the nursing supervisor. In her late fifties with tousled black hair, some gray at the roots, she had a voice that was low and broke apart on every third or fourth word. At intervals you could see her lips move but there was no sound for a beat or two, and then audio returned and she rumbled along as though nothing was missing.

Little time for explanations. For the nursing supervisor, the graveyard shift was one skirmish after another: bed shortages in the ICUs; staff shortage in the maternity ward, where mothers weren't satisfied to bring them into the world one at a time but had taken to experimenting in larger allotments—pairs, triplets, who knew what other multiples would arrive before dawn. It was the damn fertility pills. The list of problems went on, augmented by lamebrain doctors and health insurance policies that dictated what patients could go to what hospitals for what kind of care. She confided that some nights it felt as though she was wearing a Beany-and-Cecil cap with the propeller top spinning constantly. Putting down the phone, she scribbled herself a note on a clipboard holding a census report that had a dozen hieroglyphs scratched on its margins.

"So you're the brave one?" the supervisor said, examining Jan as if she'd been expecting more. "What can I do for you?"

"I'm wondering about the procedure for dealing with a death," Jan said, her tone sounding so formal that she wanted to start over. She didn't, though. "How the bodies are taken care of."

"Popular topic tonight. This concerning that extra one down in the morgue?" Covering her mouth with the back of her hand, she coughed harshly but with an eerily muted sound. Once in control of her breath, she told Jan that another guard had already visited her—the balding one—and she doubted that she could shed any more light on the mystery than what she'd already told him. She started walking and motioned for Jan to fall into step beside her.

"Would you mind going over it again?" Jan asked.

The supervisor started to object but checked herself as if this once willing to make an allowance. "Sure. It's no big secret. The doctor writes *Pronounced dead at blank time* on the patient's chart, along with a short note describing the case, although if the death was unexpected the note might not be so short. In that case, the doc has to fill out a resuscitation report. Legal reasons. Anyway, the family's notified and allowed to view the remains. Somewhere in there we clean the body and someone, usually a nursing assistant, or if it's day shift, a transport orderly, hustles the dearly beloved down to the morgue, where it's either kept for an autopsy, if the physician thinks it might be useful and the family signs for it, or it's picked up by a funeral home. Sometimes, if it's a death that happened outside the hospital and came in through the ER—say a knifing or fire—the body's transported over to the county medical examiner's facilities for them to do their thing."

They'd left the glass hallway windows of the ICUs behind and moved into a long stretch of patient rooms.

"Down in Admissions I got three names," Jan said, gaining enough confidence to sound more natural, "all deceased in the last week, who never made it down to the morgue. What could have happened to them?"

"Funeral home probably took them right off the floor. You'd have to check their charts down in Medical Records to know."

"Could one of them be our body in the morgue?"

"Around here? Sure. I've seen it all happen, even miracles."

"By any chance," Jan said, "have you heard of any staff receiving a phone call about the body in the morgue? Say around two A.M.?" She explained the calls to Admissions.

"News to me," said the supervisor.

"Hmm. So who enters the person's name in the log book that's down in the morgue? The doctor?"

"What, you think one of the high and mighty is going to hike down there and do it? If that's what you're thinking, I've got my doubts about how long you're going to be around." She didn't lower her voice even though they were passing a team center where a resident looked up from a patient's chart. "The nursing staff does it, don't kid yourself."

"Any chance they might forget?"

"Don't be an innocent. Of course there's a chance. If you've ever worked understaffed with six to eight patients to cover, you might forget a detail or two yourself."

"Do we put them in leather body bags?"

"No way. This is the county, kiddo. Strictly plastic. Leather, that's what this one's in? Then someone else put him in it."

Her beeper went off and a garbled voice broadcast an extension to call. She plucked up the nearest phone and proceeded to hammer out whether an admit from the ER with cellulitis to the left leg required an isolation room. Jan stepped over to the window and stared up at the moon, a part of her wishing she was on it. A heavy haze filled the night sky, giving the moon a phosphorescent ring that made her feel wistful—for what she wasn't sure. She stared long enough to get angry about the lump in her throat and the sensation of floundering. When the supervisor returned, Jan said, "If I gave you the initials of the staff who checked the most recent bodies into the morgue, could you give me their full names?"

"Don't go simple on me, now. I've got over a hundred and twenty nurses on duty tonight alone, and half the time I call them all Mary. Big joke, huh? I'll tell you what I can do, though. You can have a look at the work rosters for the dates and stations you want. They'll be on there. You're groping, huh? Don't let that bother you. The guy who talked to me first didn't even think to ask about those initials from the log. Why are two of you working this over, anyway?" Jan's lack of response caused a knowing glance from the supervisor. "The boys playing games with you?"

"Apparently," Jan said, relieved not to have to explain. "Anything he asked that I didn't?"

The supervisor started to grin but a cough squeezed it off. "Only if this had ever happened before."

"What'd you tell him?"

"Subversive old bitch that I am, I didn't tell him a thing, not with the way he asked it."

"Has anything like this ever happened before?"

"Not in twenty years. Somebody tried to steal one from the morgue once, but that probably doesn't count, huh?"

"What in the world did they want with a body?"

"Fraternity over at the university was having a Halloween scavenger hunt. One of the boys—a little unbalanced, I'd say—took some of the instructions too literally. Got a slap on the hands, if I remember right. Anything unusual about this extra we have?"

"He's wearing a tuxedo. Has a cigar stuffed in his mouth."

The supervisor shook her head in disgusted wonder. "Sounds like somebody's after you, lady."

4

STANLEY Charais was an unexceptional man in every way but one: his capacity for the unexpected. He'd been engaged twice—to different nurses—and bailed out directly above the altar both times. He'd once pinned a three-hundred-pound professional wrestler, by the name of Colossal Stud, to the floor in Detox. Another time he'd accompanied a wealthy widow to Rio for no better reason than her admiration of his derriere, as she put it.

What caused these sudden bouts of the unexpected was no mystery. They were the direct result of someone misjudging his age, someone such as Jan Gallagher. When she bullied him into admitting that he and Melody were having problems, he'd felt about twelve years old and could see purple spots before his eyes—a sure sign of a pending eruption of unpredictableness. She couldn't treat *him* that way.

A few minutes after leaving the morgue, he wandered over to A building and accidentally crossed paths with Gavin Larsen to whom he found himself confiding, "She's out to get you."

Larsen ho-hoed but a minute later dispatched his partner, Cindi Paige, on a bogus errand to the Psych Unit and then demanded of Stan, "All right, junior, what did you mean: she's out to get me?"

His word choice, tone, and the way he'd latched on to Stan's arm brought back the purple spots.

"Just that. She thinks you planted a corpse in the morgue." He quickly sketched in the rest of the story.

"Why in hell would I do that?" Gavin Larsen said.

"To make her look bad, I suppose."

"That crazy . . ."

You could see deep, awful thoughts cascading through Larsen's mind. Furrows climbed high up his brow. Sliding both hands in his back pockets, he parted his lips enough to bare his upper teeth. He was single—not divorced—the one confirmed bachelor on the security staff. He didn't smoke, didn't gamble, but did curse if the need arose, which it generally did when dealing with women—in the abstract or the specific. They weren't a race to be trusted. As he put it, if it weren't for bad luck, he would never have known any women at all.

"Doesn't make sense, does it?" Stan innocently agreed.

"I'm not going to goddamn stand for it."

"You ought to do something."

"You're goddamn right I'm going to do something."

"Like what?"

The question seized Gavin Larsen with the force of a blow. His face went deathly still and what sounded like a hum started deep down in his throat, mounting in force until it burst loose.

"I'm going to prove to the whole hospital what we've known all along," Larsen said. "She shouldn't be where she is. She got there because everything in this country is going to hell in a hand basket. Ninety miles an hour, straight to hell, no off-ramps, and nobody's willing to say so. Nobody but me." He leaned menacingly toward Stan. "I'll find where that body came from, and I'll do it way before Gallagher does. You'll see . . ."

Larsen pulled unexpectedly away, perhaps realizing that he'd said too much, but not willing to back down either. He peeled off toward Admissions without clarifying what would soon be proved to everyone. His exit left Stan feeling better, much better.

Over the next half hour Stan was kept busy with Galahad duty, escorting to their cars nurses who had pulled overtime. He walked tall beside them into the big bad city night so that they wouldn't get raped, assaulted, or kidnapped—all of which had been known to happen. The role of protector worked on him, eating away at how clever he felt, until he almost began to feel blamable for the maliciousness of what he'd set in motion. Believe it or not, Jan Gallagher belonged to the fairer sex. And normally—he told himself—he was an easygoing guy. Not that he suffered enough guilt to confess to anything; that struck him as too childish. No, better to do something that balanced everything out. And with that in mind, he sought out Leo Kennedy, the department's good samaritan.

Finding Leo took some time because he looked where Leo was supposed to be first, and in the obvious places last, but eventually he found him guarding the vending machines in a commons area. As Leo blew on a paper cup of coffee, Stan poured out a slightly modified version of what had happened in the morgue and with Larsen. Leo he-he-heed two or three times in a deep ruminative way. In his midforties, he was huffing and puffing toward bypass surgery. His hair remained a rooster red, thanks to the mysteries of modern cosmetology, but his mustache had never known those mysteries and was speckled white. He had an Irish brogue when it suited him and a mole on his forehead that he called Fred and sometimes carried on conversations with, although not that night.

"To sum up what you've been saying," Leo said, smiling broadly, "Jan's wondering whether someone—maybe me or brilliant old Gavin—has been doing a little sleight of hand. You went and blabbed all this to Gavin, who reared up on his hind legs and swore vengeance. And now you've come running to me, maybe hoping I can do something to smooth the troubled waters. That it?"

"Leo," Stan said, uneasy because this wasn't the way he'd envisioned Leo reacting, "I've seen that look before. What are you thinking?"

"That sometimes the only way to tame a storm is to rile things up more."

"Leo . . ."

"Stan, my boy, tell me what you'd do if you were in my shoes. If you could fill them, that is."

Nervous, Stan said, "I'm already in deep enough with her. I think she got the idea I enjoyed trying to stump her."

"And didn't you?"

"Come on. I don't mind Jan. She's OK."

"So what if you've applied for her job twice now, eh? You wouldn't act in anything less than a professional manner. Am I right, Stanley?"

"Say, I'm not the only one upset. Look at Larsen. They change the rules on you, a guy's got a right to be put out. But that doesn't mean I necessarily blame Gallagher."

Putting a hand on Stan's bony shoulder, Leo leaned closer, coffee on his breath. "Where's your chivalry, Stan? If the young woman thinks we're trying to bamboozle and humiliate her, why then, we'd better get to work. It's not polite to keep a lady waiting." He sipped his coffee and stared thoughtfully out at the traffic on Wabash Avenue, which divided Old General, also known as A building, from New

General, B building, although even New General was built nearly fifty years ago. At that early hour traffic amounted to a street sweeper beeping and grinding along the curb. In a speculative way, Leo said, "Have you ever done a security check on the cafeteria?"

"Come on, I've been here almost as long as you."

"So you have. You remember when they had the loss control problem up there? The case of the missing pork chops?"

"Who caught the cook?" Stan said. "Damn near froze to death waiting for something to happen." He rubbed his arms in memory.

"Ah. Then you remember how the walk-in freezer up there has space in the back that's never used?"

Stan stopped rubbing his arms. "What are you going to do?"

Grinning, Leo stood. "Come on, Stanley, I can't let you down. What I'm saying is, you wouldn't have come running to me if you hadn't thought I was a man of valor and action. Am I right?" When Stan looked away, Leo quickly sobered. "We can forget the whole affair if you're going to tattle."

"Say, have I ever?"

"Not to my knowledge. But then again, there's a snitch or two loose somewhere. Who was it, I've often asked myself, that fingered me for putting the *Shoot the NRA* sticker on the bumper of our fearless leader's Chrysler?"

"I didn't tell Hodges about it," Stan said stubbornly.

"Maybe not, but I've a hunch you know who did."

"Forget it, Leo. Even if I did, I wouldn't tell you."

He enthusiastically thumped Stan on the back. "That's the spirit. You're the kind of tight-lipped recruit I need for this little enterprise. This time of night there'll be nothing to it. We push it out of the morgue, glide along the tunnel quiet as tax lawyers. Nobody'll be down there to notice. It'll be child's play. Yes. What now? Is that hesitation I see? Don't you think we owe it to the rest of the staff to determine just what kind of resolve our new supervisor has?"

With Leo smothering Stan's objections, they started toward the morgue. When they arrived at room 060, Stan held the door shut with the flat of his hand and asked, "We move it to the cafeteria, then what?"

"Why, that's obvious, isn't it? In two days we move it back to the morgue. If we don't, Lord knows what kind of casserole we'll be eating next week."

"Ha-ha," Stan said dryly. "Move it out, move it back. And not a word to anyone. Ever." Stan stressed this part. In the past Leo had occasionally been unable to resist bragging about his escapades.

"Absolutely," Leo said, opening the door.

"And that's all you're going to want to do?"

Entering the cooler, Leo started rolling out the cart. "Stop hovering, Stanley. There's no need to get all upset. The person inside this bag is going to be just as comfy up in the cafeteria freezer as down in the morgue. Maybe more so. He can grab a snack if he has a mind to."

"Not funny."

"All right," Leo said, "maybe we should ask him which freezer he prefers." He started to zip open the body bag. "It'll only take a minute, and I've a hunch it will put your mind to rest." He looked down at the dead man's face, graciously saying, "Sir, my partner is wondering if you have any preference—" The mischievousness departed from Leo's ruddy face. Slack-jawed, he said, "Jesus."

"What?" Stan said, crowding closer.

"It's Doc Croft. How the hell did you get in this predicament, Doc?"

5

THE joke in Security was that Rodney Dangerfield would have been a prime candidate for their ranks. No respect was the rule. Too many people thought of security officers as police department rejects, retired boiler operators, or moonlighting Catholics with ten children to shoe and feed. But on any given shift, a security officer at General Jack had to cope with more shouting, slashing, spitting citizens than your average city cop. Within the last year: 228 arrests, 107 reported thefts ranging from a doctor's Porsche to a wall telephone, 81 attempted assaults with deadly weapons ranging from a 12-gauge pump to the incisors of an AIDS patient, 21 attempted suicides, 14 cases of arson, 2 attempted armed robberies of the pharmacy, 1 rape, and legions of minor disputes—all happening in a three-block area. And all handled by Security without a Smith & Wesson snuggling against their hips,

The average age in Security was twenty-nine, not sixty-seven. Injuries from tussles with patients or friends of patients were common, 3.6 a year per officer. To get hired, a candidate had to pass a battery of tests, including written, oral, psychological, agility, and physical; and those who weren't winnowed out by the tests had an eight-week training period to endure. Not that trainees generally had difficulty with the physical portion of their on-the-job routine, but some became disillusioned with other aspects of the position. The antagonism of fellow hospital employees who thought they were being spied on by little tin soldiers was generally an unexpected shock. And the open hostility of the largest percentage of General Jack's clientele—minority groups such as African Americans, Native Americans, and the refugees: Cubans, Ethiopians, Central Americans, or Southeast Asians—this pressure KO'd more than one candidate's ambitions. Maybe the only department that truly valued their contribution was the Emergency Room, which on some nights found it impossible to function without some law and order.

Then there was the fact that—like everyone else at General Jack—the security guards worked for the county government, which was little more than an enormous paper incinerator. For almost every duty they performed there was a form to fill out or a statistic to be tallied. If they had a suggestion for how to improve their job or some other hospital operation, the layers of management to go through effectively diverted the suggestion into the incinerator, where it at least served the useful purpose of generating a little heat, or else management subverted the suggestion until it was an unrecognizable piece of gibberish that boomeranged back at the guards in the form of a memo.

Memos! The stories that could be told about them. Long memos. Short memos. Contradictory memos. Senseless memos. How did the legions of memos affect the security officers? A slow asphyxiation.

They had to apply double wristlocks on thrashing Benzedrine ODs who needed intubation, but a recent memo cautioned them about cursing at patients. They were expected to be streetwise enough to jive-talk with assault victims, who rarely had elevated opinions of anyone dressed in a uniform, but because of a recent complaint, they had to avoid sounding condescending. They walked long, boring rounds, turning door handles and faucets and doing checklists on fire code items, and then they wrote end-of-shift incident reports that were equally long and boring.

The frustration resulting from all this may help to explain why Leo Kennedy very nearly ended up spending the night in a detention cell at the city jail and why Jan Gallagher inherited a small but undeniable shiner—as in a black eye. On the other hand, there may be a simpler reason, such as the fact that Leo's brother-in-law was a city cop who at every family gathering built himself up to be some kind of one-man task force preventing organized crime from taking over the city, and he talked to Leo as if the only men who worked in hospitals—aside from docs, of course—were all pansies hoping for a free peek at every bottom-side that came through the turnstiles. And his idea was that maybe more than a few of the MDs shared that inclination.

The news that the John Doe was one of the hospital's finest didn't provoke Jan. No exclamations. Not even a lifted eyebrow. Her first thought was that at last the gag was unfolding. Then she remembered that she'd decided this wasn't a gag.

"Not that I doubt your memory, Leo, but we'd better get someone else to collaborate. Why don't you and Stan go back down to the morgue, and I'll contact the nursing supervisor. She ought to be able to identify Dr. Croft."

Leo caught her drift immediately. Several weeks before he had had the nursing supervisor's car towed from a no-parking zone. Not that he could be expected to recognize the vehicle of every one of over three thousand employees, but when all was said and done, a memo concerning professional courtesy was posted on Security's bulletin board. When Jan picked up the phone, he commented, "If it's the one who can't see no-parking signs the size of billboards, I don't know what good it will do."

Jan hesitated. "Other suggestions?"

"You could take my word for it."

"Leo, with your history, would you?"

"Trust myself all the time." A simple nod of his red head, as if this arrangement had worked out fairly well.

"Answer this—what took you down there?"

The question made Stan shift weight in his chair, but Leo wasn't taken aback. "Why, Stanley told me about the big mystery and how you seemed to think I was involved. I didn't want to disappoint you."

"That's all?"

"Well," Leo said devilishly, "actually, we were going to pull a little switcharoo on you until I noticed it was Doc Croft. Then we deep-sixed that idea and came up here straightaway."

Jan checked with Stan, who was making a warning face at Leo. "Is that true, Stan?"

"I was trying to talk him out of it."

"Pshaw," said Leo.

"And there's still an extra body down in the morgue?" Jan asked. "Because if there isn't, you're going to be rather embarrassed when the nursing supervisor meets *you* down there. She's a busy woman, with a short temper, as you may remember."

Leo solemnly said, "Unless the good doctor riseth from the dead, he'll be waiting below. As to the lion of nursing, I think she's kind of cute with steam pouring out her belly button."

Jan nodded as if expecting such malarkey and silently elected to accompany her two officers back to the lower level. In the elevator, Leo lamented, "I used to make good money off Doc Croft. He always bet against the line." Stan kept clearing his throat as if he had a continent wedged in it. Jan unconsciously distanced herself from the two of them while remembering that she had thought the corpse's face looked familiar.

Faye Maygren took one look and said, "Yup, Dr. Croft, one of the boy wonders up on Neurology. Going somewhere special by the looks of it." She leaned over and inspected the chinstrap holding his jaw shut and the cigar in place between his lips. "He's bit into that pretty good." She straightened and cradled the clipboard against her chest. "We lose staff around here pretty regularly, but never this way before. Somebody will have to notify the family, if there is one. Don't know much about his private life. Kept to himself. Think he was single."

"There's no doubt it's him?" Jan asked.

"I argued with the hotshot often enough. He had a tendency to undermedicate and then blame it on my staff."

"Any idea how long he's been here?"

The supervisor pressed the back of a finger against the man's cheek. The skin appeared taut and resisted the pressure she exerted. "Cool to the touch. No resilience. You'll have to wait for an autopsy, and even then the time of death won't be easy to estimate, not with him lying in here. Check with the Neurological Intensive Care Unit, that's his home away from home. They'll have a pretty good idea of how long he's been missing."

Lowering her voice, the supervisor said, "You've got a real can of worms here, lady. Keep a close lid on it. Don't let a newspaper reporter within a block of it, television reporters, a mile. And I'd make double sure your two physics teachers back there"—she nodded toward Leo and Stan—"understand that directive. Administration will be howling when they find out, so you better notify whichever one of them's on emergency call. But my main advice to you, lady, is to distance yourself from this any way you can. It's called covering your ass, and around here it works like a charm."

As Faye Maygren parted the two guards in the doorway, she shot Leo a glance that could have been felt in the next county. He radiated all the more. Jan once again zipped the body bag up, stationed Leo outside the morgue, dispatched Stan on the scheduled check of the clinics, and returned to the Security office to consider her next move.

She'd had two days of orientation with the day shift supervisor and his advice had been this: "If you come up against it, go to the procedure manuals. Fifty percent of the time they'll be wrong, but at least you'll have an explanation for why you did what you did. If you see what I mean."

At the time, she hadn't. But now several fundamental questions arose for which she had no basis for making a decision, and she wasn't about to hold a consult with Gavin Larsen. It was 3:50 A.M. Whom should she roll out of a deep slumber? Her supervisor, she supposed. The administration liaison person on call seemed a wise choice. The police, certainly. But in what order?

The possibilities gave her a slight headache. Whatever order she picked would later be criticized. Any county employee could tell you that. So she went to the procedure manuals for relief. The manuals consisted of three loose-leaf notebooks, each as thick as an unabridged dictionary. Volume one stated the goals and responsibilities of the department. Volume two was a compendium of procedures for carrying out everything from bomb threat evacuations to vehicle towing. Volume three—the thickest—was a chronological listing of every memo that had come ripping down the pike in the four years since volumes one and two had been compiled. In other words, volume three revoked most of what was stated in the first two volumes if you could track down the proper entry.

She wasted ten minutes leafing through the manuals without finding any reference on how to handle a homicide. She did, however, scavenge phone numbers for her boss's home, the local police precinct, and instructions to call the hospital phone operator to obtain the number of the administration liaison person on call.

Starting with the police, she discovered the number listed in the manual was no longer connected and no forwarding number was included on the phone company's recorded message. Her situation requiring drastic measures, she resorted to the telephone directory. A policeman at the Fifth Precinct answered, "Fifth, Sergeant Bandzak."

Jan carefully explained who she was and why she was calling.

"So," Sergeant Bandzak said, "you got a dead body. That can't be something new to you people."

"The problem is," Jan said, "we don't know how he got dead."

"There's a variety of ways that can happen," Sergeant Bandzak calmly explained. "The medical examiner usually figures them out."

"That's what we'd eventually like to happen," Jan said. "But it looks like a crime may be involved."

"Look"—the officer's voice lowered—"it's four in the morning. How long do you say this guy's been cooling his heels over there?"

"We don't really know."

"What I'm trying to get at, little lady, is maybe you could call back in three hours when the day shift starts. This could wait that long, huh? We're short staffed ever since the birthday party you maybe read about in the papers."

He was referring to a birthday celebration thrown by one of the city's most eligible young heiresses, a coming-out party of sorts. Entertainment was several young cops who artfully removed their uniforms for considerable sums of money. One underfed rookie, who didn't pass the screen test, squealed to Vice, and the end result was the suspension without pay of five police officers for a period of one month's time. Four of the cops happened to serve in the Fifth Precinct.

"As far as I'm concerned," Jan said, "the ball's in your court. I'm reporting what appears to be a homicide. How you handle it on your end is none of my business."

"OK, little lady. OK. I read you loud and clear. There'll be someone there."

The wording for her call to Eldon Hodges, head of Security, was something she considered thoroughly and even wrote out in longhand so that she could read it. But when she rang his number, she reached a recorded answer: "You have the Hodges residence, coordinates 377-2424. Leave your communication at the tone."

It was the same imbecilic voice from on high that he used when making announcements at staff meetings. Closing her eyes, Jan left a message for him to phone work as soon as possible.

It required a tiny threat to get the administration liaison's home number from the hospital operator. The Communications Center had recently received a memo forbidding them to give out such information over the phone. The administrator on call was none other than Elizabeth Kavanaugh, golden girl of hospital administration even though only an administrator trainee. She had been one of the key witnesses called forward by General Jack in Jan's sexual discrimination suit. If she'd made it to her lofty position, could Jackson General be considered a discriminatory work environment? Turns out, yes, it could. Or at least the court thought so, mentioning token recruitment as insufficient for today's times and needs.

Ms. Kavanaugh answered on the third ring, sounding awake and as though caught in the middle of a voice lesson, despite the time of 4:35 A.M. Enunciating each vowel clearly, she promised to be there in thirty minutes, then made it in twenty-five, arriving on the heels of a patrolman dispatched from the Fifth Precinct. She wore a gray-blue dress suit that was cleverly cut to camouflage wide hips and stout legs that went against the illusion of petiteness she endorsed for herself. Being very short and blessed with delicate cheekbones and lips, she generally succeeded in her deception. Her pretty face had the dual quality of a two-way mirror: you could see her smiling on the surface but it felt as though someone behind that facade was scrutinizing your every move. Even at the current unheard-of hour, she had a knack for conveying that she pitied you, and she even sounded eager for some responsibilities, as if she didn't have enough to do from eight to five, Monday through Friday.

To start with, she pretended that it was absolutely no problem that Jan had gotten her out of bed at 4:35 in the morning, a time that she mentioned quite exactly. She'd simply hitched a ride in with her husband, a prominent cardiovascular surgeon whom she rarely failed to mention at least once in any conversation. He had been called in to perform an emergency triple bypass on a visiting dignitary from the Philippines. Motioning Jan to the side, she asked, "Don't you think it was a bit premature to involve the police?"

The hallway was about eight feet across, and they all stood in such close proximity that the patrolman and Leo both sucked in their guts.

"We'd identified the body," Jan said. "It appeared likely that a crime had been committed, so I phoned the police."

Kavanaugh flashed a smile at the two men before pivoting away, scowling, and tugging Jan farther down the hall to prevent eavesdropping.

"Don't be an ass," Kavanaugh said. "Are you or are you not hired to protect this hospital?"

"Of course I am."

"That *certainly* must include protecting its image, don't you think?"

Jan removed the administrator's hand from her sleeve and said, "If you're unhappy with the way I've handled this, we can take it up later. I don't think now is the time."

There was a little glitch in Kavanaugh's reaction, so that the face beneath the face was briefly revealed, but then everything melded into sisterhood. "Naturally you're right. What do you have so far?"

Jan delivered the facts and asked, "Did you want to see the corpse?"

"I can't see what possible purpose that would serve," Kavanaugh said, speaking fast enough to sound squeamish. "I will, however, notify the essential people so that we can contain whatever you've unleashed here." She started toward the nearest elevator bank, stopped, and coolly ordered in a voice loud enough for the two men to hear, "Whatever you do, no more people are to be notified. Do you understand?"

"Perfectly."

Power smile from Kavanaugh. "You can reach me at extension 3800. If anything arises for which you may need help, don't hesitate. Although I'm sure you're perfectly capable."

At committee meetings, over sugar cookies and cafeteria coffee, it sounded as though the cooperation between the city's police department and General Jack's security department was first rate. That didn't take into account city cops who thought that every security officer wanted to grow up to be just like them. As soon as Elizabeth Kavanaugh was out of sight, the patrolman and Leo started trading admirations.

"The thing that would get me down about working in a place like this," the patrolman was saying, "is that it's not first string. Take for instance, say you get in trouble over here, or you got something you can't handle, what do you do?"

The cop was maybe six feet tall, but even if you stretched him up to seven foot he'd still have a serious weight problem. The way he talked was somewhere between Fred Flintstone and Barney Rubble.

"What do we do?" Leo asked, wary of a trick question. In addition to having a brother-in-law on the city force, Leo himself had been a suburban cop for three years, so he proceeded directly to the right button and pushed it. "Why, we'd call in the little boys in blue."

"You being funny?" The patrolman squinted.

"Not me," Leo answered, completely ignoring Jan, who had returned from walking Kavanaugh to the elevators. "Not unless you want me to be. I do a pretty good imitation of the chief of police talking underwater to the city council."

"The first thing you do over here," the policeman went on, doing his level best to ignore Leo's wisecrack, "is call us in. You need somebody arrested, you call us in. You need some firepower, you call us in. Strictly second string."

"You mean like the time one of your prisoners escaped from our ER?" Leo asked.

The patrolman acted suspicious. It sounded as though Leo was suddenly agreeing with him. "Watch it."

"The guy stripped one of you first stringers of his firepower and held some little old lady with a broken hip hostage. Guess who had to collar him?"

Jan was right beside Leo now, but he continued to ignore her, as did the patrolman.

"You got time to make stories up," the cop said. "I'll listen. It's only polite."

"That's mighty white of you."

The two men squared off. Jan rolled her eyes, saying, "Leo, that's enough."

"Yeah, Leo."

"Officer," Jan said, "I assume you've been sent here to secure the scene of a possible crime?"

The cop ignored her, saying to Leo, "I hear some buzzing?"

"Hard to say with those flappers of yours," Leo said.

"Leo . . ."

"I definitely hear some buzzing," the cop said. "Who is this lady bee?"

"This is my supervisor," Leo said, taking a perverse pride in the announcement.

"Oh, I'm sure."

The patter continued on for another minute, insults to mothers and genitalia dragged out, nothing nearing intelligence being involved. Neither of the men acknowledged Jan's requests to cease and desist. Chests swelled. Eyes went gunslinger.

Finally Leo said, "Enough shit," and tried swinging his elbow into the cop's substantial gut. The cop turned out to have reflexes and blocked Leo's thrust easily, then butted the crown of his head against Leo's chest, staggering him backward. From two feet back, Leo shook his head to clear his vision and said, "That seals it." He charged, tackling the cop to the tiled floor where they punched and grappled, rolling about with enough grunts and curses to make it sound like the real thing, whatever that might be. Mortal combat. King of the hill. My wa-wa's bigger than yours.

For a moment, Jan stood back, fascinated, wondering what damage they could inflict on one another, hoping they would do some. But then the possibility of Elizabeth Kavanaugh returning to ask a question occurred to her, along with the ramifications of one of her staff being brought up on assault charges, and she tried pulling Leo off the top. That's when she caught a knuckle on her cheek. No idea which of them threw it, but it firmed up her resolution considerably. Nightstick in hand, she waited her chance, waded in, knelt to keep her balance, and thwacked Leo across the base of the skull, careful to avoid the temple, just as the training films instructed. Instant Jello.

The cop squirmed out from underneath, thinking about one last lick, actually scoping out where it would go to best advantage, until Jan suggested, "Unless you want misconduct charges, I wouldn't."

Rubbing his shoulder, he backed off, satisfying himself with an epitaph. "Bush league. Strictly."

It was shortly thereafter that Gavin Larsen arrived, alerted by some little bird that the corpse had been identified and that he was possibly missing out on all the fun. He took one look at Leo sitting on the floor, rubbing his neck; he took a second look at the city cop gloating a few feet away. The first noble words out of his mouth were to Jan.

"Gallagher, I owe you an apology. It looks as though I should have offered to help you tonight."

He sounded delighted with the discovery. Jan's face, watery eye included, screwed up as if she was about to provide an uplifting answer, but Leo beat her to it.

"She's been doing just fine without you."

Gavin Larsen took that hard, as if he'd been cheated out of some glory that was rightfully his. Leo put a hand out to the city cop, who—grinning—helped him up. *You figure it,* Jan thought as she returned to Security's office to write a report to end all reports. As she wrote, Gavin sat across from her and smoldered as pleasantly as an old tire about to catch fire. He came closest to igniting each time she wet a pencil point in her mouth and let a vacant look fill her eyes, as though she didn't know what to say next but wasn't about to ask for help.

After finishing the report, she left Gavin staring at her empty chair and went to the nursing supervisor's office to match the initials and work stations from the morgue's log book to the nursing supervisor's work rosters. She found the names she wanted and their current assignments but didn't have time to start interviewing them before the arrival of the day shift.

6

A T 6:55 Eldon Hodges arrived in his office, located in the newly remodeled administration wing; the time was five minutes before his normal punctual arrival on a weekday. That in itself was enough to set fire to his mood. But this was a weekend. A twenty-year man in the merchant marines, he put great stock in sticking to schedules. He stood barely as tall as Jan and could have fit three of her inside his waist size. Sitting down required concentration, not only because of the size of his poop deck but also because up top he balanced a black toupee that—in keeping with his maritime background—always reminded Jan of a crow's nest. Although he no longer wore a uniform, the press and stiffness of his suits left the impression that a squad of miniature midshipmen was about to march out of his briefcase and do his bidding. Also, he had a habit of standing rigidly behind his desk with a hand on the back of his chair and a dauntless look in his eyes that said, *Steady as she goes.* Finally, there were suspenders: he wore them.

Behind his back, everyone called him the Admiral, or more completely, the Little Admiral of General Jack. Never having successfully made the transition from the ocean, where he controlled everything from direction and speed to meal menus, to the hospital, where he controlled little more than the time he arrived at work, if that, the Little Admiral became fixated with results. Anyone who could achieve what they set out to do became a miracle worker; anyone who couldn't get results became a burden.

Through his bifocals he glanced from Jan—avoiding her swollen-shut eye and concentrating on her throat—to Gavin Larsen, then back to the report Jan had handed him. He stood behind his chair and rested a hand on its back as he spoke.

"Gallagher, if you accomplish this on day one, I can hardly wait for your second shift."

"I didn't put the body down there," Jan pointed out.

The Little Admiral didn't respond but stared straight ahead, between two chairs filled by Jan and the daytime supervisor, Robert Yost, a family man with prematurely gray hair that was due in no small part to daily working with the Admiral. Gavin Larsen stood glumly to the side, arms crossed, sturdy chin thrust out. The idea of an office was alien to a seagoing man like Eldon Hodges, and he'd turned its decoration over to his wife, who'd transformed it into a surprisingly homey setting with soft end-table lighting and two display cases of porcelain figurines collected in ports of call on the Pacific rim. The net result, however, was to intensify how far out of his element the Admiral was, for he was too inflexible to ever get in sync with comfy settings.

"Our official priorities shall be these," he said. "First, to cooperate fully with the police department's investigation into this case. Second, to protect the interests of Jackson

County Medical Center, completely and successfully. Questions?"

Glancing at the two men on either side of her, Jan saw blank expressions, so took it upon herself to ask, "What if those two points clash?"

"Exercise judgment. That's what we're paying you for, right?"

Yost quit taking notes to nod and Larsen lowered his chin in agreement, which led Jan to recognize that something was being said indirectly. What that something might be, she didn't know, nor did she believe that the two other dummies on her side of the desk had a perfectly clear picture, but they weren't about to admit it. Male stuff. So Jan took it upon herself to ask.

"You're saying to cooperate with the police unless there's a conflict of interest with the hospital?"

The Admiral rested his eyes on the space between Jan and Yost. The bell-jar clock on the credenza behind him chimed out the quarter hour with a maritime melody, "Anchors Away." The Little Admiral paused as if counting internal organs. "No, I'm saying to exercise judgment and follow the chain of command."

That still didn't sound like a direct yes or no, but she dummied up too, recognizing there were limits.

"Now then," the Admiral said, floating the report down on his desk and rolling up his sleeves. No tattoos of anchors or mermaids decorated his forearms; he'd been an officer. "That's the official and utterly essential. Now we discuss what we're going to do ourselves." He planted his knuckles on the desk and leaned forward. "Because I'm here to tell you that I take this as a personal insult. And I don't want some city detectives walking in on our turf and cracking this. We're going to hand this over to the PD so completely solved that even the district attorney can't fumble it away." He paused to deal a fierce and meaningful stare to each of his subordinates. Jan figured this was the part where they girded their loins. The Little Admiral went on. "I'm not going to give you any more direction than that. But I'm weighing performance on this heavily." He ceased eye contact with everyone and went back to gazing at the Strait of Magellan. "We're talking job evaluation. Am I clear?"

Definitely not. But Jan had suffered about all the clarification she could endure for one day.

"From the top then."

Jan obliged without interruption except from Larsen, who couldn't resist a cheap shot or two.

"Gavin," the Little Admiral said, interrupting Larsen's second interruption of Jan, "where were you when she was trying to cover all this?"

"In A building," Gavin guardedly said. Normally, he prided himself on refusing to make excuses. Jan didn't know if she'd ever heard him deliver any, and this one came off rusty.

"Not training Gallagher in?"

"She assigned me A building."

"And what did I assign you?"

"She didn't seem to want my help," Gavin maintained, ready to make his last stand on the point if need be.

"We'll talk about that later," the Admiral said, dismissing the topic. "Right now Gallagher's trying to tell us how and why she did what she did." Back to Jan. "Proceed."

When it was all laid out, she received neither assurances that she'd done the job properly, nor a critique on how she'd done it wrong, although Larsen's brooding eyes offered their negative assessment. At the end she got nothing from the Admiral or Yost, the Admiral's protégé. Trying to interpret their blankness was maddening, and the meeting ended with no more specific instructions from the Admiral than a rousing "Go out there and find whoever has done this thing. Results, people. Results. They are utterly essential."

He wasn't holding up a starter's gun, but it certainly felt that way to Jan, a fact that didn't make her happy. She'd never won a race in her life. Didn't like them. Thought they were invented by someone with a good pair of legs, not that hers were bad, just not fast. As to whether or not the Little Admiral approved or disapproved of her actions, her promotion, her hairstyle—she had no more inkling now than before. The Admiralty strained to always be in control of its feelings.

The city PD had a forensics team in the morgue searching for whatever the naked eye might overlook. Accompanying the boys with the magnifying glasses was a big hulking detective, one of those men who's so ugly, so hatchet faced, that if Jan looked long enough she usually began to imagine he was handsome, then qualified that impulse by saying, *In a rugged sort of way.* He wanted to ask her a few questions, if she didn't mind. Nice set of manners on him. He even introduced himself, Detective Frank White, and shook her hand firmly without any gratuitous little squeeze at the end to see if she gave at the office. So she ran it all down again, and he took notes without making any snide comments about why she'd removed the first HELP ME sign from the outer door.

"I see," he kept saying as she talked. His brown eyes watched intently, from either side of a nose outcropping worth commenting on. "I see." And when she was done, he said, "I see. Thank you. Are you the one who buffaloed our desk sergeant at four this morning?"

"I am."

"The one who coldcocked her own officer?"

"I am."

"I see."

He said all this with diplomacy, but Jan, not being used to working through the night and having had trouble sleeping the day before because of nerves, was fatigued enough to overreact by sniping, "Exactly what is it that you see?"

That made him smile, and hiding behind that face, which even a mother would have trouble with—a curved scar on his left nostril, a thick droopy mustache that made his thin eyebrows looked fire damaged, a small hairless disk near his chin—behind all that lay a perfect set of teeth, small and as even as any videotape on making your first million could demand.

"I'd like to take you out to dinner sometime," he said.

"Not a chance."

He lifted a threadbare eyebrow. "Not pretty enough?"

"You look married."

"Not true," said Detective Frank White, still smiling, though reduced, as if it had once been true, which was a fact he didn't want to think about. He handed her a business card. "If you think of anything else, give me a call."

"What's that supposed to mean?"

The smiling stopped. "It means that we could use your help in this investigation. You know this hospital, its staff. You may be able to recognize things that I wouldn't even begin to notice."

"Oh."

"One other thing."

"I had a hunch," Jan cynically said.

"Sometimes when a person finds a dead body, they feel responsible. They do things that are, well, foolish." He said this earnestly, as if advising a friend. "You be careful about that. This definitely looks like homicide."

"I can take care of myself," she said, touchy.

"I'm sure you can."

With that, he left her standing in the hallway feeling half-witted, an experience that was becoming increasingly familiar without growing on her.

Walking required commitment, she was that tired, but before she released from General Jack she wound to the third floor and the Neurological Intensive Care Unit to see if she could talk to someone about Dr. Croft. It was now Saturday morning, the floor's busiest time of the day. What with shift change and the beginning of A.M. care—medications, baths, scheduling tests—and the fact that the nurses were chronically understaffed, she didn't learn much beyond the fact that saying Dr. Croft's name soured their mouths, giving the impression he wasn't respected and cherished as a healer. The station clerk suggested, "Why don't you come back on Monday. You can talk to the great man yourself."

"Oh?" Jan said, so groggy that she was startled by the possibility.

"Yeah. That's when he comes back from vacation. We can hardly wait."

So they didn't know yet.

"Oh," Jan said, acting relieved, which puzzled the clerk. "How long's he been gone?"

"Not long enough."

"How long's that?"

"So far, fourteen days." The clerk checked a wall clock. "Want the hours and minutes?"

"Know where he went?"

"Nope. Just a few suggestions for where he could have gone."

"Don't like him?"

"Oh no, he's perfect. What wouldn't I like about him?"

Her act was cut short by a phone call. The clerk had to madly dash off orders being dictated by a physician waiting to tee off on a par three at a country club. She made silent monkey faces at the receiver while her handwriting blurred to keep up.

Stepping outside General Jack after a shift was always a shock. Something about the General's densely packed halls, the lack of windows in Security's office, the complete focusing on what transpired or expired within the hospital's boundaries—all that rubbed out memory of the world beyond. But when Jan stepped outside it all came back with a roar, as if she'd skipped a heartbeat, and made her feel giddy. But what the hell, she'd changed out of her uniform. A hazy sun warmed her face, and a row of crazy blackbirds lined up on a billboard advertising discount airfares. A breeze off the lake had even seeped through the three miles of cityscape and freshened up the leaks in manhole covers. And she'd made it through shift number one.

She navigated her dinged-up Pontiac, a holdover from husband number two, to her home in one of the near burbs. She'd driven the route so many times that her automatic pilot could handle it, which was a lucky thing, heavy as her eyelids felt. A few one-way blocks, then the on-ramp, then the freeway and the crisscrossing of semis hauling cargo from God knows where. She always felt an affinity with the over-the-road drivers and had often thought that some day she might try it, although it was another role-reversal job, which put her off. But maybe. There might be some freedom in it. No, that was probably a lie too. Who knew? Then the off-ramp and a quick stop at a Tom Thumb for milk and raisin bread. After a few blocks of maples looking an over-ripe green and panting for fall's first freeze, she hit her street, Marymount Avenue, whose quiet, well-tended properties were as far removed from General Jack as you could get without living on a postcard. For a moment she sat and stared at her canary-yellow rambler that was in need of a paint job. It too was left over from her last marriage. Sighing mightily, she braced herself for her second tour of duty, the one where she was a mother, provider, taskmaster, and ogre.

Inside the house the furnishings had been handpicked with the greatest of care out of catalogs. All the pieces carried the wear and tear of a herd that'd suffered a long cattle drive to Abilene, kids being the engines of destruction that they were. The hues were all faded browns and smudged whites, except for the odd splash of color belonging to something bought on sale, a mint green spring rocker, for instance, or several large paisley pillows, silver and red, fanned out in front of a twenty-six-inch Zenith that had sporadic horizontal roll problems. Her first official act was to turn off the Saturday morning cartoons.

"Aw, Mom."

That was Tess, age seven, wearing her Little League pajamas and hair in a ponytail. She was too young to have yet learned all the obnoxious things her older teenage sisters had to teach, but being the most intelligent of the four girls, she was learning fast.

"Enough Smurfs," Jan said. "Get dressed. Comb your hair. Go outside. Practice."

"Practice what?" Tess suspiciously asked.

"Being a kid. Go on."

The heavy way Tess trudged toward her room, you could tell she was thinking tantrum, but she decided against it after sneaking a peek at her mother's mood.

"Where's Claire?" Jan asked.

"Downstairs. Doing laundry."

"Tell her I'm home."

"She already knows," Tess said, exasperated far beyond her years.

"Tell her anyway. Tell her I'm making breakfast."

"Mom," Tess said, becoming concerned, "are you all body-achy?"

TV talk. Sometimes it felt as though she was taking part in a commercial, not the raising of a family.

"I'm fine."

"Tension headaches too, I'll bet."

"Get going," Jan warned.

"I don't want you gone all night," Tess said.

That brought Jan up short. She smiled wanly. "All right, Granny Apple, I won't be. Not all the time. Now get dressed."

Five minutes later a winded Claire appeared at the top of the stairs with a basket of neatly folded panties, training bras, and bobby socks. She thumped the load down on one kitchen chair, herself on another, and said nothing, which was the whole point, as Jan well knew. For a long minute Claire said nothing as only a woman of sixty-seven with four grandchildren to help raise could, and for a minute Jan whisked her waffle batter, pretending that she didn't know her mother was there and was busy saying nothing.

"This is worse than being married to what's-his-name," Claire said. What's-his-name was Jan's father, who'd divorced Claire after twenty-eight years to run away with a younger woman who turned out to be one year older than Claire. That's how much he'd learned about women in nearly three decades.

"What do you mean?" Jan asked, still not facing her mother so that her bruised eye remained hidden.

"He and I used to talk about this much. He'd come home from work and stand over the sink drinking a beer, and I'd haul the wash up from the basement, although never this much because I at least had sense to stop after three, and two of them boys."

Jan joined her at the table. For a woman aged sixty-seven, Claire Gallagher wasn't going to be mistaken for anyone younger. She came by her worry lines honestly, and there wasn't anything staged about the thinning of her fine hair, the puffiness to her fingers, or the early-morning knitting sessions when she couldn't sleep. She wore housedresses twenty years past their prime and looked kindly once a week on the average. Before agreeing to take on housemother chores again, she'd extracted a sworn pledge from Jan that she wouldn't get man-happy and remarry for a third time in the near future. Spotting Jan's darkened eye, she puffed her cheeks in disapproval but said nothing.

"So what do you want to talk about?" Jan asked.

"That's what he used to say," Claire said, folding a shirt before adding, "Amy stayed home last night."

"The bastard forgot?"

Amy, her thirteen-year-old, was supposed to have spent the weekend with her father, Jan's second ex.

"Not exactly," Claire said. "He called and promised her the moon next month."

"What excuse?"

"Overtime."

"Shit. Old reliable. All that overtime, but he can't make his support payments. Amazing, huh?"

Claire said nothing in that way she had of saying nothing which meant she had more to say.

"What else?" Jan reluctantly asked.

"Leah was late. The little darling looked right at the clock and denied it. Like I was senile."

"How late?"

"Hour."

"I'll talk to her about it."

"Good luck," Claire said. "Aren't you jogging this morning?"

"Too beat."

Claire leaned forward to check the bruise beneath Jan's eye. Motherly instincts stirred deep within her breast. "Well? Let's hear how you changed the world."

7

TWO weeks back, the man who had stolen the hearse and delivered Dr. Croft to General Jack drove for several hours after completing his errand. He drove to Pilot Hill, parked in line with all the neckers gazing out over the city and rifled through the billfold he'd lifted off the doc. Four dollars and plastic. With the arrival of credit cards minimum wage for muggers had dropped precipitously. Turning off his dome light, he eased out of the car and dropped the wallet down the grating of a storm sewer. Although he was the only one alone on the lane, he didn't feel that way. He felt an immense bond of brotherhood with everyone he saw; he also felt as though he owned everything he saw, including the heavens. With the aid of his stargazer's chart, he located three new constellations. He felt fucking brilliant.

He drove to a wall of condos overlooking the lake and let himself into a second-floor unit that smelled stale and boozy. Every horizontal space was crowded with either glasses holding a half inch of honey-colored ice-melt or else rings from where glasses had been parked. In the living room he lifted a highball out of a snoring woman's hand. She was a generation older than he, but the familial resemblance, particularly around their listing noses and close-set eyes, was unmistakable. When he nudged her, she woke with a gurgle, then promptly passed out again. After carrying her into the bedroom and tucking her in—fully clothed—he let himself out of the condo without turning off the TV. She liked it on when she woke.

Outside, the night had clouded over, preventing him from spotting any more constellations, so he opted for McGill's after ruling out a trip to see Tami, his start-and-stop romance of several years. At present their affair was decidedly stalled. Tami was running around with some used-car baron who looked a lot like that president from Texas, the one with the faggy name and enormous ears. The salesman was about that much older than Tami, and probably had a wife named Ladybird stashed somewhere too. All of that wasn't going to gripe him. His mood was too rare. Tonight McGill's was the perfect place; all the pro athletes went there to get laid, and he'd been mistaken for a running back more than once. Sipping fine scotch, which he bought with the four dollars lifted from the doctor's wallet, he watched a quarterback, known for throwing interceptions in big games, try to convince the wife of a teammate that he had something in his pants that she would definitely want to see, maybe touch, positively grow to love. When the teammate husband returned from the rest room, the wife immediately tattled and there followed the usual Latin-style pushing and shoving. The man who'd stolen the hearse caught the wife's eye and held up his arm to show her his wristwatch. He flashed two fingers and gestured to the stool he sat on to show they should meet there later, at two. When the wife flipped her middle finger at him, he shrugged it off and left, unwilling to let anything touch his mood.

He drove on, no particular destination in mind, but soon enough passing the house he'd grown up in, the elementary school where he'd been force-fed his ABCs, and the shopping center where he'd hot-wired a Camaro and gone on his first joyride. Troubled memories, all. He drove faster, as if to escape. After this night he expected only good memories. The bad times, the dark places, they were just about over. Not much longer now.

Three times he drove by Jackson General and parked on the street a half block away as if taunting the hospital to do something. It didn't. For once, it couldn't.

Exhilarated, he drove till dawn, still not fatigued but finally hungry. After a hearty dose of flapjacks and sausage, he pointed his RX-7 toward the western suburb of Chapwick and a barn-red townhouse that he sat in front of, waiting.

Shortly before seven a thin man with shoulders so stooped they looked broken hurried out the door with his head down, trying to prevent anyone from noticing him. The hearse thief chuckled to himself, then beeped his horn, causing the exiting man to start but not to glance toward the Mazda. Instead, he pulled his coat collar up to conceal his profile. That made the hearse thief hoot out loud. The fleeing man fumbled with keys, threw himself into a dark green Saab, and after bending over sideways so that his head barely cleared the dash, pulled away from the townhouse.

By that time a woman in a white satin robe had opened the front door of the house and studied the Mazda through the glass storm. She had fine, dark hair, like the hearse thief; a dimpled chin, like the hearse thief; but her nose didn't veer to the side like his, her lips were fuller than his, and her figure was much thicker, although in a sensual way—very much so. They were brother and sister and had once looked much more alike. That was before his sister, Vanessa, had started working as a nurse for a plastic surgeon.

After a moment Vanessa stepped away from the door without motioning him in or retrieving the morning *Star*—there were several scattered on the steps—but she didn't close the inner door either, which was invitation enough. He locked his car and joined her. Inside, the townhouse alternated between patches of neurotic cleanliness, such as the kitchen floor, which dazzled, and slovenly despair, which included the pieces of furniture in the living room that were vague shapes under the layers of discarded designer clothes.

"So how long have you been out there?" she asked while rubbing her temples in a way she had—fingertips moving in tiny circles, eyes squeezed shut—that said she was under great pressure thanks to her little brother. Her voice, on the other hand, sounded falsely accommodating.

"When you said you'd have an alibi," he said, tsk-tsking, "I never imagined. I thought Dr. Ellsworth was married?"

"So much the better," she answered, eyes opening to stare at him. Sometimes his sister had a way of looking at him that made him feel so small that she needed tweezers to pick him up. She tried that method on him now. "What about you?" she prompted.

He resisted by playing dumb. "What do you mean?"

"You were supposed to be with Mother all night. Am I right?"

"Uh-huh," he said slowly, for once having the upper hand. "She was in fine form. Never knew I stepped out. Around midnight I came back and tucked her in."

"And everything else?"

To downplay her anxiety, Vanessa turned away from him to put a brass teakettle on an electric burner. But the tight way she asked it, he knew that she felt the same about Dr. Croft as about their father, except that she was able to do something about Croft and would never be able to touch their old man, at least not directly. When they'd decided how

to handle the doctor's body, it was his sister who insisted it
be hauled back to General Jack and left on its doorstep. She
acted as though it was a way to taunt their father. Even now
neither of them quite believed he was so far gone that he
couldn't reach and touch them.

"Well?" she said, demanding an explanation. A lack of
sleep lay heavy on her face, although she'd managed to apply
makeup somewhere between her bedroom and the front
door. The cosmetics followed the townhouse's erratic patterns, fastidious around her eyes but breaking down at the
lips, which were chapped and rough, in need of another shot
of collagen to revive their poutiness.

"All in place," he assured her. "We definitely should be
getting cooperation."

"You waited like I told you?"

"Worked like a charm. Three ambulances came in and no
one saw a thing."

"So why didn't you answer when I called Mother's at
one?" She absently asked this while sifting through tea bags
in a canister. That tickled him. Old Sis, always trying to get
one up.

"You don't mean to say you were worried about me, do
you, Sis?"

"About you?" She raised an eyebrow to add a silent *Ha!*
"I figured you messed up, that's all."

His face reddened. "When have I ever—"

"Not now, please. You say everything went like we
planned?"

He calmed, irked that she'd gotten to him so easily. "Never
fear. I did a little celebrating, that's all I was up to. Mother
will swear I was with her all night."

"All right, then," she said, her tone implying that once
she'd scored her point she was willing to forget it. "I'll get
ready and we'll go down and see how he's doing."

That made him restless. "What do you mean, *how he's*

doing? He's doing exactly the same. That's the whole fucking point. There's no change at all."

"Reggie," Vanessa warned.

"I don't care," he said defensively. "You promised I wouldn't have to go down there again."

By then he was pacing. His eyes glistened as he tried to hold back tears, and he could feel his sister watching, not saying a word. Everything inside him filled with static—no more blood or tissue—just chaotic, crisscrossing energy causing his shoulders to start shaking. He sobbed convulsively, twice, and sensed his sister stepping close to cradle him in her arms, lightly patting him on the back as if he was some kind of full-grown infant having trouble with formula. He knew that all the while his sister held him she looked over his shoulder at a kitchen clock, a blank expression on her face, and he hated her for that, but not as much as he hated himself for breaking up like this in front of her.

"We've got to bring an end to it," he heard her firmly say. "You're going to have to come along."

He pushed away from her. "I-I-I . . . really think . . ."

"Forget it. If they're going to listen to us at all—"

"If? What do you mean *if?*"

Her voice rose to match his. "They're going to want to hear the same thing from both of us. So I want us both there this morning. Understood? They're going to be in shock from finding Croft. That's going to make convincing them easier. That was the whole point of sending the body back where we did. Right? They feel too safe down there. Like no one can do anything to touch them. That'll be different this morning. But we're going to have to both be there to take advantage of it."

"You said . . ." He faltered, losing track of exactly what she'd said. "Now you're saying if . . ."

"Fine," she said, brushing past him. "Fall apart when I need you."

She'd done it to him again. God, was she an expert, or

what! Everything went white at that point and he must have fainted because he came to looking up at the kitchen light. How long he'd been out he didn't know. From a back bedroom he could hear his sister sliding drawers. That she hadn't seen him collapse was a great relief. Of course maybe she had watched and simply refused to do anything. Sheepishly, he went back to her bedroom, although not past the door, which he had to close so that he couldn't see her dressing.

"All I want," he called out, "is some peace. And quiet."

"It's only death, Reg. Relax."

He silently and sarcastically mimicked her, then had an abrupt change of mood and said as if inspired, "Hey, maybe we should go into business."

"What are you talking about?" It sounded as though she was pulling something over her head.

"Murder Inc."

"Don't print any cards."

"Have Valium, will travel."

"Too much TV, Reggie."

"You bop 'em, I drop 'em."

The door opened and his sister stepped out, wearing her black interviewing suit and looking extremely formidable. He wouldn't have wanted to deal with her, and that thought made him feel better. For once, she was on his side.

"Just keep your mouth shut when we get there," she said. "And look mad, real mad."

They took her cranberry Seville and the only conversation— or attempt at conversation—came when she looked in the rearview mirror at her face and said, "When this is over, I'm going to treat myself to a chin tuck."

Reggie didn't have anything to say to that. No, the nearer they got to Jackson General, the more withdrawn he became, until finally Vanessa just drove and Reggie shrank into his seat, growing smaller and smaller with each passing block until he appeared ten years old and headed for the dentist's.

Going to see his father had always done that to him. Even now.

Nine months before, almost to the day, their *beloved* father, Lowell Asplund, had been driving home from a one-sided shouting match with his ex-wife, their equally beloved mother, Sally, who had moved across town to a condo overlooking the lake. She sublet the condo, and sublet the building's maintenance man, who actually would have put the coals to her for free—the amounts of whiskey she swilled had preserved her remarkably well—and there was one last thing she sublet, the services of a twenty-four-hour security force that radio-dispatched a guard to roust Lowell anytime—day or night—that he parked below Sally's place and stared through the windshield at her second-floor balcony window. Sometimes Lowell removed himself from his front seat to stand below her balcony and provide her with moral instructions at the top of his lungs. That's when the radio-dispatched guard usually called for backup.

Up to nine months ago, Lowell could talk. With the best of them. He'd built a successful career as a hard-nosed labor negotiator; representing sweatshops had been his specialty. He backed down from no union boss and freely offered advice to everyone. This was a democracy, wasn't it? Freedom of speech, right? But the form of government he supported at home was tyranny. Enlightened despotism, he jokingly called it. No one else got to joke about it though.

Through all the years of Reggie and Vanessa's youth, their father never once laid a hand on them. He didn't have to. He ruled completely with his tongue. In their house, the pen was mightier than the sword, and the spoken word more powerful than the written. To be verbally assaulted by Lowell Asplund was to be reduced to rubble, to a twitching mass beyond the help of a shrink's couch. Reggie developed a stutter so powerful that at times it'd seemed as though he was about to choke on his tongue. After years of speech therapy, he could still lapse. Vanessa lost the ability to cry, dried up completely. From early on she recognized that tears were what her father wanted, and so she trained herself not to oblige him; besides, her mother cried enough for both of them. Most of the time you couldn't tell if it was the crying or the booze that made their mother's eyes red. So they all lived together in perfect disharmony.

But even that wasn't sufficient for Lowell Asplund on one of his darker days. What was the use of ruling if you didn't occasionally change the rules? So it was that Reggie, who as a sophomore qualified in the high hurdles for the state track and field tournament, wasn't allowed to try out for the team as a junior but had to join a skeet-shooting team to please his father. So it was that although everyone else had to honor one another's privacy, Lowell would occasionally open Vanessa's bedroom door to watch his teenage daughter dress. Not that he ever touched her. He didn't have to. So too he openly ridiculed his wife each night at dinner, working her like a team of picadors, banderilleros, and finally the matador, whose challenge was to reduce her to tears during dessert—not before. Generally, he succeeded.

Did they never rebel? Yes, once. And the result was that Lowell went to the hardware store, returning with a galvanized bucket which he filled with water and set on the living room carpet. Reggie had brought home a kitten without asking permission. That was the great rebellion.

"Drown her," Lowell Asplund had said, nothing more.

The family curled away from him like vines withering before a brush fire. In the end, it was Vanessa who did the job, to spite her father who held a blubbering Reggie by the scruff.

So the pressures grew, the temperatures rose, and nobody ever rebelled openly again, not after the cat. They all simply prayed, separately and silently, that someday they'd be free, someday their father would be dead.

Gradually, one by one, all of them did claim their freedom—for all the good it did them. They carried the years of tyranny wherever they went. Inside their rib cages lived a snarling animal who cowered whenever their father managed to track them down. They became bitter, terribly bitter, but were clever enough to hide this from the world so that they looked and acted just like their neighbors, only more so.

Then, on a snowy Sunday evening in January, a security guard ordered Lowell to move out of the parking lot below his ex-wife's window or be arrested for trespassing. After verbally trashing the guard, Lowell roared out of the lot, clipped a fender, skidded on an ice patch, and jackknifed across two lanes of traffic, directly into the path of an oncoming snowplow. During the ensuing sirens, the arrival of the paramedics, the fire department, a special emergency team to cut the victim out of the compacted front seat—during all that his ex-wife went to the window but once and then only to pull the drapes. The rest of the time she watched "60 Minutes" and "Murder, She Wrote."

The Emergency Room doctor at Jackson General Medical Center wrote this on Lowell Asplund's medical records:

64 yr old male. Severe closed head trauma and neurodysfunction. Fixed pupils. Respiratory alkalosis. Intraventricular pressure 52 Hg, extensor rigidity.
  Secondary . . .

It went on for another page and a half, listing diagnosis and treatment.

A week later Lowell Asplund existed in a vegetative state in the hospital's Neurological Intensive Care Unit. A respirator did his breathing, dialysis machines filtered his blood in place of his kidneys. A feeding tube carried all the nutrients a body needed directly to his small intestine. To some he seemed more like a science exhibit than a person, but the medical staff, led by Dr. Jonathon Croft, refused all requests to pull the plugs on the varied apparatus keeping their patient alive.

In the state in which they lived, the courts had shown a marked reluctance to go against a doctor's opinion, and Dr. Croft firmly believed in keeping his patients alive by heroic measures. It was his conviction that the wonders of modern science and the miracle of the human body meant there was no condition that was incurable or irreversible. It was a moral imperative that he lived by. No one had the right to end a life by removing life-support systems. No one. This was not a view held by all the physicians at General Jack. Many thought the reverse, that they were playing God by keeping patients like Lowell Asplund alive, patients whose chances of climbing out of their coma were infinitesimally small, patients whose prospects for returning to anything approaching a normal life were zero. But their views didn't count because the primary physician in Neurology was Dr. Croft. So the patient remained connected to the machines and would remain attached until declared brain dead. No one knew or could predict when that might be, if ever, for as the weeks passed it became apparent that Lowell Asplund belonged to that select group of patients whom medical journals labeled the biologically tenacious. Eventually he was moved to a special ward where three other coma patients slumbered, all under the care of Dr. Croft.

At one point the patient's son barricaded himself in his father's room and sat for ten minutes with his hand on the respirator plug, unable to pull it out. Security finally forced an entry and removed him. The day before that the man's ex-wife had come for her only visit. She'd acted so pleased with her ex's inability to respond that she'd sat by his bedside for half the morning, talking to him softly, saying all the things that she'd never been able to, some nasty, many sweet.

But it was the daughter that the medical staff felt obliged to keep the closest eye on. Her bitter arguments in favor of stopping all life-support systems combined with her nurse's training to make her the likeliest candidate to subvert Dr. Croft's orders. And who knew what kind of lawsuits that would result in, for on top of all his other sterling qualities, Dr. Jonathon Croft was a litigious bastard. There was one problem with this scenario, though: the daughter refused to get any nearer her father than the doorway into his room. Some days she would stand there by the hour, staring intently, as if she could almost hear him speak. But she never went to his side, never laid a hand on his cheek. She had the staff worried.

And so Lowell Asplund lay in state, saying nothing to the nurses who came to adjust his feeding tube and check his catheter; saying nothing to his family; saying nothing about why he had been the kind of man he was. Nothing.

His family continued to pretend not to hate him, because what kind of person confessed that about someone on his deathbed? But they couldn't stop hating him so completely that they could literally taste it, a furry bitterness at the back of their mouths. Still, they remained powerless before the great man, unable to take the necessary measures to end his ordeal themselves. It wasn't fear of consequences that stymied them, but the fact that on some deeper, indescribable level their father still controlled their lives.

On the fifth story of Jackson General's parking ramp, Vanessa said, "Now, we're hoping to catch them confused this morning, but we don't want to do anything to connect ourselves to that bastard Croft. We ask to speak to whatever doctor's in charge of our father's case, and we don't say a word about Croft. Understood?"

Reggie tried to say yes but couldn't get it out.

On the elevator, Vanessa repeated, "I'll do all the talking." She kept her hand on her brother's forearm, preventing him from bolting. They worked their way down a long station of neurological rooms, twice passing elderly patients strapped into wheelchairs. Reggie gave them a wide berth. Inside the rooms they passed were nurses emptying bedpans and doctors reading charts and elderly patients watching cartoons. Twice Reggie had to stop to catch his breath.

The level of sound in their father's special ward was muffled. The staff spoke in low voices—not whispers, just not quite a normal level of speech. The beeps and whirring of machines stood out. The ringing of a telephone sounded close to an alarm, but everyone moved slightly slower, as if here, where patients hung in an eternal balance between life and death, there was no need for urgency. None of this was new. Actually the activity of the ward didn't strike Reggie as any different than usual, which made him uneasy. The staff was supposed to be reacting to the arrival of Dr. Croft's body.

Vanessa stepped up to the nurse's desk in the hall and announced to the station clerk, "We want to see whoever's in charge."

That meant a short thin nurse who'd sparred with Vanessa before. "There's no change in your father's condition," the nurse said, assuming the soft businesslike manner that many nurses developed for delivering bad news. "But you're welcome to look in on him as soon as some staff can join you."

From the time that Reggie had barricaded himself in the room there were no more unattended visits.

"That won't be necessary," Vanessa said. "My brother and I have reached a mutual decision. We want our father removed from all life-support systems. And we want it done immediately."

"Not possible." The nurse firmly shook her head no. "Not without orders from the doctor in charge of your father's case. I believe you already know that, ma'am. And I believe you already know Dr. Croft's opinion on the matter."

"Then call him."

"I think you know that's hardly possible," the nurse said. Both the brother and sister became still. "I saw you talking to him yesterday, so I'm sure you know he's on vacation for the next two weeks."

The brother tried to say something but he couldn't get it out. *Didn't they know about Croft?* The sister paled but then demanded to speak to whoever was in charge while Croft was gone. That request took some arguing, for the nurse insisted that today's attending physician would certainly not countermand Dr. Croft's orders without some change in the patient's condition. And there was no change. Absolutely none. There hadn't been for months. Finally the sister wore the nurse down and she agreed to page the doctor on call, Dr. Ellsworth. That was their second surprise. Reginald started to stutter upon hearing the name, and Vanessa became extremely tense. When the charge nurse returned to tell the brother and sister that the doctor would be there within the hour, she found them gone.

Part Two

8

JAN Gallagher consented to have breakfast with Detective Frank White on Monday, Labor Day morning, for one and only one reason: he claimed to have received an anonymous tip. She assured herself there were no personal reasons for agreeing to see him. Two or three times she repeated that assurance to make sure it was rock solid. After the Saturday and Sunday night shifts, she realized her investigation needed some oomph. About all that she'd accomplished was the healing of her bruised eye to a respectable flesh tone and the discovery that the HELP ME notes were posted as a prank by the nursing assistant who'd recently delivered two bodies to the morgue. Maneuvering the NA into confessing that much took some major laying on of guilt. With the help of the other NAs she interviewed, Jan was further able to narrow Dr. Croft's arrival to a three-day period two weeks back, a Thursday to Sunday, August twentieth to twenty-third. To land even this paltry bit of information had been a struggle, as she'd had to wheedle and goad her fellow employees into remembering whether or not there'd been a red body bag in the cooler. They all exhibited an ingrained tendency to resist the authority that Jan represented.

But the real kicker came early on Monday morning at the tail end of her Sunday night shift. Without fanfare, she was summoned to the Little Admiral's private office for an emergency staff meeting of Security's supervisors. For some unexplained reason the attendees also included Gavin Larsen and the Duchess of Administration, Elizabeth Kavanaugh, who was chaperoned by a tape recorder. With one of the muckety-mucks present, and a woman at that, everyone acted as sullen as a pre-op patient waiting to start counting backward. Their eyes kept ticking toward the tape recorder as if it might explode, taking them with it. The addition of another woman to the room didn't lessen Jan's burden, either. Their common gender made her feel responsible for whatever ungracious remarks the administrator trainee was sure to deliver.

When the Admiralty requested updates, Jan's humble offering of what she'd uncovered created an embarrassed silence. Not only didn't her sickly efforts merit words, but everyone present acted perfectly willing to blame her for eliminating one of the few solid leads they had—the posted notes.

"Three days?" the Little Admiral said, sounding as though Jan was trying to pawn magic beans off on him. Hard eyes all around.

Into that boundless vacuum galloped Gavin Larsen, declaring that maybe he could pinpoint the doctor's arrival with a bit more precision. Old friend Gavin had learned that on the Friday evening two weeks ago, August twenty-first, between the hours of ten and midnight, Emergency Room staff had discovered a red body bag in the triage area. Assuming that a funeral home would sooner or later claim it, they subsequently transported the body bag to the morgue where the nursing assistant who delivered it neglected to make an entry in the log book. In the triage area, no one had seen who abandoned the goods, which were definitely not county merchandise, leather being as pricy as it was. This meant that no one knew whether the body was being smuggled out of General to conceal where the murder occurred, or—less likely—brought into General for reasons as yet unknown.

Jan made the mistake of offering an opinion at that point. "Shouldn't we assume brought in? Admissions received several calls wanting to know if we'd found it."

"Gallagher," said a provoked Little Admiral, "does it make any sense that someone would deliver a murder victim to a hospital?"

Jan responded that as of yet nothing made much sense, so she didn't think she could answer.

"Let me answer for you," the Little Admiral said, peevish and condescending, like a kindergarten teacher at the end of his rope. "It doesn't make any sense at all. But if you murdered someone in a hospital and then had to abandon the remains—for whatever reason—before you could get rid of them, and then you didn't hear a word about it for days in the news, wouldn't you be a trifle curious? Maybe call?"

"That doesn't mean you're wrong," administrator trainee Kavanaugh quickly appended, displaying enough sympathy and understanding to make Jan blush, "but maybe we better concentrate our efforts on using some common sense. Are we agreed?"

They were agreed and then some. The Little Admiral promptly ordered the questioning of every hospital employee until they discovered where the murder took place. Why so eager to believe the event had occurred inside the hospital? The question left Jan feeling as though she didn't have a grasp of the entire picture, but she didn't speak up when

Eldon Hodges asked if there were any questions. She tried to limit her public humiliation to once a day. Seeing no raised hands, he falsely thanked everyone for their efforts, acknowledged Gavin's contribution with an approving nod, and dismissed the entire lackluster bunch of them.

On the way back to Security's subbasement office, Gavin said with dagger-tongued sincerity, "If you need any more help, Gallagher, just let me know."

At which point Jan recognized this was a grudge match, no holds barred. When she received a message from the Communications Center to phone Detective White, she did so without qualms, agreeing to a breakfast conference even though the hours of sleep she'd snared in the last three days could have been totaled on both hands.

She wouldn't have described the hospital cafeteria as romantic, which suited her fine. The scrambled eggs defied cutlery, the coffee tasted faintly of lemon dish soap, and the decor had been plucked out of an office catalog from under the heading *Post–Danish Modern.* Everything smelled steam cooked, pressed, and preserved. The clatter of voices imitated the noise of any public eatery until you singled out individual words—cauterize, arrhythmia, melanoma—by which time it was too late to flee. Jan pushed the detective through the cafeteria line and chose a corner table as removed as possible from white smocks and pale blue scrubs.

From up close she saw that Detective Frank White didn't shave too closely or knot his blue serge tie evenly. He was descended from prime breeding stock if your aim was a rugged line of yak. It must have been his droopy mustache that suggested husbandry from that far corner of the world, for nothing else about him was Oriental. His most troublesome feature? Deep-brown eyes that made a run at being sensitive. A woman with Jan's history better have learned to discount whatever she saw in a man's eyes.

"We've had a tip," Detective White started.

Having but moments before been humiliated in front of a room full of peers and higher-ups, Jan was of no mind to be toyed with. "So you said."

"And I thought I might share it with you." Like many big men, the detective overcompensated for his size with dainty table manners. While speaking, he concentrated on buttering the edges of his toast.

"In exchange for . . . ?"

"Some straight answers," he said with an irresistible twinkle.

God, she hated that kind of twinkle. She'd succumbed to it before, and who knew the limits of her strength to hold out against it again?

"Those kind of answers," the detective continued, "seem to be at a premium around here."

"So you've come to me?" she said, suspecting it wasn't an honor.

He considered her question while peeling back the cap on a single serving of strawberry preserves. "Let me put it this way: you know a Ms. Kavanaugh from Administration?"

Jan managed to say that she did without elaborating, but the automatic flare of her eyebrows must have given her away for the detective's mood brightened further.

"I thought it a possibility," he said. "She's been assigned as my liaison person with the hospital. Why I need such a contact isn't exactly clear—not yet." He spoke with a certainty that said it was his business to make it clear. Setting his butter knife aside, he held his tie against his chest and leaned forward to whisper in a husky voice, "I don't think she specializes in straight answers." Having delivered that nugget, he leaned back and continued his hitting streak by asking, "You know a Gavin Larsen?"

She stopped stirring her coffee and said, "I do."

"But wish you didn't?" the detective asked, smiling rakishly, which was a fairly ridiculous expression for a man of his size and scars. "Yesterday this Larsen approached me with a proposition. He'd tell me whatever he learned in exchange for the same from me. It was to be our little secret. You and him wouldn't be in some kind of competition, would you?"

"What makes you think that?" Jan asked, full of the glassy kind of innocence that's intended to be seen through.

"Oh nothing, just the fact that he couldn't say your name without showing his eyeteeth. He seems determined to make you look bad, although personally I doubt that's possible." The delivered compliment tickled the detective and he beamed accordingly.

"For the record," Jan said, appreciating neither his familiarity with her problems nor the flattery, although it took some effort to mistreat the flattery, "Larsen's under stress, that's all."

"From what I hear, he's not behaving like a gentleman."

"Maybe not," Jan conceded, forcing herself to look into the detective's brown eyes. "Nothing says he has to. So are you working with him?"

"Not me," he said, mildly insulted. "I like the underdog."

"I suppose that's me," Jan said without softening. "You're probably not far off the mark either, but let me tell you something up front, Detective. Any meetings between you and me will be strictly business."

"I wouldn't have it any other way," said Detective White, spoken as if he loved a challenge. "But do you mind if I ask you one personal question before we proceed? One government employee to another?"

"If you must."

"Why did you go after your promotion? In the courts and all."

The question didn't sound antagonistic or snide; "earnest" described it most closely. Great, an earnest cop. Not being the kind of person who kept a pat answer on hand for soul-searching forays, Jan stared at him, rather dumbly she supposed.

"Do you like your job that much?" he prompted.

Still no answer.

"I didn't think so," the detective said, discarding that explanation but acting as though they were carrying on a lively discussion. "So why not go elsewhere?"

"The money," she abruptly said, wanting to shut him up.

"That I don't buy," he said, nodding as though it was a good cover but not quite good enough, "not completely. Sorry. But if you're determined enough to let yourself be dragged through the courts, you've got the gas to go elsewhere."

"Easier said than done for a single parent," she answered vindictively, hating to be pressed into making excuses. "Besides, maybe I'm a feminist and wanted to prove a point."

"You don't say that last like you mean it."

"How would you know?"

"You're right," he admitted. "Maybe I wouldn't."

She said after studying him a moment, "Why are you asking?"

"It might help me answer something I've been wondering about for years," he said, smiling self-consciously. "Namely, why I don't quit my job and find something saner."

"Let's say," Jan carefully answered, "that maybe I thought I could make a contribution."

"In place of a new constitutional amendment?"

"Something like that," she said, watching him closely to see if he was mocking her. More bad news, he didn't appear to be.

He nodded as if he suspected her motives had been something noble, although he didn't act naive enough to believe altruism was the only fuel she ran on. She felt roughly the same.

"This Ms. Kavanaugh," he said, dropping the side excursion into Jan's personal history, "I think she's holding out on me."

"Now why would she do that?" Jan asked, glimpsing a bit of whimsy to his statement.

"Hey, this is a homicide, right? Maybe she did it."

Jan chuckled dryly as if she should be so lucky. "That your tip?"

"Nope, afraid not. We're not quite to the tip yet. We're getting there, though." He framed his next words with some care, taking on a jurisprudential kind of glow as he did so. "What the hospital knows about the deceased, that's an area where I could use some cooperation. Unfortunately, I've reached the conclusion that I won't be getting copious amounts, not from your Ms. Kavanaugh. It took her most of the damn weekend to get me Dr. Croft's personnel file, and when she finally did release it, I got the impression she'd weeded through it first. Everything was too orderly for a county document, if you know what I mean."

"This is all connected to the tip you received?" Jan asked, wanting to verify they were still headed in the same general direction.

"Round about."

"Uh-huh," she answered, doubting him.

Checking the nearby tables, he held his tie and leaned forward again. "I was hoping you might be able to help me out with a file from your Personnel Department."

"Gavin wouldn't do it for you?"

"Didn't ask," he said, offended.

"And once I do," Jan said, thoughtfully stirring her coffee, "then you'll tell me about this mysterious tip. Is that it?"

"No. I'll need more of your help than that would buy me."

"At least you're honest about it."

"Yes, ma'am," Detective White said, all polished manners. "Now about this tip . . . Yesterday, after news of the murder had gone out on the airwaves, after our honest citizenry had time to be shocked by our indecency to one another, after all that fell into place, we got an anonymous call telling us that a Dr. Ellsworth was our man."

She had nothing constructive to say about that.

"The name doesn't mean anything to you?" he asked, disappointed. "I believe he's on staff here at General."

"So are three hundred and fifty–plus others. Did this voice out of nowhere tell you why Dr. Ellsworth did it?"

"Didn't get around to that."

"Meaning it could be a crank?"

"A possibility," the detective allowed. "Any time you have a circus, you're going to have clowns. But considering what we're investigating, I think it deserves a look-see."

"And how do I fit in?" Jan asked, setting her spoon on the saucer and abandoning all interest in stirring her coffee.

"What I was hoping," the detective said, getting as faithful and honest as a life insurance salesman discussing whole life, "maybe you could get me a look at this Ellsworth's personnel file." Before she could refuse, he held up a hand and rushed to explain why. "True, I could ask myself or get a court order, but either way I might lose what I most want. If I request it myself, who knows who might tamper with the file before it got to me. Go after a court order and who knows who might receive a call over here as soon as I leave the courthouse, courtesy of one county employee to another. You know how it is. What I want is to be certain that I'm seeing *all* of this Ellsworth's file. That way, I'd not only get a look into his character, but I could compare his file to the dead doc's and see what might be missing."

"Or connected," Jan said, noting that she hadn't yet refused him. Apparently the detective picked up on the omission as well, for he perked up considerably.

"Now I hadn't thought of that," he said, too accommodating to be believed.

"Why are you convinced that Elizabeth Kavanaugh's holding something back?" Jan asked.

"She wouldn't go out to dinner with me."

"I see," Jan said, using the phrase that had been quite

prominent on the detective's lips the first time she'd met him. "No other reason?"

"A twinge in my gut," he said, more serious. "She strikes me as the sort who might hold a little something back for the public good. And this Ellsworth, I've done enough checking on him to know that his old man carries a big stick down at the county."

He wasn't slow, this dumb detective. Jan said, "Kavanaugh doesn't know about this anonymous caller?"

"Not unless she's the one who called."

"It was a woman then?"

"There," he said as if vindicated, "you see? I knew you were cut out for this business. A woman called us, that's right. Do we have a deal?"

"Perhaps," Jan said, not being swept along just yet. "Has anyone told you that our Admissions Department received some supposedly crank calls last week? The caller wanted to know if we had an extra red body bag down here."

"It's news to me," the detective said, not appreciating its late delivery.

"It was a man who called, though."

"I see," the detective attentively answered. "We'll keep it in mind. Two phone calls, a man and a woman. We're making headway already, I'd say. So do we have a deal?"

"What about the autopsy report on Dr. Croft? Are you willing to share it?"

"So far that's confidential," he said, squinting at her warily. "We haven't been able to locate his parents to let them know. They're on a fishing trip in Ontario. Maybe you'd like to go up there sometime. Beautiful country, I hear."

"Fat chance," she responded without blinking. "And by the way, the personnel folder you want, that's confidential too."

He chuckled as if he knew he was being suckered. "What I say stays with you?"

"Who am I going to blab to?" she asked, implying she was in this alone, which was basically true.

"You break your word," the detective said, a twinkle crowning his eyes again, "and you'll have to go out to dinner with me."

"Agreed," Jan answered without encouraging him.

"The man died from an overdose of Valium and alcohol. Not the best items to mix together, unless you want the results he got. You can read it yourself, if you want. I'll bring a copy of the examiner's report."

Intuition said she could trust him on it, which immediately made her doubt the dependableness of that judgment. "I want," she said. "How about the time of death?"

"Tricky," he answered, shaking his head in admiration of her stick-to-itiveness. "His being in the cooler messes that up. The doc's saying he breathed his last more than thirty-six hours before we got him and that's about as near as they can get it."

"The wonders of modern science have let us down?"

"Afraid so."

"Gavin got it closer," she begrudgingly said. "Or at least he pinpointed the arrival time of the body bag we found him in. Between ten and midnight, Friday night, August twenty-first, a red bag appeared in the emergency entrance. No one saw how it got there, but everyone's assuming the murderer was attempting to get the corpse away from the scene of the crime. Whoever brought it was scared off and the body abandoned. Eventually some staff transported it down to the morgue where it sat."

"And sat. Duly noted."

"That's all Gavin's work," Jan reminded him. "Maybe you picked the wrong horse to back."

"Doubtful," the detective firmly said. "So what do you think? Are we cooperating?"

"I'd say so." Over the slab of the detective's shoulder she'd seen Elizabeth Kavanaugh enter the cafeteria. At her side wasn't the prominent cardiovascular surgeon to whom she was married. At her side was Gavin Larsen.

9

LEAVING the detective to his overcooked breakfast, Jan slipped out of the cafeteria a back way to avoid being spotted by Larsen or Kavanaugh. Once in the clear, she counted dopy, fatigued steps to the parking ramp and her oversize Pontiac. She'd traveled halfway home before remembering that this particular Monday was a holiday, Labor Day, and that her brood of daughters wouldn't be packed off to school. The thought tired her even further. Breakfast again. This time she got to make it. Then there was the issue of the detective. What to do about him. What to make of him. She chastised herself for having bothered to notice that he didn't wear a wedding ring. Didn't she have more pressing dreck to trouble over than Detective Frank White's actual marital condition? Exactly what that dreck might include eluded her, but she agreed with herself to stop thinking about the man and almost succeeded. Maturity was a wonderful thing. Up her front steps she labored, trying to sort everything she had to do into neat lists.

Just because she was off duty didn't mean that she was *off duty*. Her kind of predicament, a test case of sorts, she found impossible to forget. She didn't want to let anybody down, that was her problem. She didn't want to disappoint herself, her family, her fellow employees, the entire next generation, or the woman on the street whom she'd never seen before but who had stopped to thank her. Such thinking made her disgusted with herself. Didn't she have a right to let someone down? It seemed as though she should have. All right, who? She had four daughters to act as a role model for when she could keep her eyes open, so not them, although acting as a role model might be too grandiose a plan—maybe simply getting breakfast on the table after having been up all night was more her speed. She got busy burning scrambled eggs.

If she couldn't let her daughters down, then maybe she could disappoint her mother, Claire, just a bit. Oh sure. Her mother with arthritis and trifocals and gallstones; her mother who out of a sense of responsibility had agreed to sublet her own house and come live with them to attempt to tame the pent-up hormones of her teenage granddaughters. That was out.

Her fellow employees, then. They definitely hadn't done anything deserving of special effort. But letting them down was exactly what they expected; letting them down would be admitting that she was unable to perform the job. Scratch that. She was far too willful to allow that. The next generation, then. Surely that was an abstract enough ideal. No one would notice if she eased up on an obligation or two there. But wasn't that the problem with our society? Everyone pampered themselves without considering the needs of who might be coming after them. As a mother of four, she couldn't allow herself to lighten up there. Which brought her down to the stranger on the street, the unknown woman who had come up to her and thanked her for standing up for their rights. But that chance encounter pumped Jan up, gave her some reason for enduring, made her feel as though someone actually was noticing her labors. Oddly enough, she needed that stranger's support more than anyone's.

Which left her one last person in the entire, overcrowded world to let down—herself. Except that she wouldn't be in this fix if she hadn't let herself down in the past, hadn't forgone college because of car rides that ended in the back-seat. She wouldn't be squirming this way if she hadn't allowed herself to be talked into remarrying because she was afraid . . . of what, she'd never exactly figured out. If she'd all along believed she could take care of herself, she wouldn't be sitting where she was right now. She had an advanced degree in letting herself down and didn't intend to disappoint herself again, at least not intentionally, which was the total and complete answer to Detective White's question about why she went after her promotion. But she was damned if she would shout it from the rooftops. If she wasn't going to disappoint herself, that meant starting with discovering how the dead doctor landed in the cooler. No one named Gavin Larsen was going to beat her out of that.

So much for easing up on some of her expectations. Was it her imagination, or were all of her daughters now seated at the kitchen table with their heads tilted back and their mouths agape, peeping for their mother to spoon-feed them breakfast? Upon closer inspection, she recognized it was her imagination, although the three out of four daughters who were assembled watched her expectantly from the breakfast nook, as if she'd said or done something peculiar.

"Well?" her mother said. "Katie asked you a question. Were you going to answer?"

"What, honey?" Jan asked.

"Did you bust any bad guys?"

Katie specialized in being the sweetest daughter, the one who planned to grow up to be like her mother. For that, she received undisguised scorn from her sisters, although even the oldest one at times allowed herself to be comforted by Katie, who was all of ten.

"She's not a cop," Tess, the youngest, explained. "She can't arrest people. Isn't that so, Mom?"

"Half right. We make citizen's arrests and hold the suspects for the police."

"Well," Katie said, unwilling to have her mother's stature diminished, "did you hold any bad guys?"

"Do we *have* to talk about this at the table?" asked Amy, the second oldest at age thirteen. Whatever her mother did embarrassed her greatly, and the fact that Jan had done something newsworthy, particularly since it involved what no other woman had previously been willing to do, made Amy want to hide, shrivel up and disappear, not even bother with dying, too much attention in that.

"Amy's right," Jan said from behind the steaming skillet. "Let's talk about something more pleasant."

So they searched for more suitable conversation. That took some work, with a good deal of uneasy silence thrown in until Katie asked permission to have lunch at a friend's—granted—and Tess asked if she could go too—denied because of Katie's crestfallen expression. Meanwhile, Amy refused to be coaxed into any kind of dialogue about her plans for the day. Claire warned her that she'd better have some projects lined up because no one was moping around the house the entire day. At that point Amy's eyes flooded and she blindly left the table, groping toward a bedroom shared with her older half sister, Leah, who at sixteen played the wanton woman by sleeping late. Amy wouldn't be getting any sympathy from Leah, who thought the world a very hard place indeed. Jan almost went to comfort her, but the two youngest daughters started squabbling about Katie's lunch date, causing Jan to raise her voice. The entire household, including Claire, would be grounded if everyone didn't button up so she could get some sleep. After that, she could have heard a tear drop.

Telling herself that she refused to regret the strong-arm tactics, she descended to the basement where she'd rigged a cot in the laundry room, right over the twenty-five-pound boxes of detergent. This was the quietest part of the house and was completely dark so that she could sleep through the daylight hours. For once, she was out within minutes. But she wasn't resting. No, her subconscious had a few drills to run her through, which resulted in her tossing and turning through a long lineup of dreams with outlandish images— knotted Fallopian tubes, silverware, fourth-grade class-mates—confusing messages, trampling feet, and the recurrent whispering of her name by a man with a walrus mustache. When she woke near six that evening, the one thing she didn't feel was rested.

Claire was mending socks in the small alcove that served as a dining room when Jan roused herself sufficiently to trudge up the stairs wearing a pair of jeans cut into shorts and an electric-green tube top that belonged to her eldest, Leah. Both fit her too snugly but had been near at hand in the drier.

"Cute," Claire said. With a floor lamp casting light over her shoulder, she held a sock up to check her stitches. She was a small, slightly stooped woman, hair thinning, eyes active, with a sense of smell that was dwindling as fast as she could bail gardenia perfume out of an economy bottle. The flowery currents almost blotted out the faint tang of some-thing burnt in the kitchen.

"Mother," Jan said, "do you want to know what the kind-est thing you could do is?"

"Make the world go away?"

Jan quickly countered, "All right, the second kindest thing."

"What?"

"Not say a word."

"Not even about the man who called?"

Claire was teasing now, although not completely. She was of the opinion that the best thing that could happen to Jan was that another man would never show interest in her. *You've no luck with them,* she often said, as if talking of a pair of dice that never rolled seven. And for that reason, Claire had been strenuously opposed to Jan's taking a job in a field dominated by men. *It won't work,* she foretold. A prediction that hadn't necessarily goaded Jan into taking the job in Security, but which hadn't prevented her either. Over the years her refusal to listen to her mother's advice had become a family joke, particularly whenever Claire tried applying reverse psychology by suggesting Jan do something outlandish. These attempts to back her into doing the sensible thing invariably backfired.

"Only one man?" Jan asked, assuming that Claire had made it up.

"That's right. Asked for you and when I said you weren't available, he asked me if I wanted to go out for dinner with him. A Detective White. Nice manners, compared to that cop you married. I told him I was booked."

"What'd he want?" Jan asked, unsuccessfully trying to veil her interest.

"Wouldn't say," Claire said. Her suspicions aroused, she stopped mending socks. "Gave me two numbers, home and work, but said he'd reach you if you didn't contact him. He seemed, well, persistent. I put the numbers on the bulletin board, but I hope you won't be needing them."

"Yes, Mother."

"There was one other caller too, a . . ." She strained to remember the name. ". . . Ms. Kavanaugh. A nasty little bitch, that one. Talks like she married a Kennedy."

"Close enough. What'd she want?"

"To talk to you. When I told her you were sleeping and I wouldn't wake you, she gave me permission to let you sleep. Imagine that."

"She say anything else?"

"That if you had any problems you should call her, no matter what the hour. And that you shouldn't worry, everything was going to be fine. What's that about?"

"Little excitement at work," Jan said, downplaying its importance to circumvent an *I told you so*. But at the same time she couldn't avoid admiring the treachery wrapped up in Kavanaugh's show of support.

"When I said I was sure that would make you feel much better," Claire scoffed, "she took me seriously, as though I believed she was doing you some kind of favor."

Before Jan could confirm her mother's insight, the door to the kitchen swung open and her four daughters, ages seven to sixteen, carried in a slightly burned German chocolate cake that supported one lit candle. With several off-key harmonies, they sang "Happy Birthday." It wasn't Jan's birthday, which came in April, but she'd so often invented birthdays to cheer everyone else up during the wreckage of two marriages that it had become a household tradition. In a rough year, they might celebrate ten or twelve birthdays. The sentiment and support struck home, and for all the foolish, overly emotional reasons she hated, her eyes started to tear.

She went to work a half hour early that night, hoping to pin down what Gavin Larsen had been doing attached to Elizabeth Kavanaugh's twill skirt in the cafeteria. Finding out would require subterfuge, for Larsen didn't bare his soul to anyone who happened to ask. In fact, Jan knew of but one person in whom he confided, and that was Security's evening shift supervisor, Victor Wheaton. They were an extremely odd couple, Wheaton and Larsen, and not because they were so different, although they certainly looked nothing alike, but odd because their personalities were so remarkably similar—monochrome and flat. Going directly to Victor Wheaton would gain nothing but alerting Larsen that she was on to him. But there was a way, a way named Ginger.

Of Jan's two mortal enemies in Security, the first was Larsen, the second was Ginger Foley, who currently worked the evening shift. All her other enemies in the department were either not of the caliber of those two, or else far beyond them and into the realm of immortal enemies, such as the Little Admiral. The only other time she and Ginger had ever socialized had been a brief visit in the women's locker room during which Ginger had falsely accused Jan of fucking her man—a hunkity-hunk nicknamed Studly—and warned her that she would personally tear her breasts off, if she could find them, should Jan ever do it again. Not wanting an audience for this second encounter, Jan contacted the Communications Center and asked them to radio-dispatch Ginger to the same locker room where they'd been so honest with each other once before.

While Jan was buttoning up her uniform shirt, the Ginger—as she frequently referred to herself—arrived and rested her boot on the bench where Jan sat. She was willowy and busty at once, thus overly fond of promoting nudity in the dressing room, a tendency that gave away the fact that her hair color came from a bottle labeled Lady Something or Other. When she leaned forward, vast amounts of hair spray kept her blond waves in place as she said in a chummy voice, "How they hanging, Gallagher?" Today something other than Jan's imagined interest in Studly occupied Ginger's frontal lobes.

"Super," Jan said and promptly smiled so largely it made her cheeks ache.

"That-a way. But listen, if there's any little thing I can be doing to help you come out ahead, you be sure and call it out. You know what they say about the rat race."

"What's that?"

"It's the only race."

"I'll keep it in mind," Jan said, feeling a cramp in her left cheek due to all the smiling. "Anything else?"

"A man's antiperspirant. It'll get you through the tough spots."

"Sound advice."

"And if any of our co-workers get ballsy with you, stare at their crotch."

"That all?"

"When they start to stutter, stop. You can take things too far."

"OK," Jan said, willing to be coached.

"I heard someone poked you in the eye," Ginger said, stepping to the side to appraise Jan's shiner under a different angle of light. "Doesn't look like much, though."

"It isn't."

Ginger playfully punched Jan's shoulder with enough snap to sting. "Something tells me you're going to do all right, Gallagher. Just don't burn your bra. You may need it someday." Suddenly, Ginger dropped the chumminess. "There a reason you wanted to see me?"

"I was hoping you could help me figure something out," Jan said.

"What?" Ginger exclaimed, astonished. "There aren't enough people helping you already?"

Uncertain what Ginger meant by that snideness, Jan picked her way carefully. "In this case, you'd be the only one I know of."

Ginger had to sit down with that news; it was too enormous an honor to stand up with. Her facetiousness had no subtlety to it as she said, "Oh, any way I can."

"I've noticed that Larsen's been spending time with that administrative trainee named Kavanaugh."

"Yeah?" Ginger said, sounding way ahead of Jan.

"Yeah. And I'm wondering what it's all about?"

"This some kind of condition of the heart?" Ginger asked, sounding as sympathetic as a politician in heat. "Is old Gavin two-timing you? Because if he is, I gotta admit that I didn't think he'd unlock his undies for one woman, say nothing about two."

"Oh, I think you know what this concerns."

Ginger dropped the act to say with satisfaction, "Maybe I do. Just maybe, being as how you're the woman of the second, and everything. But believe me, tough girl, what I know is going to stay locked up right where it is." She unconsciously tapped her chest rather than the side of her head, a gesture that Jan chose not to comment on. Ginger went on, "Don't matter what anybody tells me to do, you and me, we ain't getting into none of this sisterhood birdshit. You know what they say, every man for himself, and that's only the beginning for women."

"In your case," Jan said, "I couldn't agree more. That's why I asked you down here."

Ginger eagerly stood up. "A little hair pulling?"

"I had something else in mind."

"Such as?"

"How are you and Studly getting along?" Jan asked.

"As long as you keep your skinny legs together, fine." Bored, she added, "We've been through that before."

"What I'm wondering," Jan said, wanting to avoid any false starts, "is how Studly would take it if he learned someone saw you and Victor driving off together Saturday and Sunday nights."

Ginger's expression vapor-locked, but she soon got herself under enough control to say knowingly, "There's your colors. This is a shakedown, isn't it?"

"I prefer to think of it as a trade-off," Jan said. "You can keep both Studly and Victor, as long as I find out what Larsen's doing with that goddamn Kavanaugh. The way I figure it, Larsen tells Victor because there's no one else he talks to. And Victor crows to you. And you pass it on down here where nobody hears a thing but me, and I'm not going to tell anyone I had to go crawling to you for help. Trust me on that."

Sizing Jan up anew, Ginger said, "There might be something to you after all."

"You were about to tell me something?"

Ginger brayed. "So I was, although for the life of me I don't know why. That goddamn Studly's not worth the grain it takes to feed him." She sounded a little too brave while saying that. "Listen up, Admin's sweating something out on this one, something that goes a little beyond that yummy one your boys found down in the freezer. I mean, death—even a murder—ain't exactly news around here, right? I mean, they cart them in the door every day. But Admin's uptight."

"So what is it?"

"Big secret. I don't think even sorry old Gavin knows, which is eating him alive. This Kavanaugh bitch wants someone trained in muck to stick their nose into Croft's death and see what stinks. But why, I ain't been hearing, and I think I've been hearing everything Gavin knows, babe."

"They have somebody they're protecting," Jan guessed.

"Probably themselves."

"Any names come to mind?"

"You know I'm not much on names. Only peckers."

"Why'd she pick Larsen?" Jan asked.

"Maybe this Kavanaugh broad wants to help him put the boot to you, lady. In the world where I live, people carry grudges, and I heard your lawyer did some fine spadework on her. And you got to figure she's at least bright enough to see that in this case old Gavin's self-motivated. So have I laid everything out so that you understand it? Good. I wouldn't worry about it anyway. You're the chosen woman. In the end, they're not going to let anything happen to you, no matter how bad you fuck up."

"What's that supposed to mean?"

"Oh, I think you know." She chucked Jan's chin, saying, "They can't fire you. It'd look like more discrimination. But personally, I hope old Gavin figures out some way to burn your dimpled little ass. You golden girls are all alike."

Not imagining she'd learn anything more by allowing herself to be further baited, Jan said, "Then I think it's all the more important that I prove I can handle my job. Say, how do you think I'd look as a blond?"

"You've got teeth, Gallagher. I'll give you that."

Closing her locker door, Jan walked out of the dressing room and as far as the elevator with Ginger.

"Where you off to now?" Ginger asked.

"A better tomorrow," Jan said before the doors pinched shut between them.

By the time she received a status report from the evening supervisor, Victor Wheaton, who was in a bit of a hurry to be on his way, lump in his pocket and all—by then Jan's people were filing into Security's subbasement office. They looked far more rested than she was, that much was unmistakable. Taking her chair, she dispatched duty assignments with the added twist of questioning all employees, every single one, about Dr. Croft's death. Groans all around, but Jan didn't try to duck anything by blaming it on the Little Admiral. When everyone had quieted, she reminded Larsen of his special assignment in the refrigerator. No reaction, just steady eyes in every direction. She was beginning to wish she'd never resorted to that little ploy to assert her authority. It wasn't as though she could have Gavin keelhauled for insubordination, and it made her feel like a nag to keep going back to it. Furthermore, it surely didn't feel as though anyone had taken the time to tell her own crew that Administration was afraid to fire her.

The night was unmemorable, a steady stream of drunks and seizure patients who needed to be four-pointed onto gurneys so they wouldn't roll off and hurt themselves. None of the countless employees she quizzed about Croft knew a thing.

The completion of the shift brought Tuesday morning, the end of the holiday weekend, and the return of the eight-to-five office staff, which meant Jan could now take care of her errand for Detective White. Back up in the Administration wing, she waited for a chance to have a word alone with the Little Admiral's private secretary, an overly feminine young thing named Sheila who wore ribbons in her blond hair and embroidered shawls over frilly dresses that blended into a business landscape about as well as a flamenco dancer would have, not that Eldon Hodges noticed any discrepancies. Nor was the head of Security aware that his own secretary called him a drimp—a cross between a drip and a wimp—and to show who actually ran the old scow did little favors behind his back. When she reached the secretary's desk, Jan caught Sheila's attention and pantomimed taking a smoke break without speaking a word. The Little Admiral's door was open. A few minutes later, Sheila joined her out in the landscaped courtyard, Marlboros in hand.

"Was wondering if I'd see you today," Sheila said while lighting up.

"Why's that?"

"Your name's already come up once or twice this morning, usually preceded by Damn. Been doing some good work?"

"Guard of the month is my goal. What's the complaint now?"

"The usual bushwa. A man's gotta do what a man's gotta do, and there shouldn't be any woman trying to do it. How can I help you, Damn Gallagher?"

"Think you could sneak me a personnel file? Staff physician name of Ellsworth."

Sheila stopped in the middle of raising a cigarette to her lips. The number of furrows on her brow increased.

"Something wrong?" Jan asked.

"That's another popular name around here today. The drimp was yakking about him when I got in this morning."

"Saying what?" Jan asked, leaning closer.

"Sorry, couldn't catch it. He heard me come in and closed his door, then went on gabbing with one of the boys."

"Let me guess," Jan said. "He was talking to Gavin Larsen."

Sheila nodded. "How'd you know?"

"Instincts."

"God love 'em," Sheila said, then added seriously, "This important?"

"Could be," Jan answered. "You hear about what happened this weekend?"

Inhaling deeply on her cigarette, Sheila exhaled and said, "Have I ever. I had to come in Sunday to help *him* prepare for an emergency administration meeting. Some days I swear I have to tell him to zip up after the men's room."

"The thing is," Jan said, speculating, "it's beginning to look as though this Ellsworth might know something."

"Jesus, we don't need any TV soap operas to entertain us around here. You think there might be something in his folder to tell you?"

"I was hoping. Or at least something to get me started. But I have to warn you, I'm working alone on this."

"No you're not," Sheila said in a devil-may-care voice.

"Thanks. It's appreciated, but you be damn careful. A doctor killed in-house? You got to believe that Administration will be head-hunting."

"Hey, my best friend clerks in Personnel. Nobody will know a thing. Just sit tight, I'll be right back." She took a step, turned, and said, "Am I licensed to kill?"

Jan gave a firm, exaggerated nod.

A few minutes later Sheila reappeared with a newspaper too heavy to contain only today's news. "Maybe you can return it tomorrow," Sheila said. "There were some coupons I wanted."

* * *

Out in her car, Jan found that the first sheet in Dr. Ellsworth's personnel folder was a typed letter of resignation. He would be leaving Jackson General at the end of the month for personal reasons. What those reasons might include went unsaid, but they intrigued Jan mightily. She drove to a pay phone to try reaching Detective White but no luck. He was out of his office until noon, so she left a message and headed home.

With her daughters off to school and Claire parked before a morning talk show—topic of the day being several scientists who claimed the human race had three sexes, not two—Jan changed into her sweats for a morning run in the park to clear her lungs and mind. A small band of crows flew from tree to tree before her, dark heralds announcing her approach to anyone up ahead. She outwitted them by turning off along a bridle path and soon had the park to herself. If she concentrated, she could almost have her mind to herself too.

10

WITH the changing of shifts that Tuesday morning, the night workers drifted out of General Jack in less than tip-top shape. The hazy sunlight disoriented them, the long night of wakefulness made them forgetful. Before shoving off, the graveyard crews relayed to the day shift status reports on each patient. The hospital census hung at 472, a 63 percent occupancy.

Of course some of the night staff weren't allowed to go home because their replacements hadn't arrived. Perhaps someone had called in sick; or there might not have been anyone scheduled to replace them, an oversight possibly due to a shortage of workers for almost every medical position but doctors. There were more than enough candidates for the top slots at a teaching institution. Or the shortage could have been the result of yet another mess-up in the county's Personnel Department, whose hiring procedures resembled a flawed maze, two ways in, no way out.

Naturally Personnel denied any culpability while repeatedly pointing out that traditional health care workers—namely women—were discovering other fields of endeavor—law, accounting, fluid dynamics, you name it—where as a minority they would be given VP treatment and hustled on the fast track to upper management. These other careers paid better and didn't involve rotating shifts, sharp needles, or cramming NG tubes down people's noses. These other careers didn't involve taking orders from doctors either, particularly young doctors, male and female, whose umbilical cords to medical school had barely been snipped and who frequently imagined they were God's gift to humanity, a condition sometimes known as sitteth-at-the-right-hand-itis. And furthermore, of the women who remained in the field, many wouldn't consider working in an inner-city public hospital for reasons of personal safety. Needing an escort to your car after dark wasn't a confidence builder. And if pushed, Personnel got around to pointing out that men weren't flocking to fill these positions no longer desired by women. So what was Personnel supposed to do in the face of an entire shift of society's norms? And who was to say that the extra body down in the basement wasn't the result of these larger forces? Not Personnel, a very didactic department.

On that Tuesday morning, General Jack itself sat solidly in the early September sun, a collection of buildings that from the outside appeared little different from aging apartment complexes or, depending on your angle of observation, turn-of-the-century high schools. If you ignored the banners proclaiming it a level-one trauma center, the parking posters saying RESERVED FOR DOCTORS, the street signs pointing to the Emergency entrance—if you overlooked all that, the buildings might have belonged to any number of institutions. The only thing unusual about the hospital's profile was the three-story smokestack crowning an incinerator that was no longer in use because of tougher EPA guidelines. The burner couldn't fire up hot enough to destroy all the toxics in the hospital's infectious wastes.

On the other hand, the General's interior couldn't be mistaken for any other kind of building anywhere. To begin with, there was that special hospital fragrance, which unless you'd worked there for years made you feel apprehensive, maybe creepy, as though you might lose something you'd grown attached to. Next came the piped-in music, which some genius in Administration dreamed up as a way to soothe the clientele when all it actually did was serve to remind them they weren't in an upscale shopping mall where three hundred specialty shops sold nothing that was essential to human existence unless bee pollen counted as indispensable. No amount of mood music was busting General Jack's patrons out of poverty. And of course the money spent on installing and renting the music could have been used to add a staff position or two, thus actually improving patient care. Then there were the bright lights, the shiny floors, the people in uniforms, and the other people in loose robes and slippers. What other kind of building could it be?

Lastly, there were machines—everywhere. Machines whose functions were unfamiliar and thus suspicious to the general public. Machines to measure brain waves and heartbeats; machines to take pictures of what goes on inside your body; machines to listen; machines to count corpuscles, to preserve vaccines, to grow cultures; machines to store information about you and your ability to pay for the services of all the other machines. It had to be one of the highest concentrations of machines in the city.

Of all this instrumentation, the most complicated was the human machine, the biodegradable one that ran all the others and occasionally was able to steal a moment away from its duties to realize that it was more than an assemblage of parts that fit together in such and such a fashion and needed a tune-up or replacement valves from time to time. At those inspired pinnacles of revelation, when able to rise above the machine-to-machine interface, maybe the workers caught a glimpse of much of what kept them at their jobs: the sensation that they had a shot at accomplishing something grand or noble or worthwhile, something larger than themselves, maybe something lasting. How many jobs offered that kind of bonus? Not that the staff would have freely admitted this to Personnel; contract negotiations were scheduled for spring.

But just as the workers had a saintly side, they shared a venal half too, and on that Tuesday morning the machine that was functioning most efficiently of all in General Jack was the grapevine. By midmorning most of the hundreds of people working, regardless of their position, had learned all the details to be had concerning one of the hospital's finest turning up in the morgue, apparently murdered. They were ravenous for more information. Given the uneven operation of a grapevine, the cause of death was variously given as gunshot, strangulation, AIDS, and overdose. With no definitive word having yet been released from the medical examiner's office, who could say otherwise to any explanation? Staff reactions were varied but professional.

"Someone beat me to it."

"Bye-bye."

"The holier-than-thou one?"

"Who gets his locker?"

The day shift rolled on toward the evening. Patients came, patients went. The hospital grapevine spread until every employee, regardless of rank, had his or her own theory about how the body reached the morgue, yet nobody stepped forward with any alarming evidence or any silly evidence or any evidence at all. A body had miraculously appeared in the morgue, the body of a staff physician no less, and everyone was extremely interested but no one had any light to shed on the topic. A worker in housekeeping was giving four-to-five on a wronged lover, three-to-five that she was a nurse. He had some action but not enough to finance a trip to Vegas. As a rule, the employees of General Jack were far too superstitious to bet something this close to home.

11

ON Tuesday morning Gavin Larsen went to the grapevine, went to it hard. If anyone thought that after having his promotion stripped away he was going to step silently aside, if they imagined he was going to sacrifice his integrity or be available for service as a doormat, he was about to correct them, show them the error of their ways, come down on them like two tons of fire-hardened brick. This wouldn't even be a contest. He'd find out who snuffed the doc, why, prove it, and hand the answers in along with his resignation to that shovy administrator Kavanaugh, the one who acted as though she was doing him a favor by letting him spy on people. The promise of satisfaction in resigning was high octane.

Same as city cops, he'd over the years cultivated his information sources, and although the payment plans differed slightly, the principle remained the same: there were formal channels and informal ones, and real knowledge flowed underground. The problem was tapping it. Without having the authority or petty cash funds available to a cop, he'd learned to be creative, and he'd also discovered—to his amazement—that his being a loner was a major advantage for a closed society like General Jack's. People believed that he would keep their gossip padlocked and chained. For the most part, this assumption was true.

He started by arranging a meeting with the hospital chaplain, whose older brother was an MD on staff, the chief of medicine, no less. Due to a mean-spirited sibling rivalry, the chaplain's primary form of recreation was tracking the sins of General Jack's physicians. With that in mind, Gavin had some years before set up a tricky barter system with the potbellied Baptist. To get dirt, Gavin gave dirt, plus a little jolt of cloak-and-dagger that jazzed up the shabbiness of their enterprise and protected the minister's reputation as a man of utmost confidentiality. To that end, they always met in a confessional at the back of the hospital's chapel. Although General Jack was a public institution, the confessional was there to appease the Catholic diocese, which had after all donated the land on which the south block of General, called New General, had been constructed back in the 1940s. The code words they used to set up meetings were the chaplain's idea. He was a bit wacky from the continued light of the Lord, as he described it.

"Bless me, Padre." That was how Gavin identified himself to the Baptist minister sitting in the screened-off priest's chair.

"The Lord is forgiveness." Which was how the Baptist minister represented himself as the Catholic priest whom Gavin wanted.

Since neither of them was Catholic, they kept their voices low and did the best they could with the protocols, in case anyone was listening. Who might be eavesdropping was uncertain. With the falling number of available priests, the Catholic church no longer assigned a father to Jackson General except on an on-call basis for last-rite emergencies; and the chapel itself—a simple room converted from a doctors' lounge—may have been the least populated space in the entire medical complex. With the advent of modern medicine, few people relied on the old standby except when in gravest need of the supernatural. Some days the chapel's only visitor was the woman from housekeeping who feather-dusted its unadorned, nondenominational altar and ten pews.

Now it was time for dirt.

"This is about Dr. Croft?" the minister guessed. It really wasn't a shot in the dark, not with the local TV stations using the doctor's unexplained demise to parade their sense of community, and, coincidentally, to help out with the ratings.

"It is," Gavin said. "Administration thinks they have a suspect."

"Administration always has a suspect. It's the way their minds work. But there's more, right, G?" The minister insisted on initials.

"Their suspect is a doctor."

"Better. Now we're getting somewhere. I should warn you though, if it's my brother I'd make a poor character witness."

"Not to worry," said Gavin. "A different MD."

"Oh," the minister said, a trace of disappointment in his voice. But he rebounded with quick optimism. "Well, let's not get ahead of ourselves. What exactly happened to the dead man?"

"Cause of death isn't out for public consumption. The cops are holding on to it until Croft's parents can be notified. I'd say not trauma, though."

"Something internal?"

"A good guess, Padre."

"Why not suicide?"

"Doesn't have that feel," Gavin said. "No note, for one

thing. Somebody put him in a body bag, for another. Zipped it up all the way. That can't be done from the inside."

"Good points," the minister agreed. "When did the foul deed happen?"

"Another unknown, although I'm guessing two weeks ago, Friday the twenty-first."

"That would mean he lay in state for fourteen days," the minister said, unable to avoid sounding gleeful. "How could that be?"

"County efficiency," Gavin routinely explained, appending his own theory on how someone was trying to get the body out of the hospital, where the murder must have taken place, but had been scared off before succeeding. From there Gavin traced the corpse's progress to the morgue without too much ado.

"Better and better," the minister said, warming to the story. "And your suspect's name?"

"First an agreement."

"Ouch."

"Everything you know about the deceased, for starters."

"And for enders?"

"Everything you know about Administration's suspect."

"Croft first?" the minister asked, enthusiastic about the chance to show his wares.

"By all means."

"He was an unpopular man, G. Everywhere. A perfectionist. Demanded everything be done the right way, meaning his way. A very knowledgeable man, but not a tactful one. Let me give you an example. A few years back Croft testified in a malpractice suit against another physician here at General."

"Who?"

"Not important," the minister said. "Last I heard, that fellow was doing missionary work in some pest-riddled third-world country. Far removed from here. I only mentioned it to show how Croft dealt with his colleagues. Actually, his testimony would have been quite admirable if he'd done it for humanitarian reasons instead of the fact that the man hadn't done as Croft told him. Still, a lot of doctors wouldn't dream of pointing fingers at one another in public. It's not so much that it isn't polite, although there's that, but mainly it's the cost, the hours spent without pay in courtroom after courtroom, appeals on the local, county, and state levels. But it's never mattered to Croft. He's got an ego big as a Macy's parade balloon."

"So plenty of suspects," Gavin thoughtfully said. "Any leaders of the pack?"

"I thought that's what you were going to tell me?"

"No, I'm telling you who Administration's worried about. I never said I agreed with them. They haven't told me enough to know."

"Keeping you in the dark, eh? Suspects . . . You've got me there. No shortage, I should imagine. Even my brother, the Maharajah of Medicine, feuded with Croft. That's good, put him down."

"What'd they fight about?"

"Stethoscopes, tongue depressors, the usual."

"How about something serious?"

"Believe me, G, hospital budgeting is hard core for those boys. Say Neurology gets a Magnetic Resonance Imager worth a half million dollars. That means the egos in Medicine go without."

"Did that happen?"

"Oh yes," said the minister. "Last year Radiology got one, with Neurology's solid support. My brother even came whining to me about it, as if I could put in a good word somewhere up high."

"Anyone else?"

"Hmm," the minister said, grinding on it a moment. "Croft had a reputation as a nurse-izer."

In the darkened booth, Gavin strained to see through the screen. "Any particular lovelorn?"

"None that I've heard of, but recent nursing graduates are always popular."

"Any other possibilities?" Gavin asked with irony. "Now that we've narrowed it down to the physicians and nursing staff."

"There's an ex-wife," the minister helpfully said. "Three offspring too, though they're probably too young. But I knew the missus once, years ago. Used to be a nurse here, down in the ER. If an electric meat carver'd been involved, I'd say she definitely should be number one. Their divorce was major surgery. Lawyers floated on air currents above their separate residences for weeks. The offal was awful, if you know what I mean."

"Could she have done this?"

"Who knows what evil lurks . . ."

"OK, Padre, OK. Let me put it this way. How long ago was the divorce?"

"Six, no, seven years ago."

"Are we to the end of possibles?"

After a moment of reflection, the minister responded, "Amen. Now, you were going to tell me about Administration's prime suspect?"

"A staff physician named Ellsworth."

"They can't be serious," the minister said.

"You're not buying?"

"I have to say I've trouble imagining Anthony Ellsworth capable of such a thing. He's too busy trying to remember everything he knows, and believe me, he thinks he knows volumes. I mean, he's one of the most arrogant, conceited men that you're likely to find in a white lab coat. And the crazy thing is, he has no reason to be. A terrible doctor, totally inept from what I hear. And as for killing someone . . . well, the rest of us are so far beneath the Ellsworth bloodline that I have trouble believing he'd think it worth his time."

"Sounds like the kind of man whose conscience wouldn't bother him."

"You may have a point there, G, but I still stick to my first reaction. I've known that family for years. His father's on the hospital board, and all in all, I can't imagine them thinking someone else so important as to merit the attention you're suggesting. Why him?"

"That's what I'd like to know," Gavin said, vexed. "Administration's concerned there might be a connection, but like I said, they're not exactly confiding why to me. They want me to poke around and see what I can find. They'd rather not involve his name at all, if they can avoid it, and they want me to make sure they can have a clear conscience if they don't mention it to anyone."

"Like the police?"

"Exactly."

"Yet they've given you no idea what this connection might be?" the minister asked, perplexed.

"That's where I'm out in the cold, Padre."

"How can they expect you to succeed under those conditions?"

"My thoughts too."

"Can you tell me this," the minister said. "Which administrator's stringing you along?"

"The new one. Kavanaugh."

"Lo and behold," the minister dramatically said, "that means Averilli too. She's his gofer. So actually you're dealing with the top paper clip. Any others involved in this cabal—other than that dunce you work for?"

"None that I know of."

"And they haven't even suggested where you should look?"

"They want me to concentrate on Ellsworth's relationship with Croft, and I had to argue with them to get that much direction."

"That's the only possibility they're interested in?"

"It's the only one they've told me about."

"Interesting," the minister said as if transfixed by some natural phenomenon. Then he snapped to, saying, "But here you sit gabbing with me, G. I'd say you've strayed from your intended line of inquiry."

"Not from mine," Gavin said. "Maybe from theirs."

"An ax to grind?"

"Significantly. We were talking about this Ellsworth, right?"

"Yes, I drifted, didn't I? So, Anthony Ellsworth . . . works in Neurology, under Croft naturally. Despite his opinion of himself, or maybe because of it, he's not reputed to be a competent man, as I mentioned. Got his position because of his father, the county commissioner. You can safely assume that young Ellsworth and Croft didn't see eye to eye, but I don't know anything for sure on that. Seems to me I also heard a rumor he's leaving us soon, moving on to private practice. I don't imagine he'll get rich at it, not with his reputation and golden way with patients. You think that's the tie-in? His leaving?"

"Who knows? You haven't heard of any direct conflicts between Croft and Ellsworth?"

"Sorry to say, G, I haven't. I feel remiss in my duties."

"Do I need to mention that you can't tell anyone about this?" Gavin asked. "I'm supposed to be conducting a discreet inquiry."

"Goes without saying."

The minister sounded distracted even as he said it, as though a list of persons who might be interested in such a tidbit was growing in his mind as he spoke. But then that was how grapevines operated, and Gavin couldn't help secretly grinning. Administration had declined to appeal the court decision in Jan Gallagher's favor, and that chafed.

"Go in peace," the minister said.

And Gavin went, although hardly in peace. The meeting had raised more questions than it put to rest.

* * *

By the time he left the chapel, it was past nine A.M., and he would have preferred to call it a night, and a long one at that, but the minister had raised a new line of inquiry—Dr. Croft's romantic entanglements. For that, Gavin had but one genuine source—Delores. So there it was. Delores. She fed on the hospital's romances like the tabloids devoured celebrities. Her accuracy was on a par with the tabs too, but he wasn't expecting a footnoted report, only a whiff of what might have happened. The prospect of a meeting with her tied his gut into three knots, at least, but once he'd resigned himself to the inevitable, he knew he'd have to get it out of the way before he tried to sleep, or there would be no resting for him. Already feeling trapped, he began to consider how to approach his source.

Delores Webb worked as the charge nurse on the Orthopedics floor. In her midthirties, she was a master of fad diets, winner of none. For Delores, the operative word was *single.* Singleness plunged as deep as the abyss of eternity, and experience forewarned him that even putting a toe on the Ortho floor would stir up coupling instincts. Maybe a phone call would strike the right professional touch. Yes, he liked that. The distance behind that arrangement bolstered his courage and he started to dial. But once Delores came on the line, his confidence dissipated rapidly.

Her first words were, "Should I faint?"

She was referring to the fact that she hadn't heard from him for several months, not since a disastrous date that had ended with her trying to coax him up to her apartment. He'd fled as if fearing infection. They'd gone to a thriller movie, no doubt picked because it allowed her to grip his hand when the stalker music got going. Today, as always, he didn't know how to deal with her insinuations. He still wasn't quite sure how he'd been jockeyed into asking her out six months ago. It was almost as if he'd blacked out for a few seconds, and when he'd come around they were setting a time. She was formidable, this one, and he became evasive.

"I'm doing some investigating for Administration," he said, thinking that was a solid start, "and I was wondering if you had time to answer a few questions?"

"It's always business with you, isn't it, Larsen?"

She sounded irate and had called him Larsen, both good signs on one level, but not so positive on another, considering that he wanted her cooperation for a few seconds, a minute at the most. After that, maybe it would be for the best if she was perturbed and skipped his first name.

"I try to earn my wages."

"Very commendable."

"What I was wondering . . ."

"May I ask you a question, Larsen?"

He didn't know what to say and almost dropped the receiver, whose cord had somehow gotten all twisted up in his hands.

"You strong, silent types," Delores said after ten seconds of dead line.

That forced him to say, "Maybe this isn't such a good idea."

"Cold feet, huh?"

"No, but you don't seem too eager to talk to me."

After a pause, her voice shifted, becoming softer, more melodious. "I wouldn't say that."

Now he was scrambling. "What Administration has me looking into is the business with Dr. Croft. You've probably heard about it?"

Too late, though. Her scorn had vanished and she sounded like a helpmate. "In that case, of course. I'd want to do what I can."

"What I'm wondering . . ."

"Don't you think it'd be better to ask these questions in person?"

"It doesn't really seem . . ."

"That way," she quickly added, "I'll be able to get a real sense for what it is you're after."

"It's a simple question really."

"Telephones make me very forgetful," she cautioned. "I always feel as though three-quarters of the conversation is missing. No, I think in person would be best. Particularly since I've been talking to so many people about Dr. Croft."

She left that thought dangling, at which point Gavin capitulated and agreed to a meeting at her team center at his earliest convenience, in other words, immediately.

All this added another knot to his stomach; no cold sweats, though. This wasn't some cheap comedy. Upon reaching station 32F, Orthopedics, he saw that Delores had arranged her normally tousled brown hair into what he thought was called a French braid. He wasn't sophisticated enough to know exactly what that meant, but he knew that it didn't bode well. She was smiling, too, and kept him waiting long enough to allow most of her staff a chance to size him up before showing him into the office she shared with the charge nurses from the two other shifts. At present, however, they were all alone. Marooned was how he thought of it. Reaching around him to close the door, she managed to brush against him. Claustrophobia entered through his nostrils with a rush of her musk perfume. Taking a seat at her crowded desk, she motioned for him to move to a chair across from her. She had a habit of keeping the left side of her round face toward him as often as possible. He couldn't detect a difference, but maybe she thought it was her best profile. Aside from her change in hairstyle, she looked the same to him—short, busty, on the prowl. Her teeth remained orthodontic marvels—they'd better, considering the investment she claimed they represented. The number of extremely personal details he knew about her was dismaying.

"I suppose you've been all wrapped up in the discrimination case," she said. "Not that you need to provide any excuses for not calling."

Eyes averted, he mumbled in agreement.

"Would you look at me?"

He did.

"You don't have any business getting that job if she scored higher than you."

She sounded as though she was reading the Emancipation Proclamation, and part of the reason why he'd once asked her out came back to him. You couldn't expect Delores Webb to simper and faint at your feet because you were an eligible man and she was desperate. She spoke her mind, a fact that he respected even if it did contort his extremely level head.

"What if I scored higher?" he asked.

"By how much?"

"Higher. How much shouldn't matter." It'd been less than a full point, a galling subject. He'd only managed it because of his experience rating, which hadn't been a documented part of the hiring process until the Little Admiral saw that the name on top of his applicants' list read Jan Gallagher. On the test and in the panel interviews, she had aced everyone.

"It probably still doesn't matter," Delores said. "Not if you're committed to equal rights."

"Who said I am?"

"I'm talking about the courts."

"Look, this isn't what I wanted to see you about."

"Oh, I think it is, Gavin Larsen. I think it explains why I haven't heard from you in over six months. You've been too busy woman-bashing to consort with the enemy. But in case you hadn't noticed, I'm not the enemy, that woman who got your job's not the enemy . . . The enemy is your own small idea about what's right and wrong, and if you can't learn to forget about . . ."

Her words began to blur at that point, and he realized she was doing it to him again, creating some kind of gravitational or centrifugal or magnetic force that was breaking down his concept of how the world fit together. If he didn't fight it, who knew what he'd find himself agreeing to.

She prophetically concluded, ". . . you'll end up a bitter, lonely old man."

"I came to ask you about Dr. Croft."

"Right."

"You said you'd been talking to people about him?"

"That's your response to all that I said? Our entire society is breaking apart because of inequality and people's inability to talk about it, and you want to ask questions about a dead womanizer?"

"Delores, did it ever occur to you that some people are happier alone?"

"Why no, Gavin," she said, cynical now, "the thought's never crossed my mind."

She glared at him then, or at least he assumed she was, probably showing him her left profile, but he didn't actually know because he was balefully facing the window where he could see the smokestack rising above General's incinerator, the one which was no longer in use because of the dangers present in plastic wastes. It occurred to him that man-woman relationships had something in common with medical by-products. Neither could be safely vented into the atmosphere without first being exposed to fires of extremely high temperatures.

"Maybe we can get together and talk about this some other time," he suggested. What traitorous part of him was saying that?

"Don't do me any favors."

"But right now what I need to hear about is Dr. Croft. Even if he was a womanizer, he's dead. Murdered. Do you think that's right?"

"Of course not," she said, mellowing. "You're under a lot of pressure, aren't you?"

"Delores . . ."

"OK. OK. Yes, I've been talking to some people about Dr. Croft, although that's not exactly how he was known around here. We called him the Casanova of Neuro, and that's what is really strange about what I've been hearing. He didn't have even one affair going on. Hasn't had any for several months. We're talking about a man who'd been known to score the hat trick on a single shift. You ask me, there's something very peculiar about any celibacy on his part."

Gavin agreed, although not out loud. Why would a man like Dr. Croft suddenly stop chasing skirts? The answer could be vital, but he wasn't about to ask Delores for her opinion. Who knew what she'd accomplish with a question like that.

"How about a doctor named Ellsworth, on Neuro too. Can you tell me anything about that one?"

"That I wouldn't go to him with a headache. You might lose your tonsils unless there's a nurse there to protect you."

"Know any stories about him and Croft?"

"No," she said, intrigued, "should I?"

"Not that I know of, but thank you for your time."

"Is that all the better you can do?" she asked, looking at him pityingly. Gavin recognized that the topic before them had suddenly shifted from doctors to larger subjects, ones nearer and dearer to Delores' heart.

"Afraid so," he said, standing and offering her his hand, which she spurned. He didn't bother asking her to stay mum concerning his interest in these matters on behalf of Administration. Requesting such a favor would create the expectation of reciprocity, and he knew what lay in that direction. Besides, with Delores such a request was as hopeless as the task of harnessing nuclear energy. Sooner or later something leaked.

When he started toward the door, she said, "Don't bother to call."

Had he heard that parting shot right? Goddamn, that woman knew how to bend his mind. It was a wonder he made it out of the room without stumbling on anything. His tongue, for instance.

On duty he never wore a hat. Off duty he was rarely without one, usually a weathered Stetson. The vanity of bald men was a curse he'd learned to live with. When he climbed behind the wheel of his Cherokee, he knew that he looked as farfetched as any of the hundreds of men in the city who wore chaps to bed, pined for ostrich-skin boots, and watched "Bonanza" every night at eleven. Nevertheless, a feeling of stony-lonesome wistfulness stole over him, a sensation that something had been lost, something that he'd never been given a chance to find—the sight of wide-open spaces or the aroma of wet sage or the feel of campfire heat. He wasn't quite sure which, maybe all of them. Even country-western music didn't help with funks like this. By the time he'd driven into the herd of foreign-made compacts crowding the city's streets, he had a notion that it might be fun to start a stampede and drove accordingly. It helped a little. He had something of a mean streak when it came to other people, particularly crowds of other people.

Once on the freeway, he ramrodded his jeep straight south at sixty-five miles per hour for a full fifty-eight minutes. After fifteen minutes he left the city proper, and once past forty-one minutes he escaped the outlying subdivisions of the farthest burb, which left him seventeen minutes of country driving. The scenery included corn rows, soil bank, silo profiles, and farm machinery as large as road-construction equipment. But he only had eyes for the emptiness of it compared to the city. Fifty-five minutes out he passed through a stand of hardwoods two miles across and ten miles long that was owned by the Nature Conservancy and would never fall prey to developers. Gavin's home butted up against the far side of this woods.

He'd found the abandoned farmhouse and bought it plus twenty acres of swampy burdock cheap from a farmer long retired to central Florida. At the time of the purchase agreement, the roof offered a grand view of the Milky Way; the plumbing consisted of a two-seater twenty feet out the back door; and a family of skunks had grown prosperous under the spongy floor of the porch. The place was about perfect. For instance, the glass in most of the windows had been shot out by roaming sportsmen. That'd been seven years ago, before he'd signed the mortgage. Today his homestead looked prosperous and no longer sagged and bagged, thanks to Gavin's skills with a hammer and saw. He took his bachelorhood seriously, which resulted in his keeping everything orderly and clean, nothing like the rooms of men who have never learned to pick up after themselves, men who acted as though expecting a maid, in one form or another, to enter their lives any day now.

Exactly why he was devoted to living alone had nothing to do with heartbreak. He'd never in his life seriously dated a woman, and while his mother had been alive they'd gotten along fine, no hidden trauma there. In his own mind, the reason was simply that he was a loner, always had been, and buying the farmhouse had only confirmed it. When the German shepherd he bought as a watchdog had run off, he was happier without the companionship and never replaced it. He refused to feed stray cats who worked their way down the lane. There was but one other living thing he kept in the house, a jade plant, which he faithfully trimmed and watered but never said a word to. It was a plant, after all.

He'd grown up in the city, the outcome of an unremarkable childhood, unless you counted as noteworthy the fact that he emerged from adolescence without any close friends or fond memories. The first social organization he ever voluntarily joined had been the navy, and that was only to avoid being drafted into the army during Vietnam. It hadn't mattered—the government sent him to Southeast Asia anyway, part of a Seabee unit that laid down harbor facilities. That had been where he'd learned his carpentry skills. He approved of the navy's discipline, hadn't cared for the chow, and after four years returned to the city where he went through a string of zero jobs until landing at General Jack, where his maritime background made him a shoo-in with the Little Admiral.

The one thing that all the time spent alone contributed to his chosen profession—and after twelve years he thought of security work as such—was an indelible idea of right and wrong. When he had an opinion, it remained strong and fresh because no one was present to dispute him. Indestructible convictions were a handy survival trait for dealing with the rows he daily encountered at work. Where his ideas of good and bad came from was not something he questioned. In his experience, people who dallied with such issues had already lost a grip on the distinctions. You either knew it or you didn't. If you didn't, neither books nor friends nor church was going to pull you through. It was going to be a long, confusing haul to the cemetery. So, on some level, down there amongst his bones, he felt that the court order sweeping his promotion aside was wrong—completely, inalterably, everlastingly. That offended him, upset his DNA, intruded into his isolation, which was one of the main reasons he'd applied for the job of supervisor. If it was lonely at the top, that's where he wanted to be.

When he finally lay down to sleep around eleven, he couldn't nod off, so he went to the kitchen for a glass of skim milk from a spotless refrigerator. All he wanted was to vindicate himself, to prove he wasn't responsible for his demotion. The death of Dr. Croft presented the perfect mechanism for that. Tracking down how it happened would be no easy matter, certainly beyond the ken of his replacement. Once he'd laid all that open, he would quit, retire to his hermitage, and maybe take up meditation, which he'd recently read about in a magazine. Except . . . there was a catch—his mortgage. He couldn't leave his job, start over elsewhere, and expect to make the same money that the county paid him after twelve years. More money had been another reason he'd applied for the promotion. He needed his current paychecks for another twenty-three years before the house and land would be his, but if he'd kept his supervisory job, he could have paid the bank off in seventeen. He'd figured that much out before applying for the position. Above all, he couldn't bear the thought of losing the contentment he'd found out here where no one could bother him.

At one o'clock, after an hour's rest, the phone rang. Being a light sleeper, he caught it on the second jingle.

"Larsen, this is Elizabeth Kavanaugh, from the hospital. It looks as though we could use your help again. That homicide detective's scheduled a special appointment with our Dr. Ellsworth for this afternoon. We want you to be on hand to see what this is about."

On the way into the city, he cut off the first three drivers who tried to merge onto the freeway in front of him.

12

KNOWING that the Little Admiral and Larsen were in collusion demolished any chance Jan had for sleep on her day off. Signs of conspiracy were breeding everywhere. Larsen walking hand in hand with Elizabeth Kavanaugh; Sheila overhearing Larsen and the Little Admiral conferring about Dr. Ellsworth; the attitude of her fellow guards, as expressed by Ginger, that it didn't matter how badly Jan performed her duties, nobody was going to let her fail. Her first response was to get into a pointless rhubarb with her mother about, of all things, cooking oils—safflower versus olive. She followed that up with a couple hours of pillow wrestling on her basement cot, which today felt spiky and hot, like a fakir's bed. Eventually she admitted to herself there was some paranoia mixed in here. After that confession, she knew rest was out of the question if she didn't take countermeasures. This led her to calling Detective White again, who—what else?—suggested dinner. She countered with a late lunch, and they were set, much to the disgust of Jan's mother, who followed her around asking why she was putting on her best dark blazer and slacks.

The Mermaid Bar and Grill, where they met, smelled musty and salty, like the inside of a peanut shell soaked in brine. It was dim and loud, with arguments about sports and women, plus jokes about gun control, filling the air. The single room had a bar at the center and was stocked with so many cops, frocked and unfrocked, that the old business on the street about being able to spot heat a block away was driven home. Regardless of shape or size, race or gender, they all bore the inky stamp of the Law, most noticeably in the way they watched each other, not easy and curious, but vigilant and estimating. On the way to Detective White's booth, her bottom was pinched twice. Having once been married to one of the little boys in blue, she recognized the liberty of that gesture all too well. If there'd been more light, she would have caught and slapped the perverts. But who wanted to make a mistake and pick the wrong cops?

Sitting down opposite the homicide detective, she felt a sideways rumbling of romantic déjà vu and promised herself, *This guy's not getting to first base.* To his everlasting credit, the detective didn't start by playing footsie but got right down to business, or at least she assumed that's what he was getting down to.

"You have any idea how many funeral homes we have in this fair city?"

"A thousand," Jan guessed, thinking that if this was a come-on she'd never heard it before.

"Very amusing. But the total I come up with is four hundred and thirty-two all qualified to . . ."

The waitress arrived. Detective White knew her first name and didn't need to check a menu. Jan doubled his order of the Tuesday special along with a pot of strong coffee to counteract the consecutive hours she'd been awake, somewhere over twenty.

". . . qualified to handle the dead," the detective said, picking up where he'd left off.

"Funeral homes," she said, getting back on track. "There a reason we're discussing this?"

"A good one. My partner and I questioned most of the staff who worked with Croft. Didn't learn much of anything, but after that, and with a little encouragement from our captain, we started calling funeral homes, one by one, to ask if they happened to be missing a red body bag."

"Ah."

"Nobody is. We also tried the mortuary wholesalers. Not a one of them stock the kind of bag we have here."

"How about the gurney the bag was on? It's not one of the county's."

After a long, disgusted sigh, the detective said, "Beau-ti-ful. You have any idea of how long it takes to call four hundred and thirty-two funeral chapels? My associates won't be happy. But you're thinking, Gallagher, that's what counts. So, we'll run down the gurney too. Now, as promised, here's the autopsy report. We haven't located the guy's parents yet, so you're not actually seeing this, if you catch my drift. I believe you have something for me?"

They exchanged papers, Jan handing over Ellsworth's thick personnel folder, and the detective sliding two sheets of the M.E.'s report across the table. Cheery reading. Neither said a word as they flipped pages. Jan finished first, finding that Dr. Jonathon Croft went the way the detective had earlier said, an overdose of Valium and alcohol. Digging that out of the highly technical jargon wasn't easy but at last she was satisfied it was so.

The lunch plates arrived, and she picked at hers while watching the detective labor through his sheaf of papers. No speed reader, he gave the impression of searing each word into permanent memory. At last he pushed the folder away, tucked a napkin in at his collar, and grumbled, "With applications long as that, it's amazing they have time to saw bones." He started in on his meal. "The only thing I see is that he's resigning. Know anything about that?"

"Not yet," she said.

"I like your attitude, Gallagher." He arched his eyebrows to show that wasn't all he liked. "I could probably find a whole lot more to approve of too, given a chance."

"You won't be."

"You sound awfully sure about that."

"I am," she said, pushing her plate away.

"You always this hard on the opposite sex?"

She smiled resignedly and said, "Not always, unfortunately. I need to get that folder back today. Are you done with it?"

He deliberated a moment before dropping the lounge lizard act and saying without insinuation of any kind, "Yes, thanks. Something tells me that letter of resignation might not have been in there if I'd asked Ms. Kavanaugh for those records." Closing the folder, he handed it over. "Anything you can tell me about this Kavanaugh?"

"She doesn't like me."

Plenty of chance for romantic repartee there but he avoided it, saying in a neutral voice, "She seems to have taken a disliking to me too."

"Administration's uptight," Jan said with an unsurprised shrug. "About all I can tell you is that she's fairly new to her job and works with the executive administrator on special projects."

"Aren't you forgetting one thing?"

"Not that I'm aware of."

"Her husband," White said. "She mentioned him often enough. He's something or other big down there at the hospital, right?"

"A surgeon," Jan said.

"Hmm," the detective said while cutting up the roast beef

on his plate. "That leaves us this Ellsworth. He's a terribly busy man, didn't want to see me at all, but I managed to arrange an interview with him this afternoon." Growing sly, he said, "Pretty soon, actually. Maybe you'd like to tag along? I could use the help, if you want the unembellished truth. You might catch something I'll miss, being as how you know the lay of the land down there and all."

"Right now?" she said, certain that Administration wouldn't appreciate her zeal. The defeatism inherent in that thought made up her mind and she concluded by saying, "I'm game."

"First," Detective White sagely said, "we better have some pie à la mode to sustain us."

He needed two slices to fortify himself for the long and winding road. Jan was beginning to see that when he asked a woman out for dinner, it wasn't just her company he was interested in. She found herself enjoying his appetite, and of course roundly chastised herself for the thought.

The Mermaid Bar and Grill lay five short blocks from General Jack, where Jan had parked, so they elected to walk. With the air lukewarm and clammy, and the city's bouquet at its ripest, the detective didn't get any openings to comment about what a glorious day it was with Jan at his side. During the morning a gray phlegm of clouds had spread over the city, looking like something spit out of smokestacks, and if all that wasn't enough to remove any flattery lurking in the detective's mouth, there was the heavy traffic. He would have had to raise his voice for even the tiniest flattery to be heard. He had the good sense not to.

Even so, Jan felt first-date foolish beside him and kept her distance, although she wasn't able to separate herself quite far enough. As they entered the hospital, she glimpsed Gavin Larsen ducking out of sight down a stairway. Positive that Larsen had spotted who she was with, she took the incident as a bad omen. What drew Larsen to the hospital so early in the day remained to be seen, but Jan felt free to imagine the worst.

"So how are we going to work this?" the detective asked as they waited for the narrow elevator doors to open.

"What do you mean?"

"We've never interviewed anyone together before. We should have some kind of routine. It's expected. You know, good cop, bad cop, although that's strictly a rerun these days."

"What do you suggest?" she asked, suspicious.

"I'll be the case-hardened bureaucrat. Doesn't matter who did what so long as my forms get filled out. You be the angel of mercy after the truth."

"I'm in no mood for wings."

Detective White chuckled. "Understandable. How's this— I'm the bureau cop and you're along to help protect the doctor. You know, to stop me from taking up too much of the important man's time, from trampling on his—not to mention the hospital's—rights. How's that?"

"I could live with it."

"You might even enjoy it?" he asked.

"Not if a certain administrator we both know finds out, which she will, considering how news travels like a hot flash through this place. But that's OK. I'm along to make sure you don't get carried away. It's not much but it should be enough to cover my ass."

The detective stepped back and glanced down as if to say that it was a shame to have to cover what he saw, but the elevator arrived and he refrained, saying instead, "Then we're set, because I excel at playing the big dumb cop. Don't comment on that."

Surprisingly enough, she had been about to say something playful. Instead, she stepped into the elevator and kept her eyes front and center.

* * *

Dr. Anthony Ellsworth's secretary had managed to pry free a few minutes of her boss's time around three, in between a patient with a brain lesion resulting in aphasia (an inability to comprehend words) and a consultation with a family about their mother who had Alzheimer's (a degenerative disorder resulting from the loss of cerebral cells). The overly learned doctor provided this information, complete with the explanatory asides, in a burst of speech designed to impress himself. At least Jan assumed that's whom he was playing to. He didn't pay enough attention to her or the detective to be trying to wow them.

In his early thirties, Dr. Ellsworth had a homely head and eyes so large that you barely noticed he had a body, although a spindly, frail assemblage of bone and tissue was stowed away beneath his white lab coat. He carried himself as if he wore the crown of empire, and when he bestowed eye contact, he acted as if expecting tribute from the West Indies. His hair was an overly enthusiastic black and probably would have risen in a rooster tail if some attendant hadn't recently wetted it down. As he escorted them to his office, he kept glancing about as if surveying a wing of the hospital that bore his full name. Once he halted a nurse, lifted a chart out of her hands as if she was holding it upside down, and after scanning the front page, ordered a different medication for the patient. The nurse, an older, capable-looking woman, promptly corrected his highness, pointing out that the patient had suffered a severe reaction to that medication but two days before. Scandalized by the impertinence, Ellsworth responded with a brashness that a more humble physician wouldn't have resorted to and dictated a second medication. He certainly wasn't one of those caring-sharing MDs you saw smiling compassionately down from HMO billboards.

Rather than hand the chart back to the nurse, he went out of his way to place it on a countertop, and then, satisfied that he'd promoted his importance, shoved off ever faster, unaware that his eyes had taken on a fluttery motion that said quite plainly *Fragile, Handle with care, This end up.* Here was a throne under siege. Here flickered a man whose mental status was short-circuiting. Here rushed a nose that had whiffed something foul.

In his office, he alighted on his black leather chair and made an gesture worthy of Kubla Khan for the audience to begin. Jan and the detective seated themselves in the smaller chairs on the other side of his oaken desk. The well-appointed furnishings hadn't been rolled out of county storage, that much was clear. As soon as Jan and White were down, the doctor abruptly changed his mind, stood, and crossed to a window. Facing away from them, hands behind his back, he leaned forward, mesmerized by something outside. Maybe he was solving some knotty medical problems in his head, say a cure for death. Detective White brought a finger to his mustache to indicate to Jan they should let this play out. They waited, all breathless. A minute passed. The doctor's busy schedule backed up further with each flicker of the digital clock on his desk. The glass front of a stand-up photo, which showed a surprisingly attractive and well-scrubbed wife and three children, reflected the advancing minutes of the clock. At last Ellsworth summoned up the strength to turn and regard them. Jan felt as though he was sizing up two malignant nodes.

"I assume this concerns Dr. Croft?"

"It does," Detective White said, doing a credible imitation of the big-city cop who's seen and been bored by it all. His voice deepened and his eyes went into the thousand-yard-stare business. "I got about a million questions, so maybe we should get started, huh, Doc?"

The familiarity of that tag steadied the doctor's nerves and prompted him to say, "Dr. Ellsworth, please."

"Sure. Now first, my captain always likes me to inform people that we appreciate whatever they can tell us. Public relations kind of move. So I've told you, right?"

"The hospital is working with the police on this?" the

doctor distastefully asked Jan. He clearly found the homicide detective uncouth and offensive.

"Our orders are full cooperation," Jan said, wondering what color her response would turn the Little Admiral. Something bright, she hoped.

"And has any progress been made?" he asked Jan.

"Damn little," Detective White said, barging in on their private discussion. "Maybe we'll be lucky and you'll know exactly what's happened."

"No one's even told me the cause of death," the doctor said, turning fidgety again.

"Forget it," Detective White answered without pause. "I'm not allowed to release that just yet."

"You've got to apprehend whoever's done this thing," Ellsworth automatically said. He may have known what he was expected to say, but that didn't mean he was able to pack much conviction into the way he said it.

"Why," Detective White said, feigning surprise, "that's *just* what we were thinking down at headquarters." He went on more civilly. "Could you begin by telling us about Dr. Croft's position here? In lay terms whenever possible."

Ellsworth stretched his slender neck and closed his eyes. For a few seconds he regulated his breaths, looking as though he wore saffron robes at home. When he began, he beamed his professorial broadcast toward the detective.

"He was the head of the Neurology service, which involves treatment of the body's nervous system. The nervous system includes the central nervous system, which contains the brain and the spinal column, and the peripheral nervous system, which includes . . ."

The detective stepped in to ask a clarifying point. "The brain's the thing at the top of the body, right?"

The quip burned Ellsworth's smooth complexion but an instant. Speaking exclusively to Jan, he said, "You'll have to forgive me if I'm behaving oddly. Events around here have been far from normal."

"Take your time," Jan said, deciding to try mothering.

"I always do," Ellsworth haughtily answered. Still, he reacted favorably to her encouragement and, acting willing to return a kindness, went on to pompously explain all the paramount administrative, diagnostic, and teaching duties that Dr. Croft had performed.

"The two of you get along OK?" Detective White asked, ignoring the several minutes of catalog description that Ellsworth had provided.

"Passably," the doctor answered, perturbed that anyone would think otherwise.

"Play golf together?"

"I don't golf." Plaid pants and little knobby white balls sounded beneath him.

"Not every doctor does," Jan indulgently explained to the detective.

"Do anything together?" Detective White asked, undeterred.

"Outside of work?" Ellsworth said, unsure if he understood how a simple mind like the detective's worked. "No. We were not particularly close."

"How about on the job?" Detective White asked, pressing. "How'd you get along here at the hospital?"

"Now wait a minute," Ellsworth said, incensed. "What gives you the right to ask a question like that?" A pea under his mattress couldn't have disturbed him more.

"The doctor's right," Jan said, stepping in. "You're making it sound as though he's being accused of something. Is he?"

Detective White's eyes approved of her statement, but his voice sounded weary of citizens constantly standing up for their rights. "All I'm trying to establish is how the dead man got along with his colleagues."

"And nothing more?" Jan said.

"Not right this minute."

"As long as we're clear about it," Jan said. "Do you have any problems with that, Doctor?"

Ellsworth did and complained, "He seems to be insinuating that everything wasn't right between Dr. Croft and me."

"Wasn't it?" Jan asked with a hushed confidentiality.

"If you must have the truth," Ellsworth huffed, "no. We had our differences. Anyone could tell you that." His vision skipped to the family portrait on his desk, as if seeking permission to reveal what he was about to share. "Dr. Croft was not a pleasant man in many ways, a sharp tongue and opinion, but day and night we were both interested in one thing, the welfare of our patients. On that you may depend."

Jan glanced at the detective, who moved his disbelieving eyes toward the doctor to indicate that she should continue.

Respectfully, Jan asked, "What kind of differences did you have?"

"Primarily over my wake-up therapies," he said, sounding wronged.

"Wake-up therapies?" she asked, apologetic for her ignorance.

"Therapies to revive patients in vegetative states," Ellsworth said. Considering the reverent way that he pronounced this, maybe the doctor did have time for an enthusiasm or two other than himself. "I've been applying strong stimuli to help rouse them out of their comas—loud sounds like rock and roll; pungent smells, say vinegar; touch sensations, like ice. I'm convinced there will be progress."

"You've had success?"

"It's very slow work," Ellsworth defensively said. "But I'm sure there'll be some exciting breakthroughs. If not my approach, then some other. Just last year, by accident, a medical team in Wisconsin brought a vegetative patient back to consciousness for several hours with a shot of Valium."

"Valium?" Detective White said, sounding as though the plot was thickening.

"That's right, something that simple. They were doing

some dental work on a man who'd been in a vegetative state for ten years." Ellsworth reeled this off like someone striving to justify his existence.

"Did Dr. Croft share your enthusiasm?" Jan asked, sensing something amiss in the intensity of the explanation.

"Not exactly." Ellsworth's eyes drifted back to his family's picture. "I don't mean to say that Dr. Croft wasn't extremely concerned. He simply didn't agree with my approach. He didn't believe that external stimuli were the answer. On his own he was doing some important work with computer-aided diagnostics of cerebral metabolism in comatose subjects. And he was terribly excited by the ramifications of discovering that Valium might revive patients."

"Are you trying out the Valium therapy here?" Detective White asked.

"On an experimental basis, yes."

"Results?"

"It's too early to tell," Ellsworth said, hedging.

"Was there any jealousy between the two of you?" the detective quickly slipped in.

"I'm not sure I like the sound of that," Ellsworth answered, standoffish again.

"It sounds like you were rivals."

"Nothing like that," Ellsworth said, dismissing the idea as more absurdities from the realm of the common man. "We had different opinions concerning a medical issue. Quite common among men of science."

"Oh yeah," White said, "men of science." He sounded as if he'd known that explanation all along but had misplaced it. In the same haphazard tone he asked, "Did Croft have anything to do with your resignation?"

The question destroyed the doctor's insolence. For a bit, Ellsworth acted as though whapped between the eyes with something sturdy, a femur or a leaded sock. He again assumed a spacey interest in what was going on outside his office window, although this time he concentrated on it from his chair, looking as though he expected a glowing light to drift through the glass, immerse him, and carry him off to some higher plane of being. None arrived.

"Doctor?" Jan asked, worried.

Ellsworth replied in a weak but formal voice, "What business is that of yours?"

The detective grunted tiredly and reached into his pocket for a small, laminated card. "I've got something I need to read you here, Doc. I've met eight-year-olds who know it by heart, but in case it's news to you, here goes." He cleared his throat and started. "You have the right to remain silent. Anything you say can and will . . ."

And so on. By the end, Ellsworth had regained enough composure to offer Detective White this deal: "I'll answer your questions if you'll tell me who informed you of my resignation."

Detective White leaned forward and pushed a telephone across the desk, toward Ellsworth. "Call your lawyer, Doc. At a time like this, a man isn't always thinking straight."

"My thought processes are in perfect order," Ellsworth snapped, shooting a withering glance at Jan, who did her best to act troubled by this latest development. "Ask your questions."

"You don't want a lawyer?"

"Hardly."

"Why are you resigning?" Detective White asked.

"Personal reasons."

"I see," Detective White said, momentarily disgruntled. "You could have told me that without all this song and dance. Answer me this, Doctor, can you think of any reason someone would kill Dr. Croft?"

"Not a one," Ellsworth said, too sure of himself to promote believability.

"How about this?" Detective White said, ready to start all over again. "Can you think of any reason someone would accuse you of killing him?"

That scrambled the doctor's short-term memory fine. He panned from the detective to Jan and back without seeming to recognize either of them. "This is a comedy of the absurd," he advised himself. Of Jan, he demanded, "You are going to allow this line of questioning?"

"You did agree to talk to him, Doctor," Jan said, working to cover up the fact that she was beginning to enjoy herself.

"That's right," Detective White said. "So maybe you can save the taxpayers a great deal of money here and tell us where you were on a Friday evening, two weeks ago, August twenty-first."

"Who's my accuser?"

"An anonymous call."

"And based on that, on someone who won't even identify themselves, you're using up time that my patients require?"

"That's about it," White said. "A call like that, it's malicious. You may not have given it any thought, but anyone who would phone in such a message might have done a whole lot more."

The doctor shook his head in groggy disbelief, bit back something, and seemed to Jan to be making a concerted effort to avoid glancing at his family's portrait, although that impression could simply have been the result of his eyes straying about the room as he marshaled his thoughts, no doubt prepping himself for a devastating rebuttal of everything the detective had said.

"You think this caller might be the killer?" Jan asked, hoping to defuse the tension. Her question immediately drew the doctor's interest.

"A possibility," the detective said. "But what I want to know from you, Dr. Ellsworth, is whether you can think of any reason someone would accuse you of killing Dr. Croft."

For a moment Ellsworth's eyes actually kindled with hope, as if spotting a way out of his troubles, but that faded upon further thought and he said morosely, "Not a one."

"How about his colleagues?" Jan encouraged. "Any grudges there?"

"Of course not," he absentmindedly said, distracted by other thoughts.

"Psychotic patients?" White asked. "If you're dealing with the brain, you must get into that."

"In certain instances mental disorders are organic in origin, yes." Textbook words came much easier for him and revived him too, returning his commanding ways to the forefront. "In such cases we might be called in to consult with a psychiatrist. But I can think of no recent medical history that might lead to this."

"Hospital employees?" Jan asked.

"No," Ellsworth bluntly answered. Then apparently deciding he'd been too hasty, he qualified his response by explaining, "Dr. Croft could be exacting to work under, true, but he only wanted the best for the patient. I believe the staff respected that."

"Girlfriends?" White asked. "Or boyfriends for that matter?"

"None," Ellsworth immediately answered. To protect himself, he appended, "That is, none that I know of."

"Then I've got to say that we're back to square one," White said. "Which means we're back to considering whether this crank call might be important. Where were you on the evening of Friday the twenty-first, Doctor?"

Ellsworth hesitated before flipping open a scheduler on his desk and petulantly saying, "If I must." He read through several entries in his notebook before tapping his finger down on a page and saying with satisfaction, "It appears I was consulting with the family of one of my patients."

"The entire night?" Jan asked.

Ellsworth flushed. "It was a delicate case."

"Of course," White said, going overboard on understanding. "When we talk to them, we'll be delicate too."

"Talk to them?" The possibility unsettled the doctor.

"It wouldn't be an alibi if we didn't talk to them," White patiently explained.

Flustered, the doctor read off the family's name and address, then informed Detective White that he hoped he wouldn't have to be bothered again. The detective wholeheartedly agreed with that prognosis and thanked Ellsworth for sparing his valuable time. The insincerity of the groveling went unnoticed by the doctor, who was moving—somewhat shakily—toward a file cabinet in the corner of his office when they left him. Once in the hallway, Detective White observed, "He didn't seem to mind mentioning the Valium treatment."

"Or else he wanted us to think that he didn't mind," Jan answered.

"Let's not drive ourselves nuts just yet," said White. "There's plenty of time for tail chasing. You notice anything I might have missed?"

"That you don't like doctors."

"Right," the detective said, taking the criticism seriously. "I'll have to adjust for it."

13

FROM the time they left Dr. Ellsworth's office to when Elizabeth Kavanaugh came streaking out of the newly remodeled administrative wing in search of them, at the most five minutes had elapsed. At General Jack connecting the dots rarely proved difficult. Ellsworth would have frizzled for all of thirty seconds before calling the associate administrator in charge of physicians, who buzzed the executive administrator, who leaned on his administrative trainee Elizabeth Kavanaugh, who apparently had nothing better to do than chase detectives down hallways. All of these conversations were of course handled with voices pleasant as an assassin's.

While all that harmony was transpiring, Jan and Detective White were taking an elevator to the lobby. After descending past the fourth floor, they were alone in the car and the detective complimented her. "You're good."

"Why does that surprise you?"

"Tough too."

"Don't think . . ."

"How many times have you been married, Gallagher?"

"An even dozen," Jan said without pause.

"Quick too."

"It's none of your business how many times I've been married."

"Of course it's not."

"Twice," she said before she could stop herself.

"You're one up on me, then."

"And I'm not interested in going for broke again."

The elevator stopped on two and a man in a wheelchair was pushed aboard by a nurse's aide. Hanging from the patient's portable IV stand was a clear plastic bag of glucose solution, which now occupied Jan's attention in place of the detective.

"I say he knows something," White announced once they started down again.

She assumed he was referring to Dr. Ellsworth. They were in agreement on that much.

In the lobby, a dreary, overcrowded place with chairs dating back to the dawn of plastic, Jan sought out a pay phone from which to call Sheila, the Little Admiral's secretary, to see if it was safe to return the folder. True, Sheila's desk was less than thirty yards from where they stood, but Jan opted for discretion. Even though Larsen would most certainly report on her traveling companion, she didn't see any need to flaunt the fact. That wouldn't do anything to improve her position in the pecking order, nor would showing up outside the Little Admiral's office with a physician's folder in hand bolster her status. She wanted to arrange a second drop outside, in the courtyard. Next to romance and horror novels, spy thrillers were a close third on county employees' nightstands. She was next in line to use the phone when Elizabeth Kavanaugh came cutting through the lobby, her chunky legs moving surprisingly fast and with purpose. Jan might have succeeded in scrunching unnoticed against the wall if she'd been alone, but a hulk like Detective White was another matter entirely. When Kavanaugh veered toward them, she adapted with a major-league smile that sharpened itself upon identifying Jan.

"I hear you've been talking to one of our doctors," Elizabeth Kavanaugh said, bludgeoning them with her professional voice. "In the future I would appreciate it if you would clear all such matters through me."

"Ms. Kavanaugh," Detective White pleasantly said, "I'm beginning to get the impression you believe you're above the law."

That socialized her some. "Not at all, Detective. But you have to consider that our physicians are in the business of serving the public just as you are. Their minutes are valuable, as I'm sure yours are too. If you'd only contact me, I could save everyone time."

"Why, that's very kind of you."

"I told you I'm here to help." She could have been chastising a naughty boy and what's more, she was doing it shamelessly. "Was there any specific reason you needed to confer with Dr. Ellsworth?"

"Ongoing investigation, ma'am."

The point-blank way he delivered that sent a thrill of victory all up and down Jan's spine. The sensation faded when Kavanaugh's vision drifted toward her. "I hope our security officer's been giving you everything you need." The innuendo tucked away in that statement made it sound as though she'd caught Jan slipping out of a linen closet with mussed hair and undone buttons.

"No ma'am," the detective said. "But I'm negotiating."

"There should be no need of that," Kavanaugh said, overly serious. "Anything you want, that's what you get. Am I clear, Jan?"

First-name basis? So that's how it was going to be. Jan

mentally rolled up her sleeves and agreed out loud so wholeheartedly that the one-legged man on the phone glanced
irately over his shoulder.

"I'm relieved we've settled that," Kavanaugh answered,
uncomfortable with Jan's enthusiasm but unwilling to pur-
sue corporal punishment. Instead, she graciously told the
detective, "My husband's completed his surgery schedule for
the day, and I was just on my way to meet him, but there was
one item I wanted to discuss with you in private, if you don't
mind."

Jan informed them that she still needed to make her call
and would wait out in the lobby. Her using a public phone
mystified the administrator, who glanced back over her
shoulder on the way through Administration's doors. Jan did
the adult thing and refrained from waving. Once on the line
to the Little Admiral's secretary, she heard Kavanaugh chat-
ting up the detective as they passed Sheila's desk. Their
words were indistinct but the tone was all neighborly and
soap suds. While Jan listened to that backdrop of cooperation and comradeship, Gavin Larsen came slinking out of
Administration's offices as if wanting to avoid detection.
Facing the pay phone so that he wouldn't notice her, she
learned from Sheila that it wasn't a propitious afternoon to
return newspaper coupons.

"Maybe in the morning," Sheila suggested in a rushed
voice. "The drimp's been thinking I can read his mind again,
and I got one fat sucker of a report to whale on. Bye."

And the line was dead, which left Jan stranded for fifteen
minutes amidst a sea of achy citizens waiting for prescriptions from the outpatient pharmacy window. There was a
surly humor to the lobby, a general feeling of being second-
or third-class citizens, an assumption that if this had been a
private hospital they wouldn't have been waiting for an eternity. Maybe they were right, although in Jan's experience the
only difference between public and private hospitals—as

concerned waiting—was the carpet. Except in Administration, General Jack didn't have any.

When Detective White returned to the lobby, he waggishly regarded Jan and said, "You're a bad influence, Gallagher."

"That what the Duchess said?"

"Implied."

"Why did she have to talk to you in private?" Jan asked. "Other than to fix my wagon."

"That's about it, although she also wanted to know what prompted my special visit to Dr. Ellsworth."

"And you told her?"

"Official business." He said it like a taunt. "Then she wanted to know why I chose you to accompany me."

"You told her?"

"Not so official business." The rakish slant overtook his eyebrows and mustache again.

"You were mistaken," Jan said.

"I frequently am."

"Learn anything else?"

"That Ellsworth didn't mention our anonymous tip to her."

"Would you have?" she asked, unimpressed. "What else? You were in there quite a while."

"Jealous?"

"That doesn't even rate an answer."

Wincing as if she'd trod on his instep, the detective said, "I learned that if you ask an administrator why Dr. Anthony Ellsworth is leaving, you'll learn it's for personal reasons. That's pretty amazing too, don't you think? I mean, two county employees peddling the same story—what are the chances?"

"I wouldn't know," Jan said, unwilling to succumb to his good humor. "So now what?"

"I think we owe it to Dr. Ellsworth to check out his alibi."

"You clear it with Ms. Kavanaugh?" Jan asked.

The detective did an exaggerated tiptoe, arms extended for

balance, toward the lobby doors while whispering, "I forgot."

It was a ridiculous sight, considering his bulk, and it made Jan sputter-laugh, out loud, not to herself. That felt good. Unnatural, but good, and she told herself she'd better watch it because the last thing she needed at present was to get tangled up in some flinty romance. The twine holding her body and soul together was frayed enough.

The family whom Dr. Ellsworth had comforted lived in the western suburb of Chapwick, one school district removed from Jan's rambler, two mill-rates up. Detective White drove them in his unmarked Ford. A mile away from General Jack, he said after repeatedly checking the rearview mirror, "Isn't that pathetic?" Swerving to the curb before Jan could glance over her shoulder, he added, "This will only take a minute." Getting out, he strode a half block back to a red and black Cherokee driven by you-know-who Larsen. The men's conversation was short and sharp, and when Detective White returned to his car, he said, "He claimed he wasn't following us." A block later Gavin turned left and wasn't seen again on that trip.

"What'd you tell him we were doing?" Jan asked.

"Wine tasting tour," Detective White said, far too full of himself to be encouraged.

The family they were going to visit included a son, daughter, and divorced wife, but the address provided by Dr. Ellsworth belonged solely to the daughter, or at least hers was the only name on the mailbox—Vanessa Asplund. Her father, Lowell Asplund, was a long-term coma patient at General Jack.

Nobody was at home in the dark red townhouse, which was located in a subdivision called Paris Hills, where the street names made Jan expect a miniature Eiffel Tower around the next bend. Ms. Asplund lived on Rue de Vouille. The only other French influence Jan could see was an omnipresent lilac-blue siding that covered almost every unit. Otherwise, the development came right out of the same box as the rest of America. The time was by then four-thirty, so they decided to wait at the front curb on the chance that Ms. Asplund was a working woman and would soon arrive.

Their conversation stalled quickly as Jan went out of her way to avoid personal topics and the detective did nothing but heap praise on his ex-wife, who was a church-going, community-volunteering, late-night-mothering angel. The detective had two kids, a son and daughter, model Cub Scout and Brownie. Before his divorce he'd had a house on a medium-size lake. Docking privileges too. He kept laying it out, although Jan never once prompted him for any of it, never asked even as basic a question as why he'd left it all behind, which was of course the question he was waiting for. Once she inquired about that, he'd have the right to probe into the failures of her past, which she didn't plan on going into, not with her eyelids lowering every third breath. With Detective White, she might never go into it. Finally the detective asked, "Don't you want to know why she let a winner like me go?"

"No."

"You don't get off that easy," White said, implying that he hadn't. "She ran off with my partner." Still no comment from Jan, so White laid on some more. "My partner's name happened to be Janet. The two ladies have relocated in Los Angeles. They want to be screen writers. I got a house I couldn't afford, two teenagers I couldn't understand, and a big hole in my thinking on how the world was supposed to work."

Checking his expression, she decided he wasn't making this up on the fly, and worse, maybe liked sprinkling salt on his wounds. Objecting to that kind of indulgence, she said, "Shall I plunk another quarter in the jukebox?"

"What's that supposed to mean?"

"I think you know. If you want to feel sorry for yourself, you'll be doing it alone."

"Is that what I was doing?"

"A good imitation."

He chewed on that a moment before saying with bemused admiration, "You're tough, Gallagher."

Which Jan secretly hoped was true. To further prove her mettle, she commented on his statement by saying nothing. After that exchange, the detective turned on the radio for the news, although that couldn't have been particularly comforting either, not with the entire police department under investigation for racial discrimination. Detective White's only comment was an occasional cluck of his tongue.

Soon thereafter Vanessa Asplund arrived in a Seville that was color coordinated with the townhouse, both the deep dark red of a fresh scar. She parked outside the garage and crossed to her front door in a white nurse's uniform that attracted all of Detective White's attention, although it wasn't the starchy white cotton skirt that necessarily interested him. The ladies in bubble bath ads were related to this woman. Piece by piece—nose by chin by tooth—she approached perfection, but when her parts were totaled, they teetered vaguely off balance or minutely out of focus, a distortion that many men would have believed made her all the more alluring. From the neck down, all bombshell, close to the kind of ammunition that the fashion industry likes to explode on the front of glossy magazines. How she could move in all those directions and still advance forward was something of a mystery. Optical illusion, no doubt.

"Duty calls," the detective said in a sham voice intended to let Jan know precisely how attractive Ms. Asplund was. He swung so quickly out of the unmarked Ford that it made Jan feel like a poor country cousin.

When they stepped onto Ms. Asplund's small lawn and called out her name, she reacted casually, giving the impression she was expecting them. How that could be so, Jan had no idea. As a first impression, however, it served up the notion that here was a woman accustomed to misrepresenting herself, and even when Ms. Asplund explained how she knew to expect them, that first impression lingered. She acted slightly amused by finding them on her doorstep and confided that she'd never been interviewed by the police before. The fact that Jan wasn't exactly a bona fide policewoman went unmentioned by anyone as Ms. Asplund said, "He told me you'd be coming around."

"He?" Detective White asked, holding the storm for her while she unlocked the front door.

"Dr. Ellsworth. Come on in. Forgive the mess."

For once a woman who wasn't kidding about her home needing some cleanup. The living room looked as though the lady of the house did nothing but try clothes on all day. Her closets must have been empty. Every piece of furniture in the place appeared buried beneath a pile of designer garments. From plum-colored brassieres to sheer blouses to a lineup of shoes that could have shod a dance line, no space was left unclaimed except the area in front of a full-length mirror. If she did take a break from modeling garments, it was to spray herself with perfume. Several scents drifted on the air. To his credit, Detective White took it all in stride, no wetting of his lips or glazing of his eyes as they followed Ms. Asplund's bewitching backside to the kitchen, which was unexpectedly spotless and well ordered, not a draped stocking or whiff of night-siren to be found.

She put a kettle of water on to boil and told them to make themselves at home while she slipped into something more comfortable. Jan could hardly wait to see what that would be. Detective White too. While Ms. Asplund was gone, White leaned close to say, "Let me apply some of my sparkling wit on her. You just scowl, as if you don't approve."

"Of her or you?" Jan said, her tone letting him know that she didn't approve of either.

"Doesn't matter."

"What if I have a question?"

"We're not at the hospital now," the detective warned her.

"And this investigation is my responsibility. You have a question, ask it. But let me run this interview. Remember, I do this for a living, sort of."

"Point taken," Jan said, so tired she actually was relieved not to have to consider possible questions. "You ever hear from your wife?"

The detective's jaw went so slack that she immediately regretted the haymaker. Fortunately, Vanessa Asplund returned in faded jeans and an oversize T-shirt with an Ivy League emblem on its front before White had a chance to complain of whiplash. Taking one look at their hostess, Jan had a premonition that she was about to be lied to. Ms. Asplund's opening remark didn't alleviate that sensation, as she said in an accommodating voice, "I guess you want to know where Dr. Ellsworth was on a Friday two weeks ago."

"He says he was with you," Detective White answered, every inch of him suddenly a toothsome gentleman. "Is that right?"

"It is," Vanessa Asplund agreed, checking with Jan, who belatedly remembered to frown. "I was having a tough time with my father. He's in Dr. Ellsworth's care."

"And the doctor consoled you the entire night?" the detective solicitously asked.

"Yes."

"From what time to what time?" The detective asked this question so coolly that Jan almost smiled. She didn't though and kept her face stern. It appeared that White had regained his wind and was back on the job.

"I believe it was from eight or nine in the evening to about six, maybe seven, in the morning."

"Where were you during all that time?"

"Well," she pretended to think a moment before saying as if surprised herself, "I guess we were right here."

Why Jan thought the woman was pretending, she wasn't exactly sure. Perhaps it was the way she answered with such simple-hearted conviction. Maybe it was one of those *woman things* her last husband frequently complained of, or maybe the slight pout to Vanessa Asplund's full lips gave it away. Or it may have been that Jan knew because she had run the same deceit herself, although in her case she had been covering up for a wayward husband. Substitute "boyfriend" for "husband" and maybe that was the case here.

"What did you find to talk about during all that time?" Jan asked.

Detective White seconded that question. "Ten or eleven hours is quite a discussion."

"So many things. He's a very intelligent man."

"A dedicated physician," Jan said, sounding as though reading a roll call of honors.

"And there's no chance," Detective White said, slipping Jan a frown, "that he could have left at any time? Say, if you fell asleep for an hour or two?"

By then it was dawning on Ms. Asplund that some of the biggest bastards she knew were perfect gentlemen and that Detective White might be one of them.

"No," she said, deliberating as if trying to recall exactly. "I was awake the entire evening."

"Had he consoled you on other occasions?" Detective White asked.

"Exactly what are you trying to suggest, Detective?" Vanessa Asplund's tone shifted with that question. She sounded more shrewd than scandalized.

"We're investigating a homicide," Detective White said factually. "Did Dr. Ellsworth tell you that when he mentioned we might come around?"

"N-no." Her lovely face darkened, and her lovely lips stayed parted as if she didn't know whether to laugh or believe him. "I thought this had something to do with his wife."

"Why would the police be interested in his wife?" Jan asked.

"They're going through a divorce." Ms. Asplund may not have believed that herself.

Detective White said, "That's a civil matter. Why would the police become involved?"

"I hadn't thought about it," she said, bewildered. She did lost and confused so nicely that maybe it was real. "I just assumed you would be. There's child custody involved and his wife may be trying to prove he's an unfit parent by using me."

"Are you saying that he's spent more than one night consoling you?" asked Detective White, his voice dripping so much kindness that Jan suddenly quit feeling despicable for earlier taking aim at the detective's long-gone wife.

"Yes, I suppose I am."

"You were having an affair?" the detective said, wanting her to verify it.

"I guess you could say that."

"I'm glad you leveled with us, Ms. Asplund," a relieved Detective White said. "It makes me much more inclined to believe Dr. Ellsworth's story. I can see how he might have spent the night with you if you were doing more than talking." Troubled, his eyebrows bunched together. "But it raises another question for me."

"It wasn't unethical," Vanessa Asplund blurted.

"What?" Detective White said, not understanding.

"His seeing me while caring for my father. He wasn't trying to take advantage of me."

"That wasn't what I had in mind."

"No?" She refused to believe him.

"I'm wondering why he didn't tell you what we wanted to talk about," the detective explained. "That strikes me as strange."

She brought a finger to her lower lip, seeing his point immediately and maybe seeing beyond it. "He didn't say why you were coming, actually. And at the time I was too busy to ask. I just assumed it was over his marriage. That's all he had time to tell me before I cut him off. Work was a madhouse."

"Were the two of you planning on getting married?" Jan quietly asked.

"I'd rather not answer that," she said, embarrassed.

"Why not?" Detective White asked.

"It wasn't his . . . wife, was it?" Vanessa Asplund steeled herself for the worst and asked in a small voice, "That's not who got killed, is it?"

"No," White said, extremely interested in her question. "We're investigating the death of one of Dr. Ellsworth's associates. A Dr. Jonathon Croft."

"Oh my." She covered her mouth with both hands and stood still until the detective pulled out a chair for her. She sat.

"What's wrong, Ms. Asplund?" the detective asked, concerned.

She cradled herself as if feeling a sudden draft. "I think his wife is having an affair with Dr. Croft. Or at least she was."

Jan and Detective White exchanged glances, and Jan, feeling vindicated for believing that the woman had until now been lying to them, asked, "You're sure he was with you on the night of the twenty-first?"

Vanessa Asplund shivered and held herself, saying, "I'm sorry, but yes he was. What has he done?"

"We don't know that he's done anything, ma'am," the detective said, quite gently in fact.

"Have I gotten involved in something?"

"I sincerely hope not," White said. "Has he ever threatened to do anything to this Dr. Croft?"

"Anthony?" she said, shocked. "Oh no, he's one of the kindest, gentlest . . . ."

And that was the extent of what they learned from Ms. Asplund.

14

"**W**HAT do you make of it?" Detective White asked. He sat behind the wheel of his unmarked Ford, gazing gullibly at Vanessa Asplund's front door, giving the impression he'd just been sold something he didn't need or want or even recognize.

In the fading gray afternoon light, the red of the townhouse reminded Jan of blood long in a test tube. With that wholesome thought in mind, she said, "Ellsworth could have hired it done and then set himself up with an alibi."

"It could be the wife too," the detective said. "Maybe she and Croft had a falling out."

"So next we talk to the wife?"

"Next, meaning tomorrow," the detective answered, rousing himself from his afternoon fantasies and facing Jan. "I've put in ten plus and you look like hell."

"Thanks."

"You need some rest, Gallagher. We can pick this up tomorrow when we've got clearer heads. I don't even know if I should let you drive home."

"If you're planning on telling me your couch is comfortable, forget it. We don't know each other, besides which, I can't afford to leave my wreck in the hospital's ramp overnight. It'd break me."

The detective shrugged and started the car. On the drive back to the center of the city, Jan nodded off and woke to White nudging her shoulder. They were stopped in front of General Jack's parking ramp.

"You're sure you can drive?" he said, serious, no come-on.

She nodded yes and, not wanting to appear as dazed as she felt, said, "There's something else bothering me. How do you figure a woman like Vanessa Asplund falling for Ellsworth?"

"His doctor's hands?"

"I'm sure."

"Go home and get some sleep, Gallagher."

"Why are you working with me on this?" Jan said, distrustful of her motives as much as his.

"What do I know about hospitals? I need your help."

"Don't you have a partner?" she asked, rubbing her eyes. "I thought cops always came in pairs."

"He's working on Croft's personal life. His ex-wife, his neighbors. He's the one who gets to tell the parents when we finally locate them."

With her fingers on the door handle, she said, "I'm sorry for that cheap shot about your wife."

"Forget it," he said, sounding as though he had almost trained himself to do just that. "In answer to your question, yes, I hear from her. About once a week. She likes Southern California fine. Hasn't sold any scripts, though. She's writing a good one about a homicide detective." Sadly he concluded, "That's usually why she calls, to talk to her free technical adviser."

She studied him until he started grinning mischievously in self-defense, apparently enjoying the fact that she didn't entirely know what to make of him.

"Tomorrow at seven-thirty," he said. "We'll visit Mrs. Ellsworth right after she packs her kids off to school."

"Here at seven-thirty," Jan said, pointing at the street corner.

"I could pick you up."

"Here," Jan reiterated.

"You're consistent, Gallagher. I admire that in a woman."

"You're fairly predictable too. Every man I've ever known has been, in one way or another." She got out of the car before he asked her to explain that. She wasn't sure she could.

Afraid of dozing for even a second at freeway speeds, she drove city streets home, which doubled her traveling time. She didn't mind. Of late, some of her best moments were spent alone in her car, momentarily able to keep her job, her daughters, and the world at bay.

When she arrived home stillness greeted her. No television. No music of puberty being unleashed from the girl's bedrooms. No bickering or foot stomping or movement of any kind. This of course was a bad sign. Whenever a catastrophe hit, everyone sought cover. A cursory inspection of the living room and kitchen painted a bleaker picture still. Everything in the two rooms was picked up and neatly put away. That didn't happen without cause. In the hallway leading to the three bedrooms, every door but the one to the room she and Claire shared was closed, and when she peeked in there, it was empty. From across the hall, in the bathroom, she heard a sniffle. Checking that door, she found it locked and softly called out, "Mother?"

No answer. None of the other doors opened.

"Mother, are you in there?"

"I'm fine," Claire answered, her voice choked and teary.

"Has something happened?"

"Nothing."

Meaning everything. Increasingly over the last few months her mother had at odd moments become weepy and inconsolable. In a crisis, she functioned like a trooper, but let a day roll by smoothly, with nothing to occupy her, and she became withdrawn, dreamy, easily frightened, and then flowed the sluggish tears. She might be sitting in the living room with all of them, watching calorie-free sitcoms, not having spoken for two or three commercial breaks, and the flood would start. The deluges scared the girls and terrified Jan, who didn't know how to react but felt driven to do something. But what? Talking solved nothing and sometimes set Claire off on a rampage of accusations ranging from no one loving her to everyone wishing her dead. She could get vicious. And in the end nothing was resolved. So finally, at the suggestion of a psychiatric nurse Jan knew from General, they no longer interfered in Claire's mood swings but allowed her to bottom out on her own, which routinely involved locking herself in the bathroom. Later, sometimes hours later, she would either creep into her bed for a long, still sleep or else go on a cleaning jag as if bent on proving she deserved the Good Housekeeping seal.

"Claire," Jan said, "if you want to talk, I'll be in the bedroom."

Retreating across the hall, she collapsed on her bed without bothering to kick off her pumps. Soon thereafter she was jarred awake by Claire poking her thigh.

"What if you lose your job?"

"Huh?" Jan said, groggy and unsure of what conversation she was stepping into the middle of.

"I'm too old to go back to work."

"I won't lose my job, Mother."

"You might. You've never known what you're doing when you get involved with a man."

"What in the world are you . . ." But then she saw.

"Mother, believe me, there's nothing going on with the detective."

"You were with him all day when you should have been home."

"That was for work."

"The girls don't know what to think," Claire said, refusing to hear her. "And I can't manage things around here all by myself." She wiped at her eyes even though they were dry at the moment. "So you better think about what you're doing."

Claire left her then for some sport in the kitchen, pot-and-pan toss and the like, even though everything was clean. That was the signal for the girls. Gradually the other bedroom doors opened and footsteps filed down the hall. Giving up on napping, Jan rose and spent some time trying to ferret out what her daughters had done that day. Skimpy rewards. Amy's biology class dissected a dumb frog. Katie's teacher was sick and the substitute smelled bad. Leah asked if they could do the small talk another time, and Tess, busy lining up her evening's television viewing, couldn't remember a single thing that had happened. Eventually, Jan gave up, warned everyone that watching too much TV caused babies, and retreated to the basement laundry room and her cot, where she threw her body's clock completely out of whack by sleeping through her night off. Her dreams were starting to worry her. That night she wandered around on the astroplane with a state park camping sticker pasted on her forehead, but she couldn't find anywhere to pitch her tent. Every campsite was full. The campers were all clones of Elizabeth Kavanaugh.

In the morning, for a change well rested, she set the table for breakfast and readied herself to head downtown for her meeting with Detective White, but a few minutes before seven the house's only phone, which was situated on the wall between the kitchen table and the back door, rang. There was a scramble, which her youngest won. Across all fifteen feet of the kitchen, Tess shouted, "Mom, there's a *man* asking for you."

To loud groans, Jan turned off the countertop TV's sound before accepting the receiver from her daughter. It was Detective White, who told her, "Something's come up, Gallagher. The captain's temporarily pulling me off the Croft investigation."

"For how long?"

"Undetermined. I'll let you know when it's go again. Meantime, I want you to stay clear of it, and particularly clear of the Ellsworth family. One of these people is a murderer."

"Thanks for the reminder."

"Gallagher . . ."

But she'd already hung up, determined not to be dissuaded from her self-appointed rounds. Claire was peering at her suspiciously, her youngest daughters were agitating for the return of cartoons, and her oldest daughters were occupied with unfinished homework. Stepping to the nearest cupboard, she lifted down both the city and suburban directories. In the suburban she located a listing for Dr. Anthony W. and Hope Ellsworth on Bluebill Trail in West Cambridge. Satisfied, she turned toward the table, where the entire crew sat gawking about as if abandoned by their waitress. When Jan asked who was cooking breakfast, everyone groaned. The leaders of tomorrow weren't quite up to cutting a grapefruit in half and pouring cereal out of a box.

Not having to drive downtown to meet with White, whom she'd vengefully quit thinking of as Detective White, she managed to arrive at the Ellsworths' modern split-level by ten of eight. The doctor would have been long gone, but she was early enough to see a private-school van pick up three young children at the foot of the curved drive.

The subdivision appeared to have been landscaped by a golf pro who favored par fives. There were extensive lanes of short-cropped, fortified-green lawns, dotted here and there with obstacles such as shrubs, artificial ponds, the occasional sandbox. The houses were large and sprawly, with enough extensive decks and windows to suggest clubhouses at the drinking end of the back nine. Behind the wheel of her rust-flecked Pontiac, she felt as though she worked for the groundskeeper despite having touched up her face and put on her best suit and blouse. Such efforts didn't buck up her spirits, but each time she nearly convinced herself to turn around, she asked herself what Gavin Larsen was scheming away at right this minute. The answers she dreamed up were neither flattering nor comforting, and she drove on, beginning to feel trapped in a competition she hadn't bargained for but wasn't quitting either.

Mrs. Hope Ellsworth didn't answer the door in an evening gown, which considering the country-clubby surroundings almost surprised Jan. The lady of the manor wore a slate-blue business suit cut severely enough to please the joint chiefs of shaft, as Jan's father had called them after his Pacific adventures in World War II. Mrs. Ellsworth had a slim, athletic figure, which the tailor's straight lines complimented, and an attractive, alert face, framed by flossy black hair arranged in a pageboy. Her most noticeable feature was her complexion—smooth and roseate—which sharply contrasted with eyes that were the dense dark of storm clouds and behind which thoughts almost visibly arced.

"Yes?"

A careful woman, Mrs. Ellsworth said this through a locked glass door. Jan had to hold up both a driver's license and hospital ID before being accepted as who she claimed to be.

"Does this have something to do with my husband's arrest?" Mrs. Ellsworth asked, opening the door.

Jan did a double take, all her initiative having just been stolen away.

Hope Ellsworth observed Jan's floundering a moment

before dryly commenting, "Apparently not. On the other hand, it seems a little too coincidental that you should show up a half hour after his secretary calls and tells me the police have taken him into custody. What brings you here, Ms. Gallagher?"

"You've heard about Dr. Croft's death?" Jan said, feeling tippy.

"I have." The woman's words came in the short, clipped fashion of someone trying to clear her desk of nuisance work.

"The hospital's trying to determine what actually happened," Jan truthfully said, "and since your husband and Dr. Croft were close associates, I thought it might be helpful if you could answer a few questions."

"There's more to it than that," Hope Ellsworth judged, "or Anthony wouldn't have been up half the night staring out the window. And he wouldn't be needing our lawyer's services at this moment. Come in, Ms. Gallagher, I'd like to hear these questions of yours before I join our lawyer downtown."

She stepped aside, allowing Jan across the threshold. Before closing the door, she scanned in both directions to ensure that Jan was alone. A very careful woman, not one easily rattled. For someone with a husband apparently in jail, she displayed unnatural detachment. Presented with that news, Jan would have become an instant three-pack-a-day smoker, but Mrs. Hope Ellsworth gave the impression that being air-dropped into the middle of a Stephen King novel might not be enough to unravel her.

As she told it to Jan, she'd learned of her husband's arrest a half hour earlier. Since that time Jan noticed that Mrs. Ellsworth had had the presence of mind to bundle three children off to school, call a lawyer, and dress herself with the fastidiousness of a cadet. On top of all that, the living room they stepped through could have led off a parade-of-homes tour; everything from the cut daisies to the U-shaped sofa fronting the limestone fireplace was irreproachably tidy. The room had all the hominess of Euclidean geometry. The three children must have done close-formation drills in their spare time, because they certainly didn't spread chaos and destruction the way Jan's little pagans had—and did.

Mrs. Ellsworth led Jan to two wicker seats before a row of windows that faced a bird feeder full of seed but empty of feathers. On the other side of the willow holding the feeder spread a split-level treehouse that mirrored the main residence in many details and must have been built by a master craftsman. No child's hand could have accomplished it. Farther away a tennis court behind a neighboring split-level was visible. On a clear afternoon you could see to Utopia. On another day Jan would have been envious; today she was too busy spinning combinations in her head, trying to unlock some answers. Dr. Ellsworth arrested? Jan guessed she'd discovered why White had canceled their appointment.

"Your husband was arrested?" Jan asked, not knowing what else to say.

"Perhaps I've overstated," Hope Ellsworth patronizingly answered in a tone similar enough to her husband's to make Jan wonder who learned it from whom. "When he arrived at work this morning, he was taken into custody for questioning. I'm not sure that he's going to be arrested, but knowing firsthand what Anthony is capable of, I assumed that he'd manage it."

"What do you mean by that?" Jan asked, intrigued by how easily the woman slighted her husband.

As if the answer should be obvious, Hope Ellsworth said, "Anthony may be capable of diagnosing what is wrong with someone else's brain, but he's not particularly advanced when it comes to using his own. As to why he's been detained, I was hoping you could provide some details. The information I received was sketchy at best, something about a patient dying."

"No," Jan said, feeling asinine, "I don't know about that."

"A pity," Mrs. Ellsworth airily said. "Would you mind explaining again what brought you here?"

Jan repeated herself, mentioning a background check on Dr. Croft.

"I don't think so," Mrs. Ellsworth said, disagreeing with confidence. "If your reason for being here was as innocuous as you make it sound, you'd have arranged a meeting through Anthony. No, you're fishing for something else."

"If you'd rather not talk to me . . ." Jan started to say. It felt as though Mrs. Ellsworth's eyes were taking snapshots of her throughout all this.

"Something tells me this is involved with Anthony's little adulterous fling."

"You know about that?" Jan asked, baffled by the directness.

"Keeping secrets is not my husband's forte. It's one of the reasons I agreed to marry him. I knew I'd always have plenty of forewarning if he was up to something. Not all men are so transparent, you know."

"I know," Jan said, revealing enough about herself to make Mrs. Ellsworth smile.

"The truth of the matter is," Hope Ellsworth said, "aside from answering questions about automobiles now and then, and the planting of the seed, men are entirely superfluous. Poor Anthony barely knows which end of a car points forward, and my last two children were the products of artificial insemination—low sperm count. But his family has some influential connections in this city, connections I eventually intend to make use of. So I allow him his fantasies. Anthony's aware of all this. He may not believe it, but he's been told."

Apparently there was no need to approach the topic with tact, so Jan said, "Your husband claims to have been with his mistress all night on a Friday evening two and a half weeks ago, the twenty-first. Is that possible?"

Mrs. Ellsworth answered without any fury, "Very. I was

out of town on business and the children were with my parents. Anthony was on call at the hospital, or so he claimed."

So she'd neatly implicated her husband and laid the groundwork for her own alibi all in one stroke. Wanting to upset the cut and dried quality of the interview, Jan changed directions and asked, "You don't believe that love exists, do you?"

"Unfortunately there's no doubt that it does," Mrs. Ellsworth answered, bitter about the knowledge. "Personally I believe it is a form of schizophrenia. Perhaps the pharmaceutical conglomerates may one day develop a pill to remedy the situation. One can hope." Hope Ellsworth allowed herself a superior smile after that pronouncement.

"The reason I'm asking," Jan said, plodding on, "is that I've heard it rumored you were having an affair with Dr. Croft."

Mrs. Ellsworth's smile broadened without gaining any sincerity. "So now I know the reason for your visit?"

"Yes," Jan confirmed. "Were you involved with Dr. Croft?"

"How nicely you put it," Hope Ellsworth said, sounding so agreeable that it made Jan uneasy. " 'Were you seduced by one of your husband's associates, Mrs. Ellsworth? He happens to have been murdered. And we were wondering.' I can't imagine where you might have heard that."

"Not from your husband," Jan said, having the strange feeling of protecting the man from his wife. She had a hunch that someone had to do it.

"That goes without saying," Hope Ellsworth said, dismissing the statement as basic. "He's a little higher up the intelligence scale than that. Not much, a matter of centimeters, but a little higher. But Anthony might have whined to his plaything about it, and she might have told you to protect her man. Don't you think?"

"Is it true?" Jan asked.

Hope Ellsworth turned away to gaze out the window with all the serenity a superior credit rating could assure. The movement called to mind how her husband had sought out his office window when needing to compose himself, but whereas he seemed lost and searching for outside help, his wife simply appeared to be biding her time, editing her thoughts. Unlike the smudged buildings and rushing traffic beyond the doctor's office, it was a well-ordered scene outside this window. Trees and shrubs had been shaped and trimmed. Lawn chairs faced the sun. The nearest house lay far enough away to seem picturesque when viewed through the boughs of the willow.

"Don't take me for a fool, Ms. Gallagher. I can see where you might eventually push this, so I'm going to spare you some effort and tell you the truth, which if you bother to dig deeper can be easily verified." She made a steeple with her fingers and did some further hairsplitting of thoughts. "No matter what Anthony may have worked himself into believing, Jonathon Croft and I had no seamy dealings on the side. Not that Jonathon didn't make it known in the land that he was ready, willing, and able—especially able."

"So your husband may think you were having an affair with Dr. Croft?"

"A possibility," Hope Ellsworth allowed, not intending to protect her man right or wrong. "He's hinted once or twice, and lately he's been obsessed with Croft, who had a very high regard of himself. But Jonathon Croft was not my kind of man-creature. Far too arrogant and self-righteous for my tastes. My heart seems to prefer a male who is more secretive. If you wish to check this, you should be able without much trouble—and discreetly I hope—to discover that I've been having an affair with one of the VPs at work for over a year now, and that includes the Friday night in question, in case you have any suspicions in that direction. His name is Wade Harper, he's in charge of marketing at Healthway, where I'm employed. We were attending a seminar together at Healthway's parent company in Dallas, Conmed Corporation, and spent the weekend at the airport Holiday Inn. Do you want me to arrange for Wade to see you?"

"I'd appreciate it," Jan said, reeling a bit under all the honesty. "You're very matter-of-fact about this."

"I believe in meeting a problem head on," she said, and as if to prove it, stepped over to a phone and arranged for Jan to contact her lover at her convenience. Once done with that, she returned to her chair and said, "Is there anything else?"

"Are you planning on a divorce?"

"Give up Anthony for Wade?" She said it as if Jan was joking. "Now that's as irresponsible an idea as I've heard in ages. In my current conjugal arrangement I'm the chairperson of the board. Why trade that in for something less?"

Jan nodded as if appreciating her sentiments. "Why's your husband obsessed with Dr. Croft?"

"A blue-ribbon inferiority complex," Hope Ellsworth said. She might have been the judge who awarded the prize. "A man like Croft feeds on someone like Anthony."

"Is that why your husband's resigning his position at the hospital? His inability to get along with Croft?"

"No doubt that's one of the reasons," Mrs. Ellsworth said. Her lofty manner created a vague impression that she was covering something up. With the weight of logic behind her, Mrs. Ellsworth inquired, "Shouldn't the fact that he's leaving General eliminate him from your list of suspects? If that's where you have him."

"Why should it?" Jan asked, hating to admit she didn't follow the reasoning.

"Because he was removing himself from Croft's fiefdom. And once that was accomplished, he would have had no reason to care about Croft."

"I can think of one," Jan said.

"Oh?"

"If he thought you were having an affair with Croft."

"Yes," Hope Ellsworth agreed, giving this meticulous consideration. "I can see how you might think that, and I doubt that I can talk you out of it. But I for one don't believe it. Not that my husband is such a good man, simply that he's a coward." Smiling as though this last statement was unimpeachable, she said, "And now I should be leaving. Are we about done?"

"Close," Jan promised. "I still don't understand why he's resigning his post?"

"Nothing diabolical," she assured Jan. "Private practice is much more lucrative, that's all. I've finally managed to convince him of the merits of that line of thinking."

"You're sure?"

"I know my husband," Hope Ellsworth stubbornly maintained. She may have been repeating that to herself a good deal lately, which could explain why the line sounded faded. Perhaps she was unable to plot her husband's movements as accurately as she once could. "Was there anything else you wanted?"

"Do you know a Vanessa Asplund?" It was Jan's turn to move her eyes to the window.

"Should I?" Mrs. Ellsworth asked. Noticing Jan's discomfort with the question, she added, "Ah, we've reached the name of my husband's plaything. No, I've never had the pleasure. I'm sure she's leading him a merry chase, though. More?"

Jan thought not.

"Then I should like to say that if you're thinking Anthony had something to do with Jonathon's death, you couldn't be more wrong. He's been in genuine shock over it for days, and I continue to believe my husband incapable of cloaking his feelings or intentions from me.

"Now, I think you'll agree that I've been more than frank with you, Ms. Gallagher, so I've one question for you and then I must be going. I've already had to postpone one meeting because of this business that Anthony's gotten himself into. So perhaps you would be so kind as to tell me how all of this ties into some patient dying at the hospital?"

"I wish I could, Mrs. Ellsworth, but I have no idea."

"Doubtful, Ms. Gallagher. Very doubtful. Allow me to share some advice that could advance your career: never go on an interview without having prepared better answers. Now, I believe I have to go. Our attorney's meter is running."

Jan went along with that. She was in a bit of a hurry herself.

Not collecting a speeding ticket on the freeway to General Jack, that was luck. Jan headed to the administrative wing but found the double doors blocked by two immovable, expressionless day shift guards whose hearts had been deftly removed and replaced with a county memo that read—when boiled down to its essence—*No one gets into Administration.* No one who didn't belong, at any rate, which included the three news-action teams combing their wavy hair in the lobby. Who had so promptly tipped off the glamour media wasn't even worth speculating about. There were so many deep throats in Administration that voices behind closed doors inevitably sounded hoarse. Answering why Jan was drawn to General Jack at this time of day would have been much more difficult to explain than the arrival of the reporters. So, even though she would have been given a go-ahead nod by the guards, who knew her, she veered toward the lobby pay phone. After waiting out a teenager who was frantically explaining to his girlfriend that he didn't know why he'd tested positive, she was able to call Sheila.

"What in the world's going on?"

"Just a minute."

She could hear the voice of the Little Admiral, for once cantankerous instead of whiny, giving orders in the background. It sounded as though he was discovering how big the iceberg they'd hit actually was. A door closed and the voice was gone.

"Better," Sheila said.

"What's happening?"

"We had a patient expire up on 32G."

"And?"

"Two nurses claim Dr. Ellsworth did away with him."

The Little Admiral's voice abruptly cut in on their connection, summoning Sheila into his office. "Gotta go," Sheila said without identifying whom she was saying good-bye to. The line went dead, leaving Jan nothing to do but wander up to 32G.

The Neurology station didn't exactly have the somber stillness you might expect at a crime scene. First, there were patients bandaged up in the rooms she passed, their heads webbed in white gauze or entrapped in metal halo braces but their TVs blaring nonetheless. Then there were patients strapped into wheelchairs that were parked in the hallway where the staff could keep an eye on them; some of these patients rocked back and forth while constantly emitting high-pitched random vowels like *o-o-o-o* or *a-a-a-a* or *e-e-e-e*. Finally, there were patients pacing up and down the hallways, wrapped in their striped hospital robes, towing their IV stands with them as they tried to distance themselves from the other vacationers on the floor. And then there were nurses and orderlies and housekeeping personnel and dietary aides and phlebotomists and even doctors crossing in and out of rooms as if nothing had happened.

But that couldn't be. Not with a uniformed city cop standing sentinel before one door. In the hallway beyond the patrolman a knot of four suit-coated men, the largest of whom was White, stood conferring and occasionally glancing over their shoulders toward the room under guard. From inside that room came strobelike flashes of camera bulbs at intervals. Jan ambled past the group of men, making sure that she caught White's eye, but his vision paused hardly at all, and he refused to acknowledge that he'd seen her.

Able to take a hint, she departed, determined not to give up so easily. Her second ex, the cop, had always said over and over that police work was 90 percent spinning your wheels without knowing why. As much as she hated admitting that he knew what he was talking about, on rare occasions it turned out that he had possessed a kind of peasant wisdom, although she refused to believe that it actually belonged to him and preferred to imagine that his clichés were picked up in the station's locker room, much like a dust cloth attracts motes.

After leaving a phone message at the Fifth Precinct for Detective Frank White to contact her at his earliest convenience, she concentrated on the question of finding out who had passed away on 32G. Would the answer shed any light on what had happened to Jonathon Croft? She had no idea. But finding out who Anthony Ellsworth was accused of killing seemed the obvious thing to do. Unfortunately, the line to the Little Admiral's office was busy, so she couldn't get through to Sheila; and when she tried tapping into whatever Admissions might know, they referred her to Security, insisting they weren't allowed to distribute such details over the phone no matter who she claimed to be. She wasn't about to give any of her fellow guards the satisfaction of knowing how desperate she was to find out what had happened, which left Sheila as her only source. Before trying the Little Admiral's line again, she checked in at home to make sure nothing had exploded there and received a terse message from her mother.

"That cop called an hour back. Wanted you to meet him for lunch at the same place as yesterday, same time."

Jan didn't even try to reassure Claire that this was another business date. Instead she thanked her, promised she'd be home before the girls, and clicked off to avoid hearing Claire pack any hurt, abandoned-sounding accusation over the line.

The Little Admiral's extension continued to be busy, which left her nearly two and a half hours to maul herself with self-incriminations of every imaginable kind before meeting White at the Mermaid. Knowing how good she was at maiming herself, she decided that spinning her wheels would be healthier. This she did successfully. She couldn't manage to catch Sheila on the phone, nor could she trick a different admitting clerk into divulging who had punched out on 32G, nor did she manage to piece together all the facts about Dr. Croft in any sensible manner.

What she did succeed in doing was arranging an interview with Wade Harper III, who was vice president of marketing at Healthway, and also the adulterer who would supposedly alibi Hope Ellsworth. After twenty-five freeway minutes, she turned into the parking lot of a glass box tinted the color of a Lincoln head penny and fronted by an artificial pond that bubbled at its center. The main entrance had a fireplace large enough to handle redwoods. Two secretaries after the first one, she was ushered into Mr. Harper's suite, which had an exercise bike to one side, a treadmill to the other, and a grand view of the pond, cattails and all.

Mr. Harper was at least twenty years Hope Ellsworth's senior, round as a turnip and roughly as handsome—watery little eyes, a jaw formidable as a horseshoe, and hair so white you immediately thought it was a lie. The first smooth words out of his mouth let Jan know that here was a salesman capable of peddling used gauze. With both hands, he took her offered right hand in his and "prayed" that she possessed discretion, for he was a happily married man of forty years with grandchildren and no delusions or desires to abandon all or part of his normal life. He liked it, he assured her. At any moment she half expected him to ask her to sign on the dotted line.

Once seated around a coffee table with an arrangement of chrysanthemums, he described his relationship with Hope as strictly a matter of packaging. She was relatively young and definitely attractive, and he was wrapped in the vestments of power, as his lavish office and achievement awards indicated. So each traded what they had to offer.

"And you were trading on that Friday?" Jan asked. "August the twenty-first?"

"Yes we were," he said without an instant of doubt. "In Dallas. We were attending reorganization meetings at the parent company the entire weekend. Flew in on a Thursday, out on Sunday. Will you need to check that out further?"

"It's a possibility," Jan said, hoping that he was about to try talking her out of it. That could mean something. But like any superior salesman, he had a fine sense for what could be influenced and what could not.

"I understand," he said, all cooperation. "The man you'll want to talk to down there is Larry O'Brien, in Human Relations. He handled all our arrangements."

And that was all he said about it, other than writing down the contact's name and number on a sheet of paper. Even as Jan accepted the slip, she knew she'd never use it. To cover up her disappointment, she asked, "Do you know if Mrs. Ellsworth was having an affair with anyone else?"

"I don't believe she was," he attentively said, "and I'll tell you why. She's a bit of a cold fish. I don't think she actually enjoys romance. For her, it's something to use, like a stock option. She's been very clear about that. I admire her for it."

"Have you ever heard her mention a Dr. Jonathon Croft?"

"I don't believe I have, no." He watched her with keen enjoyment, as if always enthralled by a job well done.

"What do you think of her husband?"

"I've made it a point to never meet the gentleman. I believe we should all do what we can to make our lives simpler, don't you?"

"Up to now, I'd have to say no, I haven't believed that at all," Jan said.

Shortly after that she ran out of questions and was shown out of his office, although not before he invited her back if there was anything else he could help clarify. He admitted, with a lecherous wink, that he wanted to keep his protégée happy.

Upon leaving the pristine grounds, she felt sordid and disgusted. She could think of no reason to doubt the frankness of either Hope Ellsworth or Wade Harper III, although she wished she could. Weren't people, normal everyday kind of people, supposed to lie and cover up what these two so freely revealed? The question was, did their openness shroud something else? She found herself doubting that it did. She couldn't imagine either of them growing passionate over anything less than a promotion to the board of trustees. Heading back to the center of the city and her appointment with White, she found herself thinking that despite two divorces and a court case for sexual discrimination, she clung to some extremely old-fashioned values in a world addicted to change.

At one o'clock she reappeared at the Mermaid Bar and ran the gauntlet to White's booth. She felt a growing sense of rebelliousness for experiencing guilt over disobeying the detective's instructions. Did White have the right to warn her away from Mrs. Ellsworth? Sitting, she ordered the Wednesday special, which resembled the Tuesday special in execution and most details, carrots having replaced peas, and she faced White as if he was the one who owed an explanation.

The detective obliged, saying up front, "We took Dr. Ellsworth in for questioning this morning. It appears he did away with Vanessa Asplund's father."

15

THIRTEEN hours before Lowell Asplund's death, his daughter Vanessa stood at her door watching a homicide detective and his sidekick, Jan something or other, leave her townhouse. One thing that Vanessa knew after the two detectives' visit: she wouldn't need to call Anthony. All she had to do was wait. The great healer would soon enough worm his way to her side, fawning over her, pretending these were matters far, far above her understanding. *Don't worry your pretty little head.* Oh, she wouldn't, because this time Dr. Anthony Ellsworth might be more cooperative and less inclined to quote from the Hippocratic oath when she brought up her father's interminable condition. She had the police to thank for this opportunity. They were finally getting around to what she'd expected them to discover two weeks ago.

Without the police department's help, she didn't really know what she could have done, other than continuing to bop off doctors until she found one who was agreeable to granting an exit pass. If forced into that route, sooner or later someone, even if only county payroll, would notice the dwindling supply of physicians. But now an easier way lay open before her, a way that was littered with no obstacles, no impediments, only one poor, overmatched doctor who didn't yet realize how deep and still the waters ran.

As for the cops, she'd been expecting them since she phoned her anonymous tip in pointing them toward Anthony. That brilliant idea had been her brother's. *Give them a little jump start,* he'd said, meaning both Ellsworth and the cops. For once it appeared that he'd been right. The police were as capable and imaginative as she'd expected—barely at all. But she didn't want to underestimate what an arm of the government might accidentally knock over, so she'd been careful, very.

On a whim, she went into her turquoise bathroom, closed the medicine cabinet on all those wonderful pills, and started talking to her father as she faced her pretty self in the cabinet mirror. She didn't have any doubts over what a shrink would have to say about this kind of behavior. Abnormal reaction for an abnormal father, that had always been her answer to all the psycho-dribble that had oozed her way over the years.

The encouraging thing was that since she'd arranged for the removal of Dr. Croft, her chats with her father had gone much better. She'd begun to see that what she'd thought had been hatred for him all these years had actually been envy. He had been able to control his world completely and without having to resort to force. He managed it all with words and tones and looks. It was a wonder that the man hadn't become a congressman or senator, with his ability to persuade. Now he'd lost all that, and when a person had a great gift taken away by the gods, it was a tragedy larger than sorrow. She imagined the musician gone deaf, the artist blind, the athlete paralyzed, and her father without the ability to talk, to argue, to convince. In his present state, he might have been capable of thinking. The physicians could map brain activity with an EEG machine, but even if he could use his mind, he couldn't communicate his thoughts, use them to sway someone or to shape his environment. Lowell Asplund might go on breathing and excreting for years, for decades. As a nurse she knew that. But for him those were hardly measurements of life, and as a daughter, she knew that.

In the whole world there remained but one place where her father could hold forth and affect his destiny, and that was in a mirror found in his daughter's bathroom, which was where Vanessa was standing when the telephone rang.

"Have they talked to you?" It was Dr. Anthony Ellsworth, of course, straining to whisper and sound casual at once.

"You sent them, didn't you?" she said, vexed. "It wasn't pleasant. What kind of trouble are you in, Anthony? I think I have a right to know."

"Trouble? What makes you think—"

"I suppose the police came and asked me questions about where you were on the night of the twenty-first because they didn't have anything else to do."

"No, of course not," Ellsworth earnestly said. "I told you that they were investigating Dr. Croft's death. It's a routine matter, really. All you had to do was tell them I was with you that night and everything will be fine. I'm sure they'll be models of discretion."

To that she made no answer.

"Vanessa?" Ellsworth said, doing everything he could to avoid sounding worried, jittery, a touch gassy.

"I think we need to talk about this," Vanessa said.

"You did tell them my whereabouts, didn't you?" His voice went hard-line, as he tried to menace.

"Tonight and in person," she said, unperturbed.

"That's not possible."

His answer sounded breezy, which induced Vanessa to say in a burst, "You damn well better make it possible, Dr. Anthony Ellsworth. If you want me to talk to the police on your behalf, you'd better."

"What I meant is," Ellsworth said, fumbling, hoping to soothe, "what if they're watching your house? It might not be wise for us to be seen together."

"Come on. They already know we see each other, Anthony. Why would they care if we do it again?"

"I am a married man."

"Are you trying to back out of something here?"

Pause. "No."

The hesitation in his denial told her all she needed to know. "Anthony," she said with a sweetness as tried-and-true as Cleopatra's, "you're not forgetting how good it's been between us, are you?"

"There's been so much going on . . ."

"If you're thinking of dropping me," Vanessa said, her voice sounding hurt but her eyes remaining lively, "you'd better have the decency to do it in person, Ellsworth. Because if you don't, I'll come to your house to give you that opportunity."

"There's no need for that," he quickly said.

"I'm glad."

"Perhaps on my way home from work," he said, becoming formal, "we could meet somewhere."

"We can meet right here."

"I've already explained that the police might be watching."

What was this phobia about coming to her house? He had no reason to think that the police would take an interest in his affairs once she'd cleared him. But then it occurred to her that maybe the doctor wasn't actually afraid of being seen with her, maybe he was gun-shy about being with her, period. Perhaps he didn't want to hear what she might ask him, now that Dr. Croft was removed and he was in complete charge of her father's case. That made more sense. It explained why he wanted to meet somewhere neutral. With that realization came an influx of power.

"Just a minute, Anthony."

Dropping the phone receiver on the countertop, she walked in place on the kitchen tile so that he would hear footsteps. After a few seconds she stopped, then started again. Picking up the phone, she said, "I checked. The entire street is empty. So we meet here. How long will it be?"

Defeated, he answered that he'd try to be there in a half hour. He sounded so miserable and desperate that she felt as though maybe she had learned something at her father's knee after all. Now that her family's hour of delivery was at hand, she granted Dr. Ellsworth a reprieve, telling him, "Believe me, Anthony. You won't be sorry."

She didn't waste the half hour before the doctor's arrival by doing any straightening up. It'd been her experience that sloppy housekeeping secretly turned men on. Where did she lavish her efforts? On herself. She squirmed into a hot pink spandex-mesh suit designed for joggers who demanded more than cardiovascular excitement from their exercise, runners who wanted allure and sexual fantasy as they measured breaths and counted pulses. Tying a headband around her high forehead, she went into the bathroom to open wide the hot-water valves of the sink and shower. Closing the door, she soon grew sweaty as someone fresh from several miles of roadwork. Perspiration aroused Anthony, who spent a significant amount of each day washing his hands. From the homemade sauna, she went to her vanity for a musky perfume named Workout, which she rubbed along her arms and across her bare shoulders.

All of that left her barely enough time to check the street, which actually was empty, before poor, pathetic Anthony pulled his dark green Saab into her drive and beelined to her front steps like the fugitive he might soon become.

Meeting him at the door, she asked, "Do you see anyone watching the house or following you?"

"No," he answered, too miserable to check the street to see whether she was right. If he had lifted his head, he would have seen a red and black Cherokee jeep driven by some doofus wearing a cowboy hat. The guy passed by without slowing or gawking as Vanessa led Anthony by the arm inside. In no time at all she had him on a hastily cleared couch and was attempting to knead the tension out of his scrawny shoulders while assuring him that he had nothing to worry about.

"I'm not going to tell your wife about us, Anthony. You don't need to worry about that."

"She knows," he said with a tiny, brave laugh, scarcely more than a hiccup, as if that was the least of his worries.

"What do you mean?" she asked, stopping the massage. This wasn't something Vanessa had anticipated.

"Do you have something to drink?"

"Not until we're done talking, Dr. Ellsworth. What do you mean your wife knows?"

"Very well," Ellsworth said, indulging her, "I'll tell you about my perfect wife. I think she was seeing Croft. I know Croft had some new affair going on, and usually he brags about his conquests, but this time he never said a word to me about it. That's out of the ordinary. And I've known for some time that my wife's been seeing someone."

"You've told me all this, Anthony. Get back to the part where she knows about us."

"She does, that's all."

"How are you sure?"

"Quite simply. She told me."

"She mentioned my name?"

"No. But she knows I'm seeing someone."

"And what did you say when she told you?" Vanessa asked, thinking that perhaps she could make something out of this complication.

"I denied it, naturally. What do you think marriage is for?" His condescending tone began to creep in.

For now she ignored his superior attitude and said as if it was all beyond her, "I'm not a mind reader, Anthony. All I want to know is why you made it sound over the phone as though you were breaking it off between us. If your wife knows and was having an affair of her own, then I don't really see—"

"Listen, that detective who came to see you, he received a call from someone who claimed I did Croft in."

"So?" Vanessa said, straining to sound perplexed, as though she failed to comprehend the significance. "I told them where you were. You've nothing to worry about."

"What if my wife did it and is trying to set me up?"

"Don't you think that's a little farfetched, Anthony? A minute ago you were telling me your wife was having an affair with Croft."

"Maybe he jilted her. You don't know what a bastard Croft is."

Withdrawing her hands from his shoulders, she said, "Oh yes I do, Dr. Ellsworth. Or have you forgotten how you and I happen to know each other? And where my father happens to be?"

That started Dr. Anthony Ellsworth talking, and fast, which didn't leave much doubt about what topic he was straining to avoid at all costs. The last thing he wanted right now was a heart-to-heart about Vanessa's father. And with that realization Vanessa knew for certain that everything was going to be all right, that this story was going to have a happy ending after all, because there was absolutely no doubt in her mind that this was one neurologist whose fate she had absolute control of.

It had been completely different with that conceited bastard Croft, who imagined himself a cocksman par excellence, royalty and immortality all in one. With him there hadn't been any leading by the hand. He'd recognized Vanessa's motives almost before she did and unzipped his trousers to go along with everything right up to the point when she'd said, "Isn't there something we can do for *him?*"

Meaning her father, whose bedside she steadfastly refused to approach. Whenever she referred to a "him" in that stubborn, lost way, there was never any doubt whom she meant. At that moment she and Dr. Croft were naked and intertwined in a room with complimentary champagne and an exceptionally fine view of Waikiki Beach. He'd paid her way and Jackson County had paid his—to a medical convention.

"We're doing everything we can," Dr. Croft nobly assured her.

"He's suffering," she said, this time determined to force the doctor to suggest that perhaps they could do something to end her father's ordeal.

"We don't know that," Dr. Croft corrected.

"I do. I'm his daughter and I do. But I'm too weak to help him. But you, you could . . ."

"Don't even think it."

He wasn't supposed to cut her off that way, not while they lay naked beside one another, not after the passion they'd shared, and she reacted by blurting, "I want his feeding tube removed."

At that point the hospital staff had already successfully weaned Lowell Asplund off the respirator that pushed breath after breath into his lungs, so that no longer remained as a possible route of termination.

"Death by starvation is not pleasant," Dr. Croft decreed in that high-and-mighty voice he reserved for whoever disagreed with him. She'd heard it often enough to recognize it.

"He won't even know it."

"That's what you choose to believe. But he's trapped inside his brain, and we have no way of knowing what he's capable of thinking or feeling. He could be having perfectly lucid thoughts but be unable to tell us. The truth is, you're the one who's suffering, and you want me to do something to relieve your pain."

"Is that so bad?" she said, applying her tiny helpless voice.

The question made him snigger and pull her on top of him so that their eyes were no more than six inches apart. From that intimate distance, he told her, "Vanessa, you can fuck me blind. It won't buy you anything."

Of course with her self-confidence overflowing owing to the wonders of plastic surgery, she had chosen to believe otherwise and for several months tried to prove otherwise, but in the end was forced to concede that Dr. Jonathon Croft enjoyed her more as an adversary than a sex object. Bitter pill, that. She couldn't budge him. She cajoled, blasphemed, and once, in a tender moment, suggested that a lethal injection of morphine would be the most humane treatment possible. They'd been naked and face to face while she'd proposed that, holed up in another hotel room above another convention, this one in New Orleans' French Quarter, or maybe it had been Atlanta. Events had begun to blur as the number of weekend conferences grew. He'd gone right on screwing her while explaining that her father was receiving the best medical treatment available this side of heaven. Oh yes, he put it exactly that way, exalting in his role as dispenser of life and death, confident that he traveled the moral high road.

As the weeks passed and her tactics failed one after another, she began to despise Dr. Jonathon Croft with a finality that she'd thought reserved only for her father. In the end, even bold-faced blackmail achieved nothing. When she threatened to expose how he had exploited the patient-doctor relationship with her, he simply broke off all contact between them. To get back into his arms she had to beg and whimper and repeat over and over that she didn't know how she would manage without him. A man like Croft didn't have any difficulty believing that. By then Vanessa also knew how she would manage with him, for by that time she'd begun to know Dr. Ellsworth, second-in-command of Neurology and in charge of wake-up therapy for her father. So far the techniques to revive Lowell Asplund had achieved nothing, but they might soon include some experimental injections of Valium, which for unexplainable reasons had in at least one instance shown limited success in reviving coma patients. Trouble was, Ellsworth couldn't convince the family to sign for it. But wait, maybe that wasn't a permanent condition.

When Vanessa learned that Ellsworth was leaving Jackson General, being somehow forced out by Croft, she began to think more favorably of this new technique that Dr. Ellsworth wanted desperately to try. Why it was so vital for him to revive the near dead she assumed had something to do with his many inept failures with the living. Whys didn't concern her. What did was a memory from years before when she'd had a traumatic experience with the drug in question. In her early twenties, while still in nursing school, she'd been abandoned by a boyfriend of some years who wanted to move to the West Coast—alone. In response, she mixed the tranquilizer with liberal amounts of gin, the results leaving a lasting memory of sitting in an Emergency Room, swallowing cup after cup of water along with ipecac while holding a stainless steel basin in her lap. A plan began to form out of the mists.

During the time squandered trying to convert Dr. Croft to her side, she'd also been educating herself on the dilemma that death and dying presented the American medical profession. She had no choice if she wanted to debate the issue with Croft, and she'd been naive enough to believe they were actually debating. They weren't, of course. Dr. Croft knew all the answers from the git-go. It was his premise that physicians had to use every available technology to extend a life, because what came after life belonged to God, a realm where man had no business treading. The fact that he never concerned himself about God's realm at any other time didn't strike him as hypocritical.

Perhaps there was more to his opinion than met the eye. Perhaps not. But one thing was certain, his view wasn't shared by a majority of the other members of his profession, who felt he had the situation upside down. They believed that using medical technology to artificially prolong the life of a patient in a vegetative state was playing God, particularly if the family involved insisted that the patient would not want to linger on, part machine, the rest atrophying flesh. In Lowell Asplund's case, there was no doubt in the minds of his two children what their father would have wanted. He would have loathed such captivity. But even if he had drawn up a living will stating as much, it would have accomplished nothing. Their state didn't accept such documents as legal.

Life had been much simpler for doctors twenty to thirty years ago. And so had death. Back then the patient had expired when unable to fog a mirror. Technological advances ended that good and simple test. A respirator could breathe for a patient; an artificial or transplanted heart could keep pumping the old life-giving fluids. A more finely calibrated criterion was needed. Brain death was the result. By attaching electrodes to the head, physicians could measure the electrical activity therein. Every thought creates a minute pulse of energy as the brain tools along. Reading words on a page generates a minuscule electrochemical current. Under the new rules, the doctor couldn't pronounce that a patient absolutely wouldn't be writing any letters home until there was finally no electrical readout from any part of the brain. This was brain dead.

But what of the patients who had lost only their cognitive functions? The patients who couldn't recognize and interact with the world? They might still have sufficient juice in that part of the brain known as the stem to wobble the needles of an EEG and keep the organs of life—the lungs, the heart— rattling and ka-thumping. What of patients like Lowell Asplund? Comatose but not forgotten; kept alive by a plastic tube piping in home-cooked meals around the clock. Where were they in relation to the Grim Reaper?—who was beginning to bear a strong resemblance to the meter reader from the power company, what with all the gauges and readouts that now accompanied death. Such patients were on hold, indefinitely, unless some savior stepped forward to help them along. Should they be given a hand on their journey? That was the debate between Vanessa and Dr. Croft.

So the problem became one of how to circumvent Dr. Croft, whose position as Lowell Asplund's primary physician enabled him to block any attempt by General Jack's Bioethics Committee to grant the wishes of the family. The committee had been formed to handle just this kind of dilemma, but there was one major drawback to its smooth functioning: it had no power to govern, only to persuade. The physician-patient relation remained inviolate. The reason for placing such restrictions on the committee ranged from resistance within the medical community—no physician wanted to be dictated to by a panel—to the extremely practical threat of malpractice. If an attending physician didn't agree with the committee's decision, the hospital was opening itself up to a lawsuit in which one of its own staff would testify against them. So persuasion it was, and persuasion had as much effect on Dr. Jonathon Croft as distilled water does on the eye. He barely blinked. In Croft's book euthanasia was a four-letter word. Eventually Vanessa concluded this was due to vanity. He refused to admit there was someone he couldn't cure.

Transferring Vanessa's father to another hospital and physician wasn't feasible because Croft would block such a move, recognizing immediately what lay in that direction. Since their state had no right-to-die laws, he'd have the cooperation of the district attorney. This didn't leave a large number of options. It didn't leave *any* options as far as Vanessa was concerned, or at least it didn't leave any ordinary choices, only the extraordinary. By that time, she relished the idea of saying bye-bye to Croft and all his stances and values and the way he said *now,* as if giving an executive order, whenever he came during sex. She looked forward to that as eagerly as saying goodbye to her father. The strain of all the long months of constant hospital visits was taking its toll.

It'd been on a trip to New York City with Croft—another convention—that she'd let him bundle her off to do some shopping while he attended a boring lecture on spinal cord compression. She spent the afternoon buying the highest-quality body bag she could locate. Nothing was too good for her father's physician. Recognizing that the bag would have to be untraceable back home, she'd used the phone to locate the deluxe item, then sent a taxi driver in to purchase it. Caution was her byword. From there she shipped it home.

A week later she had her own boss at the Hillborough Clinic write a prescription for a patient who'd repeatedly phoned in, anxiously complaining that her most recent lipo-suction hadn't worked. In the small circles that the clinic drew its clientele from, such a tale was bad for business. Catering to the clients who could afford tummy tucks and nose bobs was a necessity, so the clinic had a messenger for home delivery of prescriptions. In this case, Vanessa in-structed the messenger to bring the order of Valium in an oral solution back to the clinic where the patient had an afternoon appointment. More lies. The rest had been pa-tience, letting her victim, as she now thought of him, set himself up.

When Dr. Croft suggested a therapeutic ten-day vacation that was to start with a night at the opera in New York and end with a tour of Italy, she readily agreed, willing to drop everything to be with him even on short notice. He believed it. Vanity was also his Achilles' heel. On the appointed after-noon, he'd pulled into her garage wearing a tux and carrying a bouquet of long-stemmed American Beauty roses. The few times he'd ever come to her address it was to provide a ride to the airport, but he always insisted on pulling directly into her garage so that no one would see him enter the townhouse. The question of doctor-patient improprieties was foremost in his thoughts. He was quite openly a bastard about such details, and it often started their trips off poorly. But this once she didn't make a fuss about his fanatical insistence that no one know about their relationship. This time she approved of the secrecy, and to show him her appreciation, invited him in for a toast with an extremely heady burgundy and a promise of some extracurricular activities. Mixing his drink in the kitchen, she felt positively exuberant and alive. She felt a bit like an airline stewardess on a flight to hell, the only place she could imagine Croft headed. They never did make it to the opera, where *Tristan and Isolde* was being performed.

Over two weeks after the missed opera, also after the freezer-preserved remains of Dr. Jonathon Croft had finally been found down at General Jack, and also after a police detective named White had interviewed Dr. Ellsworth and deposited a bug in his ear that someone was spreading nasty rumors about him—after all that waiting, Vanessa finally judged the conditions optimal for trying plan B. If there was one thing she'd learned from her father, you always had alternatives lined up and were ready to use them. She stripped Anthony Ellsworth's clothes off, and her own too because she couldn't stand the way Anthony fumbled with zippers and snaps. Then she did the doctor like he'd never been done before, nor was likely to be done again.

Coiled up with him afterward, she cooed, "Is that better? Can you relax and forget about that detective?"

"Don't mention him," Anthony answered, wearing the same satiated, boyish smirk that he always did after getting laid, as if the cookie jar was empty.

"Good. Because I've something important I want to talk to you about."

That revived the doctor, brought him closer to earth. His

good humor faded; he shifted, not quite as comfortable against her breasts.

"Later," he said.

"Now," she persisted.

Irked, he complained, "You're spoiling the mood."

"That's all right. I want your full attention."

He was sitting up now, sulking and facing away from her, but she imagined he was listening well enough.

"I want you to put an end to my father's suffering."

He complained, "We've talked about this before."

"Let's do it again."

"What you're asking is . . ." But he couldn't quite finish the sentence, couldn't bring himself to say it was illegal, and finished by lamely saying, ". . . impossible."

When he couldn't tell her why it was impossible, she sensed the battle was won. "It's not, Anthony. And you know it."

"I'm telling you it is." Still naked, he rose and did his duck-walk away from her to the fake brick fireplace, which he stood hunched over as if needing some warmth. "It can't be done. The Bioethics Committee won't approve it, not after the way Jonathon blocked it at every instance."

"I think there's a way," she coaxed. "A smart man like you."

"I'm telling you—"

"Anthony," she said, becoming strict, "do you want me to continue telling the police you were with me that night?"

"But I was."

"That's beside the point. Do you want me to go on saying that you were? That's what I'm asking."

He turned toward her to say obstinately, "But I didn't have anything to do with Croft's death."

"What if your wife did?" Vanessa said, trading on his fears. "You yourself said she might have."

She didn't have to go on and mention the possibility of his wife setting him up. Anthony made that leap by himself. She could tell by the screwed-up frown he wore.

"All I'm asking," Vanessa reasonably went on, "is that you let an old man go in peace. Is that so much?"

She amazed herself with an authentic tear. Anthony started boo-hooing too, soft little sobs racking his sunken chest. In the end it was agreed upon. She dressed him, casually suggesting that all he had to do was overdose her father on Valium combined with a booster shot of some additional kind of depressant for good measure, although in her father's weakened condition, the booster might not be necessary. But if he chose that route, she recommended Johnnie Walker Black, premium label, as that had always been her father's favorite. This course of action presented no dangers, she assured him. Hadn't he been pressing her for weeks to grant permission for the experimental Valium therapy? Once her father had passed on, she'd willingly sign the release for that therapy, backdating it, of course.

With that, she pushed her bewildered consort out the door. It felt as though she was setting a wind-up toy in motion. When she spotted the red and black Cherokee, driven by the same clod in the cowboy hat, following Anthony down the block, it was too late to stop anything even if she'd wanted to. Besides, she didn't know that she wanted to. Some additional police involvement might be just the right touch to bring the curtain successfully down and get on with her life.

Part Three

16

A professional would have concentrated on what connection, if any, existed between the death of Dr. Jonathon Croft and that of Lowell Asplund, but when Jan Gallagher arrived at work that overcast Wednesday evening she had a fresh dirt storm to duck and didn't have time to constantly remind herself that she was a professional. Someone—she couldn't imagine which slanderer named Larsen was responsible—had released a rumor that she was laying the detective to find out what he knew and to get a jump on everyone else in Security. She'd learned this from Ginger in the locker room before she had her steel-toed shoes laced.

"One healthy woman to another," Ginger had said. "Rate that detective zero to ten in the sack, would you, Gallagher?"

On top of that, the evening supervisor, Victor Wheaton,

passed on that at the end of Jan's upcoming shift the Little Admiral was holding a reception in her honor.

"Administration's conference room B. Attendance mandatory."

The self-congratulatory way he informed her made it clear that the meeting wasn't going to be the usual status report session where they passed incomprehensible memos around the table and pretended they were communicating. This put Jan in an exceedingly rare state of disgust, one that had become almost extinct since she'd jettisoned her last hubby. Heaven forbid that they should tell her the purpose of this meeting, or politely ask her to attend, or that the great Eldon Hodges, a.k.a. the Little Admiral of General Jack, should have informed her himself. None of those options would have sufficiently asserted their power. One thing was obvious though: her pal Victor possessed inside knowledge as to why she was the guest of honor. He leered enough to make sure that point got across. Rather than allow him a chance to deny knowing anything and behave as though she was over-reacting, she thanked him and left the office for the adjoining break room without requesting any details about the meeting.

"Nine o'clock," he called out.

Hellchristshitgoddamn. A nine o'clock meeting meant she had to sit around after the end of her shift for another hour and a half. Already shy of sleep after the morning meeting with Mrs. Ellsworth and the early afternoon spent with Detective White, she would be incredibly strung out when they finally got around to roasting her for whatever they imagined she had done or failed to do. Who knew what their triplicate-laden minds would come up with. She added an extra teaspoon of instant to the coffee maker's brew in her cup, put her sack lunch on a shelf rather than open the refrigerator, and returned to face her crew, which at least would be minus Gavin. He had the night off.

* * *

The eight-and-a-half-hour shift defied the passage of time. She spent most of it attempting to replay what White had passed on to her concerning Ellsworth's arrest, although worries about the Little Admiral's reception kept washing ashore.

As for Ellsworth, the doctor had been taken in for questioning because two nurses on 32G thought his behavior prior to Lowell Asplund's death highly suspect. Dr. Ellsworth had shown up on the floor near midnight, flipped through several medical charts, and then stepped in with the sleeping beauties—the vegetative patients—to check on his special charges. He spent several minutes praying over Lowell Asplund. At the time the nurses had exchanged looks but didn't say anything. There were a large number of conversations with the Almighty that went on in that room. But later both of the nurses volunteered that they had never seen Dr. Ellsworth on his knees before.

Then one of the RNs walked in on Ellsworth injecting something into the patient's arm through an IV port being used to administer an antibiotic to help the patient fight a urinary tract infection. To have a physician administer a shot was almost as uncommon as seeing one praying over a patient. When asked what medication he was giving, Ellsworth snapped it was part of the patient's scheduled treatment plan. What medication that could be, the nurses had no idea. Other than a weekly booster of vitamins, Lowell Asplund received nothing intravenously that they knew of.

After that the nurses kept a closer watch on their patient, not because they yet suspected anything but because if an MD came in at midnight to check on a patient's status, they knew which way the wind was blowing. An hour later they discovered the patient arresting. They thought Lowell Asplund had Do Not Resuscitate orders, which prevented the staff from calling a code blue to save him, and it was while one of them searched for his medical records to make sure he was DNR that the other nurse helplessly watched the diminishing heart-blip on the monitor screen and began to suspect the worst. For months Lowell Asplund had coasted along on a perfectly even keel, no fluctuations, no deteriorations, no hint of the end drawing near. Then there was the bothersome image of Dr. Ellsworth kneeling at the patient's bedside and the fact that one of them saw him give the patient an injection. Totaling all this made them suspicious enough to call Security, namely Gavin Larsen, who was supervisor because it was Jan's night off. Larsen in turned whistled—Detective White's description—for the administrator on call, Elizabeth Kavanaugh, who with great reluctance brought in the police.

But White's questioning of Dr. Ellsworth had produced no confessions. The detective described the interview as shrink-wrapped, meaning that he thought the doctor required the services of a psychiatrist or else was pretending that he did to help a defense lawyer at a later date. It had been as though he and Ellsworth were talking about a third person, a graduate of Johns Hopkins Medical School not present in the room. Ellsworth never once made a simple denial such as *I'm innocent*. Instead he worded it this way: *A doctor wouldn't have done such a thing*. Eventually they'd sent him back to Holding to wait until they received the outcome of the medical examiner's handiwork, which soon enough came back with a toxicity report pointing to a Valium OD, most likely injected directly into the bloodstream, say through an IV. They'd then held Dr. Ellsworth over for arraignment in the morning. He'd be greeted by the judge at roughly the same time Jan had her meeting with Eldon Hodges.

As for trying to fathom why her esteemed boss had extended a royal summons to meet him in a conference room, reasons ran rampant, but she settled on three possibilities. One, her handling of Gavin and the refrigerator, which was a petty enough issue to attract Eldon Hodges, who was a champion of the picky and preferred to let the big picture fend for itself. Two, her helping hand to Detective White, which would strike Hodges as ignoring the chain of command and—worse—disloyal. The fact that she had been aiding the police wouldn't matter. Three, her ill-advised visit to Hope Ellsworth, who no doubt had complained to Administration of the intrusion before Jan's Pontiac left a haze of oil-smoke in her driveway. Considering the way physicians could huff and puff, Jan guessed it'd be point three, but she prepared defenses for all of them.

At 8:55 in the morning she arrived at Security's administrative office only to be told by a replacement secretary to have a seat, Mr. Hodges would call for her when ready. More lifting of the scepter of power. Let her wait. Let her know who had reserved parking in the ramp.

The new secretary was short and dumpy, not unlike the Little Admiral except that her complexion was much worse than his. She worried over the papers on Sheila's desk, stacking them, rearranging them, then restacking them, as if believing they ultimately would be the reason for her dismissal. She may have been right. At the county they liked to keep you guessing.

But maybe it was the frank way Jan watched her that made the woman hyperactive. Jan felt a touch of guilt over that possibility but couldn't stop wondering where Sheila was. Aside from divulging that her name was Miss Pepperidge, the secretary revealed nothing, which included nothing about Sheila's whereabouts, although the question brought a blush to the pitted cheeks beneath her beige-colored pancake. The reaction made Jan resolve not to utter another word. So they sat three feet apart, a plastic in-out tray separating them as they awaited a summons from Eldon Hodges. Each seethed in her own juices about what plans the bureaucracy had for her.

With the door to the security administrator's office open, Jan knew that Eldon Hodges wasn't home. She supposed he was already in conference room B, which was sealed hermetically tight. For the next half hour she struggled to forget the rudeness of being made to wait and attempted to avoid the direction of the conference room, which was partially visible over the edge of a nearby cubicle. Too far away to hear anything, she nevertheless found herself straining to detect voices. Never in the past had she been able to see through Sheetrock into another room, yet at intervals she found herself attempting to. She was so fatigued that nothing made sense. Her eyes burned, her shoulders throbbed, and her feet were restless but her legs too weary to shuffle them. It felt as though she was attempting to kick a sleep habit cold turkey. And there was that closed conference room door . . . That was getting to her. She was almost ready to put her shoulder to that.

Finally, at 9:25 the conference room door opened. Jan braced herself but no one came to get her. Whoever stepped out had to be short for the nearby cubicle completely blocked Jan's view. A moment later, when she heard Elizabeth Kavanaugh's peppy voice instruct a secretary to page her husband's beeper and tell him that his wife would be late, Jan understood why she couldn't see anyone. Ms. Kavanaugh was barely five-two. The conference room door closed again. Knowing that Kavanaugh was in there didn't bolster Jan's serenity.

Fifteen minutes later Robert Yost, second-in-command within Security, came to get her. The flat way he asked her to accompany him brought to mind *The Invasion of the Body Snatchers*. Normally there was a begrudging rapport between the two of them, as though Yost respected Jan for standing up for her rights, but today he exposed none of that. She followed him, and upon turning the corner into the conference room had a premonition of catastrophe. But once in the room she was greeted by nicely beveled smiles all the way around the table, which was an oval with a large enough circumference to seat eight, nine including herself. Smiles? This was going to be worse than she'd expected.

17

THE eight people seated around the table could have been posing for a group photo intended to portray cooperation at its shining best. Jan recognized immediately that the flashes of pearly teeth meant they'd been dissecting her until the instant of her arrival. Eldon Hodges' grin resembled a grimace, as though he was holding in a hernia, and Elizabeth Kavanaugh clung to her smile as if afraid to let go of it. She might be unable to replace it.

Next to Kavanaugh sat a bookish yet affable man in a fussy business suit who had grace enough to stand and gesture for Jan to take the one unoccupied seat at the table. She'd never been formally introduced to him but recognized the man as Roger Averilli, executive administrator of General Jack's every needle and bedpan. His good cheer, which had the kind of skilled glint to it common at beauty pageants, was unexpected. A month ago at Jan's discrimination trial, the man had absolutely denied under oath the possibility of the slightest whiff of discrimination in any guise at Jackson County Medical Center. All the while he'd testified he had gazed as understandingly as a parent at her, a paternalistic attitude that Jan's lawyer exploited in her summation. Today that was all forgotten, or at least by him it was. Jan reserved judgment.

Then came two administrative types, both men. One was ridiculously young, well groomed, and tight-lipped, the kind of flesh made from a mold that never gets thrown away but is used over and over to create a smug yes-man. Rapid with numbers, slippery with questions. Automatically agreeable, so Jan assumed automatically disagreeable as well. Two was middle-aged and dressed in a physician's white coat, maybe to remind himself, or others, of what he'd once been. Currently, no stethoscope dangled from a pocket. He acted marginally impatient and bored with the proceedings, as if he had 102 more important places to be, but at the same time, he supported a smile, a benevolent expression that hinted he'd yet to form an opinion of Jan despite all the black marks delivered against her.

Next to them sat the evening shift supervisor, Victor Wheaton, whose happy-go-lucky chutzpah seemed slightly serpentine, and then came the day shift supervisor, Robert Yost, who conveniently acted as though seeing someone he knew passing by in the hallway, except that the door was closed.

Last came Gavin Larsen, whose smile might have glowed in the dark. But despite showing his eyeteeth, he still struck Jan as a basically humorless man. Possible answers for why he was included in this coffee klatch distressed her more than anything else, made her feel doomed, so she smiled too, big and bright, and took the seat next to Larsen without acknowledging him.

The only other thing she noticed about the room was the scent of coffee. No secret there. A stainless steel coffee urn, Styrofoam cups, and two lines of perfectly round sugar cookies filled a silver tray at the center of the table. The refreshments might as well have been made of plastic. No one had touched them.

Executive Administrator Averilli waited until Jan was down before reseating himself and saying in an ultragracious voice that could have greeted Christians at the Coliseum, the old one with the mangy lions, "Thank you for coming, Officer Gallagher."

Officer Gallagher? She braced herself for the worst.

The executive administrator continued. "We've been discussing the uncommon events here at General and are hoping you can help us understand what's happened. I'll let your manager fill you in on what we've covered so far."

All eyes rotated toward the Little Admiral so intently that it was obvious he'd been handed what everyone imagined to be the dirty end of the stick. He surprised Jan by sounding like an authentic middle manager as he spoke.

"Our primary goal here," Hodges said, after a false start and clearing of his thick throat, "is to determine what happened to Dr. Croft, and why, and of course to prevent any interruption of the services that we provide the community." He rolled on unaccosted for a minute or two, adeptly peppering his sentences with the usual phrases, *damage assessment, public perceptions,* and his favorite *utterly essential,* until finally reaching what Jan assumed was his destination. "Naturally, to achieve all this, we need to gather all the facts available to us."

He stopped there and everyone's eyes swiveled back to Jan.

"Are you asking me what I know?" Jan said.

The question caught the Little Admiral unprepared, and he answered as if unable to imagine how he could make himself any clearer. "Well, yes."

"I've put all that in my reports," she said, holding back any additional comments on how he could have asked this question without the lengthy preamble.

"But sometimes," he steadfastly said, "it is difficult to put into words, written words I mean now, everything that you've seen or thought, and what I'm asking you now is to tell us, in your own words, what you know about the investigation of Dr. Croft and, more recently, of Dr. Ellsworth."

Apparently her written words weren't her own, but she ignored that inconsistency, knowing that it never paid to get too literal with the Little Admiral. She told them what she'd learned, leaving out anything due to her association with Detective Frank White. It wasn't loyalty to White that held her back, more disobedience to the people surrounding her. Her recital made the natives restless, although they remained as cheerful as cannibals around a kettle. At the county they weren't afraid to eat their own when the time came.

"What we're searching for," Eldon Hodges said, with the slightest murmur of impatience, "is any special information you might have."

Jan nodded cooperatively, as if attempting to anticipate his next thoughts, if thinking was the proper term for what transpired between his ears, but she couldn't and so said nothing.

"We're not trying to trick you," the Little Admiral said, belatedly raising his hand in a peace gesture, "but it's important that we determine if there is any connection between Dr. Croft's death and Dr. Ellsworth, who as you no doubt have heard, remains under custody for another matter, which as far as we know is unrelated as well, but if you know otherwise we would appreciate hearing of that too."

"I don't know of any connections."

Hodges glanced at Roger Averilli as if to say he'd forewarned him it would be this way. The executive administrator nodded almost imperceptibly, disturbed by how this could be so.

"But you assisted the homicide detective when he interviewed Dr. Ellsworth," Hodges pointed out.

She admitted she had. Their agenda was becoming clearer. Apparently the police still weren't sharing what they knew. What she couldn't yet figure was why Administration was being so friendly about asking. They were digging for something, and she remained on guard, not about to accidentally give away for free whatever it might be they wanted.

"Why did he want to talk to Dr. Ellsworth?" the Little Admiral asked. "This was a full day before the doctor was taken into custody."

"For background on Dr. Croft. Ellsworth worked with him, right?"

"Why take you along?"

"He claimed he wanted someone there familiar with the hospital, in case I might notice something he didn't. I thought it might be a good idea to tag along to make sure he didn't overstay or ask any inappropriate questions."

"Did he?" No one acted convinced that her motives were that loyal.

"All by the book."

"It's utterly essential that we know if you learned anything that we should be aware of," the Little Admiral said.

A quick once-over of the table proved that everyone was on the edge of their seat for her answer, or at least pretending to be.

"Nothing out of the ordinary."

"Do you know anything about a connection between Dr. Ellsworth and a Vanessa Asplund? She's the daughter of the patient who expired yesterday in Neurology."

"Should I?" she asked, trying to imply that she didn't.

"Perhaps," Hodges replied, sounding as if her question insulted his intelligence, although that wasn't exactly his reaction either. Somehow, the way he lowered his eyes or pursed his lips, he made it seem as though her denseness was a burden to Executive Administrator Averilli. "Do you know anything about the fact that Dr. Ellsworth's file is missing from Personnel?"

"No." Maybe she said that too fast.

"Why do I think otherwise?"

"I wouldn't know. Why?"

"We've had to let one employee go," Hodges warned. "Those are confidential files."

So now she knew about Sheila. Scanning the faces around her, she found that everyone save Gavin, and now herself, continued beaming. She was straining to remain pseudo-friendly, but her heart clearly wasn't in it.

"So that's it," Jan said, more to herself than anyone at the table.

"Is there anything you wanted to tell us?"

"No," she said softly.

"You don't know anything about any of this? About what happened to Dr. Ellsworth's personnel folder? About why the detective wanted to talk to Dr. Ellsworth? About any connection between Dr. Ellsworth and Vanessa Asplund?"

The executive administrator spoke up, saying, "We would appreciate your help in this, Officer Gallagher."

"I've told you what I know," she said in a small voice.

"Fortunately," Eldon Hodges stiffly said to the rest of the group, "Security has found out a bit more than Officer Gallagher has been able to. Gavin, will you recount what you've learned?"

The Little Admiral didn't have to ask twice. This was the kind of retribution that had Larsen running his fingers over his head as if it was thick with hair. Unbuttoning a shirt pocket, he produced a small, tidy notebook, and began to read in a voice that capitalized everything that made his deeds sound valiant. There was a great deal of that. Out of the corner of her eye Jan could see scrawls on the page he read off, but she gazed straight ahead without cheating.

"At six-fifteen on Tuesday evening I followed Dr. Ellsworth from Jackson General."

"And why were you following?" Hodges asked, playing the straight man.

"I thought I might learn something about why Security Officer Gallagher and Homicide Detective White had talked to him."

"You're not satisfied that they talked to him solely about background facts?"

"No, not when the doctor was so agitated about their visit he complained to Administration. I thought it might go beyond the routine."

"Very good. Continue."

"He traveled directly to 12365 Rue de Vouille in Chapwick, the address, as I later found out, of a Vanessa Asplund. He stayed there one hour, after which he briefly returned to his office here at the hospital only to leave again, this time traveling to the Bay Plaza Drug, on East Culver Road, where he had a prescription filled. From there he made a two-hour stop at the bar atop the Regents Hotel."

"Did anyone talk to him during all that time?" Hodges asked, sounding as though the answer wasn't going to surprise him.

"Aside from the cocktail waitress, just one person."

"And who was that?"

"Himself."

"You mean," the Little Admiral said with hackneyed astonishment, "he was noticeably talking to himself?"

"He was. And drinking. He acted like a man deeply troubled."

"Deeply," the Little Admiral said, emphasizing the point for everyone's benefit. "Continue."

"From the Regents he returned to the hospital at ten twenty-eight. I followed him to the chapel, which was where I left him at ten forty-five, praying. I started my shift at eleven and as soon as able checked back at the chapel. At eleven thirty-five he was still praying, but when I returned at five to midnight, he had left. I learned later, when a code blue was called on 32G, that Dr. Ellsworth had gone from the chapel to that station, where he briefly visited the bedside of patient Lowell Asplund, who subsequently expired."

"Uh-huh, very good. And have you learned anything else pertinent to our discussion?"

"Yes, I believe I have. Dr. Croft was originally the physician in charge of patient Lowell Asplund, who was in a persistent vegetative state. There had been some ugly scenes between the staff and family members, who wanted all life support removed from the patient."

Now Jan tried to read Gavin's notes but didn't discover more than what he'd said.

"Family members such as Vanessa Asplund?" Hodges asked.

"Particularly Vanessa Asplund. The staff was extremely concerned about her. She has training as a nurse."

With that, Gavin put his notebook away and rebuttoned his shirt pocket. A moment of unrequested silence followed, but that was short-lived as Hodges said, "Do you have anything you'd like to add to that, Gallagher?"

The recital had allowed her time to restarch her demeanor and now she firmly said, "Since I seem to be on trial, do you mind if I cross-examine?"

Hodges didn't care for her attitude or the request, but Roger Averilli overrode any objections by first assuring Jan that no one was on trial, and then saying, "We'd be very curious to hear what you might have to ask."

"Gavin, how did you know that Detective White went to talk to Dr. Ellsworth?"

With a wave of his hand, Larsen dismissed the question as beneath him, but Elizabeth Kavanaugh answered for him. "I informed him. It's the policy of this hospital to pay close attention to any complaints received from its staff, and I received two angry calls from Dr. Ellsworth. One when Detective White initially arranged to see him, and a second, extremely bitter one when you and the detective were done with your interrogation."

"I've told you," Jan said, more than ever unwilling to reveal that the police had received a tip, "the detective asked what sounded like routine questions to me. But I would have to say that the doctor was definitely upset by our visit. Why, we never found out."

The answer clearly didn't satisfy Elizabeth Kavanaugh, who glanced toward Averilli with a conspiratorial look. The executive administrator frowned briefly in disapproval of the openness of her expression, then he was back to sovereign neutrality. Before anyone else could express disapproval, Jan quickly moved forward with another question for Gavin. "Why were you following the detective and me?"

It was dialogue in the trenches. They were sitting side by side but neither looked at the other. Each focused on Hodges, who watched whichever one of them was not speaking. When Gavin answered, his voice sounded crimped.

"That was your boyfriend's mistake. I happened to be driving down the same street as you."

"Two things," Jan said, with what she thought of as remarkable restraint. "First, Detective White is not my boyfriend. Second, I'm wondering why, if you were simply driving down the same street, you pulled over when we did. Another coincidence?"

Gavin responded with a question of his own. "Where were you and the detective going? The people in this room might like to know. We've jobs to do too."

"What I do after hours is the business of nobody present," Jan said, a wintery nip in her tone.

Elizabeth Kavanaugh was forgetting to smile, and although Roger Averilli kept it up, his goodwill appeared to be decomposing quickly. The session wasn't proceeding quite as they anticipated.

"I've another question," Jan said, and this one she directed to Eldon Hodges. "Is Sheila permanently fired?"

"I don't know of any temporary firing," Hodges said.

"Then you'd better can me too," she said, telling herself *chin up.* "I'm the one who asked her to remove that folder. If you need proof, I've still got it."

After a moment's deliberation, during which the Little Admiral barely refrained from checking with the executive administrator, Hodges said, "That was an error in judgment on your part. If you return the file, we'll forget it."

"And Sheila?" Jan said, unsatisfied.

"I've already made that decision."

By then Jan and Hodges were glaring so wickedly at one another that Roger Averilli intervened, saying, "Why did you want Dr. Ellsworth's folder, Officer Gallagher? Perhaps you could tell us that?"

"I've forgotten." She was working hard to show no emotion.

Victor Wheaton snorted in amusement, but no one else was slapping their knee. The conference room had gone beyond institutional bland to institutional ugly. A fluorescent bulb in a corner of the ceiling flickered distractingly. The walls were a dingy white. There wasn't a window in the place, and the door remained closed.

"Perhaps you'll remember it later," Roger Averilli said, still smiling, although not quite so graciously, showing some of the drive that got him to his current position. "We can talk about it. But right now I'm wondering about something else. Have you considered what an untenable position the hospital is in?"

"You talk as if I'm responsible."

"That's certainly not the case," the executive administrator said. "We recognized that. But we also see that you may have some information that would assist us in dealing with upcoming events. And preparation could be vital. The entire future of Jackson General could be resting in your hands."

"I doubt that people are going to stop getting sick."

"True," Averilli said, taking her wit seriously. "But the

importance of our public image cannot be overstressed. Lose that and we lose the public's confidence. We become a joke. Perhaps you can appreciate that as the head of this fine institution, I'm the one responsible for making sure that doesn't happen, of ensuring that no blame is laid on Jackson General's steps."

"Or your own?" Jan said.

"You're antagonistic," Averilli said, sounding reasonable. "I can accept that. Maybe you have good cause. I'm sure from your view, you do, although I'd remind you that taking Dr. Ellsworth's personnel folder was illegal. And besides, we're not asking you to break any laws. We're asking you to put aside your rivalries and share with us whatever it is you've learned through your association with this detective. Is that so unreasonable? After all, we are your employer."

There was a great deal that Jan could have said to that fine little stump speech. No doubt one-liners would be popping into her head for days. But all that she replied was, "Why's that so important to you?"

"For the reasons I've already stated," Averilli said. "Any institution, particularly a public one, must maintain the trust of the people they serve. That's all we're striving to protect."

"Why is Dr. Ellsworth resigning?"

For an instant the executive administrator's expression outstripped his control. His face tightened, his intentions became less than honorable. But then his public face reasserted itself as he said in an even voice, "For personal reasons. Is there anything else you'd care to share with us, Officer Gallagher?"

"No," Jan said, refusing to back down. "I've told you what I know."

All around the table everyone settled into their seats, attempting to get comfortable. No one rolled up their sleeves, but it seemed that way. It also felt as though something dark swooped over the room, a cloud or a disenfranchised soul.

Executive Administrator Averilli nodded agreeably, as if

her answer was perfectly reasonable, and then he started to talk about the health care industry and what a venerable institution Jackson General was. Scheherazade didn't have anything on the man. He spun a fine tale, which went this way: In health care, everyone pulled together. It was the one segment of the service sector truly devoted to serving. And within the industry, General Jack was a model other hospitals emulated. The poor, the indigent, the helpless could come through its doors and know they would receive care that equaled that given at any hospital in the city. And why was this all true? Not because of expensive machinery or pharmaceutical advancements or breakthroughs in surgical technique. It was all because of the dedication of General Jack's employees.

"Please consider all that, Officer Gallagher, that's all we're asking of you."

Jan shook her head in sullen admiration. What he'd said was undoubtedly on target, but she wasn't feeling particularly dedicated at the moment.

Averilli continued in a tighter voice. "And also think about what you can do to help bring about the reinstatement of the secretary who was fired for helping you appropriate Dr. Ellsworth's personnel file."

The way the Little Admiral's head snapped toward Averilli told Jan they were breaking new ground.

"Exactly what can I do?" Jan asked, feeling her way.

"I think you know the answer to that," said Averilli. "Share what you've already learned from the detective, plus make some extra effort"—he smiled self-consciously, giving the meaning of these words a tawdry spin—"to find out whatever else the detective knows, or may be thinking, or uncovers in the upcoming days. If that happened, I think you could depend on not having to feel so guilty about having lost this young woman her job. I believe we could find a way to reinstate her. Your position may be secure for some time to come, Officer Gallagher, but not everyone has that luxury, and you'd do well not to forget it."

She couldn't think of what to say. Wasn't that ridiculous? A roomful of people had just listened to the head of the hospital indirectly suggest bedding a detective to find out what he might know. At least if she correctly followed his drift, that's what he was insinuating. This was essential so that the hospital would know how to save its face. And she didn't know what to say. There was a logjam at the back of her mouth. Her whole face was going numb. She could feel them watching her but couldn't see them, even though looking right at them.

Averilli was saying something further. His voice sounded velvety and untouchable. "Think it over if you like. Let your manager know. But there's one thing I need to caution you about, Officer Gallagher. Do not under any circumstances take it upon yourself to intrude into the Ellsworth family's affairs again. I'm talking about your trip to visit Mrs. Ellsworth. If you do, life could become very unpleasant. And that would be unfortunate. Does anyone else have any points?"

The Little Admiral had one tiny thing on his mind. "In the future, I think you'd be well advised to pay your fellow officers the respect they're due. You'll get more cooperation that way than by asking them to do menial chores."

So they'd gotten around to the refrigerator too. When Averilli asked for other comments, no one spoke up.

"Then I believe we're adjourned."

They filed out of the room without speaking to one another and certainly not to Jan, who remained at the table until someone from the cafeteria pushed a cart in and collected the coffee urn. How much later that was, Jan couldn't really say. But she knew one thing—she'd been taught her lesson for the day about who actually ran the hospital, and she supposed that's what this was all about. The powers that be were showing that they *were* the powers that be. There was something else in there too, something about Dr. Ellsworth's resignation, but she couldn't put a finger on what that might be. The offer of clemency she'd received from the executive administrator left her too stupefied for coherent deductions.

18

FROM one of the Social Services secretaries Jan learned that Sheila had set up office in the Strong Arm, a watering hole popular with hospital staff because of its close proximity and Brompton's cocktails, named after an opiate-alcohol concoction that the English serve the terminally ill who have chronic pain. Having long ago given up on trying to avoid her just deserts, Jan packed up all her pride and headed to the bar, where she found Sheila staring at a plastic Coors waterfall hanging above the mechanical cash register. Both her hands were wrapped around a frosted highball glass as if it was trying to gallop away. The only light in the room came from bulbs covered by lanterns left over from a long-ago Chinese New Year. The first whiff was of garlic, from a roast beef sandwich the bar was justly infamous for. Sheila had a shawl wrapped around her shoulders; the baby-blue ribbon in her blond hair was drooping.

Sliding on the next stool, Jan concentrated on the sparkling waterfall herself, needing a minute of alpine serenity to collect her thoughts before swallowing and saying, "I can get your job back."

"Don't want it," Sheila said with perverse pride.

Jan turned toward Sheila, who continued to be mesmerized by the representation of clean, cascading Rocky Mountain spring water. "How many have you had?"

Glancing over, Sheila's eyes were much more clear and thoughtful than Jan had anticipated. "Had?"

"To drink."

"This is my second, I guess."

"Sure it is. Did you understand that I can get your job back?"

"I'm only drinking Fresca, Jan. Relax. I've been sitting here thinking. You know how that is. Days, weeks, months go by and you don't bother with it. You get up, put on your cheaters, and hi-ho, hi-ho. Then something happens and the first thing you know, you're thinking. You kind of have forgotten how, but after a while it comes back."

She drained her drink and tapped the bartop to signal for another. The bartender obliged, mixing it at the far end of the counter, which prevented Jan from guessing its ingredients.

"So what have you been thinking?" Jan asked.

"That I've been smiling and making the Little Turd's coffee for three years now, kidding myself that it was temporary, that I was going to go back to school and become a teacher, like I'd always thought I would. But one thing or another was forever getting in the way, a vacation with the boyfriend, or car payments, or insurance payments for the car—or whatever." She made a gesture toward the doorway to indicate the outside world and all the credit card temptations it contained. Her determination grew. "But this made my mind up for me. I'm selling that damn car, telling the boyfriend to forget it, and getting on with what I planned on doing with my life. So it looks like I ought to be thanking you."

"You're sure about this?" Jan said, her sense of relief far too selfish to be proud of.

"Absolutely."

"Because if you aren't, or if you want to change your mind, I can get your job back."

"How?"

When Jan told her, Sheila shook her head in disbelief but said, "Par for the course. You know how they found out I took the folder? My friend in Personnel. My best friend, I thought. You figure it out."

After staring at the waterfall a moment, Sheila spitefully continued. "When the Little Turd confronted me this morning, I went all mushy and had to leave. But then I got hot and came back to clean out my desk. That's when I heard them talking in his office."

"Who?"

"The Little Turd and Gavin, plus the Duchess of Administration and Averilli too. Administration was explaining some things to the Admiral, and the door was open a crack. Did you know that this Ellsworth they arrested was resigning?"

"There's a letter in his personnel folder," Jan dispiritedly said.

"That explains some things," Sheila said, sipping her drink and thinking. "Why they're so touchy about that folder, and all. Croft's the one insisted this Ellsworth resign, you know."

"No," Jan said, telling herself to wake up. "I didn't."

"Oh yes. To hear the Duchess tell it, he'd been trying to get rid of Ellsworth for years. Thought him incompetent. Then some malpractice thing came up and Croft threatened to testify against Ellsworth unless he resigned. You can imagine how popular that was with Admin, insurance costs for malpractice coverage being what they are, particularly after that outbreak of neonate casualties last year."

"Malpractice suit?" Jan asked.

"From what I heard, Ellsworth misdiagnosed some young kid's tumor as migraines because of family history. Didn't run the proper tests, not even when the medications he prescribed failed to do anything. He just kept circling back to his original diagnosis of migraine. The boy ended up in a coma after emergency surgery was needed. Now he's receiving free care at General, which the family is grateful as hell for, as you can imagine. Croft caught the case in review and threatened to enlighten the parents unless Ellsworth goes."

"You're sure?" Jan asked, realizing it explained a great deal of what had happened.

"I know what I heard. They're afraid Ellsworth did in Croft because he was forcing him to resign, which may not sound like such a big thing unless you're a doctor. They made it sound as though leaving General was going to pretty effectively end his days on Mount Olympus."

"I talked to his wife," Jan said. "She made private practice sound like a golden opportunity."

"No doubt," Sheila said, preoccupied with another thought. "There's more. They're afraid this Asplund's daughter found out about Ellsworth dropping Croft and used it to force him to do in her father."

"And they haven't told anyone?"

"They don't think any of it can be proven in a courtroom, so they're holding back to see what happens. Those old insurance premiums, you know, plus public image. Neck and neck there. And they don't want it in the news, because at this point that makes them look real bad, like they were trying to hush something up."

"But it sounds to me," Jan said, tentative, "as though the cops have Ellsworth for the Asplund business even if they can't tack on Croft."

"Don't count on it," Sheila predicted.

"How's he going to wriggle out of it?" Jan asked, not wanting to believe it possible.

"Don't know. That's when someone went by and said my

name, which made the Little Turd send Gavin out to escort
me off the premises, but from what I overheard before then,
the Duchess is convinced Ellsworth won't be found guilty.
She wanted Security to keep an eye out for anything that said
otherwise."

More of the waterfall.

"There's something else," Sheila said in a gritty voice. "I
probably shouldn't tell you this, but the Little Turd's been
predicting you won't last a month, and he's flat-out promised
Gavin your job as soon as you fold. Personally, I hope you
stick it to them. It's time somebody did. Show them you can
do that goddamn job better than any of them."

What could Jan say to all that? She thanked Sheila, promised to do her best, and reminded her that if she changed her
mind about getting her job back, all she had to do was call.
Jan Gallagher wasn't above eating crow. She was quite good
at it, actually. But what she thought was, Great, one more
person I can't let down.

By noon she had labored up her front steps, collected the
inch or so of junk mail clogging her delivery box, and prepared to sleep a week—except that she tripped over a suitcase
in the entryway. Setting it upright, she spied two smaller
versions of the same-style luggage lined up behind it, and
finally, last in line, Claire's parakeet cage with its night cloth
dropped over the top. Milhous was songless in the darkened
aviary. In her groggy state, Jan found herself wondering why
her mother had given a pet the middle name of a president
forced to resign. With questions like that occurring to her,
hallucinations might be forming in the dark recesses of her
mind as she stood there. Straightening, she leaned against the
wall, closed her eyes, and silently sang to herself *The itsy-
bitsy spider went up the water spout.* She stayed poised like
that until Claire said in a steely voice from the living room,
"I know you're home."

"What's going on, Mother?" Jan stayed in the entryway.

"I'm moving out."

"Do you mind if I ask why?" Jan said. She knew from Claire's voice that she was dressed in her Sunday clothes, which included her gray suit, pheasant-feather cloche, and patent leather purse. Her posture would be impeccable. She would be wearing her square red earrings.

"I like to think you know why," Claire primly said.

"Why did you name your parrot after Nixon?"

"If you're going to get involved with another man," Claire said, unwilling to get sidetracked, "you're on your own. That was our agreement."

"I've told you, it's nothing but work with the detective."

"He's called twice this morning alone. And I've talked to enough men to know what I hear in his voice."

Jan pushed herself away from the wall and entered the living room where Claire sat on the left side of the chintz love seat. Jan had been on target about everything but the earrings; it was the polished black ones, which somehow made it worse. Crossing to the right side of the couch, Jan flopped down, saying, "I'm too tired to be interested in men."

"Phooey."

"I mean it," Jan swore. "And even if I was interested, that detective's not my type."

"See?" Claire was triumphant. "One minute you're not interested, the next this one's not your type. Tomorrow you'll have found some redeemable trait. I know how you operate."

"What's really bothering you?" Jan put a hand on her mother's shoulder. Claire turned her head away and refused to say a word. "We need you here, Mother."

Claire moved her face farther away and tsked, so Jan assumed she was getting closer.

"What would the girls do without you?" Jan asked.

"Those little bitches." Said somewhat lovingly.

"What would I do without you?"

"Probably get pregnant again," Claire said, ridiculing the question. "Don't think it couldn't happen either. Your grandmother had—"

"Mother . . ."

"Don't lie to me about this detective."

"God!" Jan said, lifting her hand away. "You're a tough old biddy."

Claire's head whipped back toward Jan as if to reprimand but she didn't say a word.

"This house will fall apart without you," Jan prophesied.

"It probably would."

They stared into each other's eyes, each on the verge of flinching but both remaining steady.

"And that doesn't bother you?" Jan said.

Claire countered by asking, "Where were you this morning?"

"Meetings."

"Don't expect me to believe that. You were with that man, weren't you?"

"Mother, you just got through telling me he called twice. Now why would he do that if he was with me?"

Claire started to squawk, stalled, but got hold of herself enough to sullenly say, "That doesn't matter. You're setting yourself up for this guy. Don't deny it. I've seen all the signs before, and I want to know what's going to happen to me when you get involved. I think I've a right to know that much. Any woman who gets herself into the jams you do, there's no telling what kind of cockamamie ideas you'll come up with. And I want to know what will happen to me."

"This is about my job, isn't it?" Jan wearily said. "I thought we'd talked all that out."

"You never once thought about what it might mean to the rest of us."

"I *thought* I was doing it for the rest of you."

"Your daughter Amy is flunking all her classes."

"Then we better get her some help."

"And Katie all of a sudden wants to grow up to be a cop. A ten-year-old girl, we're talking about."

"What's so bad about being a cop?"

"And that oldest one of yours, she's getting all the same crazy ideas about men that you have, and that's not good. Believe me, that's not good at all."

"Enough," Jan forcefully said. "If it will make you feel any better, I'll make you this promise: If I get involved with some guy—a big *if*—but if I do, I won't move in with him, or him with me, until five years have passed. How's that?"

"You said you were through with—"

"Mother . . ."

"Will you write it up and sign it and give it to me so I can show it to you when you don't?"

"Yes."

Which she did on a scratch pad at the kitchen table. Claire insisted on ink over pencil and read it out loud once Jan had signed and dated it. Then Claire attached it to the kitchen message board with a seahorse magnet and started unpacking her suitcases after returning Milhous to his window perch.

By then Jan was too jumpy for sleep no matter how fatigued she felt and suited up for a jog in the park. A good workout usually drained off her anxieties. This time was no different except that she got lost a hundred yards down a path she'd been following for years. When she stopped to look around, she didn't recognize a thing, not a tree, bush, or rock. Overhead, the sky remained a shroud of gray, low and oppressive, which was all that did seem familiar. And then she found herself crying. She didn't know how she could hold all this together. What was about to fall apart? She was too exhausted to make a list. To suggest that she had it together enough to get involved with a man was ridiculous, and while wiping her cheeks, she started to laugh. Oh, she was in exceptional shape. A full minute passed and still she remained lost. Head lowered, she turned back the way she'd come, figuring that somewhere behind her she'd recognize a tree or street sign or blade of grass.

19

IT was early evening, downy twilight, when Claire
roughly shook Jan's shoulder.

"He's here."

Jan was curled up in her own bed, too tired to have
bothered retreating to her basement hideaway. From outside, in the grainy light, she could hear the mourning doves
that roosted in the spruce tree next to the window. From the
other side of the nearest wall, in the living room, came a low,
rambling voice, followed by a daughter's high-spirited laughter. The bedside clock read 7:20, which didn't help her rise
from the dead. It meant she'd nabbed barely more than five
hours' sleep. Nothing less than a ton of shuteye would have
been enough. She swung her feet to the floor, rubbed her eyes
with the heels of her palms, but still couldn't make any sense
of what Claire had said. *He's here?*

"Who?"

"The one you're not going to live with for five years."

"Huh?"

"The cop," Claire said without bothering to lower her voice. "He's out in the living room with a bouquet of daisies."

"Not roses?" Jan asked, refusing to believe.

"He wants to talk to you," Claire persisted. "Says it's business. I'll tell him to take the flowers back and let you sleep. How's that?"

She listened to the voice in the living room again, more closely this time, and guessed Claire wasn't making it up. Struggling to her feet, she fluffed her thick hair with both hands, tugged on the hem of her nightshirt pajamas, which came down only to midthigh, and shuffled across the hall to the bathroom, saying, "I'll tell him myself," but thinking *Toothpaste? Lipstick? Hairbrush?* She was actually reaching for some of Leah's perfume when she stopped herself, examined the puffy face in the mirror, and felt a mad coming on. Why should she care what she looked like? As if to prove that point, she put on her oldest robe, a terry cloth number that had been to the hospital for three births. But when she reached the living room, the six-foot-three, 220-pound homicide detective was down on his hands and knees playing jacks with Tess. That mollified her slightly. Furthermore, there weren't any hokey flowers in sight. The bouquet must have been some of Claire's flagrant embroidery.

Lumbering to his feet, White apologetically said, "Sorry for barging in on you, but I've been trying to reach you all day without luck. There're several things breaking that I thought you might be interested in."

Claire sat on the couch and made a deprecating chaperon's cluck in her throat without bothering to explain why she hadn't wakened Jan for the calls. Tess, on her seven-year-old knees, had assumed a toddler's posture near the detective's pant legs, as if she wanted to shyly hang on for protection.

She hadn't regressed that way for years. From the kitchen doorway, Amy looked on with her stock indifference, a pose that usually meant she desperately wanted something. White himself seemed oversized as he stood in the middle of the living room. His height and bulk lowered the ceiling and shrank the furniture. His spicy aftershave was everywhere, and his voice—honest to God—sounded like Steve McQueen, the golden matinee idol of Jan's youth. A scarcely noticed part of herself acknowledged that maybe Claire had known what she was squawking about when she waved the red flag over this guy. Otherwise, would finding a man in the living room seem like such a revelation? To comfort her mother, and herself, she coolly said, "You could have contacted me at work."

He shook his head no. "It couldn't wait."

"How'd you get this address?" she asked, suspicious that he'd called the hospital.

"It came to my attention that your most recent ex was a cop," he said, as pleased with this bit of detection as with anything else he'd so far accomplished. "He was able to help me out."

"I'll just bet he was," Jan caustically said. "What else did he tell you?"

"Simmer down, Gallagher. I asked the man for your address, that's all."

Jan was about to put the boot to that hypocrisy when Claire interrupted to say, "My daughter needs her rest."

Detective White apparently thought he knew how to two-step with mothers-in-law, for he became tight-laced respectful. "I'm sure she does, ma'am." To Jan, he contritely added, "If you'd rather wait until you're rested . . ." He let the sentence trail off the way one kid daring another would.

"White," Jan said, hardly amused, "you're priceless. What's so important that it brings you out here?"

"Maybe," White said, uneasy under Claire's domineering gaze, "we could go out for supper and talk about it."

"No, we couldn't," Jan answered before Claire had a chance to hack, cough, or do anything more blatant. "But we could step out on the patio and discuss it without the combined ears of the household listening in. Tess, would you show Detective White the way?"

She made a point of no primping or donning of glad rags for this session. Straight, unadorned Gallagher was all Detective Frank White was entitled to. Jeans and a clean blouse. He hadn't gone so far out of his way that he'd changed out of his work clothes himself, and she detested that stray-cat glint that overtook his eyes at intervals. Claire was right. He shouldn't be encouraged.

When she joined White on the back patio, he lounged in a lawn chair and held one of her few remaining crystal glasses. A slice of lemon decorated the glass's rim. Not liking the way he so comfortably made himself at home, she said nothing while passing him. The picnic table had been covered with a red and white checkered tablecloth held down by a bayberry-scented sand candle and a pitcher of lemonade. Her daughters' hands there, but when she turned back toward the house, every window was strangely darkened and empty, although music, something with an abundance of strings, carried outside. She had to twice make a cutting motion at her throat before the orchestration was dropped. Turning back toward the detective, she had to admit he cut a ruggedly handsome profile, the way some men do after they've been kicked around the block a few times.

"Let's hear it," Jan said, sitting with her arms crossed against a slight breeze and any innuendos the detective might muster.

"You remember those four hundred and thirty-two funeral homes?"

"Are we playing ten questions?"

Detective White good-naturedly shook his head no. "We've called them again. And it turns out that the Bundleweiss Funeral Chapel is missing a transportation cart. Not a body bag, just a cart, so we asked the director to come down and have a look-see at ours, I mean the one you found the deceased on." He offered this last apologetically, a little hangdog around the eyes, as though he didn't want to steal any of her thunder. "He checked it up and down and said it could be theirs, it certainly looked like theirs, but that it was a pretty standard piece of equipment. There're probably hundreds more exactly like it in the city. I mean, the only thing this guy thinks is a safe bet is death, forget taxes. But he went on to say that the missing cart had been in a hearse stolen off their lot a couple weeks back, on the twenty-first of August, actually. A date that might stick in your mind. The vehicle was recovered the next day with only one item missing."

"A cart," Jan said, intrigued despite her best efforts not to be.

From inside the house someone turned on the floodlights over the garage. Who that could have been, Jan had no idea. To see, the detective at first had to use his hand as a visor.

"Your mother doesn't approve of me, does she?"

"Let's stay on course here, OK?"

"Certainly," White said with enough courtesy to make Jan feel like a cheap-shot artist. "We impounded the hearse and Forensics went over it."

"It's me," Jan said, relenting.

"Pardon?"

"My mother. It's me she doesn't approve of. Did Forensics find anything?"

"Nothing," White said, more encouraged than she wanted him to be. "Only a partial print that doesn't belong to any funeral home employee and that definitely isn't Ellsworth's. But then I wouldn't have expected one that did match him. Would you? I mean, did he strike you as the kind of guy who could hot-wire a vehicle and boost it?"

Jan agreed that he didn't.

"It fills in a blank, though," White said. "Now we probably know how the murderer intended to move the body."

"Why," Jan asked in a thorny voice, "is everyone always assuming that he, she, or it wanted to get the body *out* of the hospital? Why not get the body *into* General? Admissions received calls about finding a red body bag, didn't it? And nobody's found out where he was done in yet, even with Security asking every employee and shining a flashlight in every corner of every floor."

"Actually," said a disgruntled White, "I'm slowly coming around to that way of thinking myself, even though your basic murderer's usually more interested in disposing of the goods than delivering them home."

His tardy agreement made Jan distrustful. "If you say so, it must be, huh?"

"Hey," White held his arms up in surrender, "I'm on your side, remember?"

"Why the change of heart?"

"I have reasons," he obstinately answered, "and good ones, for thinking Croft might have got done outside the hospital. And I'll share. But first I'd like to hear the latest from your place of employment. All I see are county lifers closing ranks."

"Fair enough," she said, weighing what she knew against what he might know and deciding she didn't have all that much to lose. "I've learned a couple of things that might interest you. First, my dear friend Gavin Larsen was following Ellsworth around on the night Lowell Asplund died. You might want to check with Bay Plaza Drug on East Culver Road to see what Ellsworth purchased there."

"Larsen already tipped us," White said. "We're checking."

"Well, here's something you might not have heard about," Jan said, not appreciating anything that put Larsen one leg up. "Croft's the one who was forcing Ellsworth to resign."

"Do tell?" said White, sincerely interested.

Jan eased up and told him, "It appears Croft had wanted Ellsworth out for years and found the means when Ellsworth pulled some bonehead stunt that could have been headed for malpractice. Croft threatened to testify unless . . ." She let it hang to make sure she had the detective's undivided attention.

"Unless Ellsworth resigned," White filled in with a sorry shake of his head. "The world just keeps getting older, doesn't it?"

"What I'm telling you," Jan qualified, "that's all hearsay. I can't prove a lick of it. But certain persons in Administration are afraid it explains why Croft's dead."

"I wasn't planning on ruling Ellsworth out," White said, defending his intellect. "He could be working with somebody."

"Like who?" Jan asked, immediately suspecting the detective of holding back.

"Now that gets interesting," said White, fond of this part of the story himself, "seeing as how we've all of a sudden got a second murder case down at your place of work. It seems to me they might—as my boss says—hypothetically be connected. That one might have somehow led to the other."

"You're thinking like Administration if you're putting the Asplund woman somewhere in the middle."

He shhhed her with a finger across his lips. "Bad luck to name a suspect. Scares them off."

"But you're thinking it."

"Let me put it this way: When I questioned Ellsworth about his divorce and the child custody battle that Ms. Asplund mentioned, he almost dropped his teeth. Said, no way. I didn't know what I was talking about. Made me curious, so I casually brought it up to his wife too."

"Casually?" Jan asked, remembering Hope Ellsworth's regimented presence.

"Absolutely. And she told me I was nuts."

"In those words?" Jan said, knowing otherwise and smiling at his liberties.

"Bigger words, same idea. So either the husband and wife

are in something together, which doesn't seem likely considering that they've both got a little something going on the side, or else the Asplund woman's been lied to, or else she lied to us."

"What's your pick?"

"I only do that at the track," White said. "But I can tell you that my partner's been checking into Dr. Croft's affairs. The doctor started a two-week vacation on the day the hearse was stolen. His desk scheduler is blank from five o'clock on that day. Digging into his charge cards, we found out he purchased two tickets for the opera in New York on the night we now assume he was murdered. The Metropolitan's here next month. Maybe you'd like to go?"

"Save the funny stuff."

"I'm not trying to be funny," White persuasively said. He almost took a gulp before continuing, and that vulnerable pause was touching enough to cross Jan up. The detective said, "I mean, maybe we could go out sometime. When we're done with this."

"Like on a date?" she said, twitting him because if she didn't she might give in. "To the malt shop?"

Not appreciating that poke, he said, "Target range, if you want."

"You just want to be close to me, is that it?"

"Why is that so hard to believe?" the detective asked, pinkening at the ears.

"Maybe it's not," she said, regretting her impulse. She'd insulted him when all she'd intended was to protect her flank.

"It's got something to do with my wife, doesn't it?" he asked. "Her running off with another woman."

"It's got more to do with me," Jan said, correcting him without much sympathy. She didn't intend to mix that emotion in here. "My track record isn't so great."

"It's not going to get any better sitting at home, Gallagher."

"Nor worse."

"Why don't we flip a coin?" he suggested, still hoping to carry the day.

"Why don't we get back to talking about murder?" she said, unwilling to be carried anywhere. "That's safer. If I want to hear from you about anything else, I'll let you know."

The detective was halfway into a regressive pout before he caught himself, chuckled grimly, and returned to business. "It'd be interesting to know who was going to the opera with Croft that night, don't you think?"

"Maybe."

"Don't give anything away, Gallagher." When it didn't appear that she would, the detective went on. "Croft also charged two airfares to Rome. The reservations to Italy departed early the day after the opera. Two tickets in the name of Mr. and Mrs. Croft. But when my partner asked the only Mrs. Croft we know of—the victim's divorced wife—she denied having communicated with her husband, other than through lawyers, for years. Looks to me like we've got a mystery companion on our hands."

"So you think it's Vanessa Asplund?" Jan quipped. She went on to ruminate in a crazy, moonstruck way, "Let's see. She did away with Croft down at General, slipped him into a body bag that happened to be handy, and hot-wired a hearse to drive him away in. That sounds about right to me, Detective." Her voice sobered. "Except I can't see Vanessa Asplund zipping herself up unless there's a man somewhere handy to help."

"There is," White said, grinning despite himself. "A man, I mean."

"I thought you didn't buy Ellsworth for the hearse?"

"I don't," White said. "But Vanessa Asplund has a brother, and guess what? He's got a rap sheet with two priors on auto theft. That's why I'm willing to think the doctor got his outside the hospital. Nobody we've talked to puts the Asplund woman anywhere near Croft except to argue. So it's doubtful she got close enough to him down there to share some spiked drinks, subdue him while he went under, and cart him all the way to the Emergency Room without somebody noticing. But if they did him outside, they could have wanted him inside to make it look like that's where it happened."

By then they needed the lights above the garage to see each other's expressions, which were very intent.

"The brother's print on the hearse?" Jan asked.

"Not enough there for a definite match."

"He could have been the one who called Admissions," Jan observed.

"Or it could have been Ellsworth," White countered. "Like you said, it doesn't make sense to rule him out, not if he's got motive."

"So now where are we?" she said.

"To the reason I'm visiting you."

"At last," Jan said, pretending to be thrilled.

"You may have noticed," White went on, undeterred, "that Ellsworth and Ms. Asplund are alibi-ing each other. But I've also heard it whispered that Croft was quite a lady's man himself, and then there's all this business with who his traveling companion was. Wouldn't it be interesting if this Vanessa Asplund was carrying on with him too?"

"Why, that'd be fascinating," Jan said.

"If her brother stole the hearse," White answered, wagging a finger at her in admonishment over the cynicism, "maybe she was supposed to go to the opera with Croft, and on to Rome, but maybe she never actually planned on going anywhere. I've checked the Hillborough Clinic, where she works, and know that she hadn't requested any vacation."

"Hold on," Jan said, done playing games. "Why would she be seeing both of these doctors?"

The detective gave her a worldly smirk for an answer.

"Other than an unusual appetite," Jan said.

"Maybe she was hedging her bets. If one doctor wouldn't help her, the other would."

"Don't you think," Jan said with a great deal more reasonableness than she felt, "that if she was seeing Croft, somebody would have noticed? Someone like Ellsworth?"

"Maybe he did," White said, his faith unshaken. "Maybe she wanted him to." He set his glass on the table and leaned forward to give her the lowdown. "Remember our anonymous tip concerning Ellsworth? For me, Ms. Asplund's the leading candidate for the job. What we have here may be nothing more than your common old crime of passion. You add a love triangle up with Croft trying to get Ellsworth sacked, and we might have enough spark for a fire." He snapped his fingers, feigning inspiration. "The woman could have gotten involved with Croft first, and getting nowhere there, switched to Ellsworth, who made promises concerning her father if she helped him with Croft. One of those you-scratch-my-back kind of things."

"If they're working together," Jan objected, "why the anonymous phone call?"

"God, Gallagher, murderers aren't always the most trustworthy individuals. It's their nature. The doctor might have had a second opinion about keeping promises made in the heat of the moment, and the lady decided he needed some encouragement."

Nodding reluctantly, Jan saw how it could have unfolded. "Does the brother have an alibi for the night Croft got it?"

"He does—his mother, who's a blackout drunk."

"So how are you going to prove anything?" Jan asked, almost ready to buy it.

"With a little help from my friends, I was hoping."

"Meaning?" Jan said, put on guard by the sudden onset of innocence around White's eyes.

"I was counting on good citizen Ellsworth to give us a hand, except we've run into a snag."

"What do you want?" Jan impatiently asked.

"We're hoping," Detective White said, "that if we can keep the pressure on Ellsworth for Lowell Asplund, he might become talkative about his girlfriend, and then she might become talkative about him, and so on, back and forth until we got something that counts. That's usually how we get the lovebirds."

"I thought you had Ellsworth cold?"

"We do . . . more or less."

"Meaning less?" She stared directly at him while asking this. Her voice was derogatory. He didn't exactly look away but that appeared to be his inclination.

"The DA thinks there's a slight problem with our case," the detective admitted. "It appears that Lowell Asplund's medical record has been temporarily misplaced."

"So?"

"Ellsworth is claiming that he regularly prescribed Valium for the patient. Didn't he mention some new therapy? If that's the case, then the whole matter of Lowell Asplund's death moves away from murder and closer to an accidental overdose. The district attorney wants the patient's medical record because the nursing staff insists that Lowell Asplund never received Valium and the record would prove it. With that kind of written evidence, the case goes ahead. Without it, the DA drops out, and when that happens, Ellsworth won't be talking to us about much of anything."

"Now what do *you* think could have happened to that record?" Jan said, acting as though ready to lift the table-cloth to see if it might have been misplaced under there.

"Who can say?" White said, shrugging philosophically. "The nurses claim it disappeared at roughly the same time Ellsworth left the floor. They saw him recording the injection he gave Lowell Asplund in it. Then later, when Asplund went under, they had to find his chart to make sure they had written orders not to resuscitate him. I mean, it was common knowledge they weren't supposed to try bringing him back, but they needed to have it written to cover themselves. But the record was gone and they had to call their supervisor who had to call the chief of medicine who said if there's nothing written you resuscitate. By then it was too late."

"Now if Ellsworth took it," Jan said, lecturing, "don't you think he would have destroyed it?"

"Yes, I do," White said. "But you see I'm paid to act as though maybe he didn't. I got a court order and went through his house—politely of course—and it's not there, nor is there any evidence of such a folder being burned in the fireplace or anywhere else on the grounds. So I have to proceed as if he's still got the chart." He rubbed his throat apprehensively. "I mean, we need that sucker."

"There's a million places he could have stashed it."

"Right," White said. "But we can't search that many. Not this year. Only the obvious ones."

"What are you leading up to, White?"

"His office. He might have stopped in there on his way home that night, but we didn't get around to looking there."

"That's next?" Jan asked, somehow knowing it wasn't.

White chuckled uneasily. "We messed up a bit and didn't get his office on the search warrant."

"You'll get another warrant?"

"There's a slight obstacle," White said, wearing his tippy-toe expression. "The judge we're working with, she doesn't have the highest regard for my professional abilities."

"Now why would that be?"

"A slight miscalculation on a warrant I got from her last year," he answered without trying to gloss over anything. "We busted the wrong guy's door in and the newspapers were downwind when it happened. Judge Simpson, she's fond of *all* the civil liberties. Secretly, I kind of admire her for it. But the fact is, she was reluctant to do anything for me to begin with, so I'm naturally a bit slow on going back to the well, unless I know for sure that what I need is down in Ellsworth's office. In that case . . ."

"You want me to look?" Jan guessed, feeling duped.

"That's all," White hastily assured her. "Look. I'd go myself except the DA says that office is strictly off-limits without a warrant. Anyone catches me there and it could sink everything. But for you, it could be part of a security check, right? If it's there, you wouldn't have to remove it. I wouldn't want you to. That'd get us thrown out of court. But if it's there, I go back to Judge Simpson, say I fucked up, take my punishment like a man, and no one's the wiser."

"Forget it," Jan said, provoked.

"Maybe you could think about it?"

"No way," Jan promised. "I got a little message today from Administration about you."

"Stay away?" he said, wincing.

"Hardly," she indignantly said. "They seem to think I can use my charm to learn whatever it is that you know."

The detective grinned in appreciation of that directive and rubbed his mitts together as if he could hardly wait for the seduction to begin. "I'll be an open book."

"It's no joke," Jan stated. "I need my damn job for milk, TV dinners, fingernail polish . . . all the little things that hold this family together. But I'll be damned if they can boss me around that way."

"All the more reason . . ." the detective began reasonably, only to be drowned out by Jan.

"Right now, the last thing I need is for them to think I'm running little errands for you and not telling anyone about it. How long do you think I'll keep that damn job if they catch me in Ellsworth's office going through his things? That'd be grounds for something, you can bet on it."

All humor slowly left the detective's expression, and he contemplated her a moment before standing. "Say no more, Gallagher. I understand completely. It was wrong of me to ask. Thanks for the hospitality." He made a motion as if tipping a hat and started to leave.

"Don't be so goddamn understanding," Jan told him.

"I'll try not to," he said, then added seriously, "but I know about needing a job. Keep in touch."

As he turned to leave, she asked, "My going into Ellsworth's office, is that what our going out sometime was all about?"

"No ma'am, that was another matter entirely."

Having said that, he left without renewing his invitation to dinner. Oddly enough, she felt let down. So would her daughters. Not Claire, though.

On the way to work that night she gave herself the standard lecture on no romances. She didn't even feel attracted to the guy, at least not all the time. Only during sideways glimpses. But then again, it'd been years since she'd suffered an instant meltdown over a man. But now wasn't the time for any fooling around. She was too vulnerable, what with all the other debris whipping around in her life. Except that White seemed kind of at loose ends himself, which maybe balanced everything out. Right? So they could be invalids together and between the two of them dig a hole they'd never climb out of. No, now definitely wasn't the time.

Those conflicting announcements from the rational and not so rational parts of her mind were interrupted when she stopped at a red light near the hospital and spotted Elizabeth Kavanaugh in a parked Toyota. She was having words—strict ones—with someone in the passenger seat. Leaning forward, Jan caught sight of a morose Gavin Larsen silently soaking up his instructions. His pinched features were partially hidden in shadow, but Jan saw him straighten a bit and say something, at which point Kavanaugh swiveled around toward her. Jan tried to glance away before she made eye contact. Too late. The resentment and accusation in the administrator's eyes blossomed so intensely and immediately that Jan accelerated away as the light turned green, cursing herself for cowardice.

Then, with that embarrassment still fresh in mind, she

entered the Security office thirty minutes later, where things weren't fresh at all. She was almost bowled over by the overripe stench of rotting food, which had been removed from the refrigerator and stacked on her desk. There stood open containers of fuming casserole, sub sandwiches whose lettuce had gone native, and yogurt furry enough to be mistaken for a swatch of a full-length coat. Her crew appeared to be having some fun. She sat without acknowledging a thing, dispensed duties for the shift, and told herself they'd just bought her a ticket to Dr. Anthony Ellsworth's office, consequences be damned.

20

THAT Thursday afternoon, Gavin received a telephone call from Delores. Her voice had that husky quality that turned his knees to tap water.

"Don't worry," she said, "I'm not calling for social reasons."

When she paused to allow him a chance to deny that was what he feared, Gavin's response time was sluggish.

"The reason I'm calling," Delores continued, edging into huffy, "is to let you know that the police are searching high and low for Lowell Asplund's medical record without any luck. Rumor has it that they're not very happy about it."

"Uh-huh," Gavin said, slowly regaining his powers of conversation. He remained unconvinced that this phone call had anything to do with work and everything to do with Delores' blueprints for the future.

"You might say they're frantic."

"OK. Thanks for the tip."

"I swear," Delores said, exasperated, "I've met kidney stones more talkative than you. Aren't you wondering why they want the record?"

"They're conducting an investigation."

"Or what's happened to the record?"

"If Lowell Asplund was murdered, that's not much of a mystery."

"Or where it might be?"

"Where?"

"Oh, now I've got your attention, do I? Believe me, I'm sorry to say I can't do your entire job for you, Gavin Larsen. I don't know where. You see, I have duties of my own that I'm expected to fulfill down here, duties that might not be as important or grand—"

"Delores, that's not what I was saying."

"I was only trying to help you get ahead of the competition. But from what I hear, maybe you've got all the help you need."

"What are you talking about?" Gavin asked, deeply sensitive about gossip concerning himself.

"Only that you've been seen accompanying some of our luminaries down here. In particular, one that's got a rocky marriage and grand ambitions."

"If you're talking about Elizabeth Kavanaugh, she liked my work and wanted me to help out with some additional matters that have come up."

"Gavin," she said, overly congenial, "you don't have to explain yourself to me. I hope you get your man, or woman, or whatever the case might be."

"Delores, there is absolutely nothing going on between Kavanaugh and me."

"Of course not. Although, if there was, it might explain why you're forever playing hard to get."

"Who says I'm playing hard to get?"

"You're not?" Delores promptly said. "Then maybe you'd like to get together sometime?"

And there she had him. All he had to do was say no, but he couldn't. The reason eluded him. It was all he could do to fend off her suggestion of a picnic on his ranch, as she called it. She offered to make a gourmet basket and drive herself out. He countered by suggesting dinner but no movie.

"Why Gavin," she said, deeply flattered, "how very romantic."

All he had meant was that he hadn't enjoyed their last movie, but it was too late to retract the invitation now. Who knew how she might interpret and twist whatever he said. So he decided to cut his losses and run. Dinner it was.

After that encounter, he willed himself back to sleep, which turned out to be a mistake. He dreamed, and he hated dreams. This time out he dreamed he had a full head of hair, his name was Hondo, and Vanessa Asplund was in love with him. What trash. But upon awakening an odd thought occurred to him. What if this Asplund woman had been seeing not only Dr. Ellsworth but Dr. Croft too. Why? To help Ellsworth set Croft up. Even as he thought it, the idea struck him as rubbish. Why would anyone, male or female, take on the burden of getting involved with two people at once?

He was lying in bed, considering the drivel his own mind was capable of, when the phone rang again. He was going to have that thing ripped out. It was the only way for any peace. For a full minute he ignored it. Some hidden sense told him it was Delores; not believing in extra senses, he finally picked it up to prove himself wrong. "Yes?" he tersely said.

His rudeness was no match for the woman on the other end. "Larsen?"

"Speaking."

"This is Elizabeth Kavanaugh. I want a word with you."

"Go ahead," he prompted, gazing forlornly out the window at his empty pasture.

"In person," she said, hardly sounding as though she

thought of him as a person. He got the impression from her tone that she wanted to blame him for something. "I need to be sure you comprehend the gravity of our situation."

"Where?" he asked. It felt as though he had all seven floors of Old General on his shoulders.

"Outside the hospital before your shift tonight. I'll be parked on Wabash in a silver Toyota Lexus. Let's say ten twenty-five. And Larsen, be on time. I'm trying to lead a life beyond work too."

As if he wasn't, but the line went dead before he could comment. He held on to the phone an additional minute, listening to the dial tone and staring straight ahead at a framed piece of embroidery that read *Home Sweet Home,* a gift from his mother. But he wasn't thinking about his mother at present, or any woman, or any man, for that matter. He was thinking about a world with a population of one. Eventually he realized he was sitting like a cobwebbed zombie listening to a dial tone and set the receiver down.

As for dealing with Elizabeth Kavanaugh, he didn't see that he had much choice but to meet her as she'd dictated. The one basic problem that he had with his attempts at evening the score with Jan Gallagher was this: anything he accomplished alone was bound to be attributed to a personal vendetta. To legitimize his efforts, he required someone else's involvement, and the administrator trainee had stepped forward. Kavanaugh's reasons for wanting Gallagher's head on the operating table weren't exactly secrets. He'd sat in the courtroom and watched Gallagher's lawyer demolish Kavanaugh's claim that she was living proof that Jackson General didn't discriminate. By the time the lawyer was done, everyone present knew that Elizabeth Kavanaugh had been hired in a hurry, right after Gallagher filed her discrimination suit; everyone heard that Elizabeth Kavanaugh had no real duties or responsibilities, nor could she clearly tell the court what it was she did all day; and worse, everyone had learned that Kavanaugh's husband was on staff at General, a superstar of sorts in the medical world. Her husband's position may have been Ms. Kavanaugh's only qualification for her current position. Before starting her job, she'd earned a degree in French Literature, emphasis on the troubadours, and had limited experience as a volunteer in the hospital gift shop.

That night he was on the corner of Wabash and Twentieth at the prescribed time. Kavanaugh arrived four minutes late without making any apologies.

"Get in," she said. "We've got to make this quick. My husband is home waiting."

Gavin made a point of not saying anything in greeting, a snub that went unnoticed. The car smelled of newness, and its leather seat squished softly beneath him. Elizabeth Kavanaugh was dressed in what he supposed passed for casual in her posh residence, but her peach-colored silk blouse and string of pearls looked a trifle out of place on Wabash Street where the wine of choice was Thunderbird, not Chablis. However, her expression of contempt fit right in.

"Have you learned anything new?" she asked before he'd even closed the door.

"Since this morning?" he said, implying there hadn't been time.

"You see, Larsen. That's what I mean. I don't think you appreciate the immediacy of this situation. That's why I had to make this extra trip all the way down here." She lightly socked a balled fist against the lower half of the steering wheel. "I watched you in that meeting this morning, and I don't think you understand what's at stake."

"Maybe you'd tell me."

"Careers, Larsen. Careers. Yours—and mine. I don't plan on being an assistant administrator forever."

He didn't yet see what she was driving at so said nothing.

"Do I have to lay it all out for you?" she asked.

"Please do."

"Very well, I shall. If I handle this situation right, it could mean a promotion. And if I get promoted, I'll certainly be predisposed to help anyone who helped me."

"Meaning?"

"That Security Administrator Hodges isn't doing so well," she bluntly said. "He's close—very close—to losing the Exec's confidence, and when that happens the Exec will be looking for a replacement."

"Yost is next in line."

"Don't be dense," Kavanaugh snapped. "If the Exec eases Hodges into retirement because he doesn't trust his judgment, do you think he would turn around and hire the man he picked to follow him? Not likely. He'll be searching for new talent. That could be you, if you handle yourself right and have support in the proper quarters. So let me ask again, have you learned anything new?"

"I haven't had a—"

"Wrong," she said, cutting him off. "Have you learned anything new?"

Not appreciating being led by the nose, he refused to answer.

"Politics, Larsen."

He shook his head in disbelief and glared at the windshield.

"You don't believe me?" she asked, incredulous.

He faced her and was about to say he believed her all right, he couldn't very well disagree, not after twelve years county time, but movement beyond the assistant administrator's shoulder caught his eye, and his vision shifted to it. Someone in a car that had pulled up next to them was leaning forward, straining to see him. Then his focus cleared and he said, "Shit."

"What?" Kavanaugh said, offended.

"Don't look to the left."

The first thing Kavanaugh did was glance to her left and mutter something cutting beneath her breath. A second later the car that had stopped next to them shot away, driven by

Jan Gallagher. The administrator rotated back toward Gavin, watching him a moment before saying, "Let me ask you one more time, Larsen. Have you learned anything new?"

She acted as though she'd never seen Gallagher, which had a galling effect on him. He started to stubbornly say no, he hadn't uncovered anything at all, but stopped, reconsidered, and said instead, "I'm working on several promising lines."

"Good boy, Larsen. Good boy. I'll pass that on to the Exec. Now, judging from my conversations with the police, they're getting desperate. They can't find Lowell Asplund's medical record. I had a long meeting with that overbearing homicide detective, and I got the impression he doesn't have much of a case without it. But I'd like to know for sure, wouldn't you?"

"Sounds reasonable."

"I think Gallagher knows for sure. When I told the detective I couldn't do any more than I had already done, he acted as though he knew someone who could. It'd be very nice to know what he thinks Ms. Gallagher can do for him that I can't. Don't you agree?"

"I suppose."

"So, I want you to keep a close eye on her tonight, and for the next few nights. Extremely close. And if that homicide detective shows up down here, I want to know about it immediately. Because if there's one thing this hospital isn't, it's an extension of the city police department. Am I understood?"

"That's all?" Gavin said.

"That's enough. You can go now."

And he did. Gratefully.

He didn't for an instant believe that Kavanaugh was sincere about helping to catapult him into the Little Admiral's chair. Naturally, he resented the way she'd so clumsily dangled it in front of him. It didn't appear to matter to her that he'd been the one who'd pinpointed the time Dr. Croft's body arrived at the hospital, and he'd been the one who'd reported Jan Gallagher's close working relationship with the homicide detective, and he'd been the one who'd tailed Ellsworth all over creation to discover his whereabouts on the night that patient Lowell Asplund expired. No, none of those deeds had been the topic of discussion with the administrator trainee. What had been on her mind was what Gavin had done for her lately, within the last five minutes, say.

He ground his teeth on that while putting on his uniform. On the way from the locker room to Security's subbasement office, his mood soured further when he bumped into Cindi Paige, who warned him that Leo Kennedy was planning something stupid, a prank on Gallagher. Not liking the sound of that, he went to find Leo and straighten him out.

"This isn't the time for your bag of tricks, Kennedy."

"Of course not," Leo answered. "Who could be so thoughtless?"

They were strolling side by side into Security's office. The twinkle in Leo's eyes wasn't reassuring. Then Gavin took a breath and gagged. The fermented garbage on Gallagher's desk top explained why. But before he could get a second wind and threaten to shove Leo's bulbish nose into one of the vile containers, Gallagher herself entered the office.

To her credit, she barely flinched while taking her seat. Throughout the assignment of duties, she pinned her eyes on Gavin as if to say she had a damn good idea who was responsible for the ambrosial scent lifting off her desk. But she never uttered a word about it. Instead she dispensed duties and in closing said, "Do you have anything to add, Gavin?"

Everyone's ears perked up, but Gavin let them down, saying, "No, you seem to have covered it all."

"Nothing from Administration?" she inquired.

The request was a hit with the other guards. It added a sense of mystery to the cold war they'd been witnessing, a touch of intrigue they could only guess about. Why would she think Gavin had an open line to Administration? That's what they were asking themselves. Since what she intimated was true, he naturally got busy denying it. "They don't consult with me, Gallagher."

Willie Smokeham was digging an elbow into Jackson Martin's substantial ribs, and Stan Charais was rotating his shoulders the way he did when excited. Leo Kennedy grinned in anticipation while Cindi Paige scowled at Gallagher, unable to understand what made her tick. The whole scene filled Gavin with contempt for the human race. Voyeurs, every member. A person's own set of miseries were never quite enough. You could depend on any assembled group licking their chops whenever someone else's troubles floated to the top.

Fortunately, Gallagher took it no further, although she couldn't resist a parting shot to show that he wasn't fooling anyone. As repayment for the picnic on her desk, she assigned him clock tour in New General. Checking to see if doors were locked and faucets tight wasn't a plum. But that night he nodded as if she'd done him a favor, which she inadvertently had, for the tour would afford him plenty of time to keep an eye on her. All he had to do was occasionally slip away to punch in at one of the clock locations; the rest of the time he could keep track of Gallagher without being missed by anyone. On his way to his first clock site, he saw Gallagher go into Medical Records, and he returned in plenty of time to catch sight of her striding purposefully down a hall leading away from Medical Records. Whatever was on her mind appeared important. He pursued.

Once he'd removed his hard-heeled boots and turned his belt-radio off, he found that tailing her down the tiled corridors of General Jack proved easier than following her on the street in his Cherokee. The halls were long and straight, with countless laundry bins, dietary carts, and doors to duck behind if his suspect turned. She didn't. Far too preoccupied to care about who might be skulking after her, she proceeded directly to Dr. Anthony Ellsworth's office where for an instant she became indecisive and surveyed the empty hallway behind her. Gavin had foreseen that move and stepped out of sight as soon as she paused. From his concealed position he heard her slide a master key into the lock and enter the arrested doctor's office.

That was when he felt a booster shot of adrenaline and knew he had her. If she stayed put long enough to get caught rifling through Ellsworth's papers, he definitely had her. He slipped away to the nearest phone and dialed Elizabeth Kavanaugh's home number, praying that he had Gallagher. At one-thirty in the morning, the man who answered wasn't overly civil, but Gavin insisted it was urgent. His conversation with the administrator was brief and to the point.

"She's in Ellsworth's office."

"Don't let her out," Kavanaugh said, as if he could lock her in.

When Kavanaugh arrived at the hospital twenty-three minutes after his phone call, she didn't look quite as put together as earlier but her mind was sharp as ever. "Is she still in there?"

"She is."

"Perfect. I'll handle it from here. You're along as my witness. Follow me."

When they opened the door to Ellsworth's office, Jan Gallagher was seated at the desk, a single brass light on as she sifted through a stack of patient folders high as her chin. Gavin had wanted her to look crushed or defeated or at least humiliated, but he was disappointed. Instead she acted almost relieved, as though she'd grown tired of wondering when they would arrive.

"You realize," Elizabeth Kavanaugh said, gloating so obviously that Gavin found it distasteful, "that you have absolutely no business being in this office or going through patient records. There are laws concerning confidentiality."

"Spit it out," Jan Gallagher said.

"I shouldn't need to, but if you insist. I'd say you're all through as the night shift supervisor. If you want to know the truth, I'm surprised you've lasted this long."

The way Jan Gallagher kept a stiff upper lip, Gavin couldn't take as much pleasure as he'd hoped in his victory. But at least the job was done. All in all, it'd been much easier than he'd anticipated. Gallagher had lasted a week and a day, and it looked as though Ellsworth was the murderer. Not that Gavin or anyone else would ever prove it. But at least he knew himself.

Later, after his shift had ended and all the reports had all their blanks filled in, he drove home feeling drained, but good. He slept, a wonderful, deep sleep void of dreams, only to be woken by the telephone. It was Delores.

"If what I'm hearing is right," she said, "there won't be any need for us to keep our date."

When he didn't respond, she said, "Well? Did you team up with Administration? I hear you caught your replacement doing what you would have done, if only you'd thought of it first."

When he still didn't answer, she said, "Don't bother calling me ever again, Gavin Larsen."

After she hung up, he mouthed into the dead line, "My pleasure." But it wasn't a satisfying feeling, and a strange impulse overtook him, an urge to call Delores back. That was a first. He didn't know what to make of it. He resisted but the temptation grew until he gave in and tried her number. Fortunately, the line was busy. Fifteen minutes later, the same. He didn't know what he'd say to her anyway, but suddenly it seemed so completely quiet and still out in his country retreat that he dug out a battery-powered transistor radio that he kept on hand for severe weather and turned it on just to hear another voice.

For the first time in his adult life he wasn't tickled to be alone. What it meant, he didn't know. Not yet. A distemper shot wouldn't have hurt though. He hoped to hell this wasn't some kind of midlife crisis that was going to turn him into a different man, a more social creature, some kind of balding party animal. The things that life put you through were unbelievable, and just when he thought he had everything all settled.

21

THEY promoted her. Early Friday morning, after the end of her shift, they convened in Administration's conference room B again, this time a more select, august group, one limited solely to Jan, the Little Admiral, Administrator Trainee Kavanaugh, and Executive Administrator Averilli. The room held the same flickering light, the cafeteria tray carried identical goodies, and the administrators continued to look as if they needed to be burped. Jan imagined she would have photographed something like MOST WANTED in the post office.

"This is serious," said the Little Admiral, bringing his considerable gravity to bear on the subject.

"If we choose to prosecute," the executive administrator pointed out, "there's no doubt you'd be found guilty."

"That would be the end of your career," Administrator Trainee Kavanaugh grimly predicted.

Jan smiled shamelessly and told them to do what they had to. Saying it made her feel like an extremely hard case, someone bound for a penitentiary, or worse, but she refused to knuckle under, although she didn't for an instant doubt that they would be vindictive enough to take this to court rather than slap her wrists. She did not apologize or say she was sorry or—best of all—explain her reckless actions. For the first time in a long string of days she felt good, as if accomplishing something worthwhile. What that could be was open to debate. Certainly she wasn't changing the county, nor could losing the luxury of a paycheck exactly be considered a victory. You didn't work at a public hospital like the General without knowing firsthand how far down the skids could take you. Yet she refused to cooperate and felt giddy because of it.

Much earlier that morning, in the middle of the night actually, Larsen and Kavanaugh had marched their prisoner from Dr. Ellsworth's office to Kavanaugh's, which was an unexpected cupboard space, an afterthought tucked under a stairwell. Kavanaugh had ordered Larsen to take over supervising Jan's crew and dismissed him. Then Jan and Kavanaugh went mano a mano for nearly an hour until the administrator trainee grew weary of bullyragging without results and dispatched Jan back to her job after a chilly notification that there would be a meeting first thing in the morning. For the most part, Kavanaugh succeeded in making the meeting sound ominous.

Returning to the guards' office, Jan had slammed the colorful containers of mold and freezer-burned food back into the fridge and decided that the only fitting response to what she'd just been subjected to was a return to Ellsworth's office to finish what she'd started. It struck her as doubtful that anyone would bother her a second time, and no one did. But she never located Lowell Asplund's medical record. So in some ways, she wasn't hiding anything she'd found, only what she hadn't. That made her refusal to reveal motive to the three administrators a matter of principle, which pleased her all the more.

"I hope you've thought long and hard about what could happen," the Little Admiral said.

"Of course," Roger Averilli said with compassion, "we're willing to forgive and forget. To chalk your enthusiasms up to inexperience. All you have to do is show that you intend to turn over a new leaf."

"Cooperate," said Elizabeth Kavanaugh, who by that late hour of the morning had shed all patience.

"Ask away," said Jan, curious to hear what they had on their collective mind.

The Little Admiral again became the designated interrogator. Leaning forward and resting his elbows on the table, his words marched ahead in close formation. "Why did you go to Ellsworth's office?"

"To see if I could learn what happened to Lowell Asplund."

"Who sent you?"

"No one."

"What were you looking for?"

"Anything of interest."

"What leads you to think there's a connection between Lowell Asplund and Dr. Ellsworth?" He was really bearing down on her now. Burning calories at a ferocious rate.

"It's no secret," Jan said, too fatigued to react incredulously to such simplicity. "Everyone's talking about it."

"Is that what the police think?"

"In particular a certain homicide detective?" Jan asked, throwing in a leading question of her own.

"If that's who you've been in communication with."

Averilli broke in to remind her kindly, "Our earlier offer still stands."

"Earlier?"

"To reinstate the secretary who was fired because of your indiscretions."

"I'm afraid there's really nothing I can contribute along that line," Jan said, her resolve firming up each time one of her accusers spoke. "But you've reminded me of another interesting topic."

"Which is?" Averilli indulgently asked.

"The matter of Dr. Ellsworth's malpractice suit."

A full-blown county stupor engulfed the room. Everybody forgot everything they'd ever known and many things they'd never known. The silly expressions of ignorance on their faces were dead giveaways that they'd lived through earlier meetings on this very topic. And Jan suddenly saw a path out.

To help their memories along, she said, "The suit that Dr. Croft was going to testify in unless Ellsworth resigned."

"We're not at liberty to discuss the matter," Averilli said with distaste, not bothering to ask which hole in the sieve had leaked her the information.

"But I am," Jan cautioned. "You might want to keep that in mind."

The three administrators exchanged hooded looks and shortly thereafter the kangaroo court was adjourned, although not before Jan was given instructions to take the weekend off to think about what she'd done. They would be in touch.

Both Saturday and Sunday it felt as though her punishment was to sit facing a corner. She whiled away the time squabbling with her family. She also found sufficient energy to repeatedly ask herself whether she should cooperate with them, or if it was too late for that, or if what they had here was a classic Jackson County case of live and let live. Whenever the phone rang, she shied away from answering it because of a catch lodged in her throat. Detective White called on Saturday, but she refused to talk to him, which was the one thing she did all weekend that Claire approved of. Finally, late Sunday afternoon the Little Admiral called. By then she was convinced that she would be dismissed but that wasn't the outcome at all. Effective immediately, she was promoted to a newly created position in charge of special projects for Security. It was then that she truly knew, deep in the marrow of her largest bones, that she worked for the county.

"I don't know if I can handle another promotion," she said into the phone.

"It's that or criminal proceedings."

Jan found enough voice to ask, "Why?"

"You can't very well sue us for a promotion, now can you, Gallagher?"

No, she didn't suppose she could. Nor—she was ashamed to say—did she want to bite the hand that fed her. Her refusal to admit why she'd rifled Ellsworth's office had lost its nobility after a weekend's worth of frank exchanges with Claire about why she wasn't at work. Jan refused to tell her mother the truth, and it didn't take long for the friction between them to wear thin any elation she'd felt over discovering she had some principles. By Saturday evening what she'd done simply seemed pigheaded. The practical matter of heating bills, and their ilk, soon assumed command of her thoughts. So she figured she might as well let them promote her out of harm's way, where they could keep an eye on her. A perfect county nonsolution. She was to start Monday morning at eight o'clock sharp, as Eldon Hodges felt obliged to say. Did she have any questions? When she didn't, the Little Admiral bid her good day with all the warmth of melting ice. Jan kept the news to herself and that night went to bed feeling bloated, as if she'd swallowed the entire county bureaucracy whole. Before lights out she updated Claire on her new assignment. Unwilling to go into what had happened, Jan explained it away as a scheduling thing. Nothing was a winner that day. Claire was positive Jan had arranged it so that she'd have her nights free to be with that man.

Sunday night she spent most of the time awake, staring upward into the darkness and wondering how she was going to cope with this latest humiliation. Everyone at work would automatically assume she'd been bumped upstairs because she couldn't hack her job. Why should she care if they thought less of her? She shouldn't. And wouldn't the new hours normalize her life? It would put her back into a sleep pattern with the rest of the world, which happened to include her family, who'd been put through quite enough this year. And being closer to Administration couldn't hurt. Could it? Maybe she'd learn something useful, like how to deep-six suggestions for improvements. So for once couldn't she cope by keeping her mouth shut? Unfortunately, none of these highly sensible excuses could hush the little recording that kept telling her she'd been bought, and quite cheaply too. When she woke from her half sleep on Monday morning, she didn't head out the door to work with her chin held high.

Dressed in her uniform, she arrived at Security's administrative office with Dr. Ellsworth's personnel folder, which she silently laid in the Little Admiral's pudgy hand. In return, she was assigned a desk that was wedged into the hallway across from the substitute secretary replacing Sheila. Her new duties involved updating Security's three procedure manuals. Pure make-believe work. The task was hopeless. Meanwhile, the substitute secretary, who didn't know how to type and had a poor phone voice, acted suspicious that Jan would eventually replace her. She shot several nasty looks across the front of Jan's desk, which protruded into the corridor, causing foot traffic to step lightly around it. The metal desk she'd inherited had surely been picked as an insult. It had been hauled up from storage, where no one knew how long it'd been in mothballs. The sole highlight of her new assignment was that she had a direct line of sight into the Little Admiral's office. It didn't take him long to close the door.

At midmorning Jan received a call which she had to take on the secretary's extension because her own desk didn't yet have one installed.

"New hours?" It was Detective White.

"Promoted," Jan tentatively said. Who might be listening in on their conversation was an unknown. Before the secretary had informed Jan of the call, she'd disappeared into the Little Admiral's cul-de-sac for a hushed conference.

"Did something bad, huh?"

"I can't really talk right now," she said, all disagreement and distance. She recognized it was an irrational impulse, but part of her blamed the detective for her promotion.

"Oh?" the detective said, managing to sound as though he inferred a great deal from the little she'd offered.

Not appreciating his attitude, she said, "Is there a reason you called?"

"To let you know that our mutual friend walked on Friday. I made a trip to the drugstore he visited, but it wasn't enough."

"So now what?"

"We try some other approaches."

Their conversation was interrupted by chimes in the background. The bells sounded nautical, like something from Annapolis.

"Where are you calling from?" Jan asked, glaring at the Little Admiral's closed door.

"My office."

"Not the deck of a ship?"

"The ship of justice."

"How poetic. The clock on that ship have chimes like we just heard?"

"Uh-uh. All electric here."

"Then I guess that was my supervisor calling. I'll have to go now. Oh, by the way, that question you asked? I couldn't find an answer anywhere."

"You looked?" he eagerly said.

"Oh yes."

"You're a rampaging contradiction, Gallagher. Maybe we can have a salad some time?"

"What happened to dinner?"

"I'm on a diet."

"That's good," Jan said, chuckling in spite of herself. "But not good enough. Maybe later."

Why she'd said that last bit, she told herself she had no idea, not that she believed such a line. But for now she had noses other than White's to consider, namely the Little Admiral's beak and how he was sticking it in her business. Wasn't it always the small detail that pushed her over the edge? She'd finally decided to sue for discrimination because the Little Admiral had made the mistake of telling her *Better luck next time.* She'd made her mind up about divorce number two after sitting through a meal without speaking a word to her husband. The road to divorce number one started with her husband ogling a high school carhop at a root beer stand. She'd asked Claire to move in with them after Tess, at age seven, said she was afraid to answer the door. And it was this latest invasion of her privacy—the Little Admiral eavesdropping on her conversation—that trashed any thoughts she had of dropping the matter of Dr. Croft's death and doing what she was told by higher-ups. She would take one last crack at deciphering what had happened to Dr. Croft, Lowell Asplund, and how the two might be connected.

The remainder of the morning was spent staring at the pages of convoluted, tortured syntax in the procedure manuals she was to update. She didn't actually read the words but scowled at them as if she was. Rather than reading she brainstormed on how to accomplish this miracle of drawing a line from Croft to Vanessa Asplund. All manner of ingenious, devious approaches occurred to her. Hiring an actor to make himself up as Croft and approach the Asplund woman. Kidnapping the woman and interrogating her until she broke down and confessed. But in the end, the simplest approach had the most to recommend it. She decided that if she could get her hands on a photo of Dr. Croft, showing it to Vanessa Asplund's co-workers and neighbors might produce the quickest results. Someone might recognize the man. If that happened, she would have connected the two of them outside the hospital and that could be major. If she could pin that down, she should be able to restore her good name and at the same time fumigate the carpeted halls of Administration with the truth.

Having decided on a course of action, she stood so abruptly that it startled the substitute secretary, who, when Jan apologized, squinted as if trying to deduce her ulterior motives. Without offering explanations, Jan walked down the line of offices to Public Relations where she requested a copy of the publicity photo they had on hand for Dr. Croft. The first clerk clucked her tongue as if she was kept busy all day with requests for Dr. Croft's photo. She referred Jan to a second clerk, who passed her on to a third pit bull, who instead of asking *why* Jan needed the picture, wanted to know *who* needed it. For an instant Jan considered fudging the truth and saying that she'd been sent by the security administrator, but the woman before her had a blood-hound's eyes that promised to run any answer to ground, so Jan confessed it was for herself, part of the ongoing investigation. Without another word, the senior clerk pulled out a folder, made a notation, and handed over a studio snapshot that showed a handsome Dr. Jonathon Croft in a white lab coat and dark tie gazing into the camera lens as if facing his one true love.

On the way back to her desk two voices jarred her out of her reverie over what had happened to the man in the photo she held. One voice was near frantic, the other controlling, and both were familiar. Bearing down on her were Executive Administrator Averilli and Dr. Ellsworth, whose frail face she couldn't imagine behind bars. Apparently the district attorney concurred with that judgment. Engrossed in their discussion, neither had yet noticed Jan's approach.

"What is being done about those nurses?" Ellsworth was insistently asking.

"That's a touchy . . ."

Averilli saw Jan ahead of them and tapped Ellsworth's shoulder so that he would notice too. As the men mutely filed past, Averilli smiled and nodded to indicate that Jan should carry on with her good work. Ellsworth stared straight ahead as if he didn't recognize Jan from their earlier session. Perhaps he didn't. There was a wobble to his eyes, his chin, his knees. The doctor appeared to be functioning at a level barely skimming the floor, one which was more consistent with his wife's appraisal of him than with his own view of himself. Seeing the two of them plotting together put some zip in Jan's step as she hurried once again out to the lobby pay phone. The woman on it ahead of her was telling someone on the other end that they'd found a kernel of corn in there and taken it out. Where *in there* was remained unspoken.

When Jan's turn on the phone came up, she dialed information for two numbers, Vanessa Asplund's and the Hillborough Clinic's, where the woman worked. Jan remembered the place of employment not because of a terrific memory but because a friend of her mother's had gone there to have the size of her ears reduced. Assuming that her quarry would be grieving over the loss of her father, she tried the home first. No answer. At the Hillborough Clinic the receptionist's cheery voice frayed when Jan made her request. "Vanessa Asplund?" Apparently Ms. Asplund's ears burned whenever and wherever she left a room. Thirty seconds later a voice came on the line, saying with suspicion, "This is Vanessa."

Jan cut off, returned to her desk, and informed the substitute secretary that something she'd eaten for breakfast wasn't agreeing with her. She was going to take some sick time. The secretary didn't make any get-well noises.

From General Jack, she drove directly to Vanessa Asplund's neighborhood, intending to avoid a second encounter with the bereaved daughter if at all possible. The prospect of a face-to-face meeting with a possible murderess made her twitchy. Besides, her impression of the woman had been that questions were better left unasked. Her answers only went at tangents to the truth, intersecting it occasionally enough to be confusing but not often enough to be revealing. Collect the proof, turn it over to White, let him do whatever he had to. Those were her best-laid plans.

One thing nagged though—the fact that Ms. Asplund hadn't taken the day off to grieve. It didn't bother Jan because she thought such behavior was insensitive. Exactly the opposite. If one of her parents passed on—to where she had no idea—she probably would deal with it by hiding out at work too. For the first time Vanessa Asplund had done something Jan understood.

Ms. Asplund's townhouse was near the epicenter of a subdivision whose structures were mirror images of each other, unfolding over and over, up one street and down the next. When White had driven, Jan hadn't paid much attention to their route. Now she tried to downplay the fact that she'd been so distracted on that first trip. The streets, which all bore the names of Parisian avenues, filed past with hypnotic regularity. Naturally the dwellers rebelled against such monotony by marking their small territories with flower beds, thorny shrubs, and antebellum bird feeders. None of it made much of a dent, though. Everything looked the same, déjà vu around every corner. Jan got lost twice on Rue de Rivoli before finally setting her sights on the purplish-red townhouse that was her destination. It was one of the few units that had taken the drastic step of painting over the lilac-blue siding that smothered every vertical surface for several square blocks. The contrast with the other townhouses connected to it was mildly garish.

Afraid that the warts on her aged Pontiac would scare people away from their doors, Jan parked out of sight on a cross street, Avenue Victor Hugo. Still, the results of her door-to-door canvassing were negligible. Even with the photo as an aid, no one recalled ever seeing Dr. Croft at Vanessa Asplund's, and one crusty, retired neighbor, the civil libertarian on the block, wanted to know what gave her the right to harass a fine girl like Vanessa. Moving from unit to unit as quickly as possible, she hoped to clear out well before her subject arrived home from work near five. She was about to cross Rue de Vouille to complete her circuit when a cranberry sedan, a Cadillac Seville, blocked the drive she walked down, and Jan had to fight against a strong urge to flee. The driver's window lowered, revealing Vanessa Asplund's stylish face and releasing a wave of jasmine perfume potent enough to cloak day-old death.

For several seconds Ms. Asplund stared at Jan's feet as if that was the center of her intelligence. She didn't blink or speak or, as far as Jan could tell, breathe. Her hair was stilled by hair-spray polymers, her eyelids were rimmed with heavy-handed purple lines, and the whites of her eyes were awash with sleepless red. When she spoke, she sounded mildly sedated.

"Was there something you wanted to ask me directly?"

Her gaze remained fixed on Jan's feet, which was unsettling enough for Jan to rather stupidly ask, "What are you doing here?"

Upon hearing Jan's voice, Vanessa Asplund lifted her eyes to Jan's chest. That was heavy work. "One of my neighbors called. I think I've a right to know what I'm suspected of. Wouldn't you agree?"

"Routine investigation," Jan said, regrouping. "That's all I can say."

"Isn't this harassment?" Vanessa Asplund asked, finally lifting her eyes to Jan's. Despite their fatigue, they were unwavering and horribly tranquil. Her voice contained a childish dutifulness that hinted at an unreasonable singlemindedness. "Will I have to file a complaint?"

"How well did you know Dr. Croft?" Jan asked, digging in.

"Haven't I already discussed that with you?" Her eyes lowered again.

"He was your father's physician too, wasn't he?"

"You're with the hospital, aren't you?" Vanessa Asplund mused aloud as she inspected the insignia of Jan's shoulder patch.

"As I understand it," Jan said, "Dr. Croft was originally in charge of your father's care. Did you agree with his treatment program?"

"Something tells me that you know I didn't."

"You preferred Dr. Ellsworth's approach?"

"Not likely. My father was Dr. Ellsworth's science project." A dreamy, sleepwalker quality carried her voice. "You may remember those from junior high. My father's been dead for nine months, and it's not until now that we're able to plan the funeral." She raised her eyes to Jan's again and asked with a frightening sincerity, "When do you think a person's dead?"

Jan inarticulately answered something awkward about the soul leaving.

"Ah," Vanessa Asplund said, as if Jan's answer provided much insight, "you're one of those. Well, I can guarantee that you know as much about it as any physician, probably more if Dr. Ellsworth is an example."

"Yet you had an affair with him," Jan said, refusing to be pulled along by any dark undertows.

"Does that make me a monster?"

"Did you see Dr. Croft after hours too?"

"Of course not," she said, dropping her eyes again.

"I've talked to Mrs. Ellsworth," Jan said. "I know she wasn't seeing Croft."

"Really?" Vanessa Asplund said, marginally surprised. Her every word sounded as though it contained equal parts of truth and lie.

"You told us she was."

"That's what the lady's husband reported."

"She didn't mention a divorce either," Jan said.

"Strange," Vanessa Asplund said, giving the impression she was referring to something entirely different. "It's all her husband can talk about."

"Are you planning on marrying him?"

"What could she be getting at," Vanessa Asplund asked herself out loud. Gazing upwards toward the flat gray sky, she said to Jan, "I think it's going to rain. I hope you don't get caught in it."

She drove off then, leaving Jan unable to avoid the impression that she'd been threatened. Or was that a lie too? If she had been threatened, Jan wasn't backing down, not with all the voices she had to answer to before getting to sleep at night. She continued knocking on doors right up to Vanessa Asplund's townhouse. No one added anything new.

As far as Jan could tell, Ms. Asplund paid no attention to her progress or exit, but she had to reevaluate that assessment when within fifteen minutes of her finishing the door-to-door work, a blue-black Mazda pulled into the red townhouse's drive. Jan viewed this latest development from a new position she'd taken up in her car after pretending to leave the neighborhood. The fact that Ms. Asplund had come running home when hearing of Jan's presence was intriguing, as was the veiled threat she'd delivered, although Jan had to admit that went beyond intriguing into the realm of unsettling. Now the new arrival—what could that mean? The man who climbed out of the sports car wasn't Dr. Ellsworth. Even from a block and a half away, Jan could identify that much. He was too rangy, too shaggy, too fashionable. Perhaps the brother? The townhouse's front door opened so quickly upon his approach that it appeared he'd been summoned, and that titillated her interest as well.

She had parked in front of a unit that appeared to harbor several teenage boys of driving age, a rambling wreck for each. Using the cars parked on the street for camouflage, she settled into her seat, thinking, Dear Diary, my first stakeout.

22

THE phone call from his sister couldn't have come at a worse time. He'd managed to once again reconcile his differences with his girlfriend, Tami, by making her see that with his father gone he truly was a man reborn. He'd had to speak from the previously uncharted depths of his soul for most of the weekend before Tami would buy that program. Now, on Monday afternoon, they cuddled on a low-backed sofa overlooking the doors that opened onto a lip of concrete that was supposed to be a fourteenth-floor balcony. Beyond the railing was a city park and clouds so low and heavy that he could smell their moisture. What finally convinced her of his sincerity was a proposal of marriage. He'd never tried that before. They were setting a date and drawing up wedding plans when the phone rang.

"Reginald," Vanessa said in her take-charge voice once he got on the line, "we're going to have to do it."

Since their father's death, she'd been acting as though her brother's life had a steering wheel to it, one that she was sitting behind. Do this. Do that. Then all of sudden she would shed all that breezy confidence and do something really unexplainable like break into tears on the way to view the remains of their old man. He'd had to wait in the parking ramp a solid fifteen minutes for her to compose herself. What that was about, he had no idea. He'd never seen her sprinklers work in twenty-eight years. Why now? Then just as abruptly she would switch back to ordering him around.

"Now Vanny . . ." he said.

"I want you over here right away. There's a self-promoting guard from the hospital showing a picture of Croft all around, wanting to know if anyone ever saw him."

"Nobody around there's seen Croft, have they?"

"What do you think? I introduced him to the neighbors?"

By then his fiancée's often-hurt blue eyes were watching him expectantly, apprehensive about her life going haywire again. He tried to reassure her with an all-knowing grin. If he was lucky, she bought about a third of it before going back to wanly leafing through a bridal catalog she happened to have lying around. As she flipped pages, she twisted a strand of her blond hair around a finger and concentrated on the pictures of gowns. Her face bore that special tunnel vision she had when life, particularly life with Reginald Asplund, refused to cooperate with her dreams.

"If she's asking questions about me and Croft," Vanessa was saying, "she's going to get around to you soon enough. So I think we've only got one option, little brother, and that's to solve the crime for everyone."

"Goddamn it," he said, recognizing too late that he was whining.

"I know you don't like it," said Vanessa. "I'm not thrilled either. But we knew it might come to this, so get over here.

The hospital woman's just left, and we've got to do it quick if we're going to do it at all."

His sister hung up on him. By then his bride-to-be had closed the catalog and was suffering concern verging on dread. He knew what that was all about. He'd reneged on every conceivable promise before, and she could see it unfolding all again. Here they'd gone so far as narrowing the bridesmaids' possible color down to wisteria or Vassar rose. She wasn't even the one who had wanted to plan everything right this minute, before his father's funeral, whenever that would be. The medical examiner had yet to finish all his tests. Planning the wedding now, that had been his brilliant idea. When she'd protested that it wasn't quite natural, he insisted, saying it would help get his mind off the bad stuff coming up if he had some good stuff to focus on. But now she was getting that hurt and abandoned fear in her eyes again, the look that nearly drove him buggy with longing to vanquish it.

"My sister," he said, helplessly stating the obvious. "She's really taking this business with the old man poorly. I'm going to have to go see her."

"Right now?"

"She's very upset. Look, this doesn't change anything. Believe me. We'll get through the funeral and everything will get back to normal, including Vanessa. But today I have to go see her. She's not doing too well. This can wait a few days, can't it?"

"That's what I thought in the beginning," she reminded him.

"I know. I know. Let's not fight, OK?"

She repented, taking his hand and saying, "That wouldn't be fair, would it? Do you want me to come? Maybe I can help."

That showed how much she cared. Tami and Vanessa couldn't stand each other.

"No, I think it's better if I handle this alone."

She pulled him closer as if to kiss his forehead but instead stared deep into his eyes. "You do whatever you need to. We can pick a color later."

He felt like the luckiest man alive then, living under a shining star that was the envy of the Milky Way. The sublime starlight lasted until he recalled that he'd just received marching orders from his sister. On the way over to Vanessa's townhouse he comforted himself with the thought that he wouldn't have to put up with this much longer.

Wearing a white satin bathrobe, Vanessa met him at the door before he could even ring the bell. She looked as though she'd just gotten back from the taxidermist. Petrochemicals held her hair in place and her eyes were glassy. She even smelled of varnish, although that may have been hair spray. The heaviness of her makeup made her a quick decade older, possibly two, a shock he could have forgone.

Inside, the first thing he noticed was that she had collected all the mounds of fashion and stuffed them somewhere out of sight. The only piece of furniture covered with any clothing was a damask wing chair supporting the fine black suit that they'd selected from their father's closet for his funeral. It was the suit his father had worn whenever entering big-time negotiations. The black of a judge's robe, his father had always said of the suit. Its seams had been hand-stitched by London's finest Italian tailors. The way Vanessa had it resting in the chair, sleeves on the armrests, Oxford shoes positioned in front of it on the floor, the suit looked as though the first rays of daylight had recently turned the occupant to dust.

While avoiding the funeral suit and puzzling over the aberration in his sister's normal housekeeping routine, he heard a tiny mewing. From around the corner of a sectional sofa staggered a six-week kitten, a ginger tabby no different from the one he'd years before brought home without his father's permission. He had a sudden flash of the galvanized bucket filled with water and set at the center of their old living room, followed by an image of Vanessa's teenage hand lowering that earlier kitten into the water, followed by the feel of his father's hand holding him by the scruff, forcing him to watch. The memory sickened Reginald and sent him hurtling to the toilet.

"What the hell are you doing with that thing?" he asked through the bathroom door.

"I've always wanted one," she petulantly said. "What's wrong with you?"

"Allergic reaction."

"So I'll put him away. Now get out here."

Once he was done in the bathroom and the cat was locked away in the utility room, Vanessa brewed him a cup of tea, sat him down in the dining room at the parquet table, which he hadn't seen for months because of the heaps of sweaters normally stored there, and handed him a pair of surgical gloves.

"Put these on."

He did so without asking why. After the cat and the laying out of the suit, he'd rather not know why she did any of what she did. It felt as though he was about to take a cross-continental night trip with a perfect stranger. As far as he was concerned, the less he knew about her the better. Wearing gloves herself, his sister rolled a piece of paper out of a portable typewriter at the other end of the dinner table and handed it to him.

"Read this," she ordered. "The gloves are so you don't leave any fingerprints."

The paper had two neatly typed paragraphs:

There was a time when I took my physician's oath with great seriousness. Today, my actions no longer allow me that privilege. Before I take leave of this world, I wish to confess that my hand was behind the deaths of both Dr. Jonathon Croft and Lowell Asplund: Dr. Croft because he threatened to expose me as the charlatan I now know myself to be; and Lowell Asplund because I carelessly administered an over-dose, more in an attempt to redeem my faith in myself than an effort to treat my patient.

To my colleagues I leave my behavior as an example of the road not to take. Being a physician requires more character than knowledge. To my wife and family I leave my underesti-mated love. I now find that I am unable to live with the moral consequences of my actions.

He read it once and pushed it away with a fingertip. "It puffs up like your doctor, all right. But you'll never get him to sign it."

"We won't have to, as long as he handles it and leaves prints."

"And you think the cops will buy that?" he said, disbelief thickening his voice.

"Daddy says they will, as long as they can't prove anything else."

"Jesus, Vanny." He looked away as if in pain. "What do you have to talk like that for?"

"If you don't have the stomach for this . . ." she threatened, leaving unsaid what would happen if he didn't.

"He's been talking to you?" he said, looking back, wanting to make sure he'd heard right. "He hasn't been talking to me. Think about that a minute, huh?"

"What have you done to deserve it?" his sister asked, completely serious.

"He always hated you a little less," he said, testy. "Is that it?"

"None of that matters," she answered, rising above sibling rivalries. "We're talking about saving ourselves now, not him. We've done what we could for him. But if you let up now, Daddy probably *will* start talking to you."

"He's dead," Reginald said with a shiver.

"You want to try your luck and find out?"

No, crazy as it sounded, and he thought maybe it did
sound insane, he didn't want that. Ever since the deed had
been done, moments had crept up on him when he felt positive his father was about to join him. In the bathroom, shav-
ing, he kept having to glance over his shoulder to make sure
he was alone. Think about that. No, he didn't want to think
about that.

"I'm going to call Ellsworth now," Vanessa said, taking
her brother's silence as acquiescence, "and get him over here.
I want you around in case there're any problems."

"Problems?"

"Who knows. He's not exactly the sturdiest piece. When
they let him out of jail on Friday, he called and told me we
couldn't see each other anymore, then begged for my forgiveness."

"What'd you tell him?" Reginald asked, lightening up at
the thought of some other man becoming a quivering lump
of flesh before his sister.

"That I couldn't live without him, of course. That I was
devastated."

"And what if he won't cooperate?" Reginald asked. He
recognized the way his sister was watching him, and he didn't
like her commanding expression one bit.

"Then you get to spook him," she said, poking his biceps
with a fingernail.

"That's what I figured," he said. "What's Dad say about
that?"

"That it'd be good for you."

On the phone his sister remained the champion. She caught
Ellsworth at his hospital office, and although Reginald could
only hear one side of the conversation, that was enough.

"This is your mistress, Anthony. I'm going to take an
overdose . . . It is necessary. You don't care anymore."
Vanessa managed to sound utterly devastated while at the
same time examining her nails.

A long interval followed during which Ellsworth must have pleaded his case. Bored, Vanessa made a silent, jawing motion at the phone.

"Anthony," she said loudly enough to interrupt, "I don't care about the police. I can't go on. I'm leaving a note explaining what we've done . . . Of course your name will be in it. You were involved, weren't you? . . . I don't want to talk to you . . . No, I won't meet you there . . . I've changed my mind. I will not sign the consent forms for any treatments you gave him . . . You're just saying that to stop me. It didn't sound as though you loved me this afternoon . . . That's true . . . Y-e-s . . ." She was letting him convince her. "If you've something that important to tell me, come over here . . . After dark if you're afraid of being seen. You can park in the garage, no one will see a thing."

She hung up and gave her brother one of those long, appraising looks that made him feel disposable.

"Do you think you can handle him?" she asked.

"No Vanny, I don't. Maybe you'd better."

"He's got something on his mind," she said, without paying attention to her brother's excuses. "He's coming over, but I've got my doubts he's going to want to drink with us."

She started toward the kitchen, stopped when she saw he wasn't automatically following, and beckoned him onward with a single finger, acting as if she knew some big secret about why he didn't want to come. Once in the kitchen, she opened a cupboard drawer and from under some tightly woven place mats lifted out a chrome-plated pistol that was almost big enough to require wheels to move it around. She set it on the counter between them and gave it a spin.

"What's that?" he said, not meaning to come across as simple as he sounded.

"You should only have to point it at him," she matter-of-factly answered.

"You know I hate those goddamn things."

"Grow up, little brother. You're not going to have to

shoot anybody. God, that's the last thing we want. In fact, you'll have to be extra careful not to hurt him. Broken bones or unexplained holes wouldn't go too well with our note, now would they?" She condescendingly patted him on the shoulder. "Don't worry about a thing. We're not in this alone, I can tell you that."

He preferred that she didn't elaborate on that theme. He had a good idea about who she thought was in it with them.

As usual, waiting with his sister had all the allure of marking off calendar days until parole. They had several hours to occupy until Ellsworth's after-dark arrival, and once Reginald had hustled his car out of sight around the corner and backed Vanessa's Seville out onto the street, so that the doctor could pull directly into the garage, there really wasn't much to do. After Vanessa mixed a special concoction that was intended to calm the doctor's tired nerves once and for all, there wasn't anything to do. Reginald spent the time avoiding any contact—including eye contact—with the gun, which lay exactly where his sister had placed it.

"Let's build a fire," Vanessa said on a whim. The astonishment on her brother's face prompted her to add, "In the fireplace, idiot."

Without the slightest chill to the humid air, he had a strong hunch where her impulse came from. Their father had often built a fire on wintery nights, then forced them to assemble in front of it and pretend to be a family. Reginald refused to cooperate with this fantasy, but his sister went ahead on her own. Once flames were crackling, she turned the central air on high and pulled the wing chair supporting the funeral suit close to the hearth, positioning it where their father had always resided.

Out of the blue, Vanessa said, "I might have my nose put back the way it was."

"What's gotten into you?"

"A sense of what we've missed," she said after some deliberation. A faraway look settled over her eyes. The distance wasn't across land but time. She spoke in a simple, unadorned voice that welled up on those rare instances when she was being truthful with herself—as truthful as she could be.

Other than several phone calls from their mother, who kept changing her mind about attending the funeral, the only interruption was a call from his fiancée, which he took in the bedroom for privacy. Returning to the living room, he didn't mention his engagement because his sister was busy piling birch logs on the fire and whispering to someone in the wing chair, which was empty except for the suit. After that, Reginald waited in the kitchen, sitting as far away from the pistol as possible. He'd been frightened to death of firearms ever since age sixteen when he'd almost shot his father, who was tossing clay pigeons aloft. In the long run, he might have improved everyone's quality of life if he had blown the old man away, but even now, with his father actually gone, he could barely bring himself to think it.

"What should I wear?" Vanessa called out at one point. They were the first words they'd spoken in over an hour.

"Something black," he said from the kitchen's growing shadows.

"Oh, you're a big help."

He heard her traipse back to her bedroom to try on ensembles. A half hour later he checked in and saw outfits stacked high on the bed. With Vanessa talking to herself, he edged away before understanding any of her monologue. She was still rambling on in the bedroom when Ellsworth pulled into the garage.

"Vanessa," Reginald stage-whispered before the doctor cut his motor. "Get out here."

He had to steady his right hand with his left before he was able to pick the pistol up and tuck himself away next to an antique hutch filled with Wedgwood and positioned a few feet left of the door leading to the attached garage. Through the wall at his back he heard the doctor trip over something, then heard the garage-door motor click on and rollers start clacking. The door leading into the house soundlessly swung inward as their caller inched none too eagerly into the kitchen, which was dark except for the glow of the fireplace from the next room. The doctor steadied something in front of himself with both hands. The something had the dimensions and pointed nature of a gun. That made two of them in one small room, statistics that cooled the sweat on the back of Reginald's neck.

"Vanessa?" the doctor called out with a noticeable lack of confidence.

From the hallway came a series of small rustling sounds that made first Reginald and then the doctor crouch.

Without warning, the black funeral suit appeared in the doorway leading to the living room. His sister was in it. At least Reginald vowed to himself that as far as he was concerned, Vanessa was the only person who could be in it. She'd pulled her hair back tightly, making the outline of her head mannish, and she'd put on gold-framed eyeglasses—his father's bifocals—whose bows shined in the scant firelight. The suit sagged at her shoulders and bunched up at the waist. She'd slipped on her father's shoes too, which explained her shuffling steps. Her small feet would have lifted out of the oxfords otherwise. When she spoke, a commanding quality in her voice reminded Reginald of his father. But the voice belonged to his sister. He kept telling himself that.

"Come here, Anthony," was all that she said.

"Geez," Ellsworth said, not sounding particularly learned. "Don't frighten me that way." He straightened but didn't lower his gun. "What are you wearing?"

"Why, Anthony," Vanessa said, stepping closer and choosing to ignore his question, instead focusing on the gun, "it appears that great minds really do think alike."

"Let's try to contain ourselves," the doctor weakly answered.

Shuffling forward another step, Vanessa calmly said, "Reginald, now."

Reginald couldn't budge, and even if he could have, it wouldn't have been forward. The farther his sister advanced into the room, the less certain he was of her identity. The doctor could move, though. When she first said her brother's name, Ellsworth flinched as though expecting to be struck. Then, when nothing happened, he moved backward, away from Vanessa, as he warned, "I'm not a dunce."

"Are you planning on killing me?" she asked, sounding as though it was a truly fascinating notion.

"I want to calm you down," Ellsworth said evasively. "Help you through this ordeal. The police can't prove anything with your father. I've taken care of that. We just don't want to give them any reason to keep investigating. Maybe sometime later we can start seeing each other again."

"But you are pointing a gun at me," she said.

Reginald told himself no more foolishness and steeled himself for the next time Vanessa told him to move. His right hand, braced by his left, was pointing the pistol at Ellsworth's spine, or what there was of it.

"Vanessa," the doctor said, unsuccessfully trying to establish a bedside manner, "you didn't sound rational on the phone. And it has occurred to me that there's every chance you're responsible for Dr. Croft's expiration, so of course I brought something to protect myself." She started to respond, but he cut her off. "I'd rather not know what you've done. I've enough trouble sleeping as is."

"Reginald," Vanessa said, more insistent, "now."

It still didn't feel like moving day to him. A little invisibility could have gone a long way.

"All I want you to do," Ellsworth explained, ignoring her commands to her brother as if they were delusional, "is take a few sedatives."

"Reginald!"

He saw his sister's mouth moving but could barely hear the

words. It'd often been like that with his father. The orders coming faster and faster but him unable to hear them. With something dark and bottomless opening up in his mind, he lurched forward, jabbing his pistol into Ellsworth's lower back. The doctor instinctively jerked his hands upward, discharging his gun toward the ceiling, then dropping it in surprise at the recoil. The sound of the gunshot boomed so painfully in Reginald's ears that at first he thought he'd been hit. He clasped Ellsworth in a bear hug, lifting and squeezing until he felt Vanessa clawing at him while shouting, "Don't bruise him." Opening his eyes, he saw his sister—no one else—holding the doctor's gun and so released his hold. The single shot had punctured the ceiling paneling without drawing any blood.

"Sit him down," Vanessa ordered, actually sounding concerned about the way Ellsworth was doubled over and gasping for breath. "I'll get him something to drink."

He righted a chair that Ellsworth had kicked over in their struggle and pulled his catch to it. The doctor crowded its edge, holding his side and watching Reginald with a bewildered look that was more wretched than dangerous. Cautiously, Reginald sniffed the barrel of his pistol and was relieved to smell nothing. Until then he hadn't been absolutely sure but that he might have fired too and nicked the doctor, which would have explained some of Ellsworth's discomfort.

After a few labored breaths, Ellsworth secretively asked in a low voice, "Your sister's not doing too well, is she?"

It wasn't as though Ellsworth was trying to talk his way out of anything. A fatalistic ring had captured his words. No, it was more as if he was asking a colleague for a second opinion.

"She's doing better than me," Reginald assured him.

The answer undid what little was left of the doctor's spirit. He tried to speak but couldn't. He strained to turn his head away but couldn't manage that, so worked at shifting his eyes, but they kept drifting back to Reginald. In the end, he had to satisfy himself with half closing his eyelids for a few seconds. When his eyes popped open, he wet his lips and tried speaking again, asking nonsensically, "Did you ever want to be a doctor? When you were growing up?"

Before Reginald could say that the possibility had been second on his list, right after race-car driving, Vanessa returned with a crystal decanter, holding it in both hands like an offering. She'd left the doctor's gun in the other room.

"This should help," she said, full of encouragement.

She set a heavy-bottomed glass on the kitchen counter and filled half of it with expensive whiskey.

"What about us?" the doctor asked in an forlorn voice while examining the drink out of the corner of his eye.

Vanessa smiled the way their father had when assuring the losing side that they'd just made one hell of a smart deal. That was all the answer she provided.

"If I refuse?" the doctor asked, his voice nearly nonexistent.

"That's not an option, Anthony."

"But what do you gain?"

"Inner peace," Vanessa said, shaking her head as if he should have known.

"You can't make me." The child.

"My brother would make it very painful for you," Vanessa promised with more certainty than Reginald felt. "He'd probably start with fire."

"Coat hangers," Reginald blurted, not liking the idea of singed flesh but not exactly sure what he'd accomplish with coat hangers either. When the doctor stared at him as if he didn't understand, Reginald pointed to his inner ear and said, "I'd start with coat hangers."

"First coat hangers," Vanessa said, standing corrected. "Then fire. Both painful, Anthony, believe that if you've ever believed me."

Nodding rapidly to show that he didn't doubt a word of it,

Ellsworth picked up the glass to study its contents. His lower lip quivered as he assured Reginald's sister, "I would never have done this to you."

"Are you going to make a scene, Anthony?"

"I don't want to . . ." He couldn't finish saying what he didn't want to do.

"I thought we were all adults here, Anthony."

"I always wanted to be a doctor," Ellsworth ruefully commented, going off in a direction that didn't make any sense to Reginald, although his sister was matching the man stride for stride.

"I know," Vanessa said, suddenly full of understanding. Stepping closer, she moved a sprig of hair off his forehead and lightly kissed him there. "And you've done very well, but if you want to go with any dignity, now's the time. My brother's the impatient type."

Reginald fulfilled his part of the bargain by vigorously rubbing his upper arms and looking generally intolerant of further delays.

Ellsworth tried speaking but again lost his voice. His hand started wobbling violently, and he struggled to avoid glancing at it and Reginald but couldn't resist a peek at both. Vanessa's strong fingers helped the doctor steady his hold on the glass and guide it to his lips without spilling any. She kept tilting the glass up even as Ellsworth tried to turn his mouth away without success. Then something snapped inside the man. Reginald could see the resistance receding from his eyes, replaced by a kind of second sight that brought back his arrogant self, the part of himself trained to pretend that he knew what he was doing no matter how lost. The liquor flowed past his bluish lips and an expression verging on angelic relief overtook the doctor's thin face. He drained the glass in one gulp, almost as an afterthought. He gagged but kept it down.

"Again," Vanessa immediately said, watching closely,

never wanting to forget a glorious moment of it. She poured even as he coughed.

Once he'd caught his breath, Ellsworth shook his head, giving the impression he didn't quite comprehend what he saw before himself. He muttered a toast, "To Hippocrates," that seemed to be offered to someone standing behind them. Vanessa spun around to look, acting disappointed upon finding no one. The doctor swallowed the second glass of liquor in stages, leaving the impression of savoring quality stock. It went down much more smoothly.

"And again," she said, thrilled with his efforts. She carefully dabbed a spill off the doctor's chin with a napkin. "Reginald, get Anthony's note, would you? And don't forget the gloves."

Reginald obliged without discussion, eager to escape the room. On the way he gratefully handed Vanessa his gun. By the time he'd pulled the rubber gloves on and returned with the slip of paper, the doctor was slumped on the chair, the glass again empty. Vanessa handed Ellsworth his suicide note and asked him to read it out loud, which the doctor did, slurring words and having to stop frequently toward the end to regain his focus. But basically the phrasing sounded quite natural lifting off his lips. When finished, he laughed pitifully and said, "Very nice," before passing out and crumpling sideways to the floor where he lay blinking and trying to focus on the end of his nose.

"Why and the hell are you wearing that suit?" Reginald demanded of his sister.

"He asked me to."

All his questions dried up after that.

Near midnight they folded Ellsworth onto the front seat of the Saab, curled up so that he wouldn't be visible unless you stood next to the passenger door and looked down. By then Reginald had to concentrate to detect the doctor's feeble pulse. After carefully tucking the suicide note in the doctor's breast pocket, Reginald left first, as always drawing the dirty work and driving the Saab. He was to deliver the victim and his car to Pilot Hill, one of Ellsworth's favorite views of the city. Still wearing his surgical gloves, Reginald drove well within traffic laws and hoped his sister was coherent enough to do likewise.

"Seat belt fastened?" he asked the doctor. No possibility of an answer from Ellsworth, but talking at least made Reginald feel normal, as if he was driving a drunk home. That charade helped more than he cared to admit.

When he checked his mirror to make sure Vanessa was where she was supposed to be—behind him—he saw her Seville tailgating so closely that she would be lucky to avoid rear-ending him before they were done with this errand. Then something else caught his eye, a shadow approximately a block behind Vanessa's car, a dark spot speeding beneath a street light. That was when he grew extremely serious about his driving.

Accelerating to St. Cyr, the first main thoroughfare, he came to a complete stop before turning right. This wasn't any time for a traffic violation, not with Ellsworth transmigrating from the seat next to him to some place new and untroubled.

Once onto the four-lane boulevard, Reginald nailed his gas pedal until reaching the speed limit of forty-five. Vanessa did likewise, flashing her high beams at him to show that she didn't appreciate the hot-rodding. At the moment, he didn't care about her opinions or the opinions of any deceased person she might be communing with. A block and a half back, a car duplicated their maneuvers, flicking on its head-lights once in traffic and doing its more-than-capable best to keep up. God, Reginald's heart started flopping. The thoughts in his head made a chunk-chunk-chunk sound as if his mind was broken and slowing fast. He poked the doctor's shoulder.

"You bring someone with you?"

Ellsworth barely groaned.

St. Cyr was a street of commerce, including everything from muffler repair to margaritaville, so even past midnight traffic remained heavy. Lane changes and pushing the edge of the speed limit didn't alleviate his fears. The car behind him, a four-door sedan, kept pace, trying to screen itself from sight whenever possible and hanging far enough back to prevent clear identification. Finally, Reginald abruptly swerved off onto the empty drive of a closed service station, almost losing his sister, who followed with a squeal of tires and brakes. As Vanessa turned in a tight semicircle so that she could approach his driver's window, he caught a glimpse of the older sedan, a Pontiac, before the driver could change lanes and put a city bus between them. The woman driver was wearing a white top, a uniform of some sort, and she'd been keenly interested in them until she caught sight of him returning her gaze.

Pulling up next to his window, Vanessa demanded, "What are you trying to do, you little fool?"

"We're being followed."

"Nonsense."

"It's a woman," he said, craning forward to see what the Pontiac would do, but Vanessa's car blocked his view. "Dark hair, a white top that looked like a uniform. Maybe the one from the hospital?"

"That was this afternoon," Vanessa said, her confidence slipping.

"You're sure she left before you called me?"

"Of course I am," she snapped. But she added reluctantly, "Maybe she came back."

Her growing uncertainty began to feed his. "So what are we going to do?"

"First . . . we'd better settle down," she said, sounding as if repeating instructions. "What's she seen?"

"Only me," he sneered. "Driving a soon-to-be-dead guy's car."

"OK," she said, ignoring his sarcasm and speaking slowly,

piecing everything together. "True. We're going to have to do something about that. If we split up, can you lose her?"

"Say I do, then what?"

"Well, we can't very well let Anthony be found until we know what she knows. So we hold on to him for a while. Do you think she's alone?"

"As far as I could tell."

Vanessa paused in that new way she had of hesitating, the way that said she was listening attentively to someone Reginald couldn't hear. Her confidence returned and she said, "Then I say we split up and meet back at my place. If she follows me, I'll take her sightseeing before I head home. You park the Saab in my garage—you've got keys, right?—and be ready to follow her in your car. If she goes after you, lose her—make sure of that—then head to my place and we'll wait for her to show up. If I know anything about women, she'll be back."

"What are you thinking of doing to her?"

"Little brother," she said, turning carefree, "the night is young."

As she pulled away, heading back the way they'd come, his sister looked haggard as someone driving home to a cemetery after a hard night of fluttering. With a shudder, he watched traffic for a half minute but no one followed Vanessa, which meant he was up. Edging back onto St. Cyr, he trolled along until spotting the Pontiac hiding behind a McDonald's kiddyland. The chase was short-lived. He made sure of that. Within half a mile a small gap in the oncoming traffic offered the chance he wanted, and he made a sharp left turn across the opposite lanes, shooting onto a side street. Brakes and horns, but no glass or metal. By the time traffic thinned enough for his shadow to turn, the Pontiac was history. He wheeled down quiet lanes and across a school parking lot with his lights off. Within minutes he had parked the Saab in his sister's garage. Vanessa stepped out of the house, saying,

"Now we get in your car and play a little hide-and-seek of our own."

"What's that you're holding?" he asked.

"Anthony's gun."

"Not that. In your other hand."

"Just a nylon stocking," she said, sounding as if it was nothing.

He'd heard that nothing voice of hers before and knew it was something—something that usually involved him, something he'd rather not think about.

Part Four

23

FTER the green Saab ditched her, Jan streaked on for several blocks, straining to catch sight of taillights, or reflections of taillights, flicking around a corner. Every intersection was empty, though, void of all but streetlamps and layered shadows on neat suburban lawns. With a death grip on the steering wheel, she raced down parallel side streets to more of the same. A quarter hour later she punched the horn in frustration, gave up, and returned to Vanessa Asplund's where she found the Seville now parked in the drive but the Mazda no longer installed around the corner on Avenue Victor Hugo. No Saab, either. After some basic cursing, she pointed her wreck home, announcing to herself that the investigation had officially ended for the day. It was after midnight and time to angle for bed before her mother called the governor to request the state militia be sent into the streets to find a missing mother of four.

What might be the strangest part of the evening then commenced. On the way back she felt centipede legs on the back of her neck, as though she was the one being followed. She drove on without subterfuge, refusing to cave in and check the trailing traffic. This was one rich vein of cop paranoia, which she'd often enough witnessed her second ex display, that she didn't intend to tap into. Her only stop on the way back was at a twenty-four-hour service station where she asked for the key to the women's rest room.

The lights—all of them—were burning up kilowatts at home, as if to help guide her in. With an unfamiliar Buick station wagon parked in front of her house she pulled into her garage and headed toward her own door with a sense of dread that rivaled the fright she'd experienced while chasing the Saab. Before she was halfway to the front steps, the door opened and her family's five faces crowded the frame. Mostly they looked relieved, but worried too, and one pinched face, her mother's, condemned her without needing to hear her story. Over the years Claire had collected a large number of explanations, and in all that time she'd never varied her initial response.

"Where have you been?"

"Something came up," Jan said, falling into the old patterns herself.

"You couldn't have called?"

Leah, her oldest, was openly reveling in the tightening of the screws on her mother, who had imparted so much wisdom of the ages to her concerning boys, drugs, and growing up fast. Amy was wearing her Girl Scout sash and outscowling Claire, if that was possible. Katie, all smeary-eyed because she'd been into her older sister's mascara, leapt out of the pack to hug Jan around the waist and say, "This is *it.*" What exactly she meant went unexplained. Tess, the youngest, put everything into perspective by proudly announcing, "We called the cops."

"You what?"

"You're eight hours late," Claire stated. "Of course I called the police. What did you expect me to do?"

"All right," Jan said, irked about the sudden squall of guilt beneath her sternum, "I should have called, but I thought I was on to something big and couldn't get to a phone."

"I'd like to hear about it," a male voice casually said from deeper in the house, a rather familiar male voice at that. The law-and-order, big-city-cop voice of Detective White.

"I wouldn't," Claire said, touchy. "I don't want to hear another word about that job of yours. It's making you crazy, just crazy." Turning with a flourish, she clapped her hands and ordered, "Everyone to bed. The show's over."

The chorus of groans and complaints greeting that announcement was predictable, but for the doomed there was no reprieve. Jan herded them inside, promising to provide complete news coverage of her whereabouts for the last eight hours when she tucked them in. The grousing and pleas for leniency quickly diminished as the girls retreated across the living room where Detective White sat with a saucer and cup balanced on his knobby knee. The detective, who was dressed in jeans and moccasin loafers and a plaid shirt unbuttoned at the throat to reveal a single-ply gold chain that belonged on a sunbelt Romeo, didn't act as though he could be budged out of the living room as easily as her daughters. He bid each of the girls good night and received politely worded replies from three of them, Leah alone holding out and departing with an upturned nose.

Once the adults were alone, Claire took the same proper posture on the love seat as several days before when she'd intended to evacuate the premises because of her daughter's supposed involvement with a man, a homicide detective. Now that same detective set his cup and saucer down on the worn brown carpet and smiled conspiratorially at Claire.

Before checking the bedroom hallway and closing the doors to the girls' rooms, Jan slipped her mother a look that was scorching as any she'd ever sent winging. Returning to the living room, she repositioned the spring rocker away from the TV and toward the last two people in the suburb, maybe the entire metropolitan area, she wanted to talk to at the moment.

"Making house calls?" Jan asked the detective. It wasn't a friendly question. She couldn't forget who'd helped her bad judgment along, resulting in her promotion at work and Sheila's unexpected opportunity to return to school. To Claire, she disparagingly added, "This is the police you called?"

"I thought he might know what was going on," Claire said, not about to be shamed.

"I didn't," the detective clarified. "Other than that you're not the only person involved in this fiasco who's been reported missing."

"There're others?" Jan immediately asked.

"That," Claire said, turning uppity, "can wait. I want an explanation. I think I deserve one."

"Yes," White said, artfully siding with Claire, "first let's hear about your night."

Jan sized up the playing field and weighed whoppers. She didn't appreciate the way the detective acted as if about to be entertained, nor did she feel like swallowing Claire's holier-than-thou posturing. Yet if she wanted to salvage something from the night, she might require the detective's help. And she wanted to play fair with her mother, who was toiling ceaselessly to come to grips with global warming trends— namely, the way her daughter's life kept heating up.

"Mother," Jan said, resigning herself to the need for an explanation, "the reason I'm working days is that I got a promotion that's a demotion."

"I'm sure that makes perfect sense somewhere," Claire said. "But not here."

"I'll fill you in on the details later," Jan said, still unwilling to reveal to the detective his involvement in her downfall up. "You'll have to trust me, OK?"

Claire acted dubious, to say the least.

The detective gravely asked, "This wouldn't be connected to that little favor I asked, would it?"

"No," Jan obstinately said.

The detective and Claire exchanged a cozy glance that showed how much they'd been conversing and what's more made it appear that they'd reached some limited tactical agreements about their one mutually shared interest—Jan. Seeing them on the same side further ripened Jan's mood and made her determined to be unreasonable. There were enough predictable people congesting the lanes of the world, more than enough.

"All that matters," Jan tartly said, "is that I thought I had a chance to show several people that I was capable of performing my job."

"That again," Claire said, her tone dismissive.

The detective said nothing, probably because he didn't want to upset his newly formed alliance with Claire, probably also because he knew it would all come tumbling out if only he waited. He wore that what-canary expression common to cartoon cats. Jan immediately decided to do what she could about that.

"I thought," Jan resolutely continued, "that I might be able to prove what happened to that doctor who died down at work. You remember him?"

"That's my job," White cautioned, making a slow-down kind of expression. "I wouldn't want us to get confused about that."

"That's a first," said Jan. The quip received only a blunt stare from White, so she continued. "I mean, I haven't exactly noticed you shying away from my help before now."

"Listen, Gallagher," White said, resorting to an infuriating protectiveness, "maybe I don't want you getting hurt.

What I do want is for you to tell me what you've been doing tonight. I think that's what your mother wants too. In case you hadn't noticed, you're dealing with dangerous people here."

"You're going to tell me who else is missing?" Jan asked, snubbing the detective's attempts at chivalry, if that's what they were. He could have simply been acting out of some coplike instinct to protect and control. Either way, his efforts weren't appreciated, nor was Jan enamored of the silent way Claire was nodding in agreement with everything he said.

"I'll tell you," White succinctly said, not liking it.

"All right, then," Jan answered, satisfied. She went on to describe her trip to Vanessa Asplund's neighborhood with Croft's picture, the way Ms. Asplund rushed home upon learning of Jan's door-to-door campaign, and the kind of veiled threat she delivered that made Jan suspicious enough to linger on and see what would happen. White grumbled deep in his throat. Jan continued unruffled, gathering speed as she described how within minutes of her pretending to leave the neighborhood, a man arrived, forcing her to stay.

"That's why you didn't call?" Claire said, belittling the entire story.

But White now took her more seriously, saying, "Describe the guy."

"Tall, dark shoulder-length hair. He was thin, but muscular, and drove a dark blue Mazda, one of those sports jobs."

"So she was visited by her brother," White said, relaxing as though he'd been anticipating the description of a different party. "That's who it sounds like. There's nothing criminal in that."

"There's more," Jan said. "They moved their cars out onto the street. The man hid his around the corner."

"Sounds sinister," said White.

Jan refrained from wrinkling her nose at him and said, "Then they started a fire in the fireplace."

"This time of year?" White asked, dropping his sarcastic

tone. The observation clearly intrigued him, and he rubbed his chin as though trying to figure out what they might have needed to burn.

"I could see smoke and smell burning wood," Jan said. "That's all they did that I know of until it was dark enough to stop me from seeing too many details. Then another car arrived. It pulled directly into the garage and they lowered the door behind it. You know anybody involved with this case who drives a dark green Saab?"

"News to me," White said with a slow shrug of his massive shoulders. "But I haven't exactly been paying attention to who's driving what."

"With all that sitting," Claire complained, making a wringing motion with her hands, "you couldn't have slipped away to a phone?"

"Mother, how could I know that something wouldn't have happened in the few minutes I was gone?"

To her credit, Claire reluctantly saw the sense in that and shut up.

"And did anything happen?" White asked.

"Yes. I may have heard a gunshot."

"Only may have?"

"It could have been a passing car," Jan admitted.

"Did you call the police?"

Chagrined, Jan said, "I wasn't sure, but I figured if it was a gun, somebody would be coming out."

"And did they?"

"Not for three hours. Then the one you think is the brother drove the Saab out of the garage and—"

"How could you tell?" White asked. "I thought it was dark."

Jan waved him quiet. "I'll get to that. He headed north. Vanessa Asplund went next in her car, and I followed the two of them until"—her voice trailed off—"I botched it and they saw me."

White made some magnanimous noises about its happening to the best.

"Thanks for letting me know," Jan said, raising her eyes toward the ceiling.

He frowned, realizing he'd said something wrong but was unsure of what. Cautiously, he said, "You have more?"

"Before they shook me, they pulled into an empty service station to talk. That's when I got a close-up of the car and the man driving it. It was same guy who arrived in the Mazda earlier that afternoon when it was still light."

"But his car's at the townhouse?" White asked, setting the scene for himself. "Around the corner, out of sight."

"You're getting ahead of me."

"Every chance I can," White said, nodding. "When you were close enough to see all this, was he getting a good look at you?"

"I don't think so," Jan said, faltering. The possible repercussions of that had escaped her.

The detective sneaked a peek at Claire, who stopped unraveling a thread from a button on her blouse and closed her eyes as if she could wish everything away. White hurried past the point of Jan's being spotted to ask, "Notice anything else?"

"There may have been someone on the passenger's front seat of the Saab, lying low, but I couldn't be sure."

"I see. Then what?"

"They drove off in opposite directions. I tried to follow the Saab, but he pulled a cute little trick, cutting across oncoming traffic, and lost me. I drove back to Vanessa Asplund's, and now her car was there but the Mazda was gone. No sign of the Saab, either. And here I am." She opened her hands to show she was done. "I think there was something going on."

"What do you think, Detective?" Claire asked, her voice waffling so imperceptibly that only her daughter would have noticed.

A grim satisfaction seized the detective's rugged face. "That if they saw your daughter I'd better spend the night."

Before Jan could lodge an astonished protest, Claire nodded in agreement and said the unthinkable. "Yes, I think you should."

Jan patted her throat to show she was having trouble swallowing this. "What gives here?"

"I want to sleep safely tonight," Claire said.

"We'll lock the doors."

"Not good enough."

"Mother, we can take care of ourselves."

"We can all be stubborn," Claire assured her. "I think we need help."

"Maybe you should hear why I suggest it," White said. "Before passing."

She verged on ruling him out of order until noticing how unsteady Claire's hands were. The sight of their trembling made her think twice about heroics. In her best bitchy voice, she said, "Let's have it."

"I told you someone else was reported missing, and I meant it. Shortly after seven tonight I got a call from Dr. Anthony Ellsworth's wife, who I spent some time with when we searched their lovely home." He grew cagy. "I believe you've been introduced to the lady?"

"Her boyfriend too," Jan said, unamused.

Claire squinted first at one set of lips, then the other.

"You have been busy, haven't you?" the detective said with a scowl. "He sell you anything?"

"We were talking about Mrs. Ellsworth," Jan reminded him. "And why you think we can't get through the night without you."

"Yes," White said, doing his best to act trustworthy. "So you know Mrs. Ellsworth's not exactly the excitable type?"

"I noticed."

"Tonight she was, though. Her husband came home, collected a pistol he kept for protection in the bedroom, and left

without explaining himself. Now, I don't know if it was the
gun or the not answering her questions, but something
stirred the doc's wife up. When she called me, she wanted
results, demanded them. Got kind of short with me, as taxpayers will."

"What's this leading to?" Jan asked, settling back in her
chair and crossing her arms.

"What if Dr. Ellsworth drives a Saab?" White said, gazing
dead at her as if she might not recognize the significance.

"Then chances are he was doing something he shouldn't
have with the Asplunds tonight."

"What?" the detective patiently asked. "Think hard."

"Why should I?" Jan asked, a response that made Claire
disapprovingly pucker her lips. "It sounds like you've got
everything all figured out for me."

White shrugged modestly. "Showing pictures of Croft
around—that may not have been so smart, Gallagher. We'd
have gotten to it, but now you might have triggered something."

"What are you driving at?" she asked, even though the
answer was plain. He was implying they might come after
her, which made sense if they thought she was the one person
who had tumbled onto their secrets. The possibility that he
was right was as insufferable as advice from the Little Admiral. She didn't want someone else, including White, to point
out such niceties for her. She was supposed to be on top of
all that by now. Add up her credits: mother of four, winner
of a sexual discrimination case, supervisor of an entire crew
of security personnel. Did that sound like someone in need of
help? She shifted her eyes from the detective's to her
mother's. They were watching her closely, determined to
head off any foolishness. The two of them were backing her
into a corner and that wasn't smart. Her good sense ruptured
when she was cornered.

"You think Ellsworth could find out where you live?"
White asked.

"Let me jump ahead to the end," Jan promptly said. "You're offering to protect us. I fucked up—"

"Jan!" Claire said.

"—and you're offering to be our very own Schwarzenegger."

"This is a potentially dangerous situation," the detective said, sounding like an evening news come-on.

"And you want to make the most of it?"

"You make it seem as though I'm scheming to spend the night," the detective said, disgusted and insulted at once.

"Jan," Claire coaxed, "he's trying to do us a favor."

"How old am I?" Jan pointedly asked her mother.

Claire tsked as if she couldn't imagine who'd raised her daughter.

"We don't need his help," Jan said, speaking as if they were alone.

The detective didn't aid his case by choosing that moment to say, "Your mother will be here to chaperon, if that's what you're afraid of."

"It's not."

"Claire," the detective sternly said, "talk to her."

"Don't take that tone with my mother."

Claire, sinking backward on the love seat, despondently said to the detective, "It's way beyond my talking to her."

"She's right," Jan said, standing. "It is." Crossing the living room to the front entrance with purpose, she opened the door and said with hostile politeness, "Maybe we can have dinner some time."

"Goddamn it Gallagher . . ."

"Don't try bullying me," Jan said, her voice so still and controlled that it immediately shut up the detective. She pointed a thumb at White but kept the rest of her hand clenched in a fist. "I've had enough of that. Now, unless you've something to say to me in your official capacity . . ."

"I do," White said, his self-control spotty. "Stay away from my investigation, completely away."

"Even when you ask for help?"

The detective flinched as though he'd just gotten something caught in his zipper. Circulation to his face was excellent. In that deep, husky voice that the men in her life had always saved for parting shots, he said, "Do you have a gun?"

"We'll make do."

"I hope the hell you can."

Lumbering toward the open door as if uncertain whether his shoulders would fit through, he paused to allow her a chance to take it all back. When she refused, his mulishness softened, his eyes took on a meaningful and concerned depth, and he said in a voice private enough to exclude Claire, "I hope you're not making a mistake." Managing to squeeze his shoulders out the doorway, he left without the standard look back but once in his station wagon couldn't resist a predictable revving of the motor and jamming it into reverse. Before he was halfway down the drive, Claire had twice said, "That was brilliant."

Slamming the door, Jan said, "Can we go to bed?"

"For all the good it will do. I won't sleep a wink."

"That was all crap, what he said, Mother. He wanted to scare us so he could play the protector."

"Why would he want to do that?"

"Mother, aren't you the one who's always telling me to show a little common sense when it comes to men?"

"You think he made it up?" Claire said, briefly confused.

"I do."

"I don't believe you," she said in that voice that mothers use to let you know they've been watching you longer than you've been watching yourself.

Actually, Jan didn't believe it either, and she found herself wondering if there was any way she could have made a bigger fool of herself. She supposed there was and that she was doing it right now by being too proud to wave the detective back.

24

BEFORE capping a perfect night by lying down and kidding herself that she could sleep, Jan tucked in the girls. While surreptitiously checking the window locks in their rooms, she revealed to them that for the missing eight hours she had been glued behind the steering wheel of the car where intense longings for a chamber pot had plagued her. She had to explain to her youngest what kind of pot that was. On the way out of Katie and Tess's room, she turned off the rattly window air conditioner, claiming it was nowhere near hot enough to warrant it. That was a half truth at best, for the humidity saturating the air did make the night uncomfortably close, which was the reason, Jan patiently explained to herself, that she had frequent bouts with the prickles and couldn't quite catch her breath.

The shutting down of the air conditioner worked a hardship on Katie, who'd grown addicted to the constant whir-clunk of its motor. It had been lulling her to sleep night after night throughout August. The running motor protected her, or at least cloaked the rustling of what she imagined she needed protection from. Telling her that she had to start acting more grown up, she was ten after all, started the hypocrite light flashing on the console of Jan's conscience. She spent a good deal of time reminding herself she was of voting age, though her years were more than triple Katie's. But what could she do? She needed the churning motor off so that she could hear the pitter-patter of feet—big or little—anywhere in the house. She tried to tell herself that neither Ellsworth nor the Asplunds were gestating homicidal schemes outside in the bushes. She spent some quality effort convincing herself of that.

In Leah and Amy's room, she ordered the radio off even though its volume was so low she could barely detect it.

"People are trying to sleep," Jan said.

"Is the cop still out there?" Leah asked.

"No, he saw that everything was OK and left."

"Mom, you're such a faky liar."

From the other side of the room Amy asked in an uncertain voice, "Is something scary going to happen?"

"Only if you don't go to sleep," Jan said, growling as playfully as she could manage. Pausing in the doorway, she gave one final warning. "No radio."

Leaving the girls' bedroom doors open, so that she would pick up on bad dreams or anything else, which in her own mind she left unspecified, she made a sweep through the living room, where she double-checked the front door and window locks. Stealing down to the basement, she tugged on all the lower windows. Back upstairs, she closed all the drapes and wished that sometime in the last three years she'd finished her kitchen painting project and reinstalled the blinds over the four windows above the kitchen sink which overlooked the driveway. Feeling particularly exposed in front of those windows, she quickly turned off the circular fluorescent fixture, then flicked on the front-step light and the floodlights over the garage. With the garage set back of the house, the dual seventy-five-watt bulbs indirectly lit the kitchen countertops, creating long, diagonal shadows that were the same washed-out gray as Jan's confidence.

A quick glance up and down Marymount Street revealed nothing, not even Detective White's Buick wagon waiting in the wings. Not that she expected him to be. She would have been outraged if he had been out there. Right? But not spying him made her feel entirely alone, even if she was surrounded by more family than she knew what to do with.

Ready to retire, she turned off all the inside lights. Changing her mind, she left a reading lamp on in the living room, except that the shadows it cast gave her the willies. She turned it off too. Halfway to the bedroom she shared with her mother, she stopped and did an about-face, heading to the basement to retrieve a toy Louisville Slugger collected at a state fair some years before. The bat had been leaning in a corner ever since, right next to a sparkly good-witch Halloween costume. The girls sometimes used the Louisville miniature as an oversized magic wand. Without doubt the best weapon in the house was the telephone, over which she could bugle for 911 reinforcements, but that option was bolted securely to the kitchen wall to prevent her two older daughters from disappearing with it into their bedroom where some permissive fool had installed a phone jack. Backup to that link to the outside world had to be a nightstick, the one weapon she'd received on-the-job training for. Having armed herself, she made another run at turning in and this time made it.

Shielding the toy bat with her body so that Claire couldn't spot it from her bed, Jan slid it under the edge of her box frame, slipped on her nightshirt, and retired for the evening, about as ready for sleep as a piece of cheese resting on a set mousetrap.

"You've really done it this time," Claire said out of the darkness. She didn't sound prepared to tell Jan to lean on her if she needed to.

"I thought you didn't want any men in the house," Jan said in a hushed voice, not wanting the girls to hear.

"What choice did we have?" Claire griped, rolling on her side. Her voice muffled by a pillow, she added, "I'd feel safer if you had a gun."

"And I wouldn't." Although Jan had to admit to herself that the limits of psychology and talking had never seemed more clearly defined than they did at the moment. "We'll be fine, Mother. All we have to do is make it through to morning."

Claire snorted in derision, then turned from side to side and fluffed her pillows, all four of them, for the next half hour. Finally she drifted into what would pass for sleep only if the guidelines for slumber were greatly relaxed.

When Jan's eyes grew accustomed to the shadows, she could see that Claire was hugging a golf club to her side for protection, a seven iron that she sometimes hacked around with at the park. Wasn't that a sight? Her sixty-seven-year-old mother clutching a golf club. With maudlin clarity, Jan recognized how much she owed her mother, how much she loved her mother, and how much more alone she would be when Claire was gone. All these nagging thoughts swarmed about her in the dark as she strained to hear any extra breaths in the house.

The prospect of having a stranger on board, particularly one as wobbly as Ellsworth, multiplied the number of sounds that carried to her. The fact that no air conditioner hummed through its monotonous cycle, washing out all background noise, intensified every scant vibration. A moth fluttering against the screen had her reaching for the scaled-down baseball bat. A car slowly passing the house drew her to the window. Her mother's digestive tract, which sounded as though a thunderstorm was rumbling up and down its length, kept her guessing, and an entire generation of crickets outside in the damp grass kept her second-guessing. At intervals the crickets suddenly and in unison ceased chirping. Wondering what caused the interruptions tightened her shoulders.

Checking the great outdoors didn't expand her comfort zone either. After the third trip to her bedroom window to reconnoiter the terra incognita, she swore off that excursion for the remainder of her watch. All that interrupted the darkness out there were the slowly gathering patches of fog as the nighttime temperatures coalesced the moisture suspended in the air. Down the street an amber city light cast a mucous glow across the farthest half of every surface, just the way a Victorian gaslight in foggy old London would have, except she'd read somewhere that about the only time old London was foggy was on the silver screen when Jack the Ripper was honing his skills. That pleasant correlation pushed a few buttons.

Along toward the longest hours of the night, the time when several minutes out of every hour inexplicably vanish, she heard the dog pawing the back door, wanting in. Except that she hadn't had a dog since she was twelve, a cocker spaniel named Mr. Dilly. She sat up and listened so hard her jaw ached. Claire gave off the regular breaths of sleep, and all was as it should be in the girls' rooms—fast-paced quiet. The pawing continued without interruption for perhaps half a minute, by which time Jan's heart was ready for lift-off. The heavy air carried the scraping sound as clearly as if it was on the pillow beside her ear rather than on the other side of the house. By then she'd determined that whoever wanted in was trying to slip the back door button lock. As locks went, it was more protective coloration than a deterrent, but the safety chain ought to at least slow him until Jan could . . . She didn't know quite what she could do, but realized she'd better do it fast. Swinging out of bed, she stooped and fumbled for the handle of her makeshift billy club. The bat struck a caster of her bed.

"What's wrong?" Claire said, instantly awake.

"I don't know. Maybe I heard something. You stay back here with the girls.

"What are you doing?"

"Going to call nine-one-one."

From the kitchen came the sound of the door opening but catching on the safety chain. Both Jan and Claire swiveled their heads in that direction.

"Do it fast," said Claire.

For once mother and daughter were in general agreement, but there wasn't time to marvel. Barefoot, Jan moved on the balls of her feet down the pine-floored hallway and across the carpeted living room. She kept the bat cocked in her right hand while trailing her left along the wall for a sense of reality. A leaden taste congealed on her tongue. She avoided swallowing. The shadows and furniture held their breath with her. Halfway across the living room, she realized she couldn't hear anything and froze. Then, from behind her, the sound of Claire moving the girls into one bedroom registered. The thought of protecting them was only part of what propelled her forward. A fear of being a fraud did the rest. Doing it to prove she could—that struck her as meager, but it was what she had. She told her left foot to move forward. It did. And she did, getting to the kitchen doorway and crouching to peer around the corner.

At the opposite side of the room the rear door was ajar the width of the safety chain, but no intruder was in sight, just three inches of undisturbed darkness. Through the opening a faint, damp breeze carried the tiny winged creatures of the night.

Somewhere outside, somewhere near, a low voice complained. It sounded like a man having an argument with himself. Jan held some of her best arguments the same way, and she remembered Gavin's report that Ellsworth had spent a good portion of a fairly recent evening disputing himself.

This was all well and good except that the telephone was across the room, directly in sight of the square glass panes on the upper half of the back door. The light switch for the ceiling fixture lay just around the corner from her current position, within easy reach, but she remembered what Detective White said about Ellsworth cruising home long enough to collect a gun. The gunshot she might have heard at the Asplund townhouse came back to her, and she elected not to try frightening him away by hitting the switch. She didn't want to light up the target range any better than the garage lights already did. Holding the bat with both hands, she started for the phone.

Her bare soles felt sticky on the tiled floor. The fifteen feet across the kitchen wasn't far; it was the fifteen miles that someone had spliced into the middle that made her unsteady and dehydrated. The black phone might have been a mirage on the distant horizon. It seemed to hover. She didn't get a chance to find out.

Glass cracked.

She gasped and ducked—from what she had no idea—as a tightly gloved hand poked through the broken window-pane, fumbling with the safety chain. In a moment the chain would be off. Only halfway across the room, she retreated into the shadows between the refrigerator and the kitchen table. Squatting no higher than the nearest chair, she had to order herself to take a breath.

Her guest opened the door inward as warily as someone suspecting a surprise party. He didn't step in, not right away. It sounded as though he was sniffing, or maybe sniffling. That he might be more terrified than she was hadn't occurred to her. The prospect made him seem more dangerous, not less. It made him seem more unpredictable.

She heard him swear to himself, "I don't care what he says."

He paused to listen to an answer beyond Jan's, or any mere mortal's, range of hearing.

His first step into the kitchen was a long one to avoid putting his foot down on any shards of glass that had fallen out of the windowpane. There was enough light from the garage floods to see that he wore a dark windbreaker, chinos, high-top tennis shoes, and a nylon stocking stretched over his head. The stocking took away any bookish edge she remembered about the doctor, and the shadows of the room made his shoulders much wider than they'd seemed in his office.

Using both hands, he held a semiautomatic pistol tightly in front of himself, chest height, almost like someone would hold a video camera. No marksman, he panned his weapon across the shadows before him with a jerky motion that caught on several objects. He came close to blowing away the automatic ice cube dispenser on the front of the fridge, but he overlooked Jan huddled three feet to its right. He checked behind the back door, making her extremely happy to have avoided the obvious places of concealment.

"Don't want to," he muttered in a whine.

But he raggedly advanced, almost as if pulled forward by the gun.

For a few imaginative breaths—very quiet ones—Jan felt as though controlling an invisible line coming out of the gun barrel. She was reeling her guest into place. Just a bit more. A little farther, please. Come on. Her insides felt like a hand-wound alarm clock that had been assembled incorrectly. The second hand was stuck. Everything was suspended in the dark maw of time. It felt that melodramatic, that spine-shattering.

On his fourth step into the room, Jan told her body *Now!* But there were mutinous muscle groups below her neck that refused to lend their full cooperation. She had to get tough and command herself a second time before she cut loose, whipping the business end of her Louisville Slugger down on top of Ellsworth's gloved hands before he could react. The contact sent vibrations shuddering all the way to her crazy bone. A worrisome split second of doubt grabbed her. Nothing was happening. Then lag-time passed. Ellsworth yelped and dropped the gun, jerking his hands in close to his chest. Upon impact with the floor, the gun barked once. No gutwrenching cries of pain, though. She took that absence to mean she hadn't been hit. When two of her daughters called out her name, the ringing in her ears made the girls sound stranded on the far side of a lake.

As Ellsworth regrouped and stooped for the gun, she rammed the fat end of her club into the soft stuffing of his solar plexus. The jab pumped all his wind out, and he doubled up like a caterpillar curling to protect its tender underside. His right foot clumsily came down on top of the gun, skidding it backward and further tipping his balance. An enthusiastic chop to his clavicle finished the job. Solid as a timber, he fell to the floor without displaying any acting ability.

The thrill of victory was short-lived, however. Her feet kept edging away in tiny, mincing steps, but her mind, forever practical, kept asking what had happened to the gun. Kneeling, she hunted for it before he could come around. While on his level a part of her noted that his fingers were large and muscular, not the bony twigs she would have expected Ellsworth to have. Then she spotted the automatic, several baby steps behind Ellsworth, near the threshold of the back door. She'd have to step over him to get at it, and she couldn't bring herself to do that. He might be playing possum. Angered by her timidity and his possible treachery, she yanked off his stocking mask to tell him no funny business or she'd smack another bone or two for free. When the nylon came off, it revealed not a whimpering Dr. Anthony Ellsworth but the man who Detective White claimed was Vanessa Asplund's brother. There were resemblances, Jan supposed. She wasn't interested in them. All that occupied her at the moment was Ellsworth's whereabouts. It felt as though she'd misplaced him herself.

Before she could organize a search party, a new shadow filled the back doorway. Looking up, she saw a man's suit-coated silhouette and guessed that she didn't need to go looking for Ellsworth. Her internal second hand stuck again. The doctor was scooping up the pistol and holding it on her. There was but one problem with this explanation. When the doctor spoke he had a woman's voice and even from several feet away Jan whiffed a strong dose of jasmine.

"My father's going to rest in peace," the woman said, determined about it. She sounded as though she'd run out of places to hide if he didn't. There wasn't any mistaking Vanessa Asplund's quavery voice. Recognizing her was something else. Her hair was pulled back severely; the over-sized man's suit she wore concealed the sharp curves of her figure.

"Isn't he already?" Jan asked, trying not to squeak, but doing it anyway. At least their voices drove the ringing from her ears.

"He doesn't like cats," Vanessa Asplund said, defensive and serious.

"Why's that?" Jan asked, straining to sound concerned.

"Their whiskers."

"You've asked about it?" Jan said, talking just to talk, to extend the moment, to protect herself with what she had left—her wits, feeble as they felt. The nightstick remained in her right hand, but with the element of surprise gone, what good would it do her? The training videos had skipped over dodging bullets at close range.

"How do you know about that?" Vanessa Asplund sharply asked.

Her brother groaned deep in his throat and rolled on his side, grasping his shoulder where Jan had cracked him. She may have broken his collarbone. He wasn't eager to get up.

"A guess," Jan said. "Your brother needs attention."

"No he doesn't. Not yet. Not until he does what Father said."

"The police are coming," Jan said, switching topics, realizing there were more levels to this conversation than she could hope to analyze.

"We'll be gone and you'll be the victim of a deranged mind—other than my own." She laughed shallowly. "You're going to be Dr. Anthony Ellsworth's last patient. This is his gun." She indicated the pistol in her hand with a nod. "This is his finger." She held up an index finger, causing the loose-fitting coat sleeve to slide down her arm and reveal the top of the surgical glove she wore.

"I talked to your father before he died," Jan said.

"Impossible," she answered, outraged at the lie.

"No," Jan cautiously answered, "it's true."

"Where?"

"At his bedside," Jan slowly said, puzzled by the question.

"That's not where he talks," Vanessa Asplund triumphantly said.

"He wanted me to tell you something."

"He didn't," Vanessa Asplund declared, but she paused, waiting to hear.

Jan's first impulse was to say that her father had wanted her to know that he loved her, but a deeper, troubling instinct warned her away from it. When in Rome, make like the Romans—that seemed a sounder approach.

"He wanted you to know that he didn't like a cat's tail either," Jan said.

"The tail?"

"That's right," Jan said. "We'll be able to get you some medical treatment too."

"Me?"

The kitchen light flashed on, thanks to her mother, Jan assumed, although there wasn't time to check. The sight of Vanessa Asplund lost in a man's fine black suit, cinched tight at the waist, flooding her shoulders, was rare enough, but there was more. Startled by the light, she stepped backward, nearly tripping out of the men's oxfords she wore. Her eyebrows had been thickened with liner to a masculine width, and she'd sketched sideburns down to mid-ear. Regaining her balance, she swung her extended gun hand to the left with the even glide of a robotic arm.

A movement, a reflection of herself in the four casement windows above the sink, drew her attention.

She appeared to have trouble identifying the image of herself through the gold-framed bifocals she wore. Aiming down her gun sight at the woman dressed as a man who aimed back at her, there was a hitch in her timing until recognition settled in and she called out clearly, "I'm coming."

She pulled off three shots, managing to shatter one window. Before the fourth shot, Jan swung her club in a backward arc, splintering the narrow handle across the loose coat sleeve covering Vanessa Asplund's wrists. The blow sent the pistol flying and may have broken the woman's arm. There was a crack, brittle as a thick yardstick being snapped over a knee, followed by Vanessa Asplund sucking in air and cradling the wrist nearest Jan as if holding something precious and fragile, a baby robin or a dream for a better tomorrow. Looking up from her hand, she stared in wonderment at Jan. She could have been inspecting some ingenious gadget designed to beat mortality. She wanted to figure out how it worked. Her faced was crooked slightly to the side, as if raptly listening to a voice that Jan, for one, didn't expect to hear. It was a conversation Jan was glad to miss out on.

Claire edged into the room, nudged Jan in the back with her seven iron, and hoarsely whispered, "Get the gun."

For once Jan did as her mother said without questions and retrieved the pistol, putting it in Claire's hand.

"What am I?" Claire asked, gazing repugnantly at the weapon. "Your deputy?"

But when the man on the floor groaned, Claire attended to business, ordering him to stay exactly where he was if he valued his life, liberty, and pursuit of happiness.

Jan said to Claire, "Thank you, Mother."

"Don't try to butter me up," Claire toughly said.

"I know better than that," Jan answered. "Don't let them go anywhere, OK?"

A worthless comment considering that the only vehicle the Asplunds looked fit for would have had four padded walls and no windshield. The brother remained curled tight as a dog trying to keep its nose warm, and the sister stayed tuned to some distant station, one on a wavelength way off the dial. Neither of them acted aware of the other's presence or suffering.

"They'll stay put," Claire said, adding with a softhearted gruffness, "You're almost welcome."

A fleeting smile crossed Jan's face as she dialed 911 to call in the shock troops. Once the local police bounded onto the scene, everything assumed the showtime air of television docudrama—twirling lights, two-way car radios, the crowd that pulls together out of nowhere. For a while it seemed to Jan as though everything was happening to someone else, someone trapped on TV. She wouldn't have minded if that had been the case. The only good she could see out of all this was that for once the craziness wasn't hers. For once it belonged to someone else. The thought didn't give her any pleasure.

25

TUESDAY and Wednesday passed. Jan went to her local police department and made her statement. Back home, once the camera crews and newspaper photographers cleared out, there remained a noticeable increase in street traffic that eased up on the gas pedal in front of their house. In the evenings the neighbors awkwardly hung back beyond the squared hedges, waiting for an opening to sidle over and get the real scoop. The girls were split, the older ones hiding out in their bedroom, ready to expire from shame; the younger pair hanging out on the front steps, black-marketeering in their mother's autograph.

Claire wanted to know if there was any kind of reward, and she wasn't talking about harp-time awaiting her in the hereafter. But no good samaritan stepped forward with a sackful of cash, and in the end she had to satisfy herself with the notion that at least Detective White no longer had a legitimate reason to come around. She said that as if testing Jan and became cross when Jan didn't immediately agree. But she was right about one thing—Detective White stayed away. Jan learned why on Tuesday from the local constabulary.

After being shagged off Marymount Street, he'd driven over to the Asplund townhouse and discovered Dr. Anthony Ellsworth curled up on the front seat of a green Saab parked in the garage. The doctor had misplaced his pulse and gone on to that big examination room in the sky.

On Wednesday she received a terse phone message from Detective White, who didn't identify himself but said, "The brother's confessed," before hanging up.

Several days unfurled at work without a blip, without one mention of the excitement at her place. Oh, they knew. She could tell by the different reactions in the eyes that met hers—envy, frustration, feigned indifference—but not one word. Then, at the beginning of the next week, she received a summons to conference room B. Around the table it was old home week. The same administrators, the same supporting cast from Security, the same smile replicating itself around the room. Centered on the table was a floral arrangement, which was the first whiff Jan had of a rat.

Executive Administrator Averilli rose to graciously invite her in. Administrator Trainee Kavanaugh poured her a cup of coffee. The two unnamed administrators, one in white lab coat, the other not, looked on benignly. Exactly what their function was or why they were included in the roll call remained a mystery. Perhaps they hadn't yet reached their quota of meetings for the month, or maybe they were included for critical mass. That left the members of Security—Larsen, Victor Wheaton, Robert Yost, and the Little Admiral—and although their smiles were every bit as bushy-tailed as the rest of Administration's, Jan could tell that smiling made their skins crawl.

Once again the speaker of the house was the Little Admiral, who was dressed in full regalia—navy blue suspenders, shellacked crow's nest, trimmed nose hairs. He talked quite handsomely about how he hoped Jan had learned her lesson and about how, fortunately for her, the county believed in second chances. This was received with much wise nodding of heads. But then he got down to bedrock.

"We think you're ready to resume your duties as supervisor of the night shift." He made it sound as though Jan had been malingering on sick leave.

"Wasn't I promoted out of that job?" she asked, sounding as though there must be some misunderstanding.

"Temporarily," the Little Admiral agreed. "To help you gain some perspective on your actions. But some time has passed and Gavin has managed to get your crew right as rain again, so we think it's time you took another shot at it."

Her bile rising, Jan checked every face around the table before saying, "We're not going to talk about what's happened, are we?"

"What you do on your own time," the Little Admiral charitably said, "is nobody's business but your own." It was a principle that he was ready to vote for.

With everything looking carved in the usual county soapstone, Jan said, "You all set to clean the refrigerator, Gavin?"

To her immediate left, Gavin smiled as if he'd just taken a shot between the legs. "Yes," he said, although it actually sounded like *Yes, damn it.*

Strangely enough, Jan didn't find herself relishing the moment. Actually, while looking at the contorted lines on Larsen's forehead, she realized she felt degraded by it. No matter how bottom-out low her opinion of the man, they were putting his hand in the same fire as hers. As her reaction to that built, she mirrored Larsen's resentful expression and confounded even herself by saying to the Little Admiral, "It's kind of you to offer, but I think I'll keep my promotion. The daytime hours give me more time with my family."

For an instant the room felt like a stormy dark night suddenly illuminated by a lightning strike. She caught honest reactions ranging from the Little Admiral's outrage to secret admiration from the man in the white lab coat. Maybe every heart in Administration wasn't made of rhinoceros horn after all. But then normality returned as Executive Administrator Averilli took the floor. Now that Ellsworth's malpractice suit was a moot point, Averilli apparently believed that Jan didn't have the juice to hold her new position.

"There are other considerations, Officer Gallagher. The hospital's budget is in a deficit spiral and the special-projects position created for you is definitely not essential for the care of our patients."

He made other pretty noises too, covering employee responsibilities, civic duties, and the immorality of waste. Worse, she believed that most of what he said was true. As he spoke she could feel a wind of conscience kicking up in her mind, could also feel herself being sucked back to the graveyard shift. But then her eyes caught on Elizabeth Kavanaugh's expression, which must have been somewhat akin to Marie Antoinette's before delivering her line about eating cake. With that recognition, Jan rebelled against having her own sense of right and wrong turned against her.

"This all sounds very well thought out," Jan said, the kind of pleasantry that should have made a worthy opponent take a step back.

"We do our best," Averilli answered, sharp enough to sound uncertain.

"So do I," Jan said, "which is why I have one request to make."

"We're eager to hear it," Averilli said, appearing anything but.

"I'll go back as soon as you've eliminated one other nonessential postion."

Everyone acted stumped but Kavanaugh, who drew enough hint out of the suspicious way Jan smiled at her to pulse a murderous red.

"Could you clarify?" Averilli asked.

"Administrator Trainee Kavanaugh's position."

"I'm afraid I don't understand."

"As I recall," Jan said, "her job didn't exist until quite recently, either, and there's some uncertainty about what she does."

Then the lull. Not the lull before the storm but the lull that occasionally descended upon some part of the county bureaucracy when the various substrata of employees had no idea in which direction to shuffle their papers. Everyone recognized that Averilli—in his mind—was wetting a finger and holding it aloft to detect an air current. As he searched for a way to save face while spreading his spinnaker before the prevailing winds, no one twitched a corpuscle or wet a digit of their own or did anything that would allow Averilli to remember they had been present. Kavanaugh sat stillest of all, becalmed, totally unable to puff her lips and breathe a word in her own defense. Finally Averilli detected a breeze and said, "Perhaps an evaluation of job classifications is in order."

"Until it happens," Jan warned, "I'm staying where I am, or so help me, it's back to court for all of us."

"Discrimination?" asked a resigned Averilli.

"You ought to recognize it by now," Jan said.

This time it was Jan who exited first, leaving the others stunned in her wake. She had a line of gooseflesh on her arms but kept a sober face as far as the ladies' room where she grinned widely at a mirror and said, "Whew."

That afternoon she went out to the lobby to make a private call to Detective White and inquire if he might be interested in starting over on a much slower schedule. She had to wait behind a pair of hard-of-hearing, riled-up pensioners, who were attempting to raise the U.S. president himself to straighten out the blankety-blank mess known as Medicare. She didn't mind the wait. For once it felt as though she'd proven something to herself, if no one else. She was in no hurry to lose the power of that moment. A contented euphoria possessed her. She noticed that outside it had finally started to rain, a fine mizzle that made the cars on the street glisten as if they'd just rolled off the assembly line. For a few moments that's exactly how she felt herself—newborn, washed, fresh.

But then she saw an unexpected sight. Across the street Gavin Larsen was holding an umbrella for a portly nurse. Upon closer inspection the two of them were arguing about something. From Jan's vantage point their spat had the animated gestures of a lovers' quarrel, and the rearing up of that ugly side of romance jarred loose unpleasant memories of Jan's own love-stained past. When the elderly couple stepped aside to let her use the phone, she shook her head no, to show that they couldn't make her call anyone. Not today. Today it felt too grand to be on her own, even if it was what her mother wanted.